"I've been looking all over.
Where the hell have you been?"

Charity took a step back, intimidated a little by the dark glint in Call's eyes and the anger in his face. "I-I was taking some pictures. It's such a lovely day, so much warmer than it has been, and I-I—"

"Do you know how worried Maude's been?" He dumped his daypack onto the ground and continued walking toward her. "She was afraid something terrible had happened." He reached out, caught the tops of her arms, and hauled her toward him. "She was frantic. How could you be so thoughtless?"

Charity blinked at him. "I told her I was going for a walk. I might have stayed a little longer than I intended but I didn't think she'd be upset."

"Well, she was." He held her immobile, their bodies nearly touching. "She was worried sick."

There was something in his expression. Fear, she realized. Concern for her. "Maude was worried?" she said softly. "Or you were?"

Those fierce blue eyes bored into her. His arm slid down, wrapped around her waist, and he hauled her the last few inches between them, pressing his body full-length against hers. "I was," he said, and then he kissed her.

Books by Kat Martin

Published by Kensington Publishing Corporation

MIDNIGHT SUN

KAT MARTIN

ZEBRA BOOKS
KENSINGTON PUBLISHING CORP.
http://www.kensingtonbooks.com

ZEBRA BOOKS are published by

Kensington Publishing Corp.
119 West 40th Street
New York, NY 10018

All Kensington titles, imprints, and distributed lines are available at special quantity discounts for bulk purchases for sales promotion, premiums, fund-raising, educational, or institutional use.

Special book excerpts or customized printings can also be created to fit specific needs. For details, write or phone the office of the Kensington Sales Manager: Attn.: Sales Department. Kensington Publishing Corp., 119 West 40th Street, New York, NY 10018. Phone: 1-800-221-2647.

Zebra and the Z logo Reg. U.S. Pat. & TM Off.

First Printing: May 2003
ISBN-13: 978-1-4201-4576-2
ISBN-10: 1-4201-4576-2

10 9 8 7

Printed in the United States of America

To the men and women, past and present, who risk it all for adventure. To the beauty and magnificence of Alaska and the great Northwest—and the journey of a lifetime. I wouldn't have missed it for the world.

CHAPTER ONE

Manhattan, New York

"I don't believe it. You can't actually mean to go through with this." Jeremy paced over to the dresser in the bedroom where Charity stood studying each piece of clothing she intended to take on her trip. "You can't possibly mean to quit your job, give up your apartment, and go off to some godforsaken town in the wilderness."

Charity flicked him only the briefest of glances and continued to fold her sweatshirt, a red one with a little red-and-white-checked collar she thought was particularly warm.

"It isn't as if you didn't know this was going to happen," she said. "I've been planning this for weeks. I told you the day I made the decision to leave. As you do with anything that doesn't fit into your plans, you simply chose not to believe it."

He crossed the room and reached for her, turned her to face him. "Think about what you're doing, Charity. Think what you're giving up. You've got a good job at Glenbrook Publishing. You just got promoted to senior editor, for God's sake."

"I gave them notice weeks ago, Jeremy. They've already replaced the position."

"They'd take you back in a heartbeat and you know it. You're destroying your career, but if that isn't enough— what about me?"

At five-foot-ten, with his perfectly styled, jet-black hair and deep green eyes, Jeremy Hauser was undeniably attractive. When Charity had met him at a literacy fund-raiser two years ago, she had fallen like a rock for his debonair good looks, Wall Street polish and charm. After dating him— practically living with him in his swanky East Side apartment—she knew how self-centered, how totally self-absorbed he could be.

She caught the hand he raised to her cheek and drew it away. "We've had two years, Jeremy. We've shared good times and bad, but you know as well as I do, things haven't been great with us for the last six months. Maybe putting some space between us will help decide where our relationship is headed."

Or if, as Charity suspected, it was headed nowhere at all.

"There's nothing wrong with our relationship. I'll admit I've been a little stressed-out lately. I'm up for that promotion and you know how much I want it." He gave her one of his most charming smiles. "I realize I haven't been very good company, but give up this crazy scheme of yours and I'll make it up to you—I promise."

"I'm sorry, Jeremy. I think this goes way beyond being good company. We haven't even made love in nearly a month."

He paled a little at hearing her come right out and say it. Jeremy had always been reserved in the bedroom, which in the beginning she'd found rather sweet. The truth was, sex just wasn't a driving factor in Jeremy's life. He was always too tired, too busy, too rushed. Mostly, he was just too preoccupied with his own needs to care all that much about hers.

She turned away from him, reached for a pair of Liz

Claiborne jeans and started to roll them up. Jeremy leaned over and gently blew against her ear.

"Don't go," he said softly, kissing the side of her neck. "We'll work things out, I swear it."

Charity eased away from him. "Don't, Jeremy, please. Not now."

"All right, what do you want me to do? What do I have to say to make you give up this crazy idea and stay in Manhattan? You want to move in with me? Okay, that's what we'll do. Finish packing your things and I'll have a moving truck here to pick them up tomorrow afternoon."

There was a time that was exactly what she had wanted. She had believed Jeremy Hauser was the man of her dreams. It hadn't taken long to discover he wasn't. She still didn't know how she'd convinced herself for more than a year that he would change and things would work out between them.

"I don't want to move in with you, Jeremy. I want to do exactly what I've got planned. I want to fly out of JFK on Canada Airlines tomorrow morning at 7:29 A.M. I want to land in Vancouver, change planes, and fly to Whitehorse, where, after nearly eleven hours in the air and a two-hour layover, I'll be so exhausted I'll crawl into my bed at the River View Motel without even turning on the TV. The following day, I want to pick up the Ford Explorer I've leased from National Rent-A-Car and be on my way to Dawson City."

He looked so stunned that Charity reached out and caught hold of his hand. "I know this is hard for you to understand, but I'm twenty-eight years old and I've never done a single thing that's really exciting. Just once, I want to have an adventure. Haven't you ever wanted to do something a little bit crazy? Something you've secretly wanted to do but never had the nerve?"

"No."

She sighed. "Both my sisters are doing things that are interesting and exciting. Patience is getting ready to go on the rodeo circuit and Hope is traveling around the country, writing freelance magazine articles. They're living their dreams and I want to live mine, too.''

"Patience is doing research for her Ph.D.," Jeremy argued, "and Hope is trying to salvage her flagging writing career. You have a very successful career. You're a fiction editor at a well-respected publishing house. You should be happy with that.''

"Well, I'm not, and I'm tired of arguing with you about it." She turned and ushered him out of the bedroom, tugged him across her small living room to the front door. "Go home, Jeremy." She removed the chain lock and pulled the door open. "I have a feeling that as soon as I'm gone, you're going to realize our relationship wasn't going anywhere anyway. You might even be grateful to have your freedom again.''

Jeremy's mouth thinned but he didn't argue. He wasn't in love with her and deep down he knew it—she was simply a convenience. That kind of relationship was enough for Jeremy but not for her.

"You're going to be sorry, Charity," he said, stepping out into the hallway. "Unfortunately, by the time you figure that out, it's going to be too late.''

Charity cringed as he slammed the front door. *Poor Jeremy.* Maybe someday he would find a woman who would be content to simply live her life through his. In the meantime, it wouldn't take him long to get over her. His feelings just didn't run that deep.

Charity sighed as she returned to her packing, including a pair of long underwear she had purchased on-line from Cabellas, an outdoor sporting equipment and clothing store. Unlike Jeremy's superficial idea of caring, Charity knew if she ever really fell in love it would be deep and abiding, the forever, can't-live-without-you kind of love. It was the sort of love her mother and father had shared, the sort she hoped she would be lucky enough to find for herself someday.

In the meantime, she wanted a little excitement in her life.

Though her deteriorating relationship with Jeremy had been the catalyst for her decision to leave New York, living an adventure like this was something she had dreamed of since she was a little girl. Her father, Edward Sinclair, had been a professor of history at Boston University in the city where Charity was born. As a child, she and her sisters, Hope and Patience, had grown up with tales of medieval knights and damsels in distress, Robin Hood, and Red Beard the Pirate. For all three sisters, the need for adventure burned like a fire in their blood.

At Glenbrook Publishing, Charity had edited action/ adventure novels by authors like Cussler, Higgins, and Clancy. Though the stories were purely fiction, each one fueled the hidden passion that burned inside her. Charity loved them and secretly read even the ones that were published by her competitors.

Then one day it happened—the chance for an adventure of her own. In *The Wall Street Journal,* she spotted an article titled "Twenty-First-Century Gold Rush," a story about inexpensive mining claims for sale in the Canadian Yukon. It described the rugged outdoor life and the financial opportunities offered by some of the claims. Charity felt as if her destiny had finally arrived.

Two weeks later, after hours spent searching the Web for mining information and poring over stacks of library books, she contacted a real estate broker in Dawson City where the newspaper article had been set. A dozen long-distance phone calls later, she used half of the money she had inherited when her grandfather died last year to make an offer on a twenty-acre gold claim.

A photo of the property the owner called the Lily Rose, arriving via the Internet, showed *A cozy one-bedroom cabin on a wild, rushing stream. The cabin,* the advertisement read, *has modern, indoor plumbing, a convenient kitchen, and a rustic rock fireplace. Existing furniture and mining equipment are included.*

It sounded perfect to Charity, who closed the all-cash sale ten days later.

Smiling at the memory, she stuffed a last heavy sweater into her soft-sided bag, then struggled to buzz the zipper closed. She was only taking two suitcases: one with her can't-do-without personal items like shampoo, makeup, and hair spray, the other with jeans, sweaters, tennis shoes, and hiking boots. She wasn't sure exactly what else she would need so she had decided to buy the rest once she got there.

The good news was she was keeping her apartment. Hope, the oldest of the three Sinclair sisters, had agreed to move in next week and pay the rent for the next six months. Hope had an idea for a string of magazine articles that revolved around happenings in New York, London, and Paris. Charity's small apartment worked perfectly as an affordable base of operations.

And six months was perfect. She didn't plan to move away for good. An adventure was simply that. Once it was over, she would return to New York and decide what to do with the rest of her life.

Charity grinned as she thought of the exciting journey she was about to undertake, and set the second suitcase beside the front door.

CHAPTER TWO

There's a land where the mountains are nameless
And the rivers all run God knows where.
There are lives that are erring and aimless
And deaths that just hang by a hair.
There are hardships that nobody reckons
There are valleys unpeopled and still.
There's a land—how it beckons and beckons
And I want to go back, and I will.

> —Robert W. Service

By the time the plane taxied to the gate and the passengers dispersed at the Whitehorse Airport—Canadian time 3:09 P.M.—Charity had been in the air eleven grueling hours. Her neck had a kink the size of a hen egg, her back ached, and her mouth was so dry she couldn't spit if she had to. God, she hated flying.

She consoled herself with the fact that she had arrived safe and sound. "Cheated death again," she whispered when the wheels hit the ground and she was still in one piece. The airport just north of town was small but appeared to be well run, or so she thought as she collected the first of her bags off the conveyor belt.

Unfortunately, the second bag—the one with her makeup, toothbrush, vitamins, nail file, and facial cleansers—failed to arrive. Realizing she was the last person left in the baggage claim and the conveyor belt had stopped moving, she wearily trudged over to the counter and began to fill out the necessary forms.

"Be sure to put down where you'll be staying," said the clerk behind the counter, a middle-aged woman with thinning, mouse-brown hair and a bored expression. "We'll get the bag to you as soon as it comes in, eh?"

It was the Canadian "eh?" that made her grin. She was there. She had made it to Whitehorse, first stop in her wilderness adventure. That was all that mattered.

She signed the form, thanked the woman, and made her way out to the front of the building to look for the taxi stand. As she stood at the curb, staring out at the vast expanse of open space around the airport, Charity's heart slowly sank. If there *were* any regular taxis—maybe not in a town of less than twenty thousand—they had left with the rest of the passengers. Instead, parked at the curb was a battered Buick at least ten years old with a rusted-out tailpipe and oxidized blue paint.

"Need a ride, lady?" The driver spoke to her through the rolled-down window on the passenger side of the car. He had a large, slightly hooked nose, dark skin, and straight black hair. In Manhattan he could have been Puerto Rican, Pakistani, Jamaican, or any of a dozen myriad nationalities. Here it was clear the man was an Indian. First Nation, they called them up here.

My first real Indian. She barely stopped herself from grinning. "I'm staying at the River View Motel. Can you take me there?"

"Sure. Get in." No offer to help with her luggage, no opening the door for her.

Charity jerked the handle, hoisted in her black canvas bag, and climbed into the backseat, wincing as one of the springs poked through the cracked blue leather and jabbed into her behind. She shifted, hoped she hadn't torn her good black slacks. She hadn't brought that many street clothes along. "The motel's on the corner of First and—"

"Believe me, lady, I know where it is." The car roared away from the airport, windows down, the icy, mid-May wind blowing her straight blond hair back over her shoulders.

She had started off this morning with the long, blunt-cut strands pulled up in a neat little twist, a few wispy tendrils stylishly cut to float around her face. But the pins poked into the back of her head as she tried to get comfortable in the narrow airline seat and she finally gave up and pulled them out, letting her hair fall free.

By the time the dilapidated car reached downtown Whitehorse, she looked as if she had been through a Chinook, northern slang for windstorm only not nearly so warm. The driver, a thick-shouldered man wearing a frayed, red-flannel shirt and a worn pair of jeans, took pity and carried her bag into the motel lobby while she dug some of the money she'd exchanged in Vancouver for Canadian currency out of her little Kate Spade purse. The bag was too small for the sort of travel she had undertaken, she had already discovered. She wished she had brought something bigger along.

Something that would have held her now-lost makeup kit and toothbrush.

Charity paid the driver and watched the battered old Buick pull away, then turned to survey her surroundings. As small as it was—a pin dot compared to Manhattan—Whitehorse was the capital of the Yukon Territory. According to the books she had read, the city had been founded during the Klondike Gold Rush when tens of thousands of prospectors journeyed by ship to Skagway, Alaska, then climbed the mountain passes to the headwaters of the Yukon River.

In the downtown area, a lot of the old, original, false-fronted buildings from the late 1800s still lined the street, making it look like something out of a John Wayne movie. The roads were narrow, and boardwalks ran in front of the stores, just as they did back then.

Standing on First across from the wide Yukon River, Charity thought of how many years she had wanted to come here and her throat clogged with emotion. She had told Jeremy she wanted an adventure. She had told that to her colleagues and friends. But only her father and her sisters knew that coming to the Yukon had been a lifelong dream.

Since she was a little girl, Charity had been fascinated by tales of the North. Over the years, she'd watched dozens of black-and-white reruns of *Sergeant Preston of the Yukon.* She'd read Robert Service poems until she knew them by heart, and cried through Jack London's wilderness stories.

Why that particular moment in history had touched her so profoundly, Charity couldn't say. Some people dreamed of visiting the Eiffel Tower. Some yearned to see the pyramids of Egypt. Charity wanted to see the snow-capped mountains and deep green forests of the North.

And after years of waiting, at last she was here.

Charity smiled and returned her thoughts to getting settled in. After she checked into the motel, she would find a drugstore, buy herself a toothbrush, then get some sorely needed sleep. She still had more than three hundred miles to travel before she reached her destination, Dawson City. In an isolated place like the Yukon, that could be a very long way.

She was a little nervous about the SUV she had leased. She'd been living in Manhattan for years. She rarely drove, and never anything as big as an Explorer. Still, with any luck at all, she would get there tomorrow.

Charity could hardly wait.

''Welcome to Dawson City, Ms. Sinclair.'' The real estate agent's name was Boomer Smith, a short, bald, heavyset man whose smile seemed permanently fixed on his face.

Smith Realty had been named in *The Wall Street Journal* article and she had found the company afterward on the Internet. Yesterday morning, once her second bag had been found and delivered to her motel and she had picked up her rental car, she had called the office from a gas station along the Klondike Highway—one of the two or three she had seen in the entire three hundred and thirty-five-mile route!

She and Smith had been scheduled to meet at his downtown office on her arrival in Dawson late yesterday afternoon, but the black Ford Explorer began having carburetor problems outside a place called Pelly Crossing, sort of a wide spot in the road, and it had taken several hours for the attendant at Selkirk's Gas, Bar, and Grocery to fix it.

By the time Charity reached Dawson, her back aching and her eyes burning from so many hours behind the wheel, it was raining. It was dark and cold and all she wanted to do was find a place to sleep. She bought a slice of pizza at a restaurant called The Grubstake and checked into the Eldorado Hotel. It wasn't until the following morning that she actually got a look at the town.

"Well, what do you think of Dawson City?" Boomer's words conjured a memory of her first glimpse of town through the windows of her motel room: a gold-rush-era city like something out of a paperback western. Muddy, unpaved streets lined with wood-frame, false-fronted, Old West buildings bordered by weathered, uneven board side-walks. It was a little like Whitehorse, but smaller, and every-thing here looked older, as if Dawson had stubbornly endured rather than give in to change.

In fact, the place looked a great deal as it must have a hundred years ago and just thinking about it made Charity smile.

"It's quite a town," she said. "I don't think I've ever been in a city that still had dirt streets."

"We try to keep things authentic. This town is special, you know. Chock-full of history. This is the way Dawson looked during the Klondike Gold Rush and we try our best to keep it that way."

He motioned her over to his cluttered oak desk and Charity sat down in a slightly rickety, straight-backed chair. Like most of the town, the office was done in the style of the late 1800s, with oak-paneled walls and hooked rugs, and kerosene lamps sitting around for decoration here and there.

They went through the necessary paperwork, but most of it had already been taken care of through the mail. "I believe I told you on the phone the equipment and furniture was minimal. To tell you the truth, I'm not even sure what's still there.''

''Yes, you explained that.''

''Good, then I guess we're all set. Mrs. Foote should be here any minute. I sent an associate out to her place yesterday after you called to say you wouldn't be here until today. Maude doesn't have a phone.''

''I see.'' And she was actually beginning to. Coming to Dawson was like stepping back in time a hundred years, and apparently some of the people in the area still lived as they did back then.

''Ah, here she comes now.''

The bell rang above the door as Maude Foote pushed her way in and Charity stood to greet her. She was older than Charity had expected, a woman perhaps in her early seventies, her wrinkles smoothed a little by the extra pounds she carried. She was at least four inches shorter than Charity, who stood five-foot-six, but the woman walked with her back straight and kept her shoulders squared.

''You must be Charity Sinclair.''

''That's right.'' Charity smiled and extended her hand, liking the woman's straightforward manner. ''It's a pleasure to meet you, Mrs. Foote.''

''Maude'll do. Been called that round these parts for nigh on fifty years.'' Maude looked her up and down, taking in her designer jeans and the sweatshirt with the red-checked collar. ''So what makes a city girl like you come all the way from New York to Dawson?''

Charity shrugged as if she wasn't really sure—which, in fact, she wasn't. ''It's kind of a long story. Let's just say I wanted a change of pace. I wanted to get away from the city and experience a different sort of life.''

''It's different, all right. But you ain't the first greenhorn to come here lookin' for gold, and it's for sure you won't be the last.''

Boomer Smith had recommended Maude Foote as someone who might be able to help her get started in her mining endeavor. Maude had prospected Dead Horse Creek, where the claim was located, for the last forty years and lived on a piece of property just down the road from the one Charity had purchased.

"Whatever my reasons for coming," Charity said, "the fact is I'm here. I intend to make the gold claim I purchased pay for itself. The question is, are you interested in helping me?"

Eyes a watery shade of blue took in the straight blond hair Charity had pulled back and secured with a tortoiseshell clip at the nape of her neck, traveled down her jean-clad legs to her brand-new Hi-Tech hiking boots.

"You got 'city gal' stamped all over you, but I guess you'll do. Money you offered is more than fair and I got nothin' better to do. 'Sides, that claim you bought ain't never really been worked. We just might find ourselves some gold."

Charity bit back an urge to whoop out *Yippee!* This whole thing was crazy from beginning to end and yet she had never felt more alive, more sure that in coming on this adventure she had done exactly the right thing.

"Mr. Smith also mentioned a man named Johnson who might be willing to help us. He said you would speak to him for me. Has he agreed to take the job?"

"Buck Johnson owns the property that borders yours to the north. He's been dredging for gold for twenty-odd years. Early on, he had considerable luck, but not lately. He knows what he's doin' and he needs the money. He says he'll sign on."

She bit back a grin. "Great. When do we start?"

"I ain't been out to the Lily Rose since old Mose Flanagan packed up and moved. It'll probably take some rightin' to get the place in order. We'd best pick up supplies before we head out of town. Might not get back here for a while."

At Maude's instruction, they stopped at the Dawson City General Store to buy groceries, cleaning supplies, and bedding, including sheets, towels, and blankets. They bought a four-place set of dishes, silverware, pots, pans, and utensils. Maude suggested she buy an air mattress till they found out what sort of bed was there—if any. They would pick up whatever else they might need after Charity had seen the cabin and what was inside.

Once the place was livable, they could talk to Buck Johnson, decide what equipment they would need to start the dredging operation.

As they loaded their purchases into the back of the Explorer, Charity found herself grinning. Her adventure had truly begun. She couldn't wait to see her new home.

McCall Ryan Hawkins paused at the edge of a line of firs at the top of the rise and slung his backpack down on the ground. Below him, Dead Horse Creek looked no bigger than a narrow white ribbon, tumbling over boulders and winding through rocky crevices on its way down the hill.

Call squinted through the binoculars that hung from a strap around his neck. From where he stood on the border of his wooded, two-thousand-acre property not far from King Solomon Dome, he could see old man Flanagan's dilapidated cabin perched just above the creek.

The place was even more run-down than it was before ol' Mose left. One of the front-porch steps had a hole punched through it and a shutter tilted down beside the window, creaking in the wind.

Funny how forlorn the place looked. Though Call and ol' Mose had never gotten along, so much silence seemed odd somehow. The two of them had argued over everything from Mose's decrepit mule straying onto Call's property to the noise the old fool's muffler-less pickup made rattling down the gravel road and the dust he managed to create that filtered through every window in Call's house. Call had been damned glad to see the old man go.

And yet in some bizarre way, he missed him.

At least he'd had someone to argue with.

Call shook his head, thinking the climb down from the summit must have slightly addled his brain.

Turning away from the view of the cabin, he hoisted his

backpack onto his shoulders, whistled for Smoke, the big part-wolf, part-husky dog he'd adopted as a pup, and started off down the trail, heading back from his overnight trek to the house he had built along the creek.

It had been more than four years since Call had returned to the Yukon, seeking the solitude of the forest, searching for a quiet place where he could forget the past and put his life back in order. As he walked along the trail, images of those days threatened to creep in, but he firmly pushed them away, consigning them to the part of his brain where they could no longer hurt him.

He didn't like to think of the past, to remember what had sent him into his self-inflicted exile four years ago, and so he kept walking, his strides lengthening as if he could leave the painful memories behind with every step he took down the hill.

He spotted the tall rock chimney marking his home on the creek and almost missed the two specs moving farther down the mountain that signaled a pair of unfamiliar cars coming up the road. Being an hour out of Dawson on a bumpy dirt lane and only a few sparse inhabitants along Dead Horse Creek, visitors were uncommon.

As usual, Call felt a trickle of irritation that his privacy was about to be disturbed, even for the short time it took for the cars to rumble past.

He wondered who they were and where they were going.

He wondered what the hell they were doing on Dead Horse Creek.

After making the turn off Hunker Road, Charity followed Maude's ancient blue pickup along a winding gravel lane that followed the creek. They stopped once, at the little cabin where Maude apparently lived, so the older woman could retrieve a pair of work gloves she had forgotten.

"No sense buying new ones when I already got these," she said, having declined the pair Charity had offered to purchase for her at the general store.

''How much farther?'' Charity asked as she watched the older woman's peculiar ambling gait, sort of like a sailor crossing the deck of a ship, only there wasn't any water.

''Not much. Just around the next couple of curves and up the hill a piece.''

Just around the next couple of curves turned out to be a couple of miles, each one dragging at the slow pace they were forced to travel on the narrow, muddy road. Anticipation had her squirming in her seat. She felt like a little kid on her first trip to Disney World, so eager to get there, unable to quite imagine what it would be like once she did.

As the SUV rolled on, dropping into one pothole after another, she thanked God she had rented a four-wheel-drive vehicle. A regular car simply wouldn't be able to make it. She sighed as they crawled past another bend in the road.

At least I've got time to get a good look at the country, she thought, glancing off toward the rocky hills covered with a mixture of pine, fir, and alder. The entire area was mountainous, each peak dusted with a brilliant white layer of mid-spring snow.

It was spectacularly beautiful and worth the entire trip just to see it. Charity grinned to think that for the next six months she would be living in this wild, scenic place.

They rounded another curve and the pickup's red taillights went on in front of her. Charity had noticed earlier that one of the bulbs was out. She glanced toward the stream they had been following, out across a rickety-looking wooden bridge, and spotted a small log cabin situated among the pine trees at the edge of the creek.

The Lily Rose. A little thrill shot through her. Never mind that the bridge looked like it might collapse at any moment. It could be fixed easily enough. She still had money to make the needed repairs.

Maude drove over the bridge as if it were perfectly safe, so Charity closed her eyes, summoned her courage, and pretended it really was. She clattered to the opposite side and released the breath she had been holding. Parking the Ford next to the cabin, she set the emergency brake and climbed out of the car.

The breath she took of fresh Klondike air was cold and clean and smelled of the pine trees that grew on the hill behind the cabin. She could hear the rush of water over the boulders in the creek as she walked toward the house.

She paused at the bottom of the steps leading up to the covered porch. The cabin was made of logs, as the advertisement had said, but the wood shingle roof was sagging and a broken board made it hard to climb the front-porch stairs.

"Needs a little work," Maude said—the understatement of the year. The house was a shambles, Charity discovered with a sinking heart as she opened the door and walked in. It was hard not to feel a rush of disappointment.

"A cozy, one-bedroom cabin on a wild, rushing stream," she quoted from the advertisement. "Well, the stream is wild and rushing, and I can see the *convenient kitchen* from here." Two steps to the right of the door, just at the end of the living room, such as it was.

"It ain't as bad as it seems," Maude said firmly. Reaching into the pocket of her plaid flannel shirt, she pulled out a short-stemmed pipe and stuck it between her teeth. "Just needs a little work, is all."

More than a little, Charity thought glumly, watching Maude chew on the end of the unlit pipe and imagining the small inheritance her grandfather had left her shrinking by the minute. "The place needs just about everything."

"Stove works real good." Maude pointed to the big, black woodstove in the kitchen. "And the water's piped in from the well and stored in that big tank behind the house. You don't have to carry it up from the creek." She turned the handle on the faucet over the sink to demonstrate and it sputtered dirty brown water out of its nozzle. "Ain't been used in a while. Take a minute to start runnin' clean."

Charity's stomach knotted. They wandered past a small, round table and four rickety kitchen chairs that had been painted white and now were a peeling, dismal gray, and stepped into the living room, ducking cobwebs here and there. The *rustic rock fireplace* was exactly that, but the smooth, round river stones were covered with a layer of thick, black soot and ashes spilled over the hearth onto the wood-planked floor.

"Roof might need some work, but the place is sturdy—I can tell ya that. When Mose moved in, he fixed it up real good."

He must have. It looked as if it had been sitting there for the last hundred years, which she now believed it might actually have been.

"Fireplace looks real purty on a cold winter night, but the real heat comes from that little pellet stove in the corner. It'll get hot enough to run you outta here."

Well, at least she'd be warm. They wandered into the single bedroom, which was furnished with an old iron bed with sagging box springs but no mattress, a rickety wooden dresser, and two homemade bedside tables. As the ad had boasted, there was indeed *a bathroom with indoor plumbing*—a claw foot tub with a makeshift shower above it, a sink, and tank-overhead, flush toilet. But the toilet was stopped up and no water came out of the shower when Charity turned it on.

She sank down on the lid of the toilet and gave in to a sigh of despair. "I thought it would at least be livable."

"Will be. Soon as we get it cleaned up. This used to be a real nice place. Won't take much to make it that way again."

Charity looked over at Maude, saw the determined set of her jaw, and took heart from the older woman's words. She had come here seeking adventure. She was hardly going to let a little thing like a dirty house get her down.

"You're right." She stood up from the commode. "We'll put it back in shape. It'll just take a little more time than I expected." And money, but she left that part out. "Once we get it cleaned up enough to live in, I'll go back into town and hire workmen to make the necessary repairs."

Maude smiled her approval. "Electric works real good. Mose put that in just a couple years ago."

The power ran off a generator, Charity discovered, which was turned on each morning and evening. It seemed to be the only thing working in the house.

"I'll bring in the cleaning supplies," she volunteered, beginning to get into the spirit. "We might as well get started."

Maude helped her unload the Explorer and the two of them set to work. If Charity had any doubts as to whether or not a woman Maude's age could handle the grueling job of scrubbing walls and floors, cleaning out the fireplace, dusting cobwebs, and hauling trash, it didn't take long to squelch them. Maude Foote had more energy than most women half her years. There were times Charity would have rested, but Maude's boundless energy kept her working.

"We'll burn the trash in the morning," Maude said. "There's some rotten food in it and we don't want to attract any bears."

Her head came up. "Bears?"

"Don't worry, most the time they're more afraid of you than you are of them."

Most the time?

Charity shoved the disturbing thought away and continued filling the old tin bucket she had found, with ashes from the fireplace. By the end of that first day, when Maude climbed into her battered blue truck to make the short drive to her house down the hill, the kitchen was spotless, the cupboards cleaned out, the dishes all washed and put away. The fireplace held a cheery blaze made from the last of a stack of wood they had found in one of the sheds, the pellet stove was lit and hopefully would keep the house warm through the night, and Maude had helped her rig slats to prop up the sagging box springs.

She was grateful for the air mattress but even without it, as tired as she was, Charity had no doubt she'd be able to sleep. The bad news was, until she got the plumbing repaired she would have to use the outhouse.

Just part of the adventure, she told herself, never having had the dubious pleasure. She thought of the bears Maude had mentioned, thought of having to go outside in the middle of the night, and set the glass of water she had been drinking back down on the rickety table next to the bed.

CHAPTER THREE

At the pounding on the door, Charity's eyes cracked open. Her little travel alarm clock said it was only 6:00 A.M. Groaning, she tossed back the covers. She had thought it would be cold when she got up, but the pellet stove had done its job, thank God, and the house was still fairly warm. Charity pulled on her thick terry cloth robe and stumbled toward the door.

Maude Foote stood on the porch, she saw when she peeked through the grime they hadn't yet washed off the living room windows. Charity slid back the bolt and pulled open the heavy wooden door.

"Figured you'd want to get started early," Maude said, shoving past her into the house. "I'll fire up the cookstove and fix us somethin' to eat while you get dressed."

That was the deal Charity had made. Maude had been hired as advisor, cook, and general all-around worker. Charity just hadn't figured her employee would be so eager to get to work.

With a weary sigh, she shoved back her tangled blond hair, hooking it over one ear, and stumbled back into the bedroom. She dragged on the same jeans and sweatshirt she had worn the day before and pulled on her hiking boots for a quick trip to the outhouse.

She was shivering by the time she got back inside. The shower wasn't working but she could at least wash her face. Pouring water from the old porcelain pitcher they had found in the closet into a matching basin, she plunged a washrag into the chilly water and began to scrub off yesterday's dirt.

There was a mirror over the dresser, missing most of its silver but good enough that she could see her reflection. She brushed the tangles out of her hair and clipped it back and began to feel a little better.

She wasn't used to going without makeup. Applying a little base that included sunscreen, a whisper of light brown eye shadow, and a stroke of blush to each cheek, she added a dab of lipstick and walked toward the kitchen, feeling almost her old self again.

"Thought we'd start by fixing up this here furniture a little."

"Fix it? You mean like paint it?"

"Needs it, don't it?"

Charity thought Maude must be the queen of the understatement. "Absolutely." Though she had never been particularly handy, out here there really was no other choice. "Unfortunately, we didn't buy any paint."

"I brought some I had down to the house."

Charity eyed her warily. "What color is it?"

"There's a can of bright red or kind of an olive green. You can take your pick."

Catching a whiff of coffee on the stove, Charity went over and filled her cup, giving herself time to mull the notion over. She wasn't handy but she had always had a good sense of style and taste. "Red or olive green." It sounded a little too much like Christmas, but hey, when in Rome . . .

She glanced down at the peeling white paint on the breakfast table and chairs and tried to imagine them painted bright red. She didn't think she could handle red but maybe the green, if it actually was more of an olive. She envisioned the aging dresser in the bedroom and thought of it also painted green. If the knobs were painted red along with the ornate iron headboard of the bed . . . if she used bright-red accents throughout the tiny cabin, it just might look pretty.

"We'll have to brace 'em up a little, make 'em more sturdy," Maude said.

"Okay, but sometime today I think we should go back in to town. I want to get the workmen started on the plumbing and we'd better get something done about the roof." So far the place hadn't leaked but she wasn't sure how much longer the sagging timbers would hold out. Better to be safe than sorry.

As soon as breakfast was over, they dragged what furniture they'd found in the house out onto the porch and started bracing each piece up so it wouldn't wobble.

"We're gonna run outta nails," Maude grumbled. "I'll see if I can find us some out back." She ambled off to look through one of the wooden sheds behind the cabin while Charity continued to hammer away. She was pounding, making quite a racket, when she looked up to see a man striding down the path along the creek, headed in her direction.

He was tall, at least six-two or six-three, dressed in a pair of faded jeans that molded to long, muscular legs, and a worn denim shirt that stretched over shoulders the width of an axe handle. He was lean, no extra flesh, yet his movements spoke of power and physical strength. Whoever he was, he needed a haircut. Coffee-brown hair, several inches too long, curled over his collar, and it looked as if he hadn't shaved for the better part of a week.

As he got closer, she noticed he was very tan, his eyes an amazing shade of blue with tiny lines fanning out at the corners. He was probably mid-thirties, and even with his unkempt hair and several days' growth of beard, he was a very attractive man.

Charity thought of Jeremy Hauser but only fleetingly. This man and Jeremy had nothing at all in common. While Jeremy was almost ridiculously civilized, this man looked as if he had just stepped out of the pages of a Jack London

novel, like a lumberjack, or maybe a trapper, home from
weeks spent out in the woods.

He kept on walking, his strides long and filled with purpose, and as he approached the porch, she saw that his
features were sharply defined: his nose straight, his cheeks
lean, and his jaw square. There was a slight indentation in
his chin. She wondered if he was a neighbor, started to smile
and introduce herself when his deep voice cut through the
cool morning air.

"All right, what the hell is going on?"

Ignoring the anger in his voice, Charity set her hammer
on top of the dresser and climbed down from the porch.

"Good morning. I'm Charity Sinclair. I'm the new—"

"I don't care who you are, lady, I want to know what
you're doing on this property."

She fixed a smile on her face, though it took a good bit
of effort "I'm here because I'm the owner. I bought the
Lily Rose from a man named Moses Flanagan."

He narrowed those striking blue eyes at her. "Bullshit.
Old man Flanagan may not live here anymore but he'd die
before he'd ever sell the Lily Rose. I don't know who you
think you're kidding, sweetheart, but if you're planning to
squat on his property you can forget it."

It was getting harder by the moment to hang on to her
temper. "You're wrong, Mr . . . ?"

He made no effort to answer, just continued to glare down
the length of his nicely shaped nose.

"Mr. Flanagan decided to move in with his son in Calgary.
He listed the property for sale several weeks ago with Smith
Real Estate in Dawson. I'm the person who bought it."

His features looked even harder than they had before.
"That's impossible. I tried to buy this place from Mose
Flanagan every other month for the last four years. He
refused to even consider it."

Her irritation inched up a notch. "Well, apparently he
changed his mind. The transaction officially closed yesterday
morning. I don't know why he didn't tell you the property

was for sale.'' When his black scowl deepened, she couldn't resist adding, ''Maybe he just didn't like you.''

He opened his mouth to argue, clamped down on his jaw instead, and a muscle jumped in his cheek. Apparently her goading had hit on a portion of the truth.

''So now you're the owner,'' he said darkly.

''That's right, I am.''

He looked her over from head to foot, taking in her Liz Claiborne jeans and the touch of makeup she hadn't been able to resist. She bristled at his smug expression.

''And you actually intend to move in?''

''I *am* in, Mr . . . ?''

''Hawkins. McCall Hawkins. I'm your next-door neighbor, so to speak. And I don't appreciate all that hammering you've been doing. I like things nice and quiet. I enjoy my privacy and I don't like being disturbed. It'll be easier on both of us if you keep that in mind.''

''I'll do my best,'' she lied, thinking of the noisy dredging equipment she intended to use in the stream. She gave him a too-sweet smile. ''I'd say it was a pleasure, Mr. Hawkins, but we both know it wasn't. Now if you'll excuse me, I have to get back to work.''

Turning away from him, she climbed the stairs to the porch, picked up her hammer, and started pounding on the dresser again, dismissing him as if he had never been there. For several long moments, he simply stood there glaring. Then she caught the movement of his shadow as he turned and stalked away, back down the path beside the creek.

Of all the nerve. Who the devil did he think he was?

She remembered passing his house just before she reached the Lily Rose, a newer, cedar-sided home with a large, metal-roofed garage of some sort attached to it. At the time she had wondered who lived there.

Charity bit back a curse as she thought of her irritating ''next-door neighbor.'' It didn't matter. *He* didn't matter.

She turned at the sound of Maude's laughter coming up the stairs of the porch. The older woman's gaze followed

Hawkins's retreating figure down the path. "I see you met your neighbor. Wondered when he'd show up."

"Oh, I met him, all right, and I didn't like him any more than he liked me."

Maude chuckled. "Call's all right. Long as you leave him alone. He owns a couple thousand acres on this side of the creek. Built the house he lives in when he got here four years ago. Never met a man who likes his privacy more than Call."

"If he's so concerned about privacy, he should have built his house somewhere back in the woods, instead of right out here on the water."

"I guess he liked the view."

Since she liked looking down on the wild, boulder-strewn stream herself, she didn't argue. Besides, it didn't matter. The property was hers to do with as she pleased.

And there wasn't a damn thing Call Hawkins or anyone else could do about it.

Call stalked up the front steps of his house, his temper foul and his face hard. Crossing the porch, he jerked open the door and strode in, letting the screen door slam behind him.

"Sonofabitch." He should have appreciated the quiet while he had it. Damn, he couldn't believe his bad luck. If only he'd known the place was for sale. No doubt ol' Mose was rubbing his hands in glee, thinking of the prissy little blonde moving in next door to him.

Of course, she wouldn't be there long. Life this far north was hard. The rainy season had already started. For the next few weeks, there'd be too much rain and too much mud. Then summer would come and there'd be too much sun. There'd be dust and forest fires. There'd be pine beetles and hornets and flies enough to drive you crazy. If she made it till winter—which there was no way in hell she would—there'd be snow up to her pretty little ass.

He thought of the designer jeans she wore that said she

was a city girl and not from around these parts, and tried not to think how good she had looked in them. He thought of her pretty face and the hint of makeup she had worn that emphasized her clear green eyes. What in the world had possessed a woman like that to come to an isolated place like Dead Horse Creek?

Of course he had also come north from the city, but that was different. Call had been born in this country. His father had been in the logging business in Prince George, a small town in the forests of British Columbia, and though his mother was American, she had loved the woods and the out-of-doors as much as her husband. Both Call and his brother, Zach, had been hunting and fishing this country for as long as either of them could remember. Both of them loved to backpack, canoe, and cross-country ski.

But Call, a year older than Zach, had been young back then, and he had been restless, curious about life in the city. The lure of his mother's American family in San Francisco had drawn him to the States. He'd spent four years at Berkeley, where he had roomed with a boy named Richie Gill. Call and Richie had become fast friends, both of them interested in sports and the fascinating world of computers. Eventually, they'd become partners in a successful software game that had made them both rich.

Call had entered the world of business and loved it. By the time he had sold his first company and accepted the position as President and CEO of American Dynamics, he was working sixteen hours a day, so immersed in the financial empire he was building he didn't have time for anything else.

Not even his family.

As it always did, the memory sent pain ripping through him like a ragged shard of glass. It eased as he forced the thoughts away. He never dwelled on the past anymore. He'd spent four long years trying to forget it.

"Toby!" he shouted as he crossed the polished wood floor in the living room. "Toby, are you in here?"

The younger man appeared through the doorway of the

kitchen. "I'm right here, sir. I thought I'd make us a couple ham sandwiches for lunch." Toby Jenkins had just turned nineteen, a good-looking, red-haired kid, tall and lanky, with a slender, wiry frame.

His mother lived in Dawson, ran one of the small jewelry shops in town that catered to the tourist trade. Six months ago, Toby had heard through the grapevine that Call was looking for a handyman, someone to do odd jobs for him out on Dead Horse Creek. For the first three years, Call had taken care of the place himself, but he was busier now and he needed the help. Toby lived in a small, one-bedroom cabin Call had remodeled and furnished up on the hill, far enough away so he could maintain his privacy, yet close enough so Toby could take care of the chores around the house.

"I'm not hungry," Call said. "Wrap it up and I'll eat it later."

Toby frowned. "You skipped breakfast. You gotta eat something."

Call made an unpleasant sound in his throat. The kid could be a real mother hen at times. Call figured Toby saw him as some kind of father figure, since he'd never had a dad of his own and didn't even know who the guy was. Call had been a father once. He never intended to travel that painful road again.

"Like I said—just wrap it up. I'll get around to it sooner or later."

Toby ducked back into the kitchen and Call paused for a moment in front of the big rock fireplace in the living room. The house wasn't fancy, just two bedrooms and a couple of baths, but there was a modern kitchen with the latest appliances, and the L-shaped living-dining area was nicely furnished with a comfortable, dark-brown leather sofa and chairs and accented with nineteenth-century antiques.

He'd added the metal-roofed building that housed his office and a three-car garage a little over a year ago, the first small step, as he saw it, on the road back to life.

Still, he wasn't ready to give up his solitary world completely and he certainly didn't want it breached by a woman, especially not one who spelled trouble like Charity Sinclair.

"Sonofabitch," he grumbled again, and wondered just exactly what he could do to get rid of her.

It was noon by the time Charity and Maude left for town, late afternoon by the time they returned, but Charity had found a local plumbing company to deal with the bathroom, and a roofer had agreed to do the necessary roof repairs. They'd bought a few supplies, including bags of pellets for the stove.

On one of the side streets, she had spotted an antiques store that also carried used furniture. She bought a full-size mattress and box springs that appeared to be in good condition and would fit the old iron bed, and a small sofa and chair she could decorate with the olive green dust cover she had found at the general store.

All in all, it was a good day's work, but she hadn't gotten home till almost dark and again she went to bed exhausted, too tired even to finish the Max Mason adventure novel, *Island of Doom,* that she had been reading.

Tomorrow she and Maude would finish cleaning the house and the day after that, she hoped to meet Buck Johnson and begin discussing the equipment they would need to start up the dredging operation. She wondered how many more grueling trips to Dawson she would have to endure before they actually got started.

They washed windows and scrubbed bathroom cupboards the following day, then gave the furniture another coat of paint.

"We been lucky," Maude said as she stuck the paintbrush into a can filled with thinner. "We get a lot of rain this time of year. Need to get the paint dry and this stuff back in the house before the next storm blows in."

As Maude predicted, clouds began to gather the morning of the following day. The older woman arrived just in time to help her move the furniture back inside the house before the sky opened up like a floodgate and rain fell in sheets so thick she couldn't see the creek.

It was Thursday. The workmen she had hired in Dawson had a couple of jobs to finish and weren't scheduled to arrive until the first of the week. As Charity had feared, the roof began to leak. A stream of water dripped over the woodstove in the kitchen, sending up a hiss of steam as each drop sputtered against the hot black metal.

A leak sprang up over the john in the bathroom, which didn't really matter, since it was still clogged up and totally useless anyway. The outhouse, she had discovered, was bad enough in pleasant weather. In the rain it was nearly unbearable. The roof above the little wooden building leaked even worse than the one over the house. She was soaked and freezing by the time she finished and got back inside the cabin.

Maude drove to her own house down the hill and came back with rain gear, the loan of which Charity accepted with gratitude and a mental note to buy herself some the next time she was in Dawson. It was hard to imagine putting on a heavy yellow slicker every time she had to relieve herself, but hey, stuff happened.

You wanted an adventure, she reminded herself. She thought of her favorite action hero, Max Mason, who traveled the world fighting evil, survived under the very worst conditions, and never complained. Compared to what Max went through, living up here was a stroll in the park.

Besides, next week, once the repairs were made, things were bound to get better.

Unfortunately, on Saturday, Buck Johnson showed up and she began to wonder if they ever really would.

"It's a pleasure to meet you, Mr. Johnson," she said with a welcoming smile. "I'm really looking forward to working with you."

"I never worked for a woman," he grumbled. "Maude didn't tell me the new owner was a female."

Charity straightened a little and was glad she hadn't offered to shake his hand. She came from Manhattan, after all, a city where Johnson's Planet-of-the-Apes attitude was mostly a thing of the past. "I can't see why that should matter, Mr. Johnson. I'm here to work this claim. You have experience in that regard. I'd like to employ you. That is all that matters."

Johnson grumbled something she couldn't hear. He was a big man, mid-forties, thick through the chest and shoulders, with black hair slightly graying at the temples. His forehead was wide, his nose a little too broad, and she wondered if it had been broken.

"Well, Mr. Johnson, do you want the job or not?"

"I got a kid in city college down in Whitehorse. I need the money."

"Is that a yes?"

He nodded as if he couldn't quite force out the word. "You might as well call me Buck."

"Fine ... Buck." She didn't give him her first name as she had intended. With Buck Johnson's attitude toward women, she needed him to accept that she was the boss. She hoped that in time they would come to a better understanding. "The first thing I'd like you to do is take a look at the equipment out in the shed. There isn't all that much, but some of it may be useful."

He nodded. "I'd better get to it, then." Slamming his battered old felt hat back on his head, he turned to leave— glad, it seemed, to escape outside.

As he closed the front door, Charity watched Maude saunter out of the kitchen.

"I figured you'd best deal with Buck on your own. Better he knows who he's workin' for right from the giddy-up."

"Why didn't you tell him I was a woman?"

A droopy, gray-brown eyebrow went up. "You really gotta ask?"

Charity almost smiled. "No, I guess I don't."

"We might be able to find someone else, but it'll take time and with the claim bein' so far from town, you'd have to come up with some kind of living quarters. Buck's awful handy, livin' just up the road. I figure he'll come round in time.''

''I hope so.''

''He knows what he's doin'. He's been at it more'n twenty years.''

She sighed. ''I guess that's the most important thing.''

Buck returned a little while later. The rain had turned into a fine, cold mist that clung to his flannel shirt and beaded on his ratty brown-felt hat.

''Old Mose never really worked the Lily Rose,'' he said, accepting the seat she offered at the now-green kitchen table. She had drawn a leaf pattern in red paint on the top and done the same to the backs of the chairs. She smiled to think her first handyman endeavor had turned out pretty well, considering.

''He owned a couple of other claims,'' Buck continued, ''one farther up Dead Horse Creek and another over on Bonanza Creek. He spent most of his time working those.''

''Paid off pretty well for him, too,'' Maude put in.

''From what I read,'' Charity said, ''since the Lily Rose hasn't been worked, we'll have a better chance of finding gold.''

''Oh, we'll find some, all right,'' Buck agreed. ''Can't hardly stick a pan in the water in these parts without turning up some color. Question is, how much will we find?''

A good question. She hoped it was at least enough to return the money she had invested. ''I guess we can't know that until we get started. What exactly are we going to need?''

''Like you said, there wasn't much out in the shed— leastwise, nothing much useful. Times have changed. Equipment's got a lot better in the last few years. Even gold pans aren't the same as they was when I first started. The good ones are made of plastic now and the best of those is green. Shows the color better. We'll need a few of them to start.''

''What else?''

''That old skip loader out there still works, after a fashion. Needs a little tuning, but I can handle that. We'll need a dredge—that's the most important thing—one with plenty of power but still portable enough to move up and down the creek. I can build us a sluice box. We'll need wire mesh, stuff for a riffle board, and a two- or three-horse engine for vibration.''

"All right, what else?''

"We'll need picks and shovels. A good metal detector would sure come in handy.''

She flicked a glance at Maude. "Will we be able to get all that in Dawson?'' She hoped they didn't have to go all the way to Whitehorse or order it from somewhere even farther away.

"There's a place on the outskirts of town,'' Maude said. "D. K. Prospecting Supplies. They'll have everything we need.''

"Mining is still big business up here,'' Buck put in. "And there's still plenty of gold. All you have to do is find it.''

She felt an inward thrill and a smile bloomed over her lips. "Then that's what we're going to do.''

Buck took a look at her salon-trimmed hair and the dab of makeup she couldn't resist, and apparently wasn't convinced.

"Monday,'' she said to Maude, ignoring him, "once the workmen arrive to repair the roof and the plumbers come to fix the bathroom, Buck and I will head off to D. K. Prospecting to buy the equipment we need.''

Buck made no comment, but his jaw looked tight. Charity figured he didn't like the idea of people in town finding out he was working for a woman.

Too bad, Bucko, she thought. Hadn't the guy ever heard of women's lib? Well, it was time he stopped living in the past and accepted the idea that she was the one who'd be signing his paycheck.

Monday arrived. They waited all day but the workmen never showed up. Not until late Tuesday morning. Maude said they worked on Klondike time. She said Charity might as well get used to it.

"Just the way things is done up here. Nobody hurries much. Too many other things to do."

"You mean like go camping or fishing," Charity grumbled, beginning to get the idea.

"Or canoein' maybe, or packin' back into the woods. Sun comes out, they're bound to find somethin' better to do than work."

Fortunately, Tuesday was overcast and drizzly. Charity breathed a sigh of relief when the Jed's Plumbing truck rolled up the road. An hour later, three men from Moss and Son's roofing arrived and set to work.

The plumbing snake was grinding away, the roofers pounding shingles when Charity caught sight of a dark-haired man striding toward her down the path along the creek. This time she knew who it was and though she pretended not to notice his long, angry strides, some evil little part of her couldn't wait for him to get there.

As he neared the cabin, Call spotted Charity Sinclair where she stood at the near end of the cabin. She was watching the men on the roof, her head tilted back, hair hanging down to the middle of her back, a few wisps framing her face. The long shiny strands were a bright yellow-gold, exactly the color of a nugget he had once found in the creek.

She turned as he got closer and pasted a phony-looking smile on her face. "Well, Mr. Hawkins. How nice of you to come over for another neighborly chat."

"This isn't a neighborly chat, sweetheart, and you know it. What the hell is happening over here? I thought I told you I liked peace and quiet."

"Yes, I believe you did. Unfortunately for you, I like being able to use my bathroom for something other than a place to hang wet towels and I prefer to cook my meals without rainwater dripping into my food."

He'd seen her walking back and forth to the outhouse in

her rain slicker. He'd wondered if she'd ever even seen one before. He glanced up at the sagging cabin roof. He figured it would start leaking sooner or later.

"That bad, huh?" He tried to keep the satisfaction out of his voice, but he could see by her pinched expression she had heard it.

"Let's just say Mr. Flanagan had good reason to move."

"How long till they finish the repairs?"

"Since the men seem to be working on 'Klondike time,' I have no idea. I guess it depends on whether or not the sun comes out."

He ignored a flicker of amusement, clamped down on his jaw instead. "Well, the sooner they get done, the better. All that hammering is driving me crazy."

Her smile remained frozen in place. "Maude tells me you own quite a lot of property along the creek. Perhaps you should think of relocating your house someplace farther back in the woods."

Actually, he had thought of building deeper in the forest, but he liked looking down on the water. Besides, there was a limit to solitude, even for him. At least here he'd see a car on the road once in a while. Maude Foote stopped by on occasion, and he'd had Mose to argue with.

It seemed he would have fresh battles to fight with Charity Sinclair.

"I like my house right where it is," he said, then changed tactics and added, "How much do you want for your property?"

Surprise widened those clear green eyes. She was wearing a red cotton turtleneck and he could see she had nice breasts. Her fancy jeans were filled out as well as he remembered, better maybe. Round behind, tiny waist, legs just the right length for the rest of her. His loins began to fill. It happened so rarely he took an unconscious step backward. Jesus, he couldn't believe it.

"My property isn't for sale," she said, distracting him, thank God.

"I'll double whatever you paid for it. You can buy a bigger piece of property somewhere else."

"I don't want a bigger piece of property. The Lily Rose belongs to me and I intend to keep it."

"I'll give you three times what you paid."

Her lips flattened out. Before, he noticed, they'd been full and very nicely curved. "I don't think you understand, Mr. Hawkins. The Lily Rose is a mining claim. I intend to work that claim, as I have every right to do. You can offer me ten times the price I paid—a hundred. It wouldn't make a whit of difference. I'm staying, Mr. Hawkins, whether you like it or not. If anyone's going to move, it'll have to be you!"

He drilled her with a glare and saw her tense a little at the forbidding look on his face. "You aren't telling me you intend to set up a dredging operation on this property?" Anger softened his voice, making the unspoken threat all the more intimidating. Four years ago, his employees had cowered at that menacing tone but Charity didn't back down.

"That's exactly what I'm telling you. That's what Mose Flanagan intended to do—he just never got around to it."

"Sonofabitch!"

The smile she gave him looked downright evil. "Get used to it, Mr. Hawkins. I'm staying right here and working this claim. Accept it or move somewhere else."

With that she turned and marched away. He tried not to notice that round behind, but his eyes refused to look anywhere else.

Sonofabitch, he silently repeated, thinking again of Mose and the secret laugh he must be getting out of this. Call turned and started walking. He didn't look back all the way to the house. But even if he closed his eyes, he could still see the pretty little blonde with her nice breasts and round behind.

For months, he'd been telling himself it was time to reawaken the sexual side of his life. He wasn't a monk, even if he had been living like one. A couple of weeks ago, he'd started seeing a divorcee in Dawson named Sally Beecham, a cocktail waitress at the Yukon Saloon he had known for a couple of years. Sally was a sexy little brunette and she had made it clear he was welcome in her bed whenever he was ready. He'd been telling himself that time would be soon.

But he'd never gotten hard looking at Sally.

Not like he was right now, just thinking of Charity Sinclair.

"I don't believe that guy." Charity walked over to where Maude stood on the porch. "Who the hell does he think he is?"

Maude chuckled. "Call's got a burr under his saddle, all right. At times, he can be downright cantankerous. But folks say he's got more money than he can count and that deal he was offerin' sounded pretty darned good. You might shoulda taken it."

She lifted her chin. "I'm not selling. Not now or anytime in the foreseeable future." Not for the next six months, at any rate. That was the time she had allotted herself and she wasn't going anywhere until that time ran out.

"All right then, if that's the way it is, I guess you and Buck had best be headin' into town."

Charity nodded. "I think he's out in the equipment shed. I'll go get him."

With Maude there to oversee the repair work being done to the cabin, Charity and Buck drove down to Dawson, Buck behind the wheel of the Explorer, which made the trip a little less wearing on her nerves. Still, the man was gruff and surly, and she didn't like the way he looked at her when he thought she couldn't see.

The good news was they succeeded in their mission even better than she had expected. To her amazement and everlasting gratitude, Charity discovered that the Internet had arrived in Dawson City. There were, in fact, two tiny Internet cafes where she could send and receive e-mail from friends and family back home. Better yet, she found out through D. K.

Prospecting that cell phones existed even in a rural place like Dawson.

While Buck assembled the equipment they would need, Charity signed up for cell phone service through Horizons Unlimited, tossing the bulky phone that had more power than the smaller models she was used to onto the seat of the Ford.

They were finished by late afternoon and on their way back to the cabin as dusk began to fall, the back of the Explorer filled with shovels, picks, gold pans, and miscellaneous gear, the larger equipment scheduled for delivery in the morning.

Unless, of course, the sun came out, in which case it might take a couple more days.

Charity's sigh turned into a grin. It was different up here. There was none of the hustle and bustle of Manhattan. Her life was new and strange and she was enjoying every minute of it. Except for her trips to the outhouse, of course.

She was even enjoying her battles with Call Hawkins.

His tall image rose in her mind, his hard jaw shadowed by the morning shave he'd missed, his hair too long but a nice, shiny nut-brown color. He reminded her a little of Max Mason—rawhide tough, whipcord lean, hard as nails. As much as she disliked the man, there was something about him that intrigued her.

Something besides his height and solid, broad-shouldered build. Besides the fact that he was so obviously male.

She didn't know exactly what it was—and she didn't want to find out. She had better things to do than think about a guy like McCall Hawkins.

Still, the image of him standing there in his faded jeans and denim shirt was surprisingly hard to forget.

CHAPTER FOUR

The equipment arrived on schedule—something to do with the rain, no doubt. Fortunately, even with the mud, the road up the mountain was still passable. Charity wasn't so sure it would be by the end of the day.

Men from D. K. Prospecting Supplies, Inc., unloaded the dredge and the rest of the machinery she and Buck had picked out, then headed back down the mountain before the mud got so deep they couldn't make it. There was a workshop of sorts in one of the sheds out back and Buck had ordered the building materials he needed for the sluice box to be unloaded there.

"It'll take a while to get everything put together," he said, and started off in that direction, leaving Charity to examine the portable dredge the men had unloaded that would need to be assembled.

She had seen a variety of different kinds in the prospecting magazines she had been reading. A gold dredge was a piece of equipment that worked like an oversized vacuum cleaner, sucking creek water, rocks, gravel, and anything else it encountered into a long, flexible pipe at one end and dumping it into the sluice box at the other. Once the water passed through the box, it ran back into the creek, hopefully minus the gold it had been hiding.

Maude sauntered up just then. "That thing's a real work-horse when it comes to findin' gold, but you still gotta learn the basics. If a little rain don't bother you, I can show you how to pan." The sagging skin below her jaw jiggled as Maude looked down at the item in her hand, a round, green plastic gold pan, flat on the bottom with the slides sloping up. There were notches for catching gold about five inches long, maybe an inch and a half apart in one spot on the pan.

Charity grinned. "What's a little rain when you're lookin' for color?" she said, using her best prospector's accent.

"Come on, then. Let's get to it." They were wearing their knee-length yellow slickers, though the rain had slowed to a steady drizzle. Maude left her by the stream for a moment, returned to the cabin, and came back with the big plastic washtub they used to mop the floors.

"The gold pan is your basic minin' tool," she said. "But pannin' ain't as easy as it looks."

Maude set the plastic tub in the sand at the edge of the water, bent down and filled Charity's gold pan about a third full of stream gravel, then pulled a little glass vial from the pocket of her jeans.

"There's a dozen flakes of gold in this here bottle." She shook it, showing the flakes of gold suspended in the little tube of water. She opened the vial and dumped the gold and water into the pan. "The trick is to catch 'em."

Maude began to demonstrate, first stirring the loose dirt and gravel into a state of suspension, then working the pan in a circular motion, slopping a little water over the brim with each rotation. "Gold is heavier than pret' near anything else. If you use the pan just right, it'll catch in the riffles and the gravel will slop on over."

Sure enough, when Maude was done, the pan was empty except for the little slivers of gold in the notches. "Now you try it."

Charity accepted the green plastic gold pan Maude gave her.

"Hold it over the tub like I did. When you're done, we'll count the flakes. Whatever you miss'll wind up in the washtub and we can start all over again."

Maude was right. It wasn't as easy as it looked. After several tries, Charity had retrieved only a very few flakes. Then the sun broke through the clouds for a moment and when she stared into the pan, she saw a lot more gold.

"Look, Maude! There's a whole bunch of it in here!"

Maude just shook her head. "That's fool's gold, honey. When the sun disappears, so will the glitter. Gold ain't like that. That pretty yellow color stays true all the time."

The clouds closed in again and the glitter of the fool's gold disappeared just as Maude said. Charity kept at it. But after an hour of work, she had only caught half a dozen flakes. Her pant legs were wet, the toes of her hiking boots soaked—mental note to buy an extra pair on the next trip into Dawson—her feet freezing, and still she didn't have the knack.

"It takes a hundred fifty, maybe two hundred pans to process a yard of gravel," Maude said. "A good panner can manage maybe ten pans an hour, which means you can do 'bout half a yard a day, a little more if you get real good."

Real good she wasn't, and not real fast, either. It was backbreaking labor, but if the end product was gold . . .

Charity worked for another half an hour.

"Why don't you take a rest?" Maude suggested. "Go on up to the house, warm up, and grab a bite to eat. You can try again a little later."

"You go ahead." Charity whirled the pan. "I'll be up in a minute." As soon as she got all twelve flakes. She'd come here for gold. She had known it wouldn't be easy. She had always been a determined sort of person. Why should learning to pan for gold be any different?

"Suit yourself," Maude said, turning toward the cabin, ambling up the bank in her funny seesaw gait.

Charity went back to work. By the time she finally captured all twelve flakes in her pan, she couldn't feel her feet.

But relief and a sense of accomplishment gave her a fresh shot of energy. She frowned as she stared down at the last flake glittering against the green of her plastic pan and started counting again, separating each thin piece with the end of a stick.

Nine, ten, eleven, twelve. *Thirteen*. Thirteen flakes of gold!

Charity's hands started to tremble. She looked down at the gravel Maude had scooped from the stream that now sat in the bottom of the washtub, then gazed at the bright yellow pieces wedged into the riffles of her pan. A huge grin broke across her face and she turned and started running.

"Maude! Maude, come out here and see what I found in the creek!"

Standing in front of the window in his living room, Call lowered the binoculars he'd been using, only faintly guilty for spying on his pretty next-door neighbor.

He checked the heavy chrome Rolex strapped to his wrist. Three hours and forty-seven minutes. That's how long she'd been standing out in the drizzle, working that damned gold pan. From the water stains on her clothes, he could see that her feet and legs were wet clear past her knees. She had to be freezing out there, but she hadn't quit.

Damn fool woman. Probably come down with pneumonia.

Still, he had to give her credit. They couldn't have paid him enough to stand out there in the drizzle that long.

He looked through the glasses again, saw the excitement flash in her face, watched her run frantically up the bank to the house. After all that work, it looked as if she'd been rewarded—found a little color, no doubt. It wasn't hard to do up here, but apparently that didn't lessen her excitement.

Call hadn't felt that kind of thrill himself in so long he couldn't remember.

Maybe he never would again.

Setting the binoculars down on the table beneath the window, he crossed the living room and opened the door leading into the big metal building he'd added to the house last year. It held his Jeep, a Chevy pickup he used for hauling supplies, a pair of snowmobiles, a canoe, and a wall full of other miscellaneous sporting gear.

His canvas flight bag sat near the door, ready whenever he went flying again. He owned a small floatplane, moored on the river at Dawson, practically a necessity up here. It was great for a trip into the interior, or down to Whitehorse if he had to catch a long-distance airline flight somewhere. Not that he did it that often.

The part of the building closest to the house was built as an office. This was the place he worked, now that he had started again. Of course, he worked for himself these days and he did it at a leisurely pace that would have shamed him four years ago. Back then he'd been consumed with the business of business, caught up in the never-ending race to make more and more money.

And for what?

Nothing he'd gained was worth what it had cost him.

Nothing was worth the loss of his wife and three-year-old little girl.

Don't go there, his mind warned. There was no use torturing himself when it wouldn't do an ounce of good.

In the past four years, at least he had learned that much. That no matter how much self-loathing he heaped on himself, no matter how much guilt he suffered, nothing could change what had happened on the road that snowy winter night a week before Christmas. Nothing could undo the fact that he had put his job—his ambition—ahead of his family, and because he had, the two people he loved most in the world were dead.

It had taken him nearly four years to accept their loss, but in the end he'd had no choice. His family was gone but he was alive, and he owed it to them to go on. It was time he continued the business of living, and in building this room he had made a start at doing just that.

Call pulled out the leather chair behind his desk, sat down at his computer and flipped on the switch, waiting with more patience than he used to have for the screen to light up and the desktop programs to appear.

The office was state-of-the-art: three computers, a laptop, and a couple of high-speed laser printers. The computer served as a fax and telephone answering machine and one computer was connected to a rain gauge, aerometer, barometer, and hydra sensor. With that equipment and what weather information he could download, he could do a better job than the weather service of predicting local weather.

Living this far out of town, getting on-line had posed a challenge at first, but satellite technology had come a long way, allowing him lightning-speed downloads, and more recent improvements now gave him uploading capabilities as well.

Mostly, he used the computer to keep track of his investments, to buy and sell stock, and do a little consulting. He wasn't interested in more than that. If he'd learned one thing from his mistakes, it was not to let ambition get in the way of what was important in life.

Things like watching a sunset, or feeling the glide of a canoe through the pure blue waters of a lake.

Or absorbing the warmth of a woman as she took him deep inside her.

Call's whole body tightened. Where the hell had that come from? But he only had to think of the woman in the yellow slicker working out in the rain and he knew. Damn, he wanted his life back to normal, or as normal as it ever would be. Some satisfying, no-strings sex was definitely on his agenda—with Sally Beecham, not his irritating next-door neighbor.

Call clicked his mouse and brought up his calendar, relatively empty now compared to four years ago when meetings and appointments filled his days, often lasting until well past midnight.

Between a scheduled call to Peter Held, a young chemist involved in an innovative hard-drive storage program Call had been working on, and one to Arthur Whitcomb, Chairman of Inner Dimensions, the software game company that had been his original avenue to success, he wrote himself a reminder to phone Sally and ask her out on Saturday night.

He would take her to dinner and afterward he would take her to bed.

He was going to start living again if it killed him.

Sally Beecham was a good place to start.

God, it was beautiful here. Unlike anyplace Charity had ever seen. And yet . . . in the oddest way, the country seemed familiar. The trees and the mountains, the rivers and the streams, all felt rooted in some inner part of her, somewhere deep in her cells. Perhaps it was the books she had read, for certainly she had read a lot of them. Whatever it was, it felt exactly right to be here.

This morning while Maude cleaned up the breakfast dishes, she decided to go for a walk, take a look at the piece of property she had purchased. Promising Maude she wouldn't go far, she found a winding path that led up the hill behind the house, affording her a view of the creek and the narrow valley the meandering stream cut through.

Across the valley, wispy white tendrils of low-hanging clouds clung to the sides of the mountains, and the air was so crisp and clear she could see for miles around her. The real estate man, Boomer Smith, had told her the property backed up to millions of acres of forest, and looking at it now, it was easy to believe. The trees, mountains, and sky seemed to go on forever.

Inhaling an invigorating breath, thinking of her promise to Maude not to go too far and imagining the sort of wildlife that must occupy such a vast area of uninhabited mountains and woods, she reluctantly started back down the trail.

She had nearly reached the bottom when she heard a noise on the path in front of her. An animal appeared—a coyote, she thought at first, but it seemed bigger than the few she had seen on TV and its fur wasn't yellow and brown, but gray and silver.

The hair on the back of her neck went up as the animal

paused on the trail, his pale gray-blue eyes focusing on her with sudden interest. The beast was taller at the shoulders than a dog or a coyote, lean through the chest, and long-legged, built for power and speed. *Wolf,* she thought with a sudden chill, trying to recall how dangerous they were and what she should do if she ran across one. But her mind remained blank and completely uncooperative.

She stayed stock-still, frozen in place, hoping the animal would wander away, but it remained exactly where it stood, watching her with keen, intelligent eyes that kicked her already-racing heart into first gear. Her legs were shaking. She glanced down the hill to the house. Shouting for help crossed her mind, but she wasn't sure they could hear her with the generator running.

The wolf's mouth opened, showing a set of dangerous-looking teeth. Running might be good, but the animal was standing in the middle of the path, blocking her escape, and she couldn't figure out how to get around it. Scaring it away seemed her only option. Reaching down, she fumbled for a heavy piece of wood she spotted at the edge of the path, figuring if he didn't run and decided to attack, she would at least have a chance to defend herself.

Unfortunately, the moment she lifted the length of wood and hefted it against her shoulder, holding it like a baseball bat, the wolf began to snarl and the hackles at the back of his neck went up.

Her knees went weak. What would Max Mason do? But she didn't remember reading where Max had come up against a wolf and even if he had, she wasn't as brave as Max.

Her grip tightened on the wood, the wolf began to growl, and her mouth went bone dry.

"Drop the stick," a man's voice said from somewhere behind her. "He was mistreated when he was a pup. He thinks you're going to hit him and he'll attack in self-defense."

She knew that deep voice, softer than usual, the calm tone meant to soothe her. Something like relief trickled through her that he was there and she wouldn't have to face the wolf alone. Very carefully, she knelt and laid the stick back down on the ground near her feet.

The minute she did, the wolf sat down on its haunches and began to wag its tail. Call Hawkins walked up behind her.

"Come here, boy," he said over her shoulder. "The lady isn't going to hurt you."

She stiffened a little as the wolf started trotting up the path in their direction. But his tail was wagging again and a second shot of relief swept through her. The animal sat down at Hawkins's feet as if he belonged there and her relief melted into annoyance.

She turned to look up at him. "I don't believe this. That wolf is your pet?"

His mouth faintly curved and though he still needed a shave, she thought it was a really nice mouth. Charity wondered what he would look like if he actually smiled.

"Smoke's not a true wolf—he's a wolf-husky mix. They're not uncommon up here."

She wanted to yell at him, to tell him he should have warned her about the dog, but just then the animal cocked its head in a very dog-like manner, reminding her of Swizzle, the big black lab that belonged to her family when she was a kid, and she found herself smiling instead.

"He's absolutely gorgeous." The dog was studying her with curiosity, as if he wasn't sure he should trust her but looking as though he really wanted to. "Can I pet him?"

"He doesn't usually take to strangers."

But Charity was already down on her knees, holding out her hand, and Smoke was sniffing her fingers. The dog must have realized she wasn't afraid of him anymore and he certainly wasn't afraid of her. She ran her fingers through his long, silver coat.

"What a beautiful dog you are," she crooned, casting a sideways glance at its master.

Hawkins was frowning again. Apparently he wanted his dog to dislike her as much as he did.

"You need to be careful out here, Ms. Sinclair. Smoke is tame, but there are lots of animals around that aren't. This is grizzly country. There are black bears and moose. If you're going to go hiking, you had better take someone with you who knows the terrain."

"Funny, I must have missed the line of people offering to take me on a sight-seeing trip."

He started to speak and for a moment she thought he meant to volunteer for the job. Instead, he clamped down on his jaw. "Come on. I'll walk you back to the cabin."

They weren't very far away, but she didn't point that out, just let him fall in behind her as she made her way back down the trail. She could feel him there, just behind her shoulders, purposely curbing his longer strides to keep from overrunning her shorter ones.

As soon as they reached the bottom of the hill, he whistled to his dog, who had run off after a squirrel.

"Remember what I said. Be careful out here."

She didn't answer, since she had no desire to do battle with a moose or a bear, and instead watched his tall figure retreat out of sight down the path beside the creek.

Call Hawkins was truly an enigma. Charity wondered if there was anyone else in his life besides the wolf-dog he kept for a pet.

It was late in the day by the time they were ready to set up Buck's homemade sluice box, a long, wooden trough about eighteen inches wide tilted up on one end. The bottom was lined with wire mesh and every few inches metal riffles, like the steps of a ladder, poked out to catch the gold as it washed past.

A three-horse gasoline engine on top of a foam rubber pad set up vibrations that shook the box, separating the gold from the lighter mass of dirt and rock. Turning the engine speed up or down controlled the force, jiggling the gold into the riffles in the box.

It looked pretty homemade to Charity, but hey, she had

come to Dawson for adventure and hopefully to find some gold. She never intended to embark on a professional mining career.

They positioned the box at the rear of the eight-inch dredge they had chosen after reviewing all the options, the inches signifying the diameter of the suction tube that went under the water to suck up the material in the streambed. The machine was five feet long and gasoline powered. The day they'd bought it, Buck made a deal with A-1 Fuel to set up a storage tank on the property for supplying gas to the dredge and the generator.

"Let's see how it works," Charity said.

Buck tightened a screw at the rear of the machine that helped keep the sluice box in place. "We'll have to go into the water to operate the suction pipe. I've got my waders in the truck." The stream was still icy cold, too cold to stay in for any length of time without special gear.

"I bought myself a pair the last time we went into town," Charity said, proud of her foresight. She had watched a video made by the GPAA—Gold Prospectors Association of America—so she knew how the dredge was supposed to work. "I'll just run up and get them."

She was back on the bank of the creek a few minutes later, pulling the heavy rubber waders on over her jeans. They came up to her waist—big, baggy, rubber legs that basically was just stood in. A pair of wide red suspenders went over her shoulders to hold them in place, which Charity adjusted to fit.

Buck eyed her up and down as if he couldn't quite believe what he was seeing. "You sure you want to do this?"

Undoubtedly she did look pretty funny, with her black-and-white panda bear sweatshirt peeking out from under the suspenders and the lower half of her body swallowed up by the ugly rubber waders. Thank God she couldn't see herself. She would probably be laughing so hard she wouldn't be able to walk into the stream.

"I came here for gold," she said. "Let's get to it."

Buck just grunted, stepped off the bank into the water,

and slowly made his way to the length of flexible, eight-inch hose sticking out of the dredging machine.

She had pulled her hair up in a ponytail so it wouldn't get wet and hoped that the waders would insulate her legs and feet. She looked down at the clear stretch of water unhampered by boulders that they had chosen for their initial effort—about three feet deep in this location—took a steadying breath, and waded in.

When Charity reached the place next to Buck, Maude turned on the dredging machine. It was louder than she had imagined. She thought of Call Hawkins and inwardly grinned. The suction pipe began sucking gravel up from the bottom of the stream and as it flowed through the dredge, Maude turned on the motor beneath the sluice box, making it vibrate back and forth.

"You got to be careful with these things," Buck warned, pointing to the pipe. "Don't get your hand in front of it. It can take your fingers off—or worse."

A shiver of alarm raced through her. She hadn't realized the job would be dangerous. She watched Buck's big, blunt hands work the suction pipe, making the task look easy, and thought that surely she could learn to master it without losing any extremities.

"Want to try it?"

She bit her lip, more nervous than she cared to admit. But there was challenge in Buck's eyes and a slight curl on his lips, and she wasn't about to let him know that she was afraid. Her fingers gripped the end of the pipe and she felt the incredible suction power of the dredge. Careful to keep her hands away from the opening, she held it steady as water rushed into the pipe.

She was much shorter than Buck. Too bad she didn't think of that before she bent to suck a load of gravel off the bottom of the stream. Water rushed into the top of the waders, filling them clear to the waist, making her so heavy she couldn't stand up and sweeping her right her off her feet. Luckily, Buck grabbed the suction pipe or God only knew what might have happened.

Water rushed up to her neck and a heartbeat before she went under, she made the mistake of glancing toward the bank of the stream.

Call Hawkins stood there with his feet splayed, nearly doubled over with laugher. If she hadn't been the butt of his joke, she might have thought how good he looked wearing a grin for once, instead of the scowl that usually darkened his face.

CHAPTER FIVE

Gold! We leapt from our benches.
Gold! We sprang from our stools.
Gold! We wheeled in the furrow,
fired with the faith of fools.
Fearless, unfound, unfitted,
far from the night and the cold,
heard we the clarion summons,
followed the master-lure—Gold!
      —Robert W. Service

Call laughed so hard his eyes began to tear. He couldn't remember the last time he had laughed this way—certainly not in the past four years. Nothing he could imagine was as funny as Charity Sinclair in ugly rubber waders being washed like a rag mop down the creek. If he hadn't realized she was about to get into a deep, rocky section where she could actually get hurt, he might be laughing still.

Instead, he sloshed into the stream just as she splashed by him, grabbed hold of the neck of her soggy sweatshirt, and hauled her out of the water. The sweatshirt molded to her breasts, which were even nicer than he had thought. There was a funny little panda on the front whose ears seemed to sag as she staggered to her feet, spitting and flinging water.

He couldn't help it. He started laughing again. "Nice work, hotshot."

She tried to stand up but the waders were so full of water, she floundered and toppled back into the creek. Call grabbed her again, hauled her up, and jerked down the suspenders, freeing her from the heavy, water-filled rubber pants. She shoved them down her legs and stepped out of the cumbersome gear, and he tossed them up on the bank.

Dripping water and shivering with cold, she climbed out of the stream, wet clothes plastered to her body, which was, he saw, very nicely curved. Her hair was a soggy blond mess, her teeth were chattering, and as she sloshed by him, he couldn't help feeling a little bit sorry for her.

"You all right?" he asked.

She swayed a little, steadied herself with a hand against his chest, then drew away, her expression a study in misery. "More or less."

He saw Maude Foote scurrying toward them, her wrinkled face lined with worry.

"Get a blanket, Maude," he said. "She's more cold than anything."

Her legs were wobbly. He considered picking her up and carrying her up to the cabin, but figured she probably wouldn't like it if he did. Instead, he slid an arm around her waist and she leaned into him, letting him guide her up the hill. He noticed she didn't protest. Maude met them halfway and draped an old olive-drab army blanket around Charity's trembling shoulders.

"You're not hurt, are ya?" Maude asked.

She managed to muster a smile. "Just my pride."

"It'll be easier once the weather warms up. Most folks don't start dredgin' quite this soon."

"I'll get the hang of it," Charity told her. By then they had reached the porch. Buck Johnson was already there and Call didn't miss the smug expression on his face. Buck didn't much like women, except, as he'd once put it, on their backs with their legs apart. Call had a sudden suspicion

that Buck had somehow engineered the scene at the creek
and was amazed to feel a shot of anger.

"You must be freezing," he said to Charity as her slender
body trembled against him. "You'd better go in and get out
of those wet clothes."

She nodded, looking utterly bedraggled. "Thanks for
helping me down there."

"No problem."

"I guess I did look pretty funny."

His mouth edged up as he remembered the incident again.
"Yeah, you did." She gave him a watery smile. Her lips
were pink and plump—*so soft-looking,* he thought, and his
body began to stir.

"If you hadn't helped me get out, I probably would have
floated all the way to Dawson City."

"Maybe not quite that far."

She started up the steps to the porch, sloshing water with
every step.

"Charity?" She turned to look at him, surprised at his
use of her first name. "What is it? Why the hell are you up
here?"

Something shifted in her features. He caught a flash of
uncertainty and something else he couldn't name.

"I don't know. I just had to come. There didn't seem to
be any other choice."

It was an odd answer, one she seemed as puzzled by as
he was. He watched her climb the stairs, noticed the way
the wet jeans molded to her legs and bottom, and felt a jolt
of lust he hadn't felt in years.

She's trouble, he thought again. And after what he'd been
through the last four years, trouble was the last thing he
wanted.

"I thought I was going to drown—in three feet of water."
Wrapped in her soft yellow bathrobe, Charity stood in front
of the fireplace in the living room, rubbing her hair with a
towel. "And *he* had to be there. God, it was so humiliating."

She was finally warm again, having just stepped out of a nice hot shower. Unfortunately, the plumbers had been less successful with the toilet. It still didn't work, but they were scheduled to bring out a new one on Monday.

Assuming, of course, the sun didn't shine and they decided to go fishing instead.

Maude chuckled. "Call ain't really a bad sort. He's got his own set of problems, just like you got yours."

"Actually, he was fairly decent today." She tossed aside the towel, picked up the brush she had set on the arm of the sofa, and began to pull it through her hair. "I'd probably still be in the water if he hadn't pulled me out when he did."

She could still remember the way he'd sloshed into the icy stream, as if he were immune to the freezing temperature or the creek was actually warm. He was amazingly strong and his chest was as hard as granite. She still remembered the tingle of awareness she had felt when he slid his arm around her waist.

"At least I know what I did wrong. I should have gripped the pipe farther back, put more length in the water instead of bending over so far."

Maude frowned. "Buck should have told you that."

The brush stilled in her hand. "You don't think he—"

"No, not on purpose. Not that he wasn't happy to see ya fail. Tomorrow you'll do it right, show him just because you're a woman don't mean you can't hold your own."

Charity turned. "That's what you'd do, isn't it, Maude?"

She laughed. "Honey, that's what I been doin' all my life."

It was late in the afternoon two days later that Charity saw Call again. From the start of this endeavor, her plan had been to take Saturdays and Sundays off. She had come to see this rugged country and as excited as she was with the prospect of actually finding gold, she also wanted to enjoy herself.

Friday had been a good day. As she and Maude had planned, she had pulled on her ugly waders and gone back into the stream, and this time her turn with the suction pipe had gone off without a hitch. Buck had glared at her, but eventually he would get used to the idea that they would be working on this project together.

By the end of the day she was tired but satisfied with her progress and really looking forward to having Saturday and Sunday off.

When morning finally arrived, she slept in late, then built herself a fire and sat down in front of it to read one of the new adventure novels she had received as a member of the Glenbrook Action Readers' Club. She had already made the address change to her post office box in town for the four action series books a month she got through her subscription.

The day was overcast and rainy, usual weather for this time of year, but not so cold she couldn't sit for a while out on the porch. Call's big husky-wolf, Smoke, surprised her with a visit and she fed him some ham bone scraps from the beans and biscuits Maude had cooked for supper the night before. Afterward, she climbed a little way up the hill to get the best reception possible on her cell phone.

She called her dad, as she did once a week, and told him she was well and getting settled in. She asked about Patience and her dad said she was dating a lawyer, but he didn't think it was all that serious. The conversation ended a little while later. Long distance calls were expensive up here and her dad had remarried several years ago and had a busy life of his own.

She phoned her apartment to speak to her sister, but Hope wasn't in. She called her best friend, Deirdre Steinberg, an editor at Simon and Schuster, and they talked about happenings in New York.

"Jeremy's been calling," Dee said. "He seems lost without you. I didn't tell him you had a cell phone, but maybe I should. He's desperate to talk to you. I could give him the number and—"

"Please, Dee—I don't want to talk to Jeremy, and besides, the reception out here is really bad. The phone doesn't work unless you're outside the house, so he probably couldn't reach me even if you gave him the number."

"I take it that means you're planning to stay."

"I'm staying, Dee. For the full six months, at any rate."

Something beeped on the other end of the phone. "Darn it, my other line is ringing," Dee said. "I'll pacify Jeremy for as long as I can, but call me again—soon. I worry about you, you know."

"I know, and thanks, Dee. The only thing I really miss up here is my family and friends." Charity rang off and walked back to the house, feeling a little bit lonely. It wasn't unexpected. She was miles from home and living on her own, but it was exciting, too.

In the afternoon, the rain stopped and the sun came out. Since the toilet still wasn't working, she walked out to the little wooden shed she was growing to hate more every day. She was finished and heading back to the cabin, dodging the mud puddles that lined the path, when she heard a rustle in the bushes behind her.

Charity stopped and turned, searching the thick green forest on the hill. "Smoke? Smoke, is that you, boy?" God, she hoped it was. But Smoke didn't appear and the rustling grew louder. When she spotted a patch of long brown fur moving among the branches of a tree, Charity screamed and started running.

Unfortunately, she forgot about the protruding branch of a shrub she had stepped over on her way to the latrine. Her pant leg caught. She tripped and went sprawling—right into a puddle of mud. Charity jerked her head around, too frightened to care about the murky stuff sticking to her clothes, certain that a bear was about to charge out of the woods any minute and chew her into little pieces.

Instead, a cute little furry brown creature the size of a cat jumped down from a rock and raced away, its long, fluffy tail dragging behind its small body.

Charity groaned in frustration and slammed her fist into the mud, sending up a stream of brackish water.

She was muttering, silently cursing as she dragged herself to her feet. Her clean, white turtleneck was covered with mud and so were the jeans she had dried overnight in front of the pellet stove. Mud clung to her boots and oozed between her fingers.

"I don't believe this," she grumbled, slinging mud from her arms and knocking it off her pant legs.

"Somehow I don't have the least problem believing it." The sound of Call Hawkins's voice jerked her gaze toward the trees.

He crossed his arms over that granite-hard chest. "I swear, sweet pea, if you're that afraid of a cute little weasel, what's going to happen when you run across a bear?"

A growl of frustration rose from her throat. "What are *you* doing here? And by the way, you're trespassing. Do you realize that?"

"I was looking for Smoke. He used to hang around when Mose lived in the cabin. I thought I might find him over here." He eyed her muddy clothes and she heard him chuckle, sending her temper up a notch.

Charity stomped toward him, slinging mud with every step. She didn't stop till she was inches away and staring into his face. "So you think this is funny?"

He reached out and wiped a splatter of mud off her cheek. "Yeah, I do."

"It could have been a bear instead of a weasel. I only saw the fur."

"It could have been a squirrel, too. And technically it wasn't a weasel, it was a marten."

Charity ignored the unwanted information. "What is it with you? Why do you always appear at exactly the wrong moment? You're like . . . like some kind of evil genie or something."

He laughed and she wanted to hit him. "Evil genie. I've been called a lot of things, but never anything close to an evil genie. I think I kind of like it."

She poked a finger into the middle of his chest, which was as hard as she remembered. "I know I'm new out here, but I'm not stupid. In time, I'll figure things out."

His smile slid away. The bluest eyes she'd ever seen were staring at her mouth. "I'm sure you will," he said a little gruffly.

"If you were any kind of neighbor, you'd try to help me instead of causing me trouble."

"Listen, doll face, if anyone's trouble around here, it's you."

She swallowed. His gaze moved slowly down her body and fixed on her breasts, and her nipples peaked as if they could feel it. He was breathing a little faster than he was before and suddenly so was she. She could feel the heat emanating from his big, hard body, smell his scent. It wrapped around her like smoke from a fire, heating her up from the inside out. His mouth was so close she could measure the fullness of his bottom lip. If he bent his head he could kiss her.

Something shifted in the air between them. It felt thicker, heavier. He was so tall and male, so damned handsome. Desire coiled through her limbs, tugged low in her belly. His eyes locked with hers, as blue as the tip of a flame. For several long seconds, neither of them moved.

Then Call stepped away. "You're right," he said roughly. "This isn't easy country and as you say, we're neighbors. If there's something you need, let me know."

"Wh-what?"

"I said, if—"

"I heard what you said." She eyed him with no little uncertainty. "You mean it?"

He sighed, raked a hand through his thick, dark brown hair, dislodging several shiny strands. They curled as they fell across his forehead. "I suppose so."

"Why?"

"Because at the rate you're going, you'll wind up getting hurt and I'd hate to see that happen."

"I'm tougher than you think."

His mouth curved and her stomach floated up beneath her ribs. "I'm beginning to believe that. I saw you working the dredge yesterday."

She couldn't help a smile. "I think I'm getting the hang of it."

"Keep your eye on Buck."

She didn't have to ask what he meant. "I will." Charity didn't say more and neither did he. She watched him walk away, thought how sexy he looked in a pair of jeans, and felt a renewed shot of lust. Her heart was thumping and her palms felt damp. It was ridiculous. The man was arrogant and pushy, cranky, and most of the time, downright unfriendly.

She couldn't remember ever feeling such an unwanted attraction to a man.

Sally Beecham slid into the leather seat of Call's black Jeep. The vehicle wasn't flashy, but it was obvious he had spared no expense when he bought it. Equipped with a powerful, thick-cabled winch on the front, super-wide, ten-ply tires, a roll bar, and a black vinyl top, there wasn't a four-wheel drive in Dawson that could compare. Her teenage son, Jimmy, and all his high-school friends were hoping she and Call would get together just so Jimmy could try it out, see what it could do.

Sally was hoping she and Call would get together, too, because she was crazy about him. Besides, everybody knew he was rich.

"You ready?" Call asked. She'd had to trade shifts with Betty Tisdale to get Saturday night off, and work a late shift for Betty next week, but if things turned out the way she planned, it would be worth it.

"Just let me get my coat." Sally went into the bedroom of her small, wood-frame house on Queen Street and grabbed her coat out of the closet, stopped in front of the mirror long enough to fluff out her curly black hair and make sure she didn't have lipstick on her teeth, then headed back down the hall.

Call was looking good tonight, freshly shaved, his dark brown hair still damp from the shower. God, he was handsome, and those eyes . . . One look and she practically came. In the summer once, she had seen him with his shirt off. He had a beautiful body, suntanned and lean, his chest wide and muscular, his back hard and sculpted. He had big hands and she knew what that meant.

Maybe tonight she'd find out if it was true.

Sally smiled as he led her out to the Jeep, and Call smiled back, but he seemed a little distracted.

He was that way all evening, she discovered, first through dinner in the Bonanza Room at the Eldorado Hotel, then on the drive back to her house. She wished she could scoot over next to him, but the seat belt wouldn't stretch that far and she didn't think he'd like it if she took it off, considering a car crash had killed his wife and kid.

"Are you sure you're all right?" she finally asked. "You been kinda quiet all evening."

"I've been thinking."

"What about?"

He flicked her a glance from behind the wheel. "Taking you to bed."

Her breath snagged and her body began to heat up. Little twinges started throbbing between her legs. She reached across and rested her hand on his thigh, gave it a gentle squeeze. "I've been thinking about it, too, Call."

He turned the corner, pulled the Jeep up in front of her house, and turned off the ignition. He caught her hand and eased it off his leg as he turned toward her on the seat.

"I've been thinking . . . as much as I'd like to sleep with you . . . I don't . . . I'm afraid I'm just not ready."

The heat she'd been feeling deflated like a punctured hot air balloon. "We could go nice and slow. Take it real easy. You know what they say—it's just like riding a bicycle. Once you learn, you never forget."

He looked at her with those piercing blue eyes, leaned across the seat, and very lightly kissed her. She loved the way his lips felt, sort of hard-soft, the bottom one full and sexy. She kissed him back and thought for sure he'd weaken.

Instead, he pulled away.

"I'll give you a call in a couple of days."

"Sure." She tried to keep the disappointment out of her voice. "No problem." She popped open the door and started to get out, but Call was there before her feet touched the ground.

"I'm sorry, Sally, I really am."

"Don't be." Pride straightened her shoulders. "You're not the only man in Dawson, Call, you know what I mean?"

He nodded. "Yeah, I know what you mean."

She said good night to him at the door and slipped back into the house. It was quiet inside, the rooms still smelling of the cabbage she'd cooked for supper. Jimmy was out with his friends and wouldn't be home till late.

It was early yet. It pissed her off that Call had turned her on, then left without doing anything about it. She glanced at the phone on the wall next to the stove in the kitchen.

Maybe Farley was home. He wasn't much to look at, not like Call, but he was always up for a good time. She thought of his eagerness in bed and grinned at the pun. Maybe she'd give him a jingle.

Sally reached for the phone.

As the Jeep rolled through the darkness, Call slammed his hand down on the wheel. Sonofabitch! What the hell was the matter with him? He had promised himself tonight he would satisfy the sexual desire that had finally begun to stir to life inside him again. Instead, he had apologized to Sally and headed back home.

He could tell himself it was Susan, that he felt like he was being unfaithful, even after all these years, but it wouldn't be the truth. Sex had never been that important in their marriage. At least not to Susan. Call had always had a high sex drive, but Susan had never placed much value on intimacy, aside from having kids. They'd had other things in common, other dreams and goals that had drawn them together. Since he was the kind of guy who didn't believe in cheating on his wife, he had sublimated part of his drive with work.

Not that that was any excuse for the sixteen-hour days he had put in.

Since the accident, depression and guilt had kept him celibate, but in the past few months he had finally begun to overcome those feelings and start moving ahead with his life.

The truth was, his wife was gone and he was a single man again. He was ready for some hot, uninvolved sex—he just didn't want it with Sally Beecham. He wanted it with Charity Sinclair and that posed a definite problem.

Call raked a hand through his hair. Charity wasn't a barmaid who had offered him a no-strings relationship. She wasn't some divorcee who hopped from man to man, looking for a good time. If there was ever a poster girl for the all-American, clean-cut girl-next-door, Charity Sinclair was it.

Of course, he could be wrong.

The thought started his blood pumping. He hadn't felt a single moment of lust for Sally, but he was hard just thinking maybe Charity might be up for a little casual sex. Even the low-cut blouse Sally had been wearing, showing off a set of plump, milk-white breasts, hadn't done it for him.

Not like this morning when he'd stared at Charity's luscious mouth, measured the tantalizing breasts beneath her mud-spattered shirt, and wanted to drag her down on the ground. He'd wanted to rip off her clothes, wanted to bury himself inside her.

"Jesus." Call turned off Hunker Road and started the slow, bumpy drive up Dead Horse Creek. Coming back to the real world was proving more of a problem than he'd imagined. After four years of going without, he figured just about any warm, willing woman would do. Maybe he was worried that after all this time he wouldn't be any good, but he didn't think so. Like Sally said, having sex wasn't something a man forgot how to do.

Hell, if Sally wasn't the one, there were other women in

Dawson. What about the little redhead waiting tables at Klondike Kate's? Toby had offered to introduce him, said she was a real party girl and she wanted to meet him, that she would be moving away in July and just wanted to have a little fun in the meantime.

Whatever he did, the last thing he wanted was any sort of emotional entanglement—with the redhead or anyone else. Making love to a woman who lived in the house right next to his was asking for serious trouble.

Trouble. It was Charity Sinclair's middle name.

CHAPTER SIX

Call still felt restless Sunday morning. Sitting down at his computer, he punched up his e-mail. Half a dozen messages were waiting, including one from his brother. Zach lived in Los Angeles, but planned to come north for a few weeks this summer. Call replied that his brother couldn't get there fast enough to suit him. Not the reply Zach would have received even a couple of months ago.

It was a good sign, Call thought, that he was so eager to see his sibling. It meant he really was coming back to life.

Next, he printed a lengthy attachment from the game company, Inner Dimensions, that had come in Friday morning. It showed some of the advertising being planned for their newest software game, King Cobra, expected to be the hottest ticket of the season.

There was also an e-mail from Peter Held. The kid was really excited about the progress he was making on a process that would dramatically increase the capacity for hard-disk storage. If the idea actually worked, it would revolutionize the industry. It was a notion Call had been working on four years ago. He had let the project slide after Susan died. Nothing seemed important back then.

Then his partner in the venture, Frank McGuire, had passed away of a heart attack one month later, and Call had canned the idea completely. Until six months ago, he hadn't given it another thought. But resurrecting himself seemed to resurrect some of his old endeavors.

He e-mailed Peter, gave him an atta-boy for the extra hours he'd been putting in, dealt with the rest of his e-mail, which was nothing compared to the stacks he had received in the old days, and turned off the computer.

"Breakfast is ready, Call. Pancakes and eggs." Toby stood in the doorway, his shirttail out, red hair mussed, eyes red and groggy. It looked like the kid had had a far more productive Saturday night than Call had.

"Thanks, I'll be right there." He started toward the kitchen but couldn't resist stopping in front of the window. His binoculars sat on the antique claw foot table right where he'd left them. He was beginning to feel like a real Peeping Tom, but that didn't keep him from picking up the glasses for a quick scan of the cabin next door.

He wondered what Charity would say if she knew that was how he'd been keeping track of her, and couldn't help thinking how sexy she would look with her temper shooting sparks and her pretty green eyes flashing. She was already dressed and out in the back, he saw, chopping some split logs into kindling.

He almost smiled. If he got lucky, maybe she would provide him with a little more entertainment.

He watched her working a moment more, surprised to discover she was doing a pretty good job, started to set the glasses back down, but something moved at the edge of the lens and he focused the binoculars in that direction.

The muscles at the back of his neck went tight. The big, slow-moving brown object outlined in the circle of the lens really was a bear this time.

Call grabbed his .45-70 rifle off the gun rack on the wall and hit the door running.

* * *

Charity lifted the small hand axe and brought it down on the piece of split wood she was chopping into kindling. Doing a pretty fair job of it, she thought. It was easier to light a fire with smaller pieces, she'd discovered, and this being Sunday, her last day off before the workweek began, she was looking forward to building a roaring blaze.

She whacked off another chunk and raised the axe, but a sound off to her right drew her attention. She turned just in time to see the bushes rustle, then part as if they weren't there, and a huge brown bear saunter out from between two pine trees. For a moment, she blinked, unable to believe her eyes. Horrified, she watched the animal walking toward her in a slow, ambling gait that sent shivers down her spine, its furry head ranging from side to side.

This is no weasel, she thought with a shot of fear, her fingers tightening around the grip of the little hand axe whose sharp blade was her only weapon. She held the axe up for a moment, thought about how ridiculously useless it would be against a creature that size, took a deep breath, and prepared to run.

"Whatever you do, for God's sake don't run."

Call's voice washed over her, stopping her headlong flight before it started.

"Stay exactly where you are and keep your attention on the bear."

From the corner of her eye, she saw him on the path connecting their two properties, a rifle gripped in his hands. The bear saw him, too, and the animal stopped, his big, fuzzy head going up. Call shouldered the rifle and fired into the air above the creature's head. Another shot ricocheted through the air, then a third.

The bear growled once, spun on its heavy back legs, and raced off up the hill, flinging dirt as it disappeared into the forest.

Charity stood there shaking, watching Call stalk toward

her, his face as dark as the thundercloud that had just passed in front of the sun.

"For chrissake, are you nuts? You never run from a bear or any other big game animal!"

She swallowed, too scared to give him one of her usual witty retorts. "I think I'm either going to faint or throw up. I'm not sure which."

"Shit." Propping the gun in a notch on the side of a tree stump, he eased her down on the stump beside it. "Put your head between your legs."

She just sat there, pale-faced and shaking, so Call did it for her, his big hand locking around the nape of her neck, easing her head down more gently than she would have imagined.

"Christ, what is it with you? You're a frigging magnet for disaster."

She lifted her head too quickly and a wave of dizziness washed over her. Call shoved her head back down.

"What . . . it . . . is," she answered from between her legs, "is I live here, in case you've forgotten." She slowly lifted her head, beginning to feel a little less shaky. "The bears and everyone else"—she drilled him with an includ-ing-you look—"are going to have to get used to it."

He stared at her with those fierce blue eyes, then began to survey the area around the cabin. "If that's the case, then you'd better not leave garbage out to attract them. Surely Maude told you that."

She frowned. "I didn't leave out any garbage. I might be new up here, but I don't have a death wish."

"Then what's that sitting over there?" He tipped his head toward a black plastic sack next to a pine tree, not far from the back door of the cabin. "Looks like garbage to me."

Charity got up from the stump and walked over on still-shaky legs to examine it, opening the bag that was only loosely tied shut. "It's breakfast and lunch scraps from Friday, but I thought Buck burned them along with some of the trash he's been cleaning out of the sheds. I guess he forgot."

Call gazed up the hill toward the property north of the Lily Rose, but Buck's cabin was a good way farther along the road, well out of sight from where they were. "Yeah, that must be it."

"Will he be back?"

"Buck or the bear?"

Her lips quirked. "The bear."

"Not today. Hopefully, never."

"Was it a grizzly?"

"Black bear."

"It must have been a grizzly. It wasn't black—it was brown."

He shook his head as if he couldn't believe her. "Black bears come in lots of different colors. Grizzlies are a whole different species. You have to learn which is which and you have to react to each of them differently."

"I don't know what you mean."

"I mean you have to be aggressive with black bears. With grizzlies, the best thing to do is lie down, pull yourself into a protective ball, and play dead. The bear might maul you a little, but at least you won't get killed . . . not usually, at any rate."

She sagged back against the trunk of the pine tree, her face pale again. "That's comforting."

Call sighed in exasperation. "Dammit, Charity, don't you know anything about living out here?"

"Obviously not as much as I should."

"I can't imagine what a woman like you is doing up here by herself in the first place. You did come on your own? No husband, no boyfriend, right?"

She straightened, beginning to get annoyed. "I don't need a husband to do something I've always wanted to do. Maybe I should have learned more about the animals around here and less about the history of the area, but that doesn't mean I shouldn't have come."

"This is hard country. Bad things happen up here. Unless you've been wearing blinders, by now you're beginning to see that. Why don't you accept my offer, sell this place, and go home where you belong?''

Home where you belong. They were fighting words to Charity, right along with *be a good little girl.* Her lips tightened. "You'd like that, wouldn't you? For me to sell out and go home. Then you could have your precious privacy back. You wouldn't have to worry about someone making noise when they worked next door. You wouldn't have to worry about saving some greenhorn from a bear. You wouldn't have to think about—''

She gasped as he took a threatening step toward her, his eyes snapping as he backed her up against the trunk of the tree. ''Yeah, I wouldn't have to worry about what mischief you might get into next. And whenever I saw you, I wouldn't have to think about what it might be like to kiss that sassy mouth of yours. I wouldn't have to drive myself crazy wondering what it would feel like to reach under that silly panda sweatshirt and cup your breasts, to put my mouth there and find out how they taste.''

She made a little sound in her throat the instant before his mouth crushed down over hers. Hard lips, fierce and hot as a brand, molded with hers, then began to soften. He started to taste her, to sample instead of demand. Lean, tanned hands framed her face, tilted her head back so he could deepen the kiss and she felt the rough shadow of beard along his jaw. Her mouth parted on a moan and his tongue slid inside. It felt slick and hot as it tangled with hers, and ragged need tore through her.

Oh, dear God! Heat overwhelmed her and she started to tremble. Her hands came up to his shoulders, clung for a moment, then slid up around his neck. She heard Call groan.

He pressed himself more solidly against her, forcing her into the bark of the tree. She could feel his arousal, a big, hard ridge straining beneath the fly of his jeans. His hands found her bottom and he lifted her a little, fit his heavy erection into the soft vee between her legs.

An ache started there. She inhaled his scent, like piney woods and smoke, and he tasted all male. He kissed the way a woman dreamed a man should kiss, drinking her in, making her legs turn to butter. As if he would rather have the taste of her mouth than his next breath of air.

She tilted her head back and he kissed the side of her neck, trailed hot, wet kisses to the base of her throat, then took her mouth again. Their tongues fenced, mated in perfect rhythm. Their mouths seemed designed to fit exactly together. The kiss went on and on, till her brain felt mushy and she could barely think.

Tell him to stop, a voice inside her said, but all she could think was that Jeremy had never kissed her like this. He had never made her feel like this—not once in the two years they had been together. *No one* had ever made her feel like this.

And she didn't want the moment to end.

Her brain seemed to shut down just then, leaving her body in control. Desire curled like mist through her veins. She fumbled with the buttons on the front of his denim shirt, tore one of them off in her haste to touch him. She jerked the fabric apart and slid her hands inside, pressed her trembling palms against his bare chest.

Thick bands of muscle tightened. Crisp brown chest hair curled around the tips of her fingers, and ridges of muscle rippled down his flat stomach. Call made a sound in his throat and a shudder ran the length of his body.

His mouth still clung to hers. He jerked up her sweatshirt, cupped her breasts over her white lace bra, and started to work the catch beneath the tiny bow at the front.

"Hey, Call! You over here? Call! Is everything all right?"

She whimpered as he whipped his mouth away and softly cursed. With an unsteady hand, he jerked down her sweatshirt and stepped protectively in front of her, leaving her shielded behind his body and the trunk of the tree.

"Everything's fine, Toby." His voice sounded raspy. She wondered if his friend would notice.

"I thought I heard shots," Toby said, "but I was cooking so I didn't pay all that much attention. Then I went into the living room and found the front door open. When I saw your rifle gone from the rack, I was afraid something bad might have happened."

"Our neighbor, Ms. Sinclair, came nose to nose with her first black bear." Call looked her way, gave her a quick once-over, saw that she didn't look too disheveled, and tugged her out from behind the tree. "Charity Sinclair, meet Toby Jenkins. Toby's chief-cook-and-bottle-washer over at my place, and all-around handyman. At least he is till he leaves for college in the fall. Toby, this is Ms. Sinclair, our new neighbor."

"Nice to meet you, ma'am. I heard Mose sold the place. I've been meaning to come over and say hello."

"Forget the ma'am," Charity told him. "It makes me feel too old. Charity is enough."

He nodded, smiled. He was young, maybe nineteen or twenty, with thick, dark red hair and a few scattered freckles, sort of a young John Kennedy, an attractive boy with what appeared to be a pleasant disposition. She wondered if he could tell by looking at her what had been going on when he arrived. Then she noticed Call's shirt was open and missing a button and felt her face heating up again.

Call cleared his throat. "I'll be home in a couple of minutes, Toby."

"Yes, sir. I'll have your breakfast waiting." With a wave good-bye, he set off down the path the way he had come.

When Charity turned, she saw Call watching her, his face dark, his expression closed up as it usually was. "I didn't mean for that to happen."

Oh, God. He was obviously sorry it had and it made her even more embarrassed. "Neither did I. I don't make a habit of . . . of . . . I don't exactly know what happened." She studied her feet, then stared off toward the creek. "It must have been the fear, you know? They say when your life is threatened you revert to your most basic instincts."

She risked a glance at him, saw that his jaw looked iron-hard. "Yeah, that must be it."

She glanced away, trying not to think of what they'd just done.

Trying not to wonder what would have happened if Toby hadn't arrived when he did.

"You'd better go," she said, making an effort to smile. "Your breakfast is waiting and I've got work to do."

As she started to turn, the sun peeked out from behind a cloud, casting shadows beneath his cheekbones and the little indentation on his chin. He didn't move when she grabbed the plastic bag of garbage and headed for one of the heavy iron trash cans that were supposed to be bear-proof.

She saw him walk over and pick up his rifle, his fingers wrapping around the stock with a casual ease that said he was comfortable with the weapon. He didn't walk away as she expected. Instead, he stood there watching, waiting until she disappeared inside the house.

Monday morning, she and Maude planned to work with the metal detector. She had seen them in the prospecting videos, in a variety of shapes and sizes. This one, a Garrett Crossfire, was an elliptical, plate-like metal object with a long, broomstick-type handle. While Buck chopped wood and filled the bins beneath the covered porch, Maude explained how it worked.

"You use 'em to find placer deposits in the stream or in the gravel along the creek. If you're lucky, you could turn up some nuggets in that dry creek bed where the course of the stream has changed over the years. This thing'll find 'em as small as a pinhead. You never know—ya might get real lucky and run across a vein."

Maude went on with a demonstration of how to use the machine, carrying it outside the shed toward the hill behind it. Charity tried to keep her mind on the lesson as much as she could, but her brain wouldn't fully cooperate. Instead, her mind kept replaying her heated encounter with Call the morning before.

"You gonna tell me what happened over the weekend?" Maude finally asked. "You been gnawin' on somethin' like a bear on a bone since I got here."

She tried to sound nonchalant. "As a matter of fact, I saw one on Sunday morning—a bear, that is. It wandered into the yard and nearly scared me to death."

"What happened?"

"I guess one of us left out a bag of garbage. Lucky for me, Mr. Hawkins scared it away."

Maude shook her head. "That man sure has a knack for showin' up at just the right time."

"That's the God's truth, though I can't say I'm sorry he arrived when he did on Sunday."

"You two have another run-in?"

She fought to keep the color out of her face. "You might say that. After the thing ran off, he quizzed me on bear etiquette. When I failed the test, he suggested I sell out and go back where I belong."

She thought of what happened after that—of those hot, delicious, never-ending kisses that had kept her restless and awake half the night—and kept her eyes carefully trained on the handle of the metal detector.

"Like I said before, don't pay Call no mind. It's the grief makes him grouchy as a bear with a thorn in its paw. Digs into him like a rusty pitchfork, though these last months it seems like he's finally beginnin' to get past it."

"What do you mean? What happened to him?"

"I ain't much for gossip, but I guess you got a right to know, seein' as how the two of you keep crossin' swords. The way I hear it, Call came up here after he lost his wife and three-year-old daughter."

Her heart snagged. "His wife and daughter were killed?"

She nodded. "In a car wreck, I heard. Call musta really loved 'em. He quit his high-powered job in California, bought that big chunk of property next door, and built himself a place to live. He was raised in the north, ya see. He come back here to heal.''

A lump rose in Charity's throat. She had wondered at the brief flashes of something she had glimpsed in Call's eyes. Now she realized it was pain.

''Oh, Maude, that's terrible. I can't begin to imagine how it would feel to lose your family like that.'' But as close as she was to her father and sisters, she could guess.

''I think you been good for him. Till you come along and the two of you started spittin' at each other, he spent most of his time holed up in his house or traipsing around the woods by himself. Like I said, last few months, he's been better. Been goin' into town once in a while. Hired Toby to work for him. Still, it's you who put the fire back in his eyes. I used to think I'd never seen such cold, lifeless eyes in all my days. Now, he looks at you, and they light up with fire. Makes 'em glitter like twenty-four-karat gold.''

Charity thought about that, thought that Call's eyes hadn't seemed cold at all when he had looked at her Sunday morning. In fact, they seemed to burn.

''I'm glad you told me, Maude.''

''Like I said, I ain't usually much for gossip.'' She looked at Charity as if she somehow knew what had happened between her and Call that morning. It was ridiculous, of course. Though at times Maude did seem to have some sort of mental radar.

Charity returned her attention to the metal detector but her mind remained on Call and what he must have suffered. If what Maude said was true and he was beginning to get over his grief, maybe she could help him.

''I didn't really thank him for saving me from the bear. Maybe I should.''

''He could probably use a good homemade supper. I doubt Toby is much of a cook.''

''Even if I asked him, he probably wouldn't come.''

''Maybe not.''

''I don't suppose it would hurt to ask.''

Maude reached into the pocket of her flannel shirt, pulled

out her short-stemmed pipe, and stuck it between her teeth.
"Nope. Never hurts to ask."

Charity thought about asking, she really did. But after the
way she had behaved she simply couldn't face him. For
heaven's sake, she had nearly torn the man's clothes off!
Never in her life had she felt so reckless, so wildly out of
control, but of course he didn't know that. If she went over
to his house, he would probably think she was trying to
seduce him.

Inwardly she groaned, embarrassed all over again. Still,
she thought about him, couldn't get those hot, drugging
kisses out of her head. Fortunately, she had plenty of work
to occupy her mind and keep herself busy.

They started using the metal detector, slowly working
their way along the stream. Later they would form a grid
and work the property inland. In the afternoons, when the
air was a little warmer, they worked the dredging machine,
taking turns on the suction pipe.

"Best place to look for gold is between the layers of
bedrock," Buck told her. "Sinks into the tiniest crevices.
Stays trapped there for hundreds of years . . . till somebody
comes along and sucks it out."

"What about nuggets? Where's the best place to look for
those?"

His eyes dropped down to the peaks of her breasts. "You
can find nuggets in lots of different places. They come in
all shapes and sizes. Pretty little things, they are."

Charity ignored the innuendo, knowing he only said it to
make her uncomfortable.

Buck returned his attention to the dredge. "Gold is mostly
in the bedrock and fine, black sand. Or you might run across
some alluvial gold. It washes down each year and you find
it in the gravel. Metal detector works good for that."

But so far they hadn't found any nuggets or anything else.
If they *had* dredged anything up, it was caught in the wire
mesh and riffles of the sluice box. Cleaning the box, she

learned, meant taking it apart, removing and carefully cleaning all the screens and riffles, then putting it back together again. It was a long, painstaking process, so it was done just once a week.

She was using the metal detector on Thursday morning, running it along the banks of the creek, when a pair of men's hiking boots appeared at the edge of her vision. Her gaze traveled up a set of long, nicely muscled legs encased in faded denim, past a worn leather belt, over a flat stomach that vee'd to a man's wide chest. She must have been staring, because Call reached over and shut off the metal detector.

"Hi," she said lamely.

He cleared his throat and she wondered if he was as nervous as she. "I saw you working your way along the creek. I figured I owed you an apology for . . . for what happened the other day." He glanced over her head, then looked back into her face. "I don't usually attack helpless women. I hope I didn't scare you."

She was a lot of things that morning, but afraid of those burning-hot kisses wasn't one of them. "No apology needed. What happened was my fault as much as yours. Why don't we just chalk it up to an adrenal rush with nowhere to go?"

He nodded and turned to leave.

"Actually, I was thinking of coming over to your place," she said, stopping him. "I never thanked you for saving me. If you hadn't shown up when you did, I'd probably be bear food by now."

His mouth edged into a faint half-smile. "I doubt it. You don't really need to be afraid of them. Most of the time, bears leave you pretty much alone. You just need to use a little good judgment and be cautious whenever one's near."

She studied his face, the chiseled lines and valleys, the square chin and solid jaw. There was something different this morning, but she couldn't quite figure . . .

"You shaved," she blurted out, feeling like an idiot the instant the words left her mouth.

His lips curved up. She remembered exactly the way they

felt pressing into hers and a little sliver of heat trickled into her belly.

"Believe it or not, I shave every once in a while."

"You look good." God, did he. If she'd thought he was handsome before, now she realized how disturbingly attractive he was.

"Do I?" A hint of color crept beneath the bones in his cheeks. "Then I guess I'll have to do it more often." He glanced down at the metal detector. "How's it going? Found anything yet?"

"Not yet. I don't think I've quite got the hang of this thing, but tomorrow we clean out the sluice box. Hopefully, something will turn up then."

He nodded, began to look off toward his house like he wanted to escape. Or maybe only part of him wanted to leave.

She gathered her courage and plunged in. "I still say I owe you for your very timely rescue. How about supper?"

"Supper?"

"Just a neighborly sort of thing. If you don't already have plans, that is. I was thinking maybe tomorrow evening."

He looked uncertain, torn in some way. "Well, I . . . yeah, tomorrow night sounds all right."

"You won't attack me again, will you?" she teased just to make him feel at ease, and he relaxed a little.

"Not unless you ask me real nice."

Her own smile turned wobbly. Surely she could trust herself—couldn't she? "Okay, then. Supper tomorrow evening. Seven o'clock okay?"

"Fine. I'll see you at seven." He started walking toward the path leading back to his house.

"By the way," she called after him, "how is it you always seem to know what I'm doing over here?"

He turned to her and actually grinned. "Binoculars. A good woodsman always knows what's going on around him."

Her mouth dropped open. "Binoculars! You've been watching me with binoculars?"

Call kept on walking. "They come in real handy up here," he said over one wide shoulder. "You ought to get yourself a pair."

Charity sputtered, opened her mouth, then snapped it closed again and simply stood there fuming. Binoculars! She watched him disappear down the trail, so amazed she couldn't get a single ugly name past her lips.

CHAPTER SEVEN

It was late Friday morning when Call sat down at his computer. Earlier, needing a little exercise and a chance to clear his head, he and Smoke had hiked into the forest behind the house. All the way up the trail, he had thought about Charity and the dinner invitation he shouldn't have accepted, inventing one excuse after another not to go. In the end, he had resigned himself.

It was too late to back out now, and besides, it was no big deal. The woman was his neighbor. It wouldn't hurt to be polite and he could practice his social skills, which, after four years of living like a hermit, were bound to be a little rusty. In the meantime, he would catch up on some of his work.

Call flipped on his computer and brought up his e-mail messages. One from Arthur Whitcomb at Inner Dimensions and another from Harry Turner at American Dynamics, where Call had been working as CEO before he quit. He replied to their questions, made a couple of suggestions, then clicked onto a message from Peter Held in Seattle.

The kid was in exceptionally good spirits. A headhunter, he said, had stopped by earlier that morning with an incredible job offer. He described the outrageous sum the job was supposed to pay and the unbelievable benefits.

Did I tell you I was good? the e-mail said. Peter had rejected the offer, of course. He owned a percentage of Mega-Tech. If the technology he was developing worked as well as they hoped it would, he was going to make millions.

Call e-mailed the young chemist back. *Who are you kidding? You couldn't stand a cushy job like that. You'd be bored in a week.* Which was the truth. Peter was a lot like Call had once been—ambitious and so full of energy he hummed with it. Graduating at the top of his Yale University class, Peter Held was brilliant and innovative, the only guy Call knew who could fill Frank McGuire's very sizeable shoes. It was Peter, one of Frank's disciples, who had contacted Call six months ago with the idea of resurrecting the hard-disk storage project.

At first Call had declined, but Peter had been so persistent—and so certain he could make it work—that Call had finally agreed, even given him a fat percentage. Call wasn't sure if he had come up with the millions necessary for research because of the money he could make, or just to see if the kid could really do it.

Call leaned back in his chair. Whatever the reason, Peter was hard at work and he was making very good progress. Call wondered which of his competitors had offered Peter the job and if maybe they were getting a little nervous.

Friday night arrived. The day had been lovely, bright blue skies and fluffy white clouds, just the hint of a breeze. The best part was, when they had cleaned out the sluice box, they'd found not only a nice little cache of gold flakes, but six small, glittering gold nuggets. Buck didn't seem all that impressed, but Charity was thrilled.

Maude said it was a very good sign and if Charity wanted, she could probably sell them to one of the jewelry stores in Dawson City.

Charity declined.

Whatever happened during her months in the Yukon, she would always remember the day she had found her first real gold nuggets, small as they were.

Her mood was buoyant as she set the little green table in the kitchen, using the plates and flatware she had bought at the general store that first day. During her cabin cleaning, she had run across a lovely old glass kerosene lamp and a bottle of oil with enough left in it to fill the bowl. The lamp glowed prettily in the center of the table next to the pine bough and pinecones she had arranged around the base.

She glanced at her wristwatch. Two minutes to seven. She heard a rap on the door an instant later. She had expected him to be on time. Call Hawkins wasn't the kind of guy who would be late.

She smoothed her sweaty palms down the long, navy-plaid wool skirt she wore with a pair of soft black leather dress boots. A white cotton blouse with little blue flowers embroidered on the front tucked into the top of the skirt and a wide leather belt encircled her waist.

Nervously, she opened the door. "Hi. Come on in."

Call looked nervous, too. "After I told you about the binoculars, I wasn't sure I'd still be welcome."

She smiled. "I remembered what happened that morning with the bear and decided to think of it as having a guardian angel."

A corner of his mouth curved. "Now I'm an angel. I think I like that better than evil genie." He stepped into the cabin, the top of his head nearly grazing the door frame. The cabin felt smaller the instant he closed the door and she realized what a big man he really was, lean but tall and broad-shouldered, very solidly built.

"I brought you a present," he said.

"You did?" He held out his hand and she accepted what appeared to be an aerosol can in some kind of leather case.

"Pepper spray. I figured it might come in handy."

"Pepper spray? I've heard of olive oil spray and butter spray, but never—"

He burst out laughing. His teeth were white and straight,

and his mouth . . . *Don't go there,* she told herself. *Don't even think about it.*

"I'm sorry," he said, still chuckling. "I forgot you don't know much about . . ." He fought to keep a straight face. "I should have told you pepper spray is used as protection from bears. You strap the holster on your belt when you go hiking."

She should have been mad, since he was laughing at her again, but she thought of how rarely he must have laughed in the last four years and couldn't quite make it happen.

She held up the can to examine it. "How does it work?"

"You just point and spray. It's to use in case a bear charges you. You wait till he gets about twenty feet away, hold the can up, and fire a stream of spray into his face."

"You're kidding, right? You're making fun of me again."

He shook his head. "I'm telling you the truth. Scout's honor." He held up two fingers.

A boy scout. She knew they had them in Canada and she could bet that he had been one.

"Let me get this straight. You're telling me I'm supposed to stand in front of a charging bear and spray it with a can of pepper?"

Call fought back a grin. "It isn't my idea of a good time, but it works. At least it usually does."

"You're not speaking from personal experience?"

"I've only had to use it once, but it did the trick. When that little stream of spray hit that grizzly in the face, he couldn't get out of there fast enough."

Good Lord, the man had faced down a grizzly bear with a can of aerosol spray! She stared at that hard, rugged jaw, thought of Max Mason, and didn't doubt it for a second.

She grinned as she set the pepper spray down on what passed for a kitchen counter—a board with a strip of linoleum glued to the top. "That was very thoughtful. You know what they say in the Yukon—a can of pepper spray beats a bouquet of flowers any old day."

He smiled, began to survey the interior of the cabin. "The place looks really good." He was dressed in a new pair of jeans and a tan, long-sleeved pullover shirt with a wide navy strip across the shoulders.

He had shaved again, and for the first time she noticed he had also cut his hair. It wasn't short, but it was neatly trimmed. He looked handsome and virile, and incredibly sexy, and suddenly she wondered if inviting him over was such a good idea after all.

"I know how run-down this place was," he was saying. "You did a really good job fixing it up."

"Thanks. I had fun doing it. Mostly."

There was something in his other hand and he set it down on the table. "I also brought a bottle of wine. I hope you like red."

"I love red. I love wine, in general."

"Me, too."

"And martinis. I love martinis but I never drink them. They make me do things I regret in the morning."

His eyes turned a deeper shade of blue. "I'll remember that. Next time I'll bring a bottle of Kettle One."

She flushed, but the heat she was feeling wasn't just in her face.

Call looked over at the pot simmering on the stove and she thought that every time he looked at her, she felt a little like that pot.

"Smells good. What is it?"

"Nothing fancy, just beef stew. I also made some biscuits." She gasped at the reminder and darted past him toward the stove. "Son of a—gun." She started to reach in and yank out the pan, but his hand shot out and snagged her wrist.

"Careful." He slowly released his hold, but she could feel the ghost of those long, strong fingers as if they were still there.

Not such a good idea at all.

Grabbing a pot holder, she pulled out the pan, unhappy to see the biscuits were already black on the bottom.

"I'm still not used to cooking on a wood stove. Maude fixes most of the meals."

"I'm starved. Anything will taste good to me. Why don't I open the wine while you check the stew?"

Charity nodded and turned toward the stove.

Call watched his pretty little blond neighbor at work. Her hands were slightly unsteady, her movements more awkward than normal. She was nervous, but then so was he.

At least three times, he had started to send Toby over with one of the lame excuses he had invented on the trail. Aside from a sexual relationship, he didn't want to get involved with a woman, and after what had nearly happened between them last Sunday, he was afraid his attraction might lead to more than just lust.

Even in the wild days before he was married, he couldn't remember a woman ever turning him on the way she did. She kissed like an angel and tasted as sweet as sin. If Toby hadn't shown up when he did, there was every chance he would have had her on the ground, her jeans down around her trim little ankles, and been buried to the hilt inside her.

Of course, he was a man who hadn't had sex in four years. Perhaps it was nothing more than that. He wanted her. Badly. The way she had responded, it was clear she wanted him, too. He needed to get his life back to normal and that included having sex.

Especially having sex.

He wanted to have it with Charity Sinclair.

Call used the wine cork he'd had the foresight to bring and opened the wine, a nice bottle of St. Michelle cabernet.

"Where are you from?" he asked as the cork made a soft pop and came out.

"Manhattan." She turned away from the stew and her chin inched up. "I was an editor at one of the big publishing houses. You probably think that's funny, too."

He set the bottle down on the table. "I think it's pretty amazing. I admire the courage it must have taken for you to come to a place like this."

Charity sighed and gave the stew another stir with the

wooden spoon. "I've always wanted to come here. I can't remember a time I didn't. It was a lifelong dream. I know everything about the Gold Rush and more than you might guess about looking for gold."

"Gold fever? That's what brought you here?"

"Not really." She gazed out the living room window, at the snow-capped mountains stretching endlessly beyond the creek. Evening was upon them, but this time of year it was light nearly eighteen hours a day. It wouldn't be dark for hours. "It's nearly impossible to explain. It's like an itch I needed to scratch, like a compulsion of some sort. I had to come." She shook her head. "It sounds ridiculous, I know. I don't even understand it myself."

She looked upset and he realized she had agonized over coming here for years. A dream, she had called it. An odd one, for sure, but he had to admire her courage in undertaking such a difficult endeavor.

"You look nice tonight," he said. Feminine and pretty in a long wool skirt instead of jeans, her shiny blond hair swept up in a soft knot on her head. He wanted to pull out the pins and run his fingers through it, see if it felt as silky as it looked.

His body tightened. He swore a silent curse as he went hard inside his jeans. He wanted to forget the stew, haul her into his arms, and start kissing her again. He wanted to do a lot more than that.

"This country is everything I dreamed it would be," she was saying. "I just wish I knew more about the animals and the land. That isn't really something you can learn from books."

"No, I don't suppose it is." He poured wine into the pair of water glasses she set in front of him on the table, handed one of them to her, and lifted his own in a toast. "To Klondike stew and next-door neighbors."

She grinned. "To burned biscuits and new beginnings."

Call smiled and they both took a drink.

The stew was great and the conversation easier than he

expected, at least in the beginning. She told him about her father and sisters and her job as an editor in New York.

"I did mostly action adventure and intrigue," she said. "Clive Cussler; Stephen Coonts; Dale Brown; the Max Mason, Grim Reaper series—that kind of thing. I love to read and especially those kinds of books." She tipped her head toward a bookshelf fashioned from a pine board perched on two granite boulders. The shelf was beginning to fill with paperback novels. "I buy them through the mail. Which reminds me, I need to check my post office box. I'm hoping a new batch came in during the week."

"I like reading, too. I've spent a lot of time doing that in the last few years." Call told her he had come to the Yukon four years ago, after he quit his job in Silicon Valley as CEO of American Dynamics.

"It's a company that's involved in developing sophisticated software. Before that I owned a company that manufactured games. I got involved in the field when I was a student at Berkeley. My roommate and I came up with a game called Warriors and Maidens. It turned into the beginning of the Black Knight Fantasy Series."

Her eyes rounded above the rim of her wineglass. "You're the guy who invented Warriors and Maidens?" she said with a sort of awe.

"One of them. Richard Gill was the other. At the time, it just seemed like a way to have fun. We came up with the game—and the rest, as they say, is history."

"I can't believe it. I love that game."

The conversation progressed. Call didn't offer anything too personal and neither did Charity.

It was the most enjoyable evening he'd spent in years, but as night finally arrived, as the sunlight waned and the fire in the hearth burned low, filling the cozy little cabin with warmth and a soft yellow glow, the tension began to thicken between them.

Charity was pretty and sexy, the all-American girl with the peaches-and-cream complexion and freckles on her nose. With her rosy cheeks and luscious mouth, she was every man's ideal sweetheart. He wanted to take her to bed, and it must have shown on his face.

Certainly it was evident in the fit of his jeans. Unlike his disastrous date with Sally, he'd been hard for most of the evening. His mood turned sour. He wanted to have sex with Charity, but that was all he wanted. Anything beyond satisfying his lust wasn't part of his plan.

Charity must have noticed his change of mood because her mood shifted as well. "It's getting late," she said, rising from the sofa and glancing toward the door. "We both need to get some sleep."

There wasn't much chance of that for him. Part of him was eager to leave, to get as far away from temptation as he could manage. The more he got to know her, the more certain he was that she wasn't the type for casual sex. The other part wanted to haul her into her tiny bedroom and make use of Mose's old iron bed.

Instead, he thanked her for supper and started for the door. Unfortunately, as he reached it, his mouth opened up and words spilled out that he hadn't intended to say.

"You said something earlier about wanting to know more about the animals and the land up here. I could show you around a little . . . if you're interested, I mean."

She worried her bottom lip and he remembered how sweet it tasted. Desire tore through him so fierce he had to fist his hands to keep from reaching out for her.

"I wouldn't want to impose."

He cocked an eyebrow. "It's a little late to worry about that, isn't it? You moved in next door. You started running that damnable dredging machine. You've already imposed on my peace of mind." *Not to mention what you're doing to my body.* "Why stop with that?"

Her lips twitched. "Point well taken. In which case, I suppose I may as well accept your offer and let you show me around. When do we start?"

He thought of spending more time with her, thought of the lust he was fighting right now and inwardly groaned. The hell with it. It was too late to back out now.

"You don't work tomorrow or Sunday, right? Why don't we start in the morning? We'll hike up to a little lake I know not far from here."

"Sounds good—if you promise not to make it an endurance competition. I don't know if I'm ready for that."

"You look like you're in pretty good shape to me." He couldn't stop his eyes from a thorough perusal of her body, and a jolt of heat slid into his groin. He cleared his throat. "It really isn't that far."

Charity smiled. "All right, then—tomorrow it is."

He nodded, already regretting his impulsiveness. "We'll have breakfast at my place before we leave. Six o'clock too early?"

"On Saturday? Are you kidding? Saturday and Sunday are the only days of the week I get to sleep in." She sighed. "But I really do want to see the country, so I guess I'll have to tough it till Sunday."

"Six, then." He stood for a moment in the doorway, wanting her, knowing he had to leave. "Like I said, thanks for supper. Good night, Charity."

"Good night, Call."

He closed the door behind him, pissed at himself for not kissing her.

And damned glad he hadn't.

CHAPTER EIGHT

Six o'clock on a weekend was ridiculously early. Charity almost turned over in bed and pulled the pillow over her head. But she'd told Call she would be there and she was curious about him, intrigued by the thought of what she might discover in the house where he lived.

Last night had been surprisingly pleasant. Call had been a perfect gentleman. He'd been interesting and charming, smiling more easily than he had when she had first met him, though he never once ventured into the personal side of his life.

Charity hadn't pressed him. They were only fledgling friends, after all. Considering what had happened last Sunday, even that tentative relationship was somewhat strained. But she hadn't missed the incendiary sparks in those intense blue eyes whenever he looked at her last night. They made her light-headed, made her stomach clench with desire, made her want to accept what he so obviously wanted to give her.

For a while last night, she'd been able to pretend indifference. He was simply a neighbor, she told herself. She was grateful for his help with the bear. But as the evening progressed, her eyes kept straying to the heavy bulge at the front of his jeans. She kept looking at his mouth, remembering the burning heat of it moving over hers.

By the end of the evening, if he hadn't left when he did, she might have asked him to stay.

God protect me from marauding bears and men with beautiful, pain-ravaged eyes.

She had never been so madly attracted to a man—or more certain that any sort of involvement would be a terrible mistake. Call was still recovering from the loss of his wife and child. True, it had been four years, but for some people grief lasted a lifetime. Call wasn't ready for a serious relationship, and considering her dismal record with men, neither was she.

Charity sighed as she dragged herself out of bed, slipped on the silky long johns she had ordered from a Winter Silks catalog, then pulled on her jeans. Call Hawkins, with his lean, hard body, burning eyes, and scorching kisses, posed more of a danger than any man she had ever met.

And yet she was drawn to him in a way she couldn't explain. Thoughts of him stayed with her as she dressed in a turtleneck tee shirt, pulled a warm flannel shirt on over it, and tucked both into her jeans. With her hair drawn into a ponytail, she grabbed her jacket off the back of the sofa and headed for the door. At the last minute, she remembered the pepper spray, raced back and snagged the can off the counter, then crossed the porch and headed for the path along the creek.

Call opened the door before she had time to knock.

"You're only five minutes late," he said lightly. "For a woman, I consider that right on time."

"Actually, for a woman, it's fifteen minutes early."

He chuckled. "Come on in."

His cedar-sided, wood-framed house wasn't all that big, but it was masculine, tastefully done, and expensively furnished. The dark brown sofa and chairs in the living room were made of butter-soft leather, the tables polished walnut, the floors wide-planked and covered with patterned rugs.

He gave her a quick tour, showing her the guest bedroom

with its own private bath, and the powder room just off the entry.

"Pretty impressive."

"It's comfortable."

"Compared to Mose Flanagan's cabin, I'd say that's an understatement."

They didn't linger in the master bedroom, but she felt a little tickle of heat at the sight of the big, king-sized bed. With its sleek wooden headboard, suede-trimmed orange-and-brown wool duvet, and matching suede pillows, it looked more than a little enticing. There were large framed pictures on the walls, mostly landscape lithographs of the mountains and rivers of the North. She noticed there wasn't a single family photo anywhere in the room.

Call led her into the kitchen—black granite countertops and stainless steel appliances.

"Propane?" she asked, enviously eyeing the stove.

"Yeah. There's a thousand-gallon tank out back. A-One refills it every couple of months. I don't like it to get too low." He led her over to the breakfast area and pulled out one of four chairs at the walnut table.

"Hungry?" he asked.

"In my other life I never could eat this early, but Maude insisted. Now I wake up starving."

"Good. I made pancakes and bacon. There's coffee in the pot. The cups are in the cupboard overhead."

"I thought Toby was chief-cook-and-bottle-washer." She poured them each a cup.

"He is, but the evil genie weakened and gave him the weekend off."

She laughed.

"Actually, unless I need him, Toby spends weekends with his mother down in Dawson."

"He seems like a really nice kid."

"He's a great kid. We met kayaking one summer. He had a little trouble his senior year in high school. Got arrested for drinking and fighting. Lost his scholarship to college.

He's walking the straight and narrow now. He'll be going to school in Calgary this fall. I think he's going to be okay."

He didn't say he was paying for Toby's schooling, but Charity had a suspicion that he was.

They ate breakfast, which was surprisingly good, making general conversation. Afterward, she helped him wash off the plates and put them in the dishwasher.

"Before we leave," she said, "are you going to satisfy my curiosity and tell me what's in that big metal building attached to the house?"

"Why don't I just show you?" He reached over and caught her hand. His grip was strong and solid and a tingle ran up her arm. Leading her through a door in the kitchen, he stepped into a large, carpeted, wood-paneled room and flipped on a switch. An overhead fluorescent light illuminated the room below.

"You run your generator all day long?"

"Don't have to. The place is solar-powered. The panels are on the back side of the roof."

She cocked an eyebrow. "All the modern conveniences."

"You might say that. I told you I like my peace and quiet." He led her farther into the wood-paneled room. "This is my office. The rest of the building is a garage, but this is where I work."

"You work?"

Amusement lifted a corner of his mouth. "You figured I just sat around all day and watched satellite TV?"

With that rock-hard body, he was hardly a couch potato. "I thought you were retired. You offered to triple my purchase price so I knew you had some money. I figured you spent the day dog-sledding or something."

He sat down in a black leather chair behind a built-in walnut desk and flipped on the switch to one of three computers that were stationed around the room.

"Actually, I only started working again last year. I was getting bored, I guess. I started doing some consulting for Inner Dimensions, the computer game company I used to own. I stay in touch with American Dynamics—that's the firm I ran before I quit—and in the last six months, I've started working on some projects I was involved in before I moved up here.

She ran a hand over the surface of his polished walnut desk. "Like what, for instance?"

"Well, before I left San Jose, I backed a little company called Datatron. It only has a handful of employees and for years they didn't accomplish anything spectacular. A few months back, I started dabbling with the company again, infusing a little fresh capital. I hired a couple of young programmers with some very innovative ideas." He clicked the mouse and the Web page for Datatron flashed up on the screen, its insignia a three-dimensional D, rotating in bright yellow and blue.

"What's it do?"

"Datatron collects information off the Internet and turns it into market intelligence. By using sophisticated software to search the Net, it compiles data on a specific market product or company."

"Sounds interesting," she said, her eyes fixed on the screen. "How's it work?"

Call moved the mouse, bringing up another page. "Say we take something simple, like fish sticks. In a matter of hours, Datatron can discover everything you want to know about the product. Who produces them, who buys them. Which brands sell best. What sort of advertising those companies use. That's just an example, of course. The product can be simple or extremely complex. But the fees Datatron charges are reasonable, and the companies who pay for the service save millions in labor and time."

"And they get this stuff by tapping into information on the Web."

"That's right."

"Kind of like spying."

He smiled. "I guess you could call it that, though we stay within legal parameters. As a matter of fact, lately we've taken some considerable flak in that regard. I guess some people don't like the idea that we know what they're doing."

She watched his big, dark hand working the mouse. "I don't think I'd like it, either."

"There isn't much they can do about it. As long as we don't pierce their firewalls, what we do is completely legal."

Charity dragged her gaze away from that strong, male hand and looked up at him. "Is that a note of pride I hear in your voice?"

He smiled. "To tell you the truth, this was kind of my baby. It's been fun to watch it moving forward again."

"I see." She saw more than he knew, but Call didn't mention his wife or the accident that had brought him up here, and Charity didn't ask. "So . . . one part rustic woodsman, the other sophisticated entrepreneur. I wonder which is the real you."

The remnants of his smile slowly faded. The haunted look she had seen before returned to his eyes and she wished she could call back the words.

"I've been interested in business since I was in high school. But there are times I wish I'd never invented that game, never become successful, never gone to the States in the first place. Things might have been different if I had just stayed up here."

She knew what he was thinking. She was beginning to recognize the darkness in his eyes, to know it meant he had returned to the past, remembering his wife and daughter. She ached at the pain he couldn't quite hide.

Charity glanced around the office. Like the rest of the house, it was tastefully done: furniture of polished walnut, the floor covered in deep-pile, light-brown carpet, the equipment state-of-the-art. But also like the house, it was stark and impersonal, as if its occupant wanted to erase the past and live only in the present.

She paused when her gaze lit on a wall of bookshelves filled with computer games. Above it hung a screen nearly four feet wide with a pair of control sticks mounted beneath it.

"All right," she teased, "now I know what you really do all day."

Some of the darkness faded from his features and the muscles across his shoulders relaxed. "Actually, I do spend part of my day playing games. Right now, I'm giving Inner Dimensions some feedback on a game called King Cobra."

Her eyes lit up. "Can we play it?"

He shook his head. "No way. Not today. I promised to show you the country and that's exactly what I'm going to do." He opened the office door and waited for her to walk out.

Charity glanced wistfully over her shoulder at the gigantic game board. "Okay, but I'm not letting you off the hook. It isn't like there's all that much to do up here. One of these nights, we'll have to play."

Call's expression changed and the blue of his eyes seemed to glow. "Yeah," he said, "one of these nights we'll definitely have to play."

Charity's stomach contracted. She didn't think he was talking about computer games.

Something happened. She wasn't sure what.

By the time they left the house, Call's mood had shifted again. His congenial attitude turned brooding. His jaw was set, the muscles across his shoulders rigid, his blue eyes intense. She wasn't sure what had caused the change, and the harsh set of his features warned her not to ask.

She wished she hadn't agreed to come on this hike as much as he obviously wished he hadn't offered to take her. Still, she continued up the trail, trying to pretend she was somewhere else, anywhere but with him.

At first the climb was easy. A meandering path that started in the forest behind Call's house and gently sloped upward, zigzagging back and forth across the mountain, giving her an astonishing view of the snow-dusted, granite-domed mountains surrounding the valley like a crown. A little farther up, they wove their way deeper into the forest and the soft scent of pine enveloped her. Bluejays squawked in the branches and played tag overhead.

Everywhere she looked, beauty surrounded them, and though the trail was a little bit muddy, it wasn't that difficult to climb. She watched Call's broad back, watched his long legs moving like pistons up the trail ahead of her, and wished they could have made the climb in the genial mood they had briefly shared that morning.

Instead, he seemed a different, harder man than he had been before.

Charity sighed and walked faster, trying to close the gap that continued to widen between them.

Call looked back down the trail. "Come on, you're falling behind." They were nearing the crest of the hill. At the top, they would start down, making an easy descent to the lake in the bottom of a narrow, pine-covered valley.

Call waited till Charity caught up with him, then started walking again. He wanted to get there as quickly as he could, then get her back down the hill to her cabin. He wanted to kick himself for volunteering to take her in the first place.

Dammit, the woman was driving him crazy. Just watching her climb the hill made him hard. Hell, he'd been hard off and on since breakfast when he'd watched her lick syrup off her lush bottom lip. Then they'd prepared to climb the trail and he had helped her into the straps of the small daypack he loaned her—a mistake that caused her perky little breasts to rub against his chest and sent a shot of lust straight into his groin.

He had let her see his office, which he wished he hadn't done, and she'd surprised him with her interest. Susan had never had the slightest interest in his work. She was a housewife and mother, all she had really ever aspired to be and exactly what he had wanted in a wife.

Nothing like Charity Sinclair, who had traveled thousands of miles on some wild, harebrained search for adventure. And yet he couldn't help but admire her for doing something she had always wanted to do.

Call frowned as he climbed the trail, thinking of Charity, trying his damnedest not to. He was nearly at the summit when he realized she wasn't behind him, that his back trail was empty and Charity was nowhere to be seen. For an instant, his heart simply stopped. Then she rounded a granite outcropping and stepped into view, and relief hit him so hard he felt dizzy.

She came to a halt directly in front of him, her cheeks rosy, strands of gleaming blond hair hanging down, her pretty face glowing with exertion.

"All right, that's it." She dumped the little daypack onto the ground at his feet. "If you're trying to prove your legs are longer than mine, you've done a masterful job. If you want to show me you can walk uphill twice as fast as I can, you've accomplished that, too. I thought this would be fun, but it isn't. I'm going back down the hill."

She turned and started walking, and Call cursed himself. He caught her in two quick strides.

"Wait a minute, dammit. You can't just go running off down the trail by yourself."

"Who says I can't? You? It seems to me I've been hiking by myself for most of the morning."

He glanced guiltily away. It was the truth and both of them knew it. He raked a hand through his hair, shoving it back from his forehead. "You're right. I'm sorry. I shouldn't have gone so fast. I wasn't trying to prove anything, I just . . . I didn't want . . ."

"Do you really dislike me that much?"

Dislike her? Not hardly. "I don't dislike you at all. I just . . ."

"What, Call? You just what?"

"I just . . . I'm physically attracted to you and I know it's a mistake."

She blinked and looked up at him. "Why? Is there something wrong with me?"

"Of course not. You're pretty and smart and sexy as hell, but . . . Look, Charity, there are a lot of things about me you don't know. Things that would make a difference if you did."

She seemed to ponder that. "Like what, for instance?"

"Like I haven't . . . you know . . . had sex in a long time. When I'm around you, that's damned near all I can think about. Wanting you, I mean."

She smiled, relaxed a little. "I'll take that as a compliment."

He sighed. "I suppose in a way it is, but the simple truth is, all I want to do is take you to bed. I'm not looking for any kind of a relationship aside from that."

Charity frowned. "So just a quick screw and you're done with me, is that what you mean?"

It was exactly what he meant, but he hated the look on her face when she said it. "Yeah, I guess it is."

She nudged the backpack with the toe of her hiking boot, looked up into his face. "I know about your wife and daughter, Call. I know they were killed in a car accident four years ago. I know that's the reason you came back to the Yukon."

His stomach knotted so hard he had to suck in a breath of air. He should have known she would find out. He probably should have told her himself, but he didn't like to talk about the past, even after four long years.

Charity continued to study his face. "Maybe I'd feel the same way if something like that had happened to me," she went on when he made no comment. "Maybe I'd never want to get involved with anyone ever again."

He ignored the pity in her eyes. He hated it when people felt sorry for him. It was one of the reasons he had locked himself away. He tried to look nonchalant, purposely hardened his words. "Since you know so much, you can understand why I feel the way I do. I don't suppose you'd be interested in a one-night stand?"

Charity shook her head. "Afraid that isn't my style."

"I didn't think so."

"I guess that means we aren't going to finish this hike."

He felt torn. He had promised to show her the country, teach her a little about surviving out here. And for some strange reason, he felt a little more in control. She wasn't going to make love to him. He didn't have to worry about getting in too deep. He could forget about Charity and find someone else, someone he could keep at a distance. The redhead, maybe, down at Klondike Kate's.

He took a deep breath and released it. "Now that we've

cleared the air, I don't see why we have to stop. I promised
to show you the country. The lake isn't that much farther
. . . if you still want to see it."

She looked as uncertain as he. "I guess we should . . .
since we're almost there. But I think I'll take the lead this
time."

He thought of following that round behind up the trail
and shook his head. "Not a chance. But I promise I'll slow
the pace."

"And you'll tell me about the plants and animals as we
go along?"

He nodded. "Anything you want to know."

"All right, then, let's get going."

Call looked into her pretty face, watched the breeze softly
ruffle shiny gold hair against her cheeks, thought of how
soft she looked on the surface and how strong and determined
she was underneath, and felt something tighten in his chest.

The redhead, he told himself.

The redhead—and soon.

CHAPTER NINE

The hike was fun, after all. At least until they got back down to the bottom of the hill. The lake was as beautiful as Call had promised, a clear blue mirror that reflected the tall, snow-dusted, pine-covered mountains around it. She saw her first moose and calf across a deep ravine—a safe distance away, Call said.

"Believe it or not, the moose is one of the most dangerous animals in the forest. Even a female like that one. She weighs more than a thousand pounds and there's an invisible scent stream connecting her to her baby. If you come between them, it causes a break in the scent and the moose thinks her calf is in danger. She'll do anything to protect it."

Charity thought taking on a crazed mother moose sounded almost as bad as a charging bear. "They're magnificent creatures. So homely they're beautiful. I wish I'd brought my camera along."

"They're a little too far away for a photo, unless you have a telephoto lens. Don't worry, there are lots of moose up here. Sooner or later you'll get your picture."

They ate lunch sitting on a boulder beside the lake, the conversation relaxed, as it had been earlier that morning.

"You think this is pretty," Call said, "you ought to see some of the inland lakes. Whenever I get restless, I fly my floatplane in for a couple of days. It's the best way to travel up here."

She turned away from her view of the lake. "You have a floatplane?"

He nodded, took a bite of the roast beef sandwich that was part of the lunch they'd brought along. "A DeHavilland Beaver. I've been flying since I was fourteen. My dad insisted my brother and I learn, since it's just about the only way you can get around up here."

"I've never flown in a plane that lands on water. It sounds like fun."

He shrugged as if *fun* wasn't something he knew much about, and his mood slid downhill from there. By the time they finished exploring the lake, descended the mountain trail, and Call walked her back to the cabin, he was remote and withdrawn again.

She thought of asking him in for a cup of coffee, but he seemed reluctant just to be there, stopping at the bottom of the front porch stairs while she began to climb up.

"I'm sorry about what happened earlier," he said, stopping her on the step. "You didn't deserve to be treated that way."

"You made up for it. I learned a lot today."

"If you need anything, you know where to find me." There was a note of finality in his voice that made something ache inside her chest.

"Thanks," she said. Call was determined to keep his distance, determined to stay away. For the first time, Charity realized how much she didn't want that to happen.

He started to turn and leave.

"Call?"

When he looked back at her, Charity reached out and touched his face. Standing on the step, she was exactly his height. She couldn't resist leaning forward to kiss his cheek. "Thanks for the hike."

He stared at her for several long moments, nodded, turned,

and started walking. Charity stared after him until he disappeared down the path along the creek.

"Your breakfast is ready," Toby said to Call, leaning though the open office door. "I made waffles—your favorite. And I've got some of that Saskatoon syrup you like."

"Someday, you'll make someone a great wife, Toby," Call grumbled, forcing himself to his feet though he wasn't really hungry.

Toby just grinned. Call walked past him into the kitchen and sat down at the breakfast table. Toby was babying him again. For nearly a week he'd been foul-tempered and edgy, and he hadn't been sleeping well. Apparently Toby had noticed the shadows under his eyes and his surly disposition.

Call raked a hand through his hair as the boy set a steaming plate of crisp golden waffles in front of him, then sat down in the chair across the table.

"So ... what's going on with our gorgeous next-door neighbor?"

Call nearly choked on the bite of bacon he'd just taken. "Nothing's going on. She lives there. I live here. That's all there is to it." And Call was determined to keep it that way. To ensure that it did, he hadn't seen Charity since last week, hadn't even picked up the binoculars to see what she was up to. Since then, he had been able to block thoughts of her for, oh, maybe an hour or two at a time.

Christ, the woman drove him crazy and she wasn't even near.

"Man, she is really something," Toby went on between bites of waffle. "I wonder how old she is."

Call glanced up, caught the interest in Toby's eyes. "Too old for you, so forget it."

"Hey—I like older women. And that one is definitely hot."

Too damned hot, Call thought, trying not to remember what it felt like to kiss her.

"If you're really not interested, maybe I could—"

"I told you to forget it," Call snapped, then looked over just in time to see Toby grin.

"That's what I thought."

Call just grunted. He was busily shoving food into his mouth when his satellite phone began to ring. Call slid his chair back and went into his office answer it.

"Hi, boss, sorry to bother you."

He recognized the voice on the end of the line. "Peter? What's up?"

"We got a problem, Call." Peter never phoned. Call went instantly alert. "There was a fire in the lab last night."

"How bad was it?"

"Real bad. The place is nearly destroyed. The fire department did one helluva job or it would have been."

Call could hear the depression in Peter's voice. "We've got insurance," Call said. "You don't have to worry about that. What about your research?"

Peter sighed into the receiver. "We're okay in that regard. I had backup copies of all the work in progress in the fire-proof safe. It just sets us back, is all."

"Got any idea how it started?"

"Fire department thinks it was electrical, but they're still checking into it. With all the chemicals and stuff, the place went up like a fireworks factory on the Fourth of July. Damn, we were right on the verge of a major breakthrough. Now we'll have to rebuild the lab and God knows how long that will take."

Call pondered that. "It's bound to take awhile. Maybe in the meantime we can set up somewhere else."

Peter's voice lifted. "You think so?"

"Let me see what I can do. I'll get back to you, Pete."

Call spent the next three days mostly on the phone. By the end of the fourth day, he had made arrangements for the use of the kitchen in the back of a bankrupt Chinese restaurant. The place had stainless steel countertops, water, and natural gas, the basics they would need to set up the lab. Peter was ecstatic.

"You know, we're gonna have to change our name," Peter said lightly.

"Oh, yeah?"

"Maybe something along the lines of Mega-Tech Disk Storage, Wontons, and Chow Mein."

Call chuckled. "I'll give it some thought."

"Thanks, Call," Peter said seriously. "You won't be sorry. This is gonna work. I promise you."

They ended the conversation and Call hung up the phone. He wondered if there might be more to the fire than a simple accident. If there was, the arson squad would probably turn something up. In the meantime, he refused to spend any more of his valuable time worrying about it.

He grabbed his jacket and left the house, no longer used to spending so much time in his office. As much as he enjoyed the challenge, it was a trap he would never fall into again.

At least Peter's troubles had helped keep his mind off Charity. He almost found himself wishing another problem would come up.

Another week passed and Charity saw no sign of Call. It bothered her more than it should have. She knew what he wanted from her—the only thing he wanted. As she had told him, a one-night stand just wasn't her style. And even if it were, she didn't think a single night with a man like Call would be nearly enough.

Still, she couldn't get him out of her head no matter how hard she tried. It irritated her, made her grumpy and out of sorts. God, she wished she had never met him.

Of course, if she hadn't, she probably would have been eaten by a bear.

The end of the third week arrived. It was late June, the sun out all day and much of the night, the weather warming, though a touch of snow still lingered on the high mountain peaks.

"You sure been testy lately," Maude said on Friday afternoon as they finished emptying the sluice and walked up the hill toward the cabin. "Couldn't have anythin' to do with you missin' that cantankerous neighbor of yours."

Charity fought to keep her expression bland. "Call? Why on earth would I miss him? I don't even like him."

Maude chuckled. "Used to feel that way 'bout my late husband sometimes, but most the time, I sure did love that man."

Charity sighed. "Okay, so maybe I miss him a little." More than a little. She missed him a lot. Even missed having him watch over her with those damned binoculars of his. She didn't think he was doing that anymore. He didn't want anything more to do with her.

"Maybe you should invite him to supper again."

"I can't do that."

"Why not?"

She hesitated, unwilling to reveal so intimate a conversation. Then again, Maude was her only real friend up here and Charity knew she could trust her. "Because Call's made it clear he only wants one thing." Knowing she probably shouldn't, she repeated the conversation she and Call had had on the way to the lake. "Sex isn't something I take lightly, Maude. It's just not the way I think."

"Maybe he don't take it lightly neither. Maybe he just thinks he does."

"You're not suggesting I go to bed with the man?"

"I ain't saying whether you should or shouldn't. You're a grown woman, and a smart one, too, from what I've seen. You'll do what you think is best. But I don't think Call would be so attracted to you if he thought you was a one-night kinda gal."

"Well, I don't suppose it makes any difference now. It's clear he doesn't want to see me and it's certainly better if I don't see him."

"Whatever you say," Maude muttered, but she didn't look convinced.

"I need some air," Charity said, plucking her windbreaker up off the porch. "I've been thinking of taking some pictures to send to my sisters and my dad. It's a beautiful day. I think I'll take a hike up the trail behind the house before I end the day. Can you and Buck hold the fort?''

"Sure. I'll put him to work cleanin' out that other shed. We could use a little extra storage round here. You be all right out there by yerself?"

Charity smiled. "I'll take my pepper spray." Thanks to Call, she felt a lot more comfortable hiking in the woods. She had been doing it a little every day, setting off in different directions, exploring her surroundings. There was a new trail she had discovered that she wanted to take and today she needed to get away. She was grateful Maude seemed to understand.

Charity went to get her camera and the small daypack she had purchased in town last week, then set off up the hill behind the house.

Maude checked her watch. Charity had been gone longer than usual. She'd been hiking every day for the past two weeks, but she was usually home in less than an hour. She'd been gone nearly two hours today and Maude was beginning to worry.

She glanced up the hill, but saw no sign of anyone coming down the trail. Maude wasn't in any kind of shape to go looking for Charity herself and she didn't want to send Buck. She didn't want to give him the satisfaction of having to fetch his lady boss home.

Besides, she had a better idea.

Maude didn't like to meddle, no siree, but once in awhile, it was all right to give folks a nudge.

Truth was, Charity was probably fine, but it wouldn't hurt to check on her and she knew just the man for the job. Heading down the path, she sauntered up the stairs to Call's house and pounded on his front door.

She knocked again, worried that he might not be home, but then the door swung open and there he stood, his jaw hard-set and needin' a shave, his eyes full of that haunted look she had seen on his face so often. She'd been right to come, she thought. Call looked even more unhappy than Charity and Maude had a hunch she knew why.

He collected himself, a little surprised to see her. "Hello, Maude."

"Afternoon, Call. Sorry to bother you, but I was beginnin' to worry about Charity and—"

"Charity?" He glanced over her shoulder, back toward Mose's log cabin. "What's the matter? Is she all right?"

"Far as I know she's fine, but she went for a walk a couple hours ago, and she ain't come back yet. I was gettin' kinda worried."

He straightened, making him look even taller than he usually did. "You let her go off by herself?"

"She's been hikin' most every day since you took her up to the lake. She probably just lost track of time. If my old knees weren't so weak, I'd go after her myself. I thought of asking Buck, but—"

"I'll go after her," he said darkly and she knew he didn't like the idea of Buck out there with Charity any more than she did. "I'll take Smoke along. Maybe he'll be able to pick up her trail."

"I figured you might say somethin' like that. I brung this along." It was the short cotton sleep shirt Charity wore to bed. Call reached for it and his hand shook as his fingers tightened around it. Maude patted herself on the back, thinking for an old woman she could be mighty wily sometimes.

"She won't have gone far," Maude said. "She always takes the path behind the cabin, but you know how it branches off up there. It's kind of steep in places. If she fell or something . . ."

His features darkened. "Don't worry, I'll find her."

Maude waited while he strode back into the house to collect his gear, then returned a few minutes later. She sauntered away as he whistled for Smoke and the two of them set off up the trail.

* * *

Damned woman. Nothing but trouble. Bull-headed. Too blasted independent. Determined to put herself in danger. She was probably lost—frantic to find her way home. Or maybe she was hurt, lying up there somewhere with a broken leg or something.

Sweat popped out on his forehead, the worried kind of sweat that was far worse than the kind you got from climbing up a steep trail. What if something really bad had happened? What if . . .

Call blocked the thought that came with a stabbing reminder of Susan and Amy, the knock on the door of the condo they had rented in Lake Tahoe, the sheriff who stood grim faced, hat in hand, in front of him.

This is different, he told himself. Charity wasn't Susan and he was going to find her. He'd brought his first aid kit. If she was hurt, he would deal with it, then get her safely back home.

He turned off the main trail, taking first one branch and then another, but so far Smoke hadn't picked up her scent, though he had sniffed the night shirt with interest. The dog wasn't a bloodhound, but he liked Charity, roamed over to her house at least once a day, and Call figured the animal would track her once he realized she was somewhere near.

Half an hour passed before they cut her trail. Call spotted fresh, female-sized bootprints leading off down a slightly overrun path, and he and Smoke followed in that direction. He lost track of her once and his pulse began to race, but Smoke was running ahead and he seemed to know where he was going. Call prayed he wasn't chasing a squirrel or a snowshoe hare.

He remembered the bear that had wondered into Charity's yard and how frightened she had been, and his worry kicked up. Then he remembered the pepper spray and the other things he'd taught her. Hell, he remembered everything about her. He'd thought of Charity a thousand times in the

last three weeks. Thought of her when it was the last thing
he wanted to do.

Thought of her even when he was with the redhead.

Call pushed that unwelcome memory away and concentrated on the task at hand. He studied the footprints on the
trail, but they disappeared into an outcropping of granite.
When Smoke trotted back to him instead of running ahead
on the trail, his worry increased tenfold.

She's out there, he told himself. *Just stay calm and you'll
find her.*

And once he did, he was going to wring her pretty little
neck.

CHAPTER TEN

Charity aimed her camera at a darling little ground squirrel she spotted just off the trail and snapped a picture. She had almost finished her second roll of film. She had taken some really great photos today, some wonderful panoramic shots of the snow-tipped mountains and high granite peaks, some shots of the cabin in the valley below and the ribbon of water that glistened in front of it. She had pictures of the deep pine forests she was just beginning to feel comfortable hiking through and some great shots of squirrels and birds.

An hour ago, she had discovered this tiny meadow, just beginning to come alive with wildflowers, and couldn't resist taking off her boots. The soft green grass felt cool against her bare feet as she wandered around the meadow, then returned to where the boots sat, along with her socks, in front of a fallen log.

It was time she headed back to the cabin—past time, in fact—but she only had a couple of frames left and she wanted to finish the roll. She couldn't wait for her dad and sisters to see the photos. She knew they would appreciate the beauty of this place just as much as she did.

She was winding the film forward to the thirty-fifth frame,

aiming it off toward a gnarled pine branch that presented an interesting artistic angle, when she heard the snap of a twig behind her. She jumped, then laughed as Smoke broke out of the trees and raced toward her, tongue hanging out, tail wagging.

"Hello, Smoke." She knelt and hugged his neck, ruffled his thick, silver-black fur. "What are you doing way out here, boy?"

"I might ask you the same question." In faded jeans and a denim shirt, Call stalked out of the woods behind his big dog. God, he looked so good. Tall and a little forbidding, unbelievably handsome though he badly needed a shave. She hadn't realized how much she had missed him. Well, maybe she had, but until now she'd been able to pretend it wasn't all that much.

He started walking toward her and for the first time she noticed the hard set of his jaw, the little muscle bunching in his cheek. "I've been looking all over. Where the hell have you been?"

She took a step back, intimidated a little by the dark glint in his eyes and the anger in his face. "I-I was taking some pictures. It's such a lovely day, so much warmer than it has been, and I-I—"

"Do you know how worried Maude's been?" He dumped his daypack onto the ground and continued walking toward her. "She was afraid something terrible had happened. She thought you might be lost up here, or that you might be hurt. Maybe you were lying out here in pain, unable to get help." He reached out, caught the tops of her arms, and hauled her toward him. "She was frantic. How could you be so thoughtless?"

Charity blinked at him. "I told her I was going for a walk. I might have stayed a little longer than I intended but I didn't think she'd be upset."

"Well, she was." He held her immobile, their bodies nearly touching. "She was worried sick."

There was something in his expression. Fear, she realized.

Concern for her. "Maude was worried?" she said softly. "Or you were?"

Those fierce blue eyes bored into her. His arm slid down, wrapped around her waist, and he hauled her the last few inches between them, pressing his body full-length against hers. "I was," he said, and then he kissed her.

His mouth was hard and insistent, as if he staked his claim in some way. Then the ruthless kiss softened, turned into something almost tender and in less than a heartbeat Charity was engulfed in a white-hot blaze. She moaned as she melted against him and her arms slid up around his neck. He took her deeply with his tongue and the hot, slick feel of it sent tremors crawling over her skin.

Capturing her face between his hands, he kissed her one way and then another, kissed her as if he couldn't help himself. As if he could not stop.

"I tried to avoid this," he said between hot, drugging kisses. "I did everything I could to stay away." He nipped the side of her neck, trailed kisses down to her collarbone, kissed her madly again. "Christ, what is it about you?"

She didn't know what it was, she only knew she was as wildly on fire as he was. The kiss went on and on. She had never known a man who liked kissing so much, or one who was so damned good at it. He took her mouth again, plundered it, flooding her with heat, and her knees went weak. His hands found their way beneath her sweater. He shoved it up, unfastened the clasp at the front of her bra, and palmed her breasts. She gasped at the feel of his long fingers molding the fullness, stroking over her nipples.

She heard Call groan.

Charity clung to him, kissing him as fiercely as he kissed her. One night with him—one afternoon—it no longer mattered. She had to have him. She wanted him as badly as he wanted her.

She tugged his denim shirt out of his jeans, began to work the buttons up the front with trembling fingers. Call grabbed the tails and jerked upward, sending buttons flying. He dragged her sweater over her head and tossed it away, slid her bra straps off her shoulders and the lacy pink cups fell into a pile at her feet.

"God, I want you. I've wanted you since the first moment I saw you."

Hot, wet-tongued kisses followed. Deep, erotic kisses that drove her insane. His denim shirt hung open. She shoved it off his shoulders, ran her hands over the hard planes of his chest. He was lean and solid, covered with a layer of muscle that bunched and tightened when he moved. Curly brown chest hair cushioned her fingers and ridges of muscle on his stomach went taut beneath her hand.

Call reached for the snap on her jeans, popped it open and buzzed down the zipper. "I'm taking you here. Right now. I'm not going to stop this time."

"I don't . . . I don't want you to stop."

Something like relief washed over him. He kissed her again and the next thing she knew she was lying beneath him in the soft green grass, protected by the shirt he'd spread open on the ground. His hands skimmed urgently over her body, but there was gentleness, too. He cupped her breasts, teased her nipples, then bent his dark head and took one into his mouth.

Charity moaned as sensations flooded through her. Call laved her other breast, sucked it deep into his mouth, and a shivery burst of heat slid into her stomach. His hand moved lower, over her belly, inside the open zipper of her jeans, beneath her bikini panties into the tuft of pale hair at the juncture of her legs. He parted the folds of her sex, began to stroke her, and she thought she would die of the pleasure.

Charity moaned.

"It's all right, baby. I'm not going to hurt you."

She wasn't afraid—just the opposite. She wanted to feel his hands and his mouth all over her, wanted him inside her, wanted to be so close she couldn't tell where one of them ended and the other began. She felt as if she had morphed into someone else, some wild creature she didn't even know. As if her body were some alien, newly unearthed part of her that she could no longer control.

She didn't notice when he slid her jeans and pink satin panties down over her hips, but roused a little when he dragged a small foil packet out of the wallet in his hip pocket and tore it open. She caught the sound of his zipper sliding down.

A hand she didn't recognize as her own reached out for him, wrapped around the thick, heavy weight of his sex, held him while he slid on the condom, then guided him between her parted legs.

"God, Charity . . ." With a single deep thrust, Call buried himself inside her.

The moment he did, she started to come.

"Christ." His muscles went rigid. In some vague corner of her mind, she realized he was fighting for control.

Charity cried out his name and clung to his neck, unable to believe how quickly she had reached her peak. She knew the moment he gave up his struggle to hold himself back, felt him begin to move, felt the deep thrust and drag of his shaft against the walls of her passage. She felt the power of the man above her and the deep, saturating pleasure as a second climax shook her.

Beneath her hands, hard muscle tightened and Call groaned. The sinews in his hips flexed and moved as he pumped himself inside her, then came with incredible force, his body going rigid, his shoulders glowing with a sheen of perspiration.

For long seconds, neither of them moved. The only sound in the forest was the wind luffing through the trees, their labored breathing, and the soft thud of their heartbeats.

Then Call muttered something beneath his breath. Gathering his long limbs, he lifted himself away from her and regained his feet. His shaft was still hard, big and thick and jutting forward through his open fly as if they hadn't just made wildly passionate love. Call rid himself of the condom, zipped his faded jeans, and turned to find her groping for her sweater, pulling it on to cover her naked breasts.

Swearing, he reached down and snatched up her jeans

and pink satin panties, which were tangled together and refused to come apart.

"Here."

She blushed as he unwound the fabric, handing her first the panties, then the jeans, which she hurriedly pulled on.

She didn't look at him. Her cheeks were hot and her lacy pink bra still lay embarrassingly on the ground. She snatched it up and stuffed it into the pocket of her jeans.

Charity swallowed, made herself turn and face him, tried to muster some sort of smile. "I . . . um . . . I don't suppose we can blame this on your relief at finding me alive and safe."

He shook his head, his eyes still fixed on her face. "I don't think so."

"Just lust then, I suppose."

He shrugged those wide shoulders and she wished he would put his shirt back on so she didn't have to remember all that smooth muscle moving beneath her hands.

"So it's just a one-night stand."

His head came up. Eyes as blue as the sky bored into her. "In case you haven't noticed, the sun is still up."

"The sun is always up in this place. What does that have to do with anything?"

He pulled on his shirt and she suddenly wished he were bare-chested again. "It has to do with the fact that the night hasn't even begun."

Her eyebrows shot up. "You're not . . . you're not saying what I think you are."

"I'm saying exactly what you think I am. If you believe what just happened is anything besides a warm-up, sugar, you had better think again. If I wasn't worried that Maude might send the Mounties up here to find us if we don't get back soon, we'd start over again right here."

"B-but you said . . . we both said—"

"I know exactly what we said. It's a little late to be worrying about that now." He looked at her and his deep voice softened. "Besides, I never really believed one night with you would be enough."

Relief trickled through her. Whatever was happening between them, it wasn't over yet. She gave him a reluctant smile. "I never believed it either."

"Come on." Call reached out and caught her hand. "It's Friday. We've got the whole weekend ahead of us. Maybe by Monday, we'll have had enough of each other."

"Maybe," she said. But Charity didn't really believe it and from the burning glance Call gave her, she didn't think he did either.

Call woke up with the first rays of light slanting in through the ruffled bedroom curtains. He was lying on his back in the old iron bed in Mose Flanagan's cabin. The bed was too narrow and his feet hung over the end, poking through the scrollwork at the foot of the bed. Charity lay sleeping, draped across his chest, her long blond hair fanned out over his shoulder.

With each of her soft breaths, he could feel the fullness of her breasts, remember the way they plumped in his hands. After a stop at his place to give Maude and Buck time to finish work and leave for the weekend—and retrieve the box of condoms he had purchased before his disastrous non-date with Sally—he had returned to Charity's cabin.

As he had said, their night together had not yet begun, and when it did, he meant to make more of it than the hasty round of sex they had shared in the meadow. Not that it wasn't good. It was, in fact, one of the hottest encounters he'd ever had. But the wild, passionate lovemaking they had shared last night made it pale in comparison.

His hand skimmed over Charity's naked shoulder, lifting silky strands of hair away from her cheek. He let it slip through his fingers, testing the softness, admiring the shiny golden color. Though they had made love most of the night, he had awakened painfully hard, the way he always used to in the mornings.

Susan hadn't liked morning sex. Somehow he knew Charity wouldn't mind being roused that way, that she would enjoy the intimacy as much as he did. She stirred, made a soft sighing sound as he lifted her a little and positioned her above him. He ran his palms over her tight, round bottom, then nudged her legs apart so he could slide in.

Her eyes flew open at the feel of his hardness easing inside her, then her lids drooped closed and she kissed the side of his neck.

"Good morning," he said, nuzzling an ear as she relaxed and let him ease farther in.

"Ummmh," was all she said.

She was wet and warm, pliant as he started to move. He gripped her hips, eased out, and slowly filled her again. God, she felt so good. He moved out and then in, gently at first, setting up a rhythm, feeling her heartbeat quicken. Her body tightened, began to move with his, meeting each of his strokes. It took only minutes for her climax to hit. He felt the muscles of her womb contract around him, knew that she was about to come, and fought hard for control.

He had never known a woman so responsive, so quickly aroused. So easily satisfied. Funny thing was, instead of ending the interlude more quickly, it made him want to slow things down, give her even more pleasure.

He hung on through her first rocking climax, driving into her with long, deep strokes that had beads of perspiration breaking out on his forehead. Goosebumps rose on her skin as she came a second time and he allowed himself to join her. Afterward, she stayed right where she was, her head tucked beneath his chin, her arms around his neck, and slowly drifted back to sleep.

It was Saturday morning. Their one-night stand was over. He had prayed it would be enough but known deep down it wouldn't. He wanted to make love to her in every way he could think of. It was lust, pure and simple, and yet he was afraid. He hadn't felt nearly the same with the redhead. All he'd accomplished with her after four long years was a little sexual relief and the unwelcome knowledge that another woman wasn't going to get Charity Sinclair out of his blood.

The way it looked, nothing was going to do that but time. *Give it a week or two,* he told himself, remembering his old college days when spending two weeks with the same woman had set a new personal record. But those were the days before he married. Before he became a husband and father. Before Susan and Amy.

Just thinking about them sent a shaft of pain straight into his heart. He clamped down on the memories before they could flood in and renewed his vow never to get involved that way again.

With that thought in mind, he eased Charity off his chest, gently unwound himself, and quietly left the bed. Pulling on his clothes, he crossed the room, closed the bedroom door, and left the cabin.

Sex with Charity was one thing. Having a little fun was all right, too. It was time he had some fun. Past time. But any sort of relationship beyond that was out of the question.

He had to make sure she understood.

Call looked back at the cabin, ignored a longing to stay, and kept on walking down the path toward home.

Charity woke up late that morning. Every muscle in her body felt pleasantly sore and she was relaxed in a way she hadn't been in years. Call had done that. Charity had always enjoyed sex. Jeremy had made her feel embarrassed about how much.

"You're insatiable," he'd said. "You make me feel inadequate and I know damned well I'm not. Maybe you ought to take some Prozac or something, calm yourself down."

As if her sex drive was unnatural somehow. As if she wanted too much from him.

In time, his attitude had accomplished exactly what he intended. Sex became a low priority, something to fit in when Jeremy's busy schedule allowed.

But Call wasn't that way. Call Hawkins was all hot-blooded male, passionate in bed, a skillful, unselfish lover who took one minute and gave the next. Maybe that was the reason she responded to him as wildly as she did. One long glance and she was on fire. One touch and she burned.

It was a little unnerving.

Charity sighed and opened her eyes, rolled over onto his side of the narrow bed. Her eyes cracked open as she realized the bed was empty.

"Call?" The bedroom was empty as well, and he wasn't in the bathroom. Drawing on her terry cloth robe, she padded into the living room, hoping to find him there.

The pellet stove burned low. She added some fuel and closed the heavy iron door, trying to ignore the icy feeling in her stomach. Call had wanted a one-night stand. She had given him exactly what he wanted.

She sank down on the sofa, ran a shaky hand through her hair, toyed with the fringed, olive-green throw cover.

You've got no one to blame but yourself, a little voice said. Call had been honest from the start. He wanted a no-strings relationship. It appeared that was exactly what they'd had.

With a sigh, she wandered into the kitchen. Her appetite was gone. It was too much trouble to stoke up the stove just to make coffee so she filled the aluminum pot and set it on top of the pellet stove. It would take a little longer to perk, but it was Saturday and with Call already gone she had plenty of time to herself.

She thought of the passionate night they had shared and wondered how he could so easily walk away. It was his past, she believed, the pain that had never really left him, the kind of pain he would do anything to avoid again.

Charity straightened. Whatever his intention, Call was a different man than he had been when she had first met him. Maude had noticed it, too. Charity believed she had something to do with that change and letting him back away from any sort of involvement wasn't the answer.

We have the whole weekend ahead of us, Call had said. But he had left after only one night. Charity straightened her shoulders, turned, and headed for the shower. A whole weekend, he had said. Well, she meant to take him up on it. If nothing else, she'd have two days and nights of hot sex with a macho hunk like her fantasy man, Max Mason. Hey, didn't Call even look a little like him?

And maybe with a bit of luck, it would turn out to be more than that.

Charity turned on the shower—which worked surprisingly well since the plumbers had fixed the hot water heater—adjusted the nozzle, and climbed in.

If he rejected her, she was going to be mortified. She prayed he would welcome her instead . . . though it might take a little persuasion. Whatever happened, she wasn't giving up just yet. As she rinsed the soap from her hair, Charity wondered what Call would do when he saw her coming up his front-porch stairs.

CHAPTER ELEVEN

There's gold, and it's haunting and haunting;
  It's luring me on as of old;
Yet it isn't the gold that I'm wanting
  So much as just finding the gold.
It's the great, big, broad land 'way up yonder,
  It's the forests where silence has lease;
It's the beauty that thrills me with wonder,
  It's the stillness that fills me with peace.
                              —Robert W. Service

Saturday morning slid past. It was nearing the end of June and the weather had finally begun to warm. Rainy days interspersed more and more with brilliant azure skies and bright northern sun.

Call wandered around the house, trying not to think of Charity in bed in the cabin next door. He had forced himself to leave just after dawn, though he hadn't had nearly enough of her. He needed some space, needed to distance himself. In a couple of days, he would drop by and see her. By then she would know he'd been telling her the truth, that all he wanted was a physical relationship. If she still seemed agreeable, they would pick up where they left off this morning.

The thought made him instantly hard. Dammit, what the

hell was the matter with him? He hadn't been this randy
since he was a kid. In college he'd been considered a major
cocksman, but it had only taken a couple of years to learn
it was quality, not quantity, that counted.

That was just about the time he met Susan—tall, dark-
haired, and willowy, drenched in class. He had recognized
a thoroughbred when he saw one. And Susan was a Went-
worth. That meant old money, San Francisco society. She
was also intelligent and caring, the perfect wife for a man
with plans for an ambitious career.

Then Amy had been born two years after their marriage
and he had settled down even more. God, he had loved that
child, his precious little princess. And she had loved her
daddy with all her innocent, three-year-old heart.

Call's chest constricted. If only he'd been able to see
where his endless ambitions would lead. The child of his
heart might still be alive, along with the woman he had
loved. But he had been younger then, not as clear-headed.
That didn't happen until after the accident. Not until he had
moved back here. Not until it was too late.

The ache in his chest expanded. Call crossed the kitchen
and reached for the door to his office, shoving the painful
memories back into the dark corner of his mind where he
usually kept them. Taking a seat at the chair behind his
walnut desk, he flipped on his computer.

Outlook Express brought up his e-mail. There were a
couple of new messages in the In-box, the first from Peter
Held.

*Man, you are incredible. I can't believe you've already
got the lab up and running. We're close to a solution, Call.
I can feel it in my bones.*

Call was typing in a reply when a light rap sounded at
the door. He turned to see the brass knob turning, then
Charity Sinclair walked in.

She flashed a brilliant smile. "I knocked out front but
you didn't answer. I figured you were probably in here so
I came on in. I guess no one locks their doors up here."

"There's usually no need," he said darkly, furious she

had entered his domain without an invitation. Annoyingly glad she had.

"You forgot your wallet when you left this morning." She handed it over as he came to his feet. "Of course I could have waited for you to come back and get it, but I thought you might need it before then."

"Thanks," he said gruffly, feeling like a fool for thinking she had come over just to see him.

Charity glanced around the office. "So what shall we do today? It's really nice outside. I thought maybe we could make a trip into town, take in a matinee or something. I need to pick up a few supplies. We could kill two birds with one stone."

He just stood there staring. He'd thought leaving her this morning had delivered the message: *Sex is fine but we aren't going to let this get personal.*

"If you don't like that idea," she went on, "how about taking me flying? You said you had a floatplane. I'd love an aerial view of the country."

A muscle tightened in his jaw. "You expect me to take you flying."

She looked at him as if he were smiling instead of frowning. Her own smile seemed a little uncertain. "It was just a suggestion. The show's okay, too. I know there's a cinema in Dawson but I don't know what's playing. I imagine up here you can't be too picky."

"What if I just took you back to bed?"

She cast him an interested glance. "I figured we'd get around to that sooner or later, but—"

"All right," he said, regretting the words the moment they left his mouth. "I'll take you flying."

Her smile was warm and full and her eyes lit up, the clearest shade of green, the color of a lake after the snowmelt. "Great! Where are you going to take me?"

"Where do you want to go?"

Her lashes swept down, long and thick and darkened with a trace of mascara, a hint of city girl she refused to give up. He felt the pull of a smile he refused to let surface.

"Can I pick any place I want?"

"Within reason."

She looked up at him hopefully. "I've been dying to go to Skagway. I suppose it might be too far, but—"

"Skagway? Why would you want to go there?"

"Alaska's where the Gold Rush really began. I considered driving down there from Whitehorse when I first arrived in the Yukon, but I was too excited about getting to the Lily Rose."

He turned away, not liking the curl of warmth he felt when she looked at him that way. "It's almost a three-hour flight, but the scenery's incredible. We'll have to check the weather." He sat back down in front of the computer and started pounding on the keyboard, then waited while the necessary information came up. "Weather looks good for the next couple of days."

He turned to find her peering excitedly over his shoulder. "Pack an overnight bag," he said a little gruffly, one half of his brain calling him a fool, the other looking forward to the trip in a way he hadn't in a very long time. "We'll spend the night and come back tomorrow evening."

"You're really going to take me?"

"I said so, didn't I?"

"Fantastic! It won't take me long to get ready. I'll be back in twenty minutes." She practically raced out the door, leaving him still sitting at his computer, trying to figure out what had just occurred.

So you're taking her to Skagway, his brain said. *So what? You'll get to go flying, which you love, have dinner in a great restaurant followed by some very hot sex, then come home.* He relaxed a little. It was just a date. He'd made up his mind to start living, to get out in the world again. He had already made a start. This was just a way to continue.

Call answered the e-mail from Peter and replied to a message from Bruce Wilcox, his VP at Datatron, the Internet market research company he owned. The company was being threatened with an invasion-of-privacy suit. Call had worried something like this might happen, though legally they were well within the law. He replied to a couple of other brief messages, shut down the computer, and went to pack a bag for the trip.

As he tossed in a cashmere sweater he hadn't worn in more than four years, he ignored the little voice that warned he was going to be sorry.

Call's plane, Charity discovered, bobbed in the water at a small, private dock on the Klondike River. It was a single-engine model, the body and pontoons painted fire-engine red with orange stripes sweeping along the sides.

"It's a DeHavilland Beaver," Call explained. "They're the best planes ever made for this kind of country."

After making an inspection of the aircraft, he helped her climb aboard, then followed her in and they strapped themselves into their seats. Call completed his final checklist and the engine roared to life, discharging an odorous cloud of exhaust.

She heard the rush of water over the pontoons as they taxied out into the river, then the roar of the engine; the whirling propeller added a different sound. The aircraft built up speed, gliding through the current faster and faster. Then the plane broke free of the surface of the water and seemed to leap into the air.

Charity's heart lifted with it, as if it had also taken wing. The view from the sky was breathtaking. Unlike a larger, faster airplane, the Beaver flew low enough for the passengers to enjoy the landscape spreading out below them. The earth continued to fall away and a wide swath of muddy, gray-green river where the Klondike merged into the Yukon appeared, along with vast stretches of deep green forests. Pines stretched over low, rolling hills and marched up the sides of majestic, snow-covered granite peaks in the distance.

Dawson City disappeared behind them, the vanishing grid of wooden buildings, trees, and narrow dirt streets soon just a light spot on the landscape.

"We'll pick up those supplies you need tomorrow when

we get back to town," Call promised, sitting behind the controls with the authority of a pilot who felt completely at home in the air. "In the meantime, just relax and enjoy the ride."

Exactly what Charity intended to do. Once they were airborne, Call filed a flight plan over the radio as a safety precaution, then headed south toward the little town of Skagway, a port on the inland strait of the Alaskan Peninsula, a hundred and ten road-miles south of Whitehorse, where they would stop to refuel.

Call flicked a glance to where she sat buckled into the seat next to his. "So tell me again why you were so determined to go to Skagway."

She smiled at such an easy question. "Because it's the gateway to the Klondike, the place where it all began. In the 1890s, Skagway was a boomtown. From what I've read, a lot of the old buildings are still there. It's supposed to be sort of a living museum."

"Skagway's a very interesting place. When you're raised up here, you cut your teeth on Gold Rush stories and a lot of them start there. Every old prospector in Dawson has at least one to tell. Mose Flanagan used to be full of them." A corner of his mouth edged up. "So what do you know about Skagway?"

Charity thought of all she had read, of the hundred thousand gold seekers who landed there, prepared to make the grueling trip over the mountains to Dawson City, lured by dreams of Klondike gold. She knew so much she could bore him to tears, but of course she wouldn't do that. Not everyone was as fascinated with the Gold Rush as she was.

"I know the first Stampeders arrived by steamship in July of 1897. It wasn't a town back then, just a couple of old log cabins. Three months later, twenty thousand people lived in Skagway. The streets were lined with tents, hotels, cabins, stores, and saloons."

"Not bad. What else?"

"In the beginning, five thousand gold seekers used the White Pass Trail to get to Whitehorse and go on to Dawson and the goldfields. But by the end of September the trail was completely impassable. It was clogged with the bodies of six thousand horses and mules.''

Call's gaze shifted to hers. "I've hiked the trail. It's rugged as hell. I can understand why very few animals made it.''

"You've been to Skagway, then?''

He nodded. "A couple of times. My dad took our family there when we were kids. He was as fascinated by the Gold Rush as you are.''

"Where's your family now?''

For a moment he didn't answer. He never liked to talk about anything personal. She thought that maybe it made him feel exposed. Or maybe the past was simply too painful.

"My dad died of a heart attack when I was in college,'' he finally said. "Mom still lives in Prince George. She's remarried. She seems content with her husband—though I'm not too fond of the guy myself. Zach—my older brother—is a lawyer in L.A.''

"A lawyer, huh? Remind me to refrain from the usual attorney jokes.''

One dark eyebrow quirked with what might have been amusement, but he didn't ask her to tell him one.

"My mom died when I was ten,'' Charity continued, hoping to prod him into sharing a little more of his life. "My dad's remarried. Were not as close as we once were, but we're still good friends.''

When he didn't jump in with any more information, Charity let the subject drop. They talked about the Lily Rose and she told him that their amateur dredging operation was holding its own, though she was hardly getting rich.

"On Fridays, when we clean the sluice box, we usually find enough to pay wages and buy supplies for another week.''

"That's the way it goes with prospecting,'' Call said. "People always believe the next pan will be the one that makes them rich.''

"I didn't come to get rich.''

His eyes found hers across the cockpit. The engine buzzed and a hint of exhaust tinged the air. "Why *did* you come, Charity?"

Now *there* was a difficult question. For a moment she said nothing, just studied the view going past outside the window. "Mostly, I came for adventure, as I said." She explained about her father and the stories he used to read to them when they were kids.

"My sisters and I made a vow. We swore we would each have one exciting adventure before we started a family or settled permanently into a career. Patience has always been interested in the American West. She's working on her Ph.D. at Boston University. She wants to travel the rodeo circuit next summer and write her thesis on women of the West."

"Sounds like an interesting subject."

She smiled. "My older sister, Hope, writes freelance articles. She figures something exciting will turn up sooner or later."

"So coming up here was your adventure," he said.

"Coming to the Yukon was something I had always wanted to do, but . . ."

"But . . . ?"

"But in my case there was more to it than that. It may sound crazy but I had to see this place, be part of it. It's been a driving force in my life for as long as I can remember. Even when I lived in the city, there were times I could see it so clearly it was almost as if I had been here before. The forests and the mountains—they aren't strange to me, they're familiar. As if I've always known them."

"Because you've read so much about them?"

She glanced out the window, but she wasn't seeing the sky or the endless sea of pine spreading over the empty miles below. "Sometimes it's as though I actually remember this place. I don't think it's because I read about it in a book."

Call frowned. "What are you saying? That you lived in the Yukon in some other life?"

She could hear the skepticism in his voice and she didn't

blame him. "No, nothing as far-out as that. I'm too pragmatic to believe in that sort of thing." She studied the rows of dials in the wide black panel in front of her: altimeter, barometer, air speed, a dozen little gauges that jiggled and pointed and turned.

"The truth is, I haven't the foggiest idea what drew me up here. I just feel like the history of this place is somehow part of me. That's the reason I had to come."

Call watched her a moment more, then his hands relaxed on the steering column. Apparently, he didn't think she was entirely insane. They talked about his brother, who was a year younger than Call and a dedicated bachelor. They talked about business and the projects he was involved in.

"A couple of them are becoming problematic. Datatron's on the verge of a lawsuit. Legally we should be in the clear, but tempers are running hot."

"You're talking about the company that digs up information over the Net."

He nodded. "That's the one. Financially, they're doing great, but sometimes people get unhappy when you're nosing around in their business affairs."

"You told me it was legal."

"*Legal* doesn't necessarily mean people like it. A couple of companies have threatened to sue. So far, they're only blowing smoke. We'll have to wait and see if there's going to be any fire."

She cocked her head in his direction. "Which I have a feeling you would very much enjoy putting out."

He shrugged his shoulders. "I used to like the challenge of running a business. I guess in some ways I still do."

The plane buzzed along at something near a hundred and thirty miles an hour and Charity settled back in her seat, enjoying the conversation and the view. Call dropped down a couple of times to show her something special along the route. He pointed out a huge bull moose near the edge of a marshy stream, this year's set of antlers just emerging from the velvet that marked their new growth.

She leaned back again after that, content to watch the pleasure she saw in Call's face as he handled the controls.

"You really love flying, don't you?"

He slanted a look her way. "For years I was too busy to fly my own plane. American Dynamics owned a company jet with two full-time pilots on staff. I traveled with them most of the time. I owned a twin-engine Baron for a while, but I used it so rarely that I finally sold it. A couple of years after I moved to Dawson, I bought the Beaver and had it completely rebuilt. Yeah, I really love to fly."

They made a rest stop and refueled in Whitehorse, then crested a last, tall range and dropped down over Skagway, which sat at the mouth of the Skagway River where it dumped into the sea. The town nestled in a flat spot on the ocean, surrounded by jagged granite mountains higher and more brutal than those around Dawson City.

Those craggy, forbidding peaks, Charley marveled, formed the barrier between success and failure for the men who traveled to the Klondike in search of gold.

"Imagine—a hundred thousand people set off from here for Dawson," she said as Call expertly circled and began to spiral down toward the bay. "Only about a third of them made it."

Easing back on the throttle, he set the small plane down with a light splash followed by a rush of water over the big pontoons. Call taxied to the seaplane dock, where they left the aircraft moored. After a brief stop at customs, they made their way to the white, front-wheel drive Chevy Call had rented from Avis via his cell phone.

Sourdough Taxi did the Rent-A-Wreck thing, said a nearby billboard, but Call, it seemed, wasn't the rent-a-wreck type.

"I don't like hassles," he said. "I want something reliable that will get us where we want to go." Not only could he afford a nicer car, it was just his way to be efficient and thorough about everything. His home and property were immaculately clean and well cared for and his plane was in top condition.

Jeremy had been that way, but he carried it to ridiculous extremes, lining his shirts up an inch apart in the closet, keeping every pair of his expensive shoes in a little felt bag that fit into a shelf on the wall. For heaven's sake, the man sent his dress shirts from Manhattan all the way to New Jersey because he liked a particular laundry. Charity inwardly grinned, trying to imagine Jeremy with a three-day growth of beard.

Settling back in the seat of the Chevy, she relaxed as Call aimed the car toward the main part of town. Though it was crisp and clear today, it had rained in Skagway the night before and the streets were still muddy. The vehicle navigated the roads with ease and soon they were driving through town, parking on one of the side streets.

"First we'll take a look around, then we'll find a place to spend the night." His gaze connected with hers and she didn't miss the message: *Not that you'll be getting much sleep.*

Charity ignored the hot look in his eyes and the answering warmth in the pit of her stomach. She had come to see Skagway. She wouldn't be living up here all that long. This might be her only chance.

They spent the afternoon wandering through shops and boutiques. In spite of the tourist bent the town had taken on to survive over the years, the place retained a good deal of its late-1890s appearance. Long-board sidewalks and wood-framed buildings reminiscent of Dawson stretched along Broadway, the main street of town, and establishments with names like The Purple Moose, Lynch and Kennedy Dry Goods, Mile Zero Bed and Breakfast, and the Miners' Saloon.

"This wasn't the original landing site for the gold seekers," she told Call as they looked into the window of a little boutique called The Klothes Rush. "It was a town named Dyea in a bay just a few miles from here."

"I've been there. There isn't much left. A few historical markers, a couple of old cemeteries. Where Skagway survived, Dyea faded away. The Chilkoot Trail starts there."

"The Chilkoot." Charity stared off toward the mountains as if she could see it. "The meanest thirty-two miles in history. The main route into the Yukon." She looked up at him. "You think maybe we could go there?"

"We can hike partway up in the morning if you want. I always keep outdoor gear in the plane. The trail's damned tough, though. Not like going to the lake."

"No. It climbs thirty-seven hundred feet, some of it nearly straight up. Can you imagine twenty thousand people trying to make that climb in the dead of winter?"

"I've seen old photos. There's one above the bar in the Miners' Saloon. Come on, I could use a cold beer."

They went into the bar, which had been built in 1898, a survivor, like many of the buildings, of the town's Gold Rush glory days. It looked as it must have then, the bar a long slab of scarred, battered oak running the length of the narrow room, the floors wooden and worn, the walls covered with red flocked paper that was frayed in places. Yet it didn't seem seedy, just old and somehow charming.

Charity climbed up on one of the wooden stools in front of the bar. Call sat down on another, propping a heavy leather boot on the long brass rail. While the bartender fetched them bottles of Alaskan Amber, Charity studied the picture behind the bar, a three-by-four-foot blowup of a famous black-and-white photo she had seen once and never forgotten.

Taken by a journalist in route, the picture showed a wall of ice and snow too steep for horses, notched with twelve hundred icy steps. The Golden Staircase, they called it. From the bottom of the hill on the left, an endless line of exhausted men trudged upward, stumbling half-frozen to the summit on the upper right, the would-be miners so heavily laden they could barely stand up, their hands, feet, and bearded faces white with frost and numbed by the unbearable cold.

A frozen vision of hell.

Even at a distance, the photo betrayed the men's exhaustion. The picture was so moving a lump formed in Charity's throat.

"Amazing what those men were willing to endure," Call said.

"There were women there, too." Though she tried not to think what they must have suffered.

"Not many women, I don't imagine, but definitely a few. They must have really been something."

"That photo was taken in the winter of '99. The year before, there was near-starvation in Dawson. The Mounties declared any man traveling to the goldfields had to take a year's worth of supplies—about two thousand pounds. Some of the men walked more than a thousand miles back and forth up that hill just getting their goods across the border."

"And they were still more than three hundred miles from the goldfields."

Charity took a sip from her icy bottle of beer. "They cut down trees at Lake Lindemann and floated the Yukon to Dawson. Unfortunately, a lot of them drowned in the rapids at Miles Chasm. They called it Miner's Grave."

Call eyed her as he sipped his beer. "You really know a lot about this stuff."

She stared up at the photo. "You've heard of the 'call of the wild,' haven't you? I guess that's what happened to me."

"Lady, you definitely have a wild streak—at least in bed." He cast her a hungry glance, set his empty beer bottle down on the bar. "As soon as you're finished we'll find a place to stay."

Charity met the challenge in his gaze, set her half-full bottle down on the bar. "I'm ready whenever you are."

Call's eyes turned a scorching shade of blue. "Sweetheart, I've been ready since you strolled into my office at nine o'clock this morning."

CHAPTER TWELVE

They left the bar and checked into a motel on sixth and State called Sgt. Preston's Lodge. It had all the modern conveniences: phone, TV, and king-size bed. The minute they walked into the room, Call slammed the door, turned, and backed her up against it.

"I thought we'd never get here." A big hand slid into her hair. He fisted the heavy strands and dragged her mouth up to his. The kiss was hot, deep, and thorough, the kind of kiss that made her toes curl up inside her shoes.

"I've been wanting to do that all day," he said, kissing the side of her neck, "but this time we're going to take things slow and easy."

He kissed her again, more gently now, more of an erotic tasting. Charity gave a little sigh of pleasure and kissed him that same way, sliding her arms around his neck, running her fingers through his thick dark hair.

"I want your clothes off," he said between soft, nibbling kisses. "I want to see you naked and stretched out on the sheets."

Her pulse accelerated as he popped the buttons on the front of her blouse and eased it off her shoulders. He unsnapped her bra and tossed it away, worked the zipper on her jeans and slid them down her legs.

She stepped out of the walking shoes she wore instead of her hiking boots. Call peeled down her socks and stripped off her jeans.

"God, you've got the prettiest legs. I've always been a leg man and yours are definitely a ten."

She laughed. "I'm glad you think so." She gave him a long, soul-burning kiss. "I want you naked, too." She started unbuttoning his shirt, impatient to run her hands over the long, sinewy muscles she remembered from the night before.

She eased the light cotton fabric off his shoulders and marveled at what a fabulous chest he had, wide and darkly suntanned, with bands of smooth, hard muscle. Desire burned through her, made her breasts begin to ache. He was kissing her neck, trailing moist kisses along her collarbone, when a muted ringing crept into her awareness.

"What the hell is that?" Call muttered, kissing her one last time before lifting his head to survey the room for the irritating noise. It wasn't the phone beside the bed, they realized, as the muffled ringing started again.

"Oh, my God, it's my cell phone!" She broke away from him and raced toward her purse, carelessly dropped at the foot of the bed. "I tossed it into my bag before we left. Force of habit, I guess. I always carried one with me when I lived in the city."

She pawed through her purse, a big, black leather bag she had bought at the mercantile to replace her little Kate Spade, tossed out her wallet, then her lipstick and powder compact, and finally located the phone. Conscious now of her near-nudity, she turned her back toward Call, flipped open the phone, and pressed it against her ear.

"Hello."

"Hello, Charity. It's good to hear your voice."

Her pulse took a leap, started an uncomfortable thudding. "Jeremy." She flicked a glance over her shoulder and didn't miss Call's frown. "H-how did you get my number?"

"I got it from Deirdre. I can't believe you haven't called me since you got up there."

"I-I thought it would be better this way. I thought we'd both be happier if we just left things alone for a while."

"Well, I wish you'd phoned. I've missed you, babe. I can't believe how much. I want to know when you're coming back home."

She sank down on the bed, sweeping her hair over her shoulder out of the way. She kept her back to Call, hoping to gain a little privacy, but she could feel his fierce blue eyes burning into her from where he stood just a few feet away.

Jeremy went on about the city, about the concerts and plays she had missed, as if he couldn't imagine how she could live without them. With Call so near, Charity could barely concentrate on what he was saying.

"Umm, listen, Jeremy, this isn't a good time to talk. I'm out of town right now. I won't be home for a couple of days, but as soon as I get back, I'll call you."

"Tell me you're coming home. Tell me you've had enough of this crazy adventure of yours."

She sighed into the receiver. "Jeremy, I really have to go. I'll call you. I promise." Pressing the disconnect button, she hung up the phone and stuck it back into her purse.

Call stalked over to the foot of the bed. "Who the hell is Jeremy?"

She didn't like the way he towered over her, so she stood up and faced him, her arms crossed over her naked breasts. "He's the man I was seeing before I left Manhattan."

"Seeing? As in sleeping with?"

"We went together for almost two years. I had a life, Call. I had a job and an apartment and a man whose company I enjoyed." For a while, at least.

"*Had.* That's past tense. If it's over, why is he still calling you?"

"I-I didn't exactly end things when I moved away. More like, left them up in the air. But the truth is, Jeremy and I aren't really right for each other. There was a time when I really wanted us to be. In the beginning I hoped we'd get married and have a family. Unfortunately, things didn't work out.''

"Why not?"

"I don't exactly know. Maybe I needed to come here first.''

He eyed her for several long moments. "But you wanted to marry him. You wanted a husband and kids.''

"Isn't that what most people want?"

He hesitated, glanced away. "I wanted that once. Not anymore.'' He tipped his head pointedly toward the bed. "That's all I want now. Hot, mindless sex for as long as it lasts, until we both get tired of each other. Friendship, maybe, after that.''

"Friendship.'' She dropped her arms and straightened, thrusting her breasts out in front of her. All she wore was a pair of tiny, red-silk, thong panties. "Do you really think we could ever just be friends?''

Call's eyes turned hot and a muscle leapt in his cheek. Sliding an arm around her waist, he hauled her against him. "Not now, that's for damned sure. Right this minute, friendship is the last thing I want from you.'' He kissed her hard and a few seconds later she was lying beneath him in the middle of the big king-sized bed.

Their lovemaking wasn't slow and easy, as Call had planned. It was hot, frenzied, multiple-orgasm sex like she'd never had with anyone but him, the kind that left her weak and barely able to move.

She knew their wild encounter had something to do with the phone call she had received from Jeremy, but she wasn't sure exactly what it was.

They didn't leave the room until just before time for the restaurants to close and only then because both of them were starving. The days were even longer this time of year, nearly twenty-one hours of daylight. Charity had never really gotten used to it and even after the fabulous sex, she wasn't sleepy at all.

Instead, she and Call headed down the wooden boardwalk to an Italian eatery called The Portobello. Once inside, a waiter seated them at a table near the windows of what turned out to be a surprisingly sophisticated restaurant. Done in dark green and red, with painted cement floors and lots of Italian bric-a-brac on the walls, it had a cheery atmosphere that immediately wrapped around them.

"I've never seen you in anything but jeans," Charity said, admiring the way he looked in brown wool slacks and a tan cashmere sweater. With his hard jaw and lean, tanned features, God, the man was gorgeous. "You clean up good, Hawkins."

His gaze ran over her body, taking in the short, A-line, apricot jersey dress that clung softly to her curves. She had purposely left her hair down, hoping it would please him. His eyes fixed on her mouth. "So do you, Sinclair," he said a little gruffly.

Seated at the table across from her, he lifted his glass of red wine. "To good Chianti, a beautiful woman, and a night on the town in Skagway."

Charity also lifted her glass. "To handsome men and Klondike gold."

They clinked their glasses together and each took a drink. The meal was delicious, a buttery shrimp scampi for her, a smooth chicken piccata for him. The wine was rich and mellow, the candlelight enticing. At first they laughed together, each of them relaxed and enjoying the evening, but as the meal progressed, Call's mood began to shift. He grew more and more silent, more pensive and brooding.

"You shouldn't be thinking of work," she said, hoping the problem was with one of his companies and not with her.

Call straightened in his chair. "Business doesn't interfere in my life—not anymore. It never will again."

But his mood went steadily downhill and all the way back to the room he stayed silent. Charity was afraid she knew what he was thinking.

* * *

Call was thinking he must have been out of his mind to agree to this trip. Charity Sinclair had a way of getting under his skin, of touching him in ways he didn't want to be touched, of making him feel things he didn't want ever to feel again.

In bed, she drove him crazy. He'd never met a woman who liked sex as much as he did and yet she had an underlying innocence that told him she hadn't been with many men.

"I can't believe it," she'd said with a dreamy smile that afternoon, after an incredible round of lovemaking. "I've read about women having more than one climax, but I never thought it would happen to me."

What guy wouldn't be turned on by that? The bad news was that instead of getting his fill of her, as he had imagined he would, he wanted her even more than he had before. Every time he looked at her he got hard. He wanted to make love to her every way he could think of. Christ, he couldn't seem to get enough of her.

Worse yet, when they were finished, instead of the usual male urge to get the hell out of Dodge, he wanted to sleep with her, feel her body curled against him, wake up with her in the morning. Considering he was determined never to let his emotions get entangled with a woman again, it scared the holy hell out of him.

Call sighed into the silence of the motel room. It was nearly three in the morning and he needed to get some rest. Charity slept the sleep of the dead, snuggled against him in a way that made him feel masculine and protective.

His feelings for her were growing and that could only spell disaster. He had no plans for marriage. Charity wanted a husband and kids—and she deserved to have them. But a family was the last thing Call wanted. An image of Amy popped into his head—curly, brown hair, big blue eyes, baby face smiling as she raced into his arms for a good-bye hug before she climbed into the BMW for the fatal trip down the mountain with her mother. It was the last time Call ever held her.

His eyes burned. He swallowed past the lump in his throat and tried to think of something else, anything to erase the image. The memories had been coming more often lately. Making his way back into the world of the living had disturbed the ghosts of the past and he wanted nothing so much as to bury them again.

Maybe he was moving forward too quickly, taking things too fast. When they got back to Dawson, he would do what he should have done before. He'd stay away from Charity, let things cool down a little between them. It would be better for both of them, he told himself.

But he still couldn't fall asleep.

A harsh, late-June sun radiated through the windows of their ground-floor motel room as Charity dressed in jeans and hiking boots for the morning outing they had planned. Over her shoulder, she cast a glance at Call, worrying at his continued silence. He was up and showered before her eyes cracked open, moving around the room with a restlessness that hadn't been there the day before.

It was obvious he hadn't slept well. There were smudges beneath his eyes and his features looked drawn.

"Are you hungry?" She cast him a glance on her way out of the shower, a little disappointed he hadn't come in to join her. "Because I feel like I could eat the hide off a bear."

"I'm a little hungry, I guess."

But he didn't seem hungry. He seemed distracted and edgy, as if he couldn't wait to get out of there. They ate a killer breakfast at the Gold Dust Café—crisp bacon, eggs over easy, fluffy homemade biscuits drenched in butter and slathered with strawberry jam, the old-fashioned kind of meal that was hard to find in New York City. But Call mostly picked at his food.

She wished she knew what was wrong. Maybe if she gave him some space he would talk to her about it, but Call was the strong, silent type and she didn't really think so. Instead, he paid the bill and they climbed into the rental car for the eight-mile drive around the bay to the site that had once been the starting point for the famous Chilkoot Trail.

As they rounded a curve in the road that hugged the mountain beside the bay, she could see the vast mud flats that had welcomed Stampeders, the first ordeal they faced when they arrived.

"Well, this is Dyea," Call said, as if now that she had seen it maybe they could go home.

The flats stretched out, brackish and ugly. Weary steamship passengers had to get themselves and their supplies across the thick, waist-deep mud before the tide came in— an often impossible task.

"As you said, there isn't much left."

Call drove her through what had once been a thriving boomtown, now a series of dirt roads winding among the trees, bare spots where buildings once stood, markers relaying the history of the town, and signs pointing toward a couple of forgotten cemeteries.

From the town site he drove to the trailhead. They parked the Chevy next to several other cars, most with out-of-state plates.

"There are more people here than I thought there would be," she said as she opened the door.

"June, July, and August are the big tourist months. Technically, we need a permit to climb the trail but we won't be going that far so it shouldn't be a problem."

The Chilkoot was different from what most people expected. The beginning of the climb was damp, almost rainforest tropical. Huge cottonwoods interspersed with spruce ran along the Taiya River. Broad-leafed ferns hung over the trail, and the rocks were slick with moss. The sound of rushing water accompanied them as they climbed over boulders and wound their way through damp foliage, following the trail steeply upward.

They passed a man and his wife in hiking shorts and boots, their backpacks heavily laden with gear, obviously intending to travel the length of the trail, a four- to five-day trek even at this time of year.

An hour into the climb, Call stopped and turned to look back at her. "Seen enough?"

"I-I was hoping we could go on a little farther." It was obvious he wanted to go home, but something was nagging her, teasing the back of her mind, a feathery impression just out of reach.

Call turned and simply started walking again, making the hike look easy. So far, it hadn't been bad. With the exception of a steep climb over a couple of bluffs, much of the trail was flat. The tough spots lay ahead.

They kept on moving, passing a Japanese tourist with a digital camera around his neck. He chattered something in Japanese that she couldn't understand and gave them a friendly smile, which Charity returned. Call merely nodded. At a place called Finnigan's Point, he stopped again.

"We've been hiking for nearly two hours. We aren't equipped to spend the night, Charity, and like I said, even if we were, we'd need a permit."

Charity could read his impatience in the set of his jaw, but her mind was somewhere else, someplace farther away. He said something more, but his voice sounded distant, like a bee buzzing next to her ear. Instead, her mind was focused on the images that had started crowding into her head.

"What is it?" Call asked, his words finally reaching her. "Your face is pale. Are you sick?"

She looked up at him and realized her heart was pounding. "I remember this place. I can see it in my mind—the view out over the valley . . . the glacier on the mountain behind us. I can't believe it, but I do."

"That isn't surprising. You said yourself you've read everything you could find on the Gold Rush."

"Yes, but this is different. I remember the trail up ahead,

how steep and rocky it is.'' She frowned, trying hard to recall. ''It's not exactly the same, though. In my mind it's all covered with snow.''

Call's gaze followed hers up the trail. ''You've seen photos like that. You saw one last night behind the bar in the Miner's Saloon.''

Charity bit her lip. ''I know I did, but this isn't the same. It sounds crazy, but I remember something that happened here. Something bad, I think. Someone was hurt or . . . or maybe they died. It's there in my mind. I can almost remember but not quite. It's like a name on the tip of my tongue.''

She turned toward the path climbing upward. ''It wasn't here, though. It was farther along the trail, up toward the summit.''

He saw that she was frowning, reached out and squeezed her hand. ''Listen to me. You're remembering something you read. There's no way it could be more than that. It's no secret that people died on the Chilkoot Trail, a lot more than one. But you can't be remembering something that happened before you were born.''

She sighed as the vague memory faded. She wished she could call it back, see it clearly in her mind, but even the wispy threads no longer remained.

''You're right. I must have read it.'' But she didn't believe she had and she could see by his frown that Call knew she wasn't convinced.

''Come on,'' he said. ''It's time we started down. We've still got a long flight home once we get back to Skagway.''

Falling in behind him, she let him set the pace for the hike back down the mountain to the trailhead. All the way there she thought about the memory that had almost popped into her head, a feeling of icy cold and a shadowy sensation of grief.

As far back as she could recall, she'd been fascinated with tales of the North. It was a place that seemed familiar though it was thousands of miles away. Coming here felt . . . right somehow. As if she were connected in some way.

There was something there in her mind, she was sure of it, lurking in the shadows, just beneath the surface.

Whatever it is, it's the reason I came here, the reason I had to come. If only she could find out what it was.

They reached the trailhead and made their way back to the car. She had just settled into the passenger seat when the cell phone in her purse set up a muffled ringing. Charity turned and grabbed her bag off the backseat where she had left it and fished out her phone, praying it wasn't Jeremy Hauser calling again.

"Hi, Charity, it's Toby," said the voice on the end of the line and she worked to hide her relief. When she glanced at Call she saw that he was frowning and wondered if he was thinking of Jeremy, too.

"Hi, Toby," she said and saw a faint relaxation in Call's features.

"I'm sorry to bother you," Toby said. "I tried reaching Call but half the time he leaves his phone in the plane or doesn't turn it on. I found your number in his office. Is he there?"

"He's right here, Toby." She handed over the phone and Call pressed it against his ear. With the car still sitting in the parking lot, Call spoke to Toby, nodding once or twice at whatever the younger man said.

"Phone Wilcox back," Call instructed. "Tell him I'll be in touch as soon as we get home. And relax. One thing I've learned—in business, there's always some kind of emergency. It's rarely catastrophic." He ended the conversation, reached down and cranked the key in the ignition.

"Problems?" she asked as the engine sparked, then started to purr.

"Bruce Wilcox phoned, my VP at Datatron. I guess the Feds showed up at his house this morning."

Charity arched a brow. "Sounds serious."

"Apparently the two new whiz kids I hired as programmers pierced the firewall on a couple of big companies. I'll have to deal with it, but whether it happens today or tomorrow won't make any difference."

She watched him casually wheel the car up onto the road. ''I take it that isn't what you would have done in the past.''

Call's gaze met hers. ''No, it wasn't what I would have done in the past.''

CHAPTER THIRTEEN

The little DeHavilland Beaver lifted out of the bay that afternoon. It was a different journey home from the one that had brought them to Skagway.

All morning, Call had been edgy and tense. *It's Datatron,* she told herself, but had trouble making herself believe it. Whatever it was, he sat in the cockpit, stiff and reserved, his jaw hard, the muscles in his shoulders rigid. Or maybe he was thinking of the conversation they'd had on the trail. After all, she was more than half convinced she had remembered something that happened a century ago.

Sitting next to him as the plane buzzed through the mountains over rugged White Pass Trail, she studied his profile, the way his mouth looked harder than it had on their journey southward.

In silence, he guided the aircraft through the craggy, forbidding peaks between Southern Alaska and the Yukon. Beneath them, the White Pass and Yukon Railway wound through the narrow gorge that led to the goldfields, a refurbished, narrow-gauge railroad built originally in 1899. The train, which ended the struggle up the grueling Chilkoot

Trail, chugged today over hundred-foot trestles and looked frightening even from the air.

Thoughts of the Chilkoot sent a rush of adrenalin through her. Could it really have been a memory? She certainly felt as if it had been.

She cast a glance at Call and his brilliant blue eyes collided with hers, watchful and a little wary.

"You don't really believe you remembered something from a hundred years ago."

Embarrassment washed through her, making her cheeks go pink. Part of her wanted to say no, that couldn't possibly have happened. She wanted to erase the cool, disbelieving look on his face. But lying just wasn't in her nature.

"I don't know. It felt like a memory, something I'd experienced a long time ago. There was snow all around—an avalanche, maybe—and I felt this terrible crushing sort of sadness, as if something really bad had happened."

He eyed her skeptically. "What else?"

"What else? Are you kidding? It was just a flash. I can't believe I remembered anything at all."

"Even if there was some kind of accident or something, it couldn't be a memory. It happened before you were born."

He was right, of course. But if she closed her eyes she could still see the endless white of mountains covered in snow, feel the overwhelming sense of grief. There had to be some explanation.

They flew along in silence for a while. She had brought a novel along, but the views were different heading north and she didn't want to miss anything.

Instead, she allowed her eyes to feast on the harshly magnificent, unforgiving terrain that spread out for miles around them. Call pointed to a ridge off to the east, swooped down in that direction, and she spotted a herd of caribou migrating single file up a narrow trail along the side of a hill.

"They're beautiful," she said over the noise in the cockpit. "I've never seen a caribou before."

She smiled at him; then a series of popping, sputtering

sounds distracted her and she noticed Call was no longer looking at the animals. Instead, he was frowning, staring at the dials in front of the controls, and the engine wasn't humming along smoothly as it had been. The roar of the motor was breaking up, interspersed with moments of silence, kind of a sick, sporadic coughing.

Her pulse took a violent leap and her heart started thrumming. "What's wrong? What's happening?"

"Looks like there's a problem with the fuel intake."

An instant later, the engine fell utterly silent and her heart sank like a stone. "Oh, God."

"The fuel gauge shows full but the engine's not getting any gas." He looked over, must have noticed the chalky color of her face.

"We're going to be all right," he said firmly, trying to restart the engine, switching fuel tanks and trying again. "This thing lands on water, remember? There are lots of lakes up here. We just have to find one."

She gave him a shaky nod, turned to look out the window, began a frantic search of the ground below. Ground that was getting closer every second.

It was quiet in the cockpit. Too quiet. Nothing but the whistle of wind over the wings and the rustle of paper as Call spread open the map he yanked from between the seats.

"H-how much time do we have?"

Call continued scanning the map, searching for a lake in the surrounding area. "We're losing altitude at about four hundred feet a minute. We were flying roughly five thousand feet above the ground when the engine shut down."

"Okay . . . so that would mean . . . ?"

"That means we've got about ten minutes before we're down."

Ten minutes. Oh, God. When you were about to crash to your death, ten minutes seemed less than a heartbeat. As she searched the forest below, praying for an opening that exposed a river or lake big enough to land in, they were the longest minutes of her life.

Call tossed the map aside and altered their course, aiming

the plane a little to the east. "There's a small lake at the edge of the foothills west of Yukon Crossing. We'll set her down there."

Charity continued to study the ground, her nails biting into her palms.

"Sonofabitch."

Charity's head snapped up. A puff of smoke curled out of the engine and flames erupted in its wake, licking up from the area around the propeller, blowing backward, over the nose toward the windshield.

"The engine's on fire," she said dumbly, as if he couldn't see that for himself. An instant later, thick black smoke began to roll up from under the instrument panel. "What . . . what do we do?"

"There's a fire extinguisher behind my seat. Can you reach it?"

She grabbed it with shaking hands, hauled it into her lap. "What now?"

"Nothing yet. Just put it down by your feet."

He sounded calm and that helped control the panic crawling through her. She could hear him on the radio, sending out a Mayday and relaying their current position. When a voice crackled to life on the other end of the line, she tossed a look toward heaven and said a silent thank-you that at least someone had heard them.

"Roger that, N94DB. We're tracking you, Hawkins."

"We're going to set down about twenty miles west of Yukon Crossing." He gave the coordinates of the lake.

"Roger that. We'll get there as quickly as we can."

The smoke in the cockpit grew more and more dense and Charity started coughing. She opened the window as Call had done and gulped in a breath of clean air.

"Just hang on a little while longer," he said. "We aren't that far from the lake. I need you to help me spot it."

He was turning the plane again, dropping down a little faster, worried the fire was going to get worse. Miles of forest rushed past, tall pine trees so close together a man could barely walk between them.

"See anything?"

Her heart was racing. They were going to go into the trees and if they did—*don't even think it*. "Not yet."

"Keep looking."

She strained to see through the black haze pouring up from beneath the dash, making her eyes tear up and her nose run. A dozen thoughts crowded her head. She wished she'd had time to tell her family how much she loved them. She wished she could see them one more time.

"Anything yet?"

They were only a couple of hundred feet off the ground. "No. Nothing. Yes! There it is! I can see it in that clearing, just a little bit to the east."

"Damn, it's more like a duck pond than a lake. This is going to be close."

She looked over at him, saw the tension, the concentration in his features. "Is there anything I can do?"

He must have heard the quiver in her voice because his own voice softened. "You're doing great, honey. Just hang on tight and be ready to get out as fast as you can once we stop moving."

She nodded, though she knew he couldn't see her through the black haze in the cabin. The lake rushed toward them. The bad news was she could already see the other end and they weren't even on the water. The tops of the trees slapped against the fuselage just before they shot out over the tiny lake.

"Brace yourself."

She did the best she could, closed her eyes and offered a little prayer. The plane slowed, seemed to hover for an instant, then started skimming across the surface of the water. Even at the reduced speed, she could see there wasn't going to be enough room for them to make it.

"Put your head down!"

She ducked as the big pontoons shot up onto the bank at the far side of the lake. The wings caught between two trees and ripped away with a metallic shriek. The body of the plane slid through the narrow opening, then the nose crashed into a granite boulder and Charity slammed forward in her seat. Fire shot up from the engine. The world seemed to blur and something hard banged into the side of her head. Then everything went black.

Charity's head was pounding. She must have been out for at least a couple of minutes. When her eyes cracked open, she was in Call's arms and he was running, carrying her away from the plane. A little way into the forest, he ducked behind a pine tree and carefully lowered her to the damp, black earth.

"Are you all right?" he asked and she could hear the worry in his voice.

"I'm . . . I'm okay." He swallowed, touched her cheek, then turned and started running back toward the plane.

Her stomach knotted. Using the tree for support, she levered herself to her feet, terrified the plane would explode and after surviving the crash, Call would still be killed. She watched him reach into the cockpit, pull out the fire extinguisher, then start shooting it into the flames licking out of the engine.

His shirt was torn, his face streaked with soot, but he seemed to be making progress. Reaching back into the plane, he pulled out a second extinguisher, shot some of the white foam under the dash, then returned to work on the engine.

As he set the empty canister aside, grabbed the canvas bag that held his emergency gear, and started walking toward her, Charity's knees went weak and she sagged against the trunk of the tree.

Call dropped the bag at her feet. When he saw the bloodless color of her face and noticed how hard she was shaking, he reached out for her, drew her gently into his arms.

"It's all right, baby, it's over. You're safe now. Everything's going to be fine." She could feel his heartbeat, his pulse racing nearly as fast as her own.

She swallowed, fought back tears of relief. "Will they . . . will they be able to find us?"

"They know where we are. They'll send a search plane or a chopper. I've got flares in my emergency gear."

She nodded, pressed herself tighter against him, felt his arms tighten in return. "Call?"

He eased back a little, cradled her cheek in one of his big, tanned hands. "What is it, baby?"

"I think I'm going to cry but I don't want you to think I'm a sissy."

He smoothed back her hair, looped it over her ear. "I won't think you're a sissy. You were great up there. Terrific. I wouldn't want to crash my plane with anyone else."

She did start crying then and Call just held her, letting her cry against his shoulder. His wool shirt felt rough and warm beneath her cheek and the smell of smoke seeped up from the fabric. It felt good just to be standing there in the circle of his arms.

She cried herself out in a couple of minutes, sniffed a little, and wiped her eyes on the tail of his shirt. "Thanks for the shoulder."

"Considering I'm the guy who got you here, it's the least I could do."

She managed a wobbly smile. "You were great, Call. I think you saved our lives."

He shrugged, looked a little embarrassed. "I just did what I've been taught to do."

She didn't argue, but she thought that under the same circumstances someone else might not have done half so good a job.

And less than half wouldn't have been nearly enough.

CHAPTER FOURTEEN

Summer in California was usually warm, perfect golfing weather, even hot in some places. In San Francisco, heavy clouds hung over the city and a damp mist wrapped around the tall, glass-walled structure that was the Global Tower on Market Street.

Gordon Speers was used to the erratic San Francisco weather. He liked the misty air blowing in off the sea, liked the way the early morning sunlight crept through the valleys created by the mountainous streets. It was the only place in the world he would want to live.

"You're sure no one saw him leaving the area?" Though it was Sunday afternoon, Gordon had come into his office to work for a couple of hours. And he had been looking forward to this particular call. Leaning back in the expensive Eames chair behind his desk, he pressed his leather-cased cell phone more firmly against his ear. "He had no trouble getting in?"

"Are you kidding?" said the voice on the other end of the line—his partner, Anthony King. "People don't even lock their doors up there. Grossman walked out on the mooring dock wearing a pair of mechanic's overalls, hooked the device into the fuel line, and walked back out. It actually worked better doing it in Skagway. Harder to make any sort of connection.''

They'd had a man in Dawson for over a week, getting the lay of the land, trying to figure out the best way to get the job done with as little notice as possible. The plane trip was a lucky break. A talkative mechanic, a friend of Hawkins's in Dawson, knew where he was going and when he was scheduled to return. Tony's man simply followed on a commercial flight, got the job done, and disappeared out of the area.

''Check your wristwatch,'' King said. ''By now, Call Hawkins is history.''

Gordon felt a mild sensation of relief. ''Let me know when you get confirmation.'' He hung up the phone, a private number few people had. His partner, Tony King, was one of them. Gordon was the brains of the company he had founded eighteen years ago, but he wouldn't be where he was today without Tony.

It was King's job to work behind the scenes, to use his powerful connections to get things done. And he was ruthless enough to make sure they did.

A week ago, they had made the decision to eliminate a problem that had recently arisen—or perhaps it might be better said, reared its ugly head again. Four years ago, McCall Hawkins had been a powerhouse in the computer industry, CEO of American Dynamics, not to mention his numerous other successful business interests. He was smart, fiercely competitive, and ferociously aggressive. He had power and position and one of his companies was about to stumble onto something that would ultimately destroy Gordon Speers and everything he had worked for.

Everything he expected to gain in the very near future.

Gordon had refused to let that happen. After several offers to purchase the fledgling company were refused, a more permanent solution had been pursued. As it happened, after a very timely and very unfortunate auto accident that took the lives of his wife and daughter, Hawkins retired from the industry and the problem was solved.

Or at least it *had* been.

The bad news was, sometime this year, Call had started working again, making his way back into the computer field, dredging up long-dead projects.

It was a scenario Gordon couldn't afford to ignore.

He sighed as he shoved back his chair and walked over to the wide glass windows of his office. The fog was rolling in off the bay, beginning to blanket the city. On the street below, cars had begun to pull on their headlights.

Too bad about Hawkins, he thought. Too bad the man had foolishly turned down his offer of employment ten years ago. He could have been a valuable asset to the company.

Now all he would be was food for the insects.

It seemed a terrible waste of talent to Gordon.

Call spread out the blanket he took from his emergency gear and sat down next to Charity to listen for the search plane. Over and over, his mind replayed the moments before the engine had failed, searching for some explanation.

He knew the plane was in top condition. He kept it tuned like a fine Swiss watch; his mechanic was Bob Wychek, one of the best in the North. Eventually the problem would be discovered, even if he had to have the plane dismantled down to a pile of nuts and bolts. Of course, he'd damn near have to do that just to get it out of the lake.

The main thing was he was able to walk away in one piece and so was Charity.

A shudder ran down his spine. Charity could have died. It would have been his fault. He swallowed the dread that threatened to engulf him and looked down to where she slept against his shoulder.

Shock, fear, and the fading adrenalin rush had left her exhausted. Her face and clothes were covered with soot and smudges of grease streaked her hair. Her flannel shirt was torn and a trickle of blood had dried near her temple.

It made his stomach churn to think how close she had come to dying. If they hadn't spotted the lake when they did . . . If he hadn't been able to force the nose between the trees . . .

Sweat popped out on his forehead and his stomach heaved. For a minute he thought he was going to be sick.

"Call?" Charity straightened away from him. She was looking worriedly into his face and he realized she had been watching him for some time. "Are you all right?"

He climbed unsteadily to his feet, wiping the sweat off his forehead with the sleeve of his shirt. "I'm fine. I just need to move around a little." He needed to move around a lot, he thought, spotting a game trail and starting in that direction, making his way into the shadows of the forest. He needed to take himself as far from Charity as he could get.

He was starting to care for her, starting to feel the kind of emotional attachment he never wanted to experience again. He couldn't deal with those sorts of feelings, not now. Maybe never again.

He had to cool things down, had to stay away from her, at least for a while. Long enough to get his head on straight. A little way up the trail, he stopped, still worried about her, not wanting to go so far he couldn't keep an eye on her.

"Call!" He heard her voice the instant before he heard the whop-whop-whop of the chopper. Running back down the trail, he grabbed a flare gun out of his emergency gear, broke it open, loaded, and fired. The flare arched high into the air. They must have seen it glowing in front of them. Call watched the chopper turn and begin to circle in their direction.

"They see us!" Charity cried excitedly. "They're coming this way!"

The chopper, a newer model Bell, was equipped with landing pontoons. It hovered for a moment, then began its descent into the lake. The surface of the water rippled under the downdraft. The chopper finally settled onto the water, sending a string of waves up onto the shore, then the whine of the engine died away. A few minutes later, the rotor slowed to a stop above the machine.

The crew launched a yellow rubber raft and Call watched it row toward them.

"What about your beautiful plane?" Charity asked, staring at the mass of twisted red metal lying in a smoking heap at the end of the lake.

Call stared at the plane, thought about the nearly fatal crash, and his chest felt tight. "I'll send a crew in to dismantle it. It'll have to be lifted out by chopper, same as us."

The little boat bumped the shore and a burly man jumped out and hauled it up on the bank. "Will Jonas," he said, introducing himself. "Everybody on the plane okay?"

"Call Hawkins." The men shook hands. "Cuts and bruises. The lady hit her head. She might have a slight concussion."

"I don't think so," Charity said. "I don't feel dizzy or anything."

Maybe not, Call thought, but he bet she had one helluva headache.

"We'll have it checked out at the hospital," Will Jonas said.

Charity backed away from him. "No way, I'm fine— really I am. I've just survived a plane crash. My clothes are ruined. I'm covered in greasy soot. I'm not about to be tortured by a bunch of overzealous doctors. I just want to go home."

Call could see she wasn't going unless he forced her and he didn't want to do that. "There's a clinic in Dawson. I'll pay for the extra time it'll take to fly us directly there." He turned a hard look on Charity. "And I'm taking you in as soon as we get to town."

She opened her mouth to argue, saw the implacable look on his face and knew he wasn't going to back down any further than he already had.

"*Men,*" she said with a faint lift of her chin, and climbed into the raft.

Call almost smiled.

He wasn't smiling later, when one of the doctors at the clinic told him she shouldn't be left alone for at least twenty-four hours.

"It doesn't appear to be anything serious," said Dr. Jackson, a young, dark-haired physician who worked alongside his doctor wife. "But with any sort of head injury, someone needs to keep an eye on her for a while."

Call nodded, but he was thinking about his plan to stay away from her and watching it crumble before his very eyes. He could hardly dump her at Maude's—not when it was his fault she'd been hurt in the first place.

The thought made his stomach roll again.

In the end, Call took her home with him. Old Mose's cabin would be cold, since they had been gone for the last two days, and he wasn't in the mood to sleep on the couch.

"You can stay in the guest room," he told her, hoping his lack of enthusiasm didn't show. "You're not in any shape for bedroom athletics tonight and that's exactly what will happen if you sleep with me." They were traveling in the Jeep, less than a mile or so from the house. He'd never had a woman stay there before but there didn't seem to be any other option.

Charity glanced toward him, where he sat behind the wheel. "Thanks, I appreciate your concern, but I'm going home."

Call drilled her with a look. "Not a chance. You heard what the doctor said. Someone needs to check on you. You're staying with me, so you might as well resign yourself."

She sighed dramatically but didn't argue, just followed him into the guest room once they reached his house. He showed her the bathroom with its gleaming tile shower and some of her reluctance slid away. In the end, much to his chagrin, he thought she rather enjoyed herself. Toby fussed over her and made her his special chicken-vegetable soup. Afterward she polished off a bowl of chocolate ice cream while Toby kept her company in a chair next to the bed.

Call could hear the two of them laughing and it grated on his nerves.

He told himself to ignore them, but the kid stayed so long, Call's temper began to heat. Standing in the doorway, he watched them playing checkers, his irritation mounting every time Charity laughed at something Toby said.

"Don't you have some pans to wash or something?" he growled before they had a chance to start another game. Toby gave him an unrepentant grin, winked at Charity, and left the guest room.

"You've had a rough day," Call said, wishing she didn't look so damn good in the extra-large tee shirt he had loaned her. "Why don't you try to get some sleep?"

Propped on pillows in the guest room's comfortable queen-sized bed, Charity seemed to be sizing him up. "I want to ask you a favor."

Wariness trickled through him. Unless the favor was taking her to bed, he wasn't interested. "Yeah? What favor is that?"

"You remember what happened on the trail this morning?"

This morning seemed like years ago. "I know what you think happened. You think you remembered something from a hundred years ago."

"Okay, maybe it's crazy. But maybe it isn't. I've never understood why I've always been so intrigued with this place. Sometimes if I read something or just thought about coming here, it would make me cry. When I was standing on that trail I felt like I remembered being there. I could almost remember something that happened."

"Something from another life," he said darkly.

"No. I told you I don't believe in past lives. I was thinking ... maybe those memories belonged to someone in my family, someone directly related to me. A relative of mine who actually came up here back then."

"You're saying the memories—if you had them—might be inherited from one of your ancestors. That's pretty far-fetched, don't you think?"

"Why? Animals inherit instincts. People inherit certain talents—like being a math whiz or a musician. Or take circus families, for instance. You know how they say they've got sawdust in their blood? Theatrical families are like that, even cowboys. What if there really is something in their blood? Memories that are inherited from generation to generation, a connection to the past that pulls them in that same direction?"

He cast her an unconvinced glance. "So what's the favor?"

"I want to find out if someone in my past was one of the people who came to the Yukon in search of gold. If they did, then maybe I was born with some of their memories. Maybe that's the reason I wanted to come here so badly."

It was an interesting theory, he had to admit, not that he believed it. "Yeah, well, too bad there isn't any way to prove it."

Charity looked up at him with big blue eyes. He noticed the small white bandage on the side of her head and a wave of guilt washed over him.

"Maybe there is a way," she said. "It's only a hundred years. If I could track my family back that far, maybe I could find a link to one of the Stampeders who climbed the trail."

One of his eyebrows went up. "You're talking about genealogy."

"Exactly."

"And the favor is . . . ?"

"I want to use one of your computers."

"No."

"Why not? You've got three of them. You can't use them all at once."

Because that would mean you'd be over here all the time and that is the last thing I want. His mouth tightened. He couldn't do this, dammit. He scrambled through a dozen lame excuses, finally settled on one. "I wouldn't be able to concentrate with you in the room with me." Now *that* was the truth.

Charity gave him a syrupy smile and replied in a thick Southern accent. "Why, Call, sugar, that is the sweetest thing you have ever said."

"Dammit, Charity, that office is where I do business."

"Come on, we're neighbors. Besides, you owe me. Aren't I lying in this bed because you crashed the plane I was flying in?"

He could feel the blood draining out of his face.

"I'm sorry," she said quickly, sitting up in the bed. "I was only kidding. What happened wasn't your fault—we both know that. The engine went out, for God's sake. You don't owe me anything. In fact, you rescued me, probably saved my life."

Call eased her gently back down. "It might not have been my fault, but I do owe you." He sighed, raked his fingers through his hair. "You can use one of the damned computers."

Charity grinned. Leaning forward, she gave him a smacking kiss on the cheek. "You're a real pal, Hawkins."

He fixed her with a glare. "Yeah, well, wait till you hear the favor I want in return."

Tony King sat at a table in a small, out-of-the-way bar off Market Street, not far from Gordon's office. "What can I say? The guy got lucky." He was only in the city for a couple of days, just long enough for a brief meeting with his partner, do a little business of his own, and get back to L.A.

"Hawkins seems to have more than his share of luck."

"The lab fire should have slowed things down. If it had, we would have had more time to prepare. This isn't the kind of business you can rush. Not and get away clean."

"No, I'm sure it isn't." Gordon leaned back in the red leather captain's chair across the table, took a sip of the single-malt Scotch, Glenmorangie that he favored. He was a tall, distinguished-looking man with silver hair that had been blond when Tony first met him. Tony had dark hair and olive skin. Women were drawn to Gordon's polished charm, but they liked Tony's hard-edged style just as much.

"I should have known Hawkins would step in after the fire," Gordon said, "and find some way to keep things moving. But the project is so small, I assumed he would leave it to Held."

"In the old days he would have. He wouldn't have had enough time to handle it himself."

"Whatever the case, the lab is up and running. Which means we'll have to deal with the problem fairly soon." He set the Scotch down on the small round table. "I don't need to remind you how much we've both got invested in this. Our sources say Held is close to a breakthrough. Once the announcement is made, our long-range plans are finished. We'll lose everything we've worked for the last eighteen years."

The edges of Tony's mouth flattened out. "We aren't losing anything. I'll take care of this—just like I always do."

"I'm sure you will," Gordon said.

Tony knew his partner meant it. Gordon trusted him to get the job done and Tony intended to see that it was. "I'd better get moving. I've got a lot to do before I catch that plane."

Gordon sipped his drink. "Give my love to Alice and the kids."

Tony didn't answer. He never thought of his family when he was doing this kind of business. Leaving Gordon to pay the bill, he made his way out the door into the San Francisco street. He needed to talk to his man, Stan Grossman, needed to get things rolling again.

Stan had warned him about trying to move too quickly. There was too much at stake to risk a screwup. This time Tony would listen.

CHAPTER FIFTEEN

It was Monday morning, a workday, and Charity wanted to go home. At Call's instruction, Toby had driven down to Maude's to tell her about the plane crash and that Charity was safe and staying with Call until she felt up to going back to the cabin. Toby also drove up the hill to Buck Johnson's to tell him they wouldn't be working today.

Toby had returned and was cheerfully cooking breakfast by the time Charity got up. Call was in his office, working, no doubt, on the problem at Datatron. Her headache was gone. If she'd had a concussion, it must have been minor. Still, she hadn't slept well last night. Not with Call in the room next door. Though he checked on her several times before morning, it wasn't the same as having him in bed with her. Funny how quickly she'd grown used to sleeping beside him.

Sometime near dawn, she had finally fallen asleep and Call didn't wake her till late that morning. A lingering shower revived her spirits, along with a delicious stack of Toby's hotcakes.

Carrying her ruined, soot-covered clothes in a bundle, dressed in her hiking boots and the tee shirt she had worn

to bed last night, she accepted the loan of Call's raincoat
and let him walk her back to the cabin, his big wolf-husky
trailing along at his side.

There was a car parked in the driveway. She hadn't seen
what appeared to be a rental car, a light blue Ford Taurus,
drive up the hill, and apparently neither had Call.

"Looks like you've got company," he said.

"Looks like. I wonder who it is." Just then, the door
swung and a man stood framed in the opening. Charity froze
in her tracks as Jeremy Hauser stepped out on the porch.

For a moment she just stood there, her stomach churning,
trying to convince herself she was still asleep and this was
a very bad dream.

Please God, I promise to be a good girl if you'll just
. . . She didn't finish the mantra. The fervent prayer hadn't
worked when she was a kid wanting a new pony and it
wasn't going to make Jeremy disappear.

He came down the porch stairs and started walking toward
her, the smile on his face fading as he assessed the tall man
at her side, her still-damp hair, and the odd fit of her borrowed
clothes.

"What the hell?" His gaze moved from her to Call and
back. He looked her up and down, surveying the borrowed
raincoat, the bare legs exposed beneath the drooping hem,
and the sockless hiking boots on her feet.

Jeremy's jaw tightened. "Tell me you didn't just climb
out of this guy's bed."

"Actually, I . . . um . . ."

"Actually, she did." Call's eyes were dark and glinting,
the edge of his mouth barely curved.

"It wasn't like that, Jeremy, not exactly. I was in this
plane crash, you see, and the doctors thought I might have
a concussion. I-I wasn't supposed to be alone so I slept in
Call—Mr. Hawkin's—guest room." She turned a pleading
look on Call.

"Call Hawkins," he said, not bothering to offer his hand.
"And you must be Jeremy Hauser."

"That's right." Jeremy reached over and caught her arm,

drew her stumbling toward him. "I flew three thousand miles to see you, Charity," he said. "We really need to talk."

She glanced over her shoulder and didn't miss the black scowl lining Call's face.

"Don't mind me," he said with a scowl. "I was just leaving." Turning, he started back the way he had come. Charity watched him stalking away, Smoke trotting along beside him, then dragged her eyes back to Jeremy's face.

He was better-looking than she remembered, his eyes a deeper shade of green. As always, his jet-black hair was perfectly styled, his features almost elegantly refined. He was immaculately dressed in a conservative orange-and-brown sweater and a pair of khaki slacks. She wished he would just disappear.

"When . . . when did you get here?"

"About fifteen minutes ago. I took a night flight from JFK and got into Whitehorse early this morning. I caught a small commuter to Dawson, rented a car, then went to see that real estate man you mentioned, Boomer Smith. He gave me directions out here. The door was open so I went in."

He didn't say anything about the cabin. The place was hardly Jeremy's style.

"You all right?" he asked. "I mean, that thing about the plane crash . . ."

"I'm fine. I bumped my head but it's okay now."

Jeremy nodded. He was never one to worry much over someone else's health.

"You must be exhausted," she said, thinking of the long flight he had made to get there. "Why don't we go inside and I'll make us some coffee." Casting a last glance at Call, who disappeared out of sight down the path, she climbed the steps and walked into the cabin with Jeremy.

The last person on earth she wanted to see.

It was cold inside. She busied herself getting the place heated up, kneeling in front of the stove, adding wood pellets and starting a blaze.

"It doesn't take long to warm up. Give me a minute to put on some clothes and I'll come back and make us some coffee." She started past him, but Jeremy caught her arm. He pulled her against him, bent his head and tried to kiss her, but Charity turned away.

Jeremy let her go. "Oh, I get it. You and the lumberjack, right? All that crap about sleeping in the guest room was exactly that—crap."

"Jeremy—"

"The least you could have done was tell me. You let me fly three thousand miles—"

"I had no idea you'd fly all the way out here just to see me. I thought we pretty much ended things when I left New York."

"You said you wanted an adventure. You said putting some space between us might help us decide where our relationship was headed. Well, that's exactly what it did. After you left, I realized how much I loved you. I thought by now, maybe you had realized it, too."

How long had she waited to hear him say those words? Now that he had, she no longer wanted to hear them.

She sank down on the sofa and Jeremy sat down beside her. He reached over and took her hand. "Look, babe, I understand what happened. You were up here by yourself. You were lonesome and the guy took advantage. Sometimes those things happen. It doesn't matter—I forgive you. What's important is that—"

"You forgive me? Are you going to sit there and tell me you haven't slept with anyone since I left?" She knew him better than that. Jeremy was needy. He wouldn't have lasted two weeks without a woman to take care of him.

"Well, I . . . Like I said, it doesn't matter. I never cheated on you when we were together and I don't think you cheated on me. You're the woman I love. I came here to ask you to marry me."

Oh, God. Charity sat there, stunned, as Jeremy pulled a blue velvet box out of the pocket of his slacks and flipped

open the lid. A brilliant-cut solitaire set between two diamond baguettes gleamed on a bed of white satin.

"It's beautiful, Jeremy, really exquisite . . . but . . ." He
pulled the ring out of the box and slid it onto her finger.
Her hand trembled. She wished she knew what to say.

She looked up at him, very gently slid the ring off her
finger, and pressed it into his palm. "I care for you, Jeremy.
We meant something to each other, once. I haven't forgotten
that. I'm flattered that you asked, but I don't want to marry
you."

The hand holding the ring tightened into a fist. "Don't
tell me you want to marry *him?*" He said it like a dirty
word and Charity's mouth went dry.

"Of course not." She didn't, did she? "Call's a very . . ."
Nice was hardly the word for Call Hawkins. Arrogant, obsti-
nate, domineering. Capable, intelligent, protective, the sexi-
est man she'd ever met. "He's just a friend."

"A sleeping-together sort of friend."

"The point is—"

"The point is, you and Paul Bunyan have some kind of
thing going and I'm no longer in the picture."

Some kind of thing? She thought about the way Call had
looked when he had seen Jeremy walk out on the porch.
She wondered if he had any sort of feelings for her beyond
sexual attraction and began to realize how deeply her feelings
ran for him.

"I'm sorry you came all this way for nothing, Jeremy. If
I'd had any idea what you were thinking, I would have
called and tried to explain. But I didn't and it's too late
now."

"I can't believe this."

"Neither can I," she said before she could stop herself.
"Well, you're here and for the present there's nothing either
of us can do about it. It's beautiful up here. Before you go
back, maybe we could take a ride and I could show you
some of the country."

He looked around the little cabin, but still made no comment. "I suppose I might as well," he said with a pained expression. "I'd planned to stay all week. Now I'll have to reschedule, try to get a flight out sometime tomorrow." He dragged out his cell phone, started to punch in numbers.

"Um, I'm afraid that won't work. You'll have to walk up the hill a little to get any sort of reception."

He gave her a look that said *What the hell kind of place is this?* Making his way outside, he climbed up the hill to make the call and came back a few minutes later.

Charity couldn't help thinking that for a man who was supposed to be madly in love, he was taking this very well.

"I was able to make connections tomorrow," he said. "You don't mind if I spend the night, do you?"

Of course she minded! Having Jeremy as a houseguest was the last thing she wanted. But hey, the man had come all this way to propose. She could hardly toss him out on his ear.

Inwardly, she groaned. A whole day and night with Jeremy Hauser. There was a time she would have leapt for joy if he had spared that kind of time for her. Now she just wished it was time for him to go home.

In the end, Jeremy didn't leave until late the following day, catching the little Air North commuter from Dawson to Whitehorse, where he would have to spend the night. From there he planned to catch a very early plane to New York via Vancouver.

Charity had never been so glad to see anyone leave.

As she swept the porch, she thought of the uncomfortable evening they had shared and heaved a sigh of relief that it wouldn't be repeated.

"That bad, was it?" Maude had arrived for work at her usual early hour and wound up cooking breakfast for both Charity and Jeremy. Charity could tell by the older woman's expression that Maude had guessed they were once romantically involved, even if the wrinkled sofa throw cover made it obvious he had slept on the couch.

"It wasn't the best, that's for sure. Hard to believe there was a time I actually thought I was in love with him."

"Well, he seemed nice enough. A little stiff in the rump, maybe, but a real good-looker. Snappy dresser, too."

"Real snappy. That was Ralph Lauren he was wearing. That's really dressing down for Jeremy."

Maude stuck the stem of her unlit pipe in her mouth and talked around it. "So he's outta the picture, is he?"

"Definitely. He asked me to marry him and I wasn't the least bit tempted."

Maude chuckled. "Always nice to be asked, though."

Charity started sweeping. "I suppose so." But she was thinking of Call, not Jeremy Hauser.

"Somethin' I been meanin' to ask."

Charity stopped working. Maude never asked anything. "What is it?"

"My granddaughter's comin' in next week. Gonna be stayin' with me for a couple of months this summer. I didn't know she was comin' when I took the job, but my son wrote and asked, and I said it was all right. I was wonderin' if you'd mind if she came down with me once in a while."

"Of course I wouldn't mind. How old is she?"

"Just turned eighteen. Her name's Jenny. She's just graduated high school. Robert—that's my boy, Robbie, he's Robert now—wants her to go on to college, but she says she ain't sure that's what she wants. That's why he's sendin' her up here, give her time to make up her mind."

"Where's she live?"

"Los Angeles. Robbie moved down there with his dad, my ex-husband Fred, when he was still a kid. Robbie's got a fancy job there now, makes all kinds of money."

Charity set the broom aside, wondering if Maude ever got to see him. "Bring her whenever you want. I could use the company."

"Maybe she could work some, pick up a little extra spendin' money."

"Actually, that's a good idea. I could use a hand with some of the chores." Finished with the porch, Charity joined Maude at the bottom of the stairs. "It's only been a few days, but I feel like I've been away from work for a month. Buck's been running the backhoe down by the creek. Why don't we pull him away from that and do a little dredging, see what we can find today?"

"Now you're talkin'."

Buck had been playing around with the backhoe all morning, digging up chunks of dirt from the side of the hill down at the end of the claim, then hauling it back and dumping it next to the sluice box so he could shovel it into the machine. Charity didn't like him mining that way. Digging up the ground, she felt, was too detrimental to the environment. It was the same reason she didn't use mercury to process black sand concentrates, the way some amateur miners extracted minuscule particles of gold.

The dredge was better, simply sifting through the mud and gravel beneath the creek, then dumping it back into the water. And the truth was, as much fun as it was to find gold, she hadn't really come here intending to get rich.

She glanced down the creek toward Call's house. She could see the cedar walls and the gleam of sunlight on one of the windows. She wondered if he was still angry over Jeremy. She wondered if he knew her one-time lover had spent the night and thought how she would feel if the situation were reversed.

She chewed on a nagging cuticle, her worry beginning to build. Call wouldn't come over. Not when he thought she was still involved with Jeremy. She needed to talk to him, explain what had happened, but she wasn't quite sure what to say.

Hi, Mr. One-night-stand. Just wanted you to know I broke it off completely with my ex. Why? Because you're the guy I'm crazy about. I'm all yours now—isn't that just terrific?

She groaned to think how happy that would make him. She had to face him sooner or later, but she wasn't ready yet. In the meantime, she would work a little, clear her muddled thoughts.

Her mind must have still been foggy. Walking toward the creek, she didn't realize Buck was about to sling a shovel of dirt into the sluice box. As she took a step closer, he turned, and an instant later, she was covered head to foot with dirt.

"Sorry," he said, taking a step away, propping the shovel against the skip loader. "Didn't hear you walk up."

She wiped dust out of her eyes, brushed off her jeans and shirt, bent over and shook out her hair, ridding herself of most of the grime. "My fault. I should have said something so you'd know I was here."

With anyone else, she would have laughed. It was an accident, no big deal. With Buck, she was always on guard.

"Damn fool," Maude grumbled. "Never could hear worth a lick."

"I said I was sorry."

"It's all right—no harm done." Charity turned to Buck. "Let's work the dredge for a while, see what we can stir up."

He made a curt nod, talkative as ever. Turning, he lumbered up the hill to the shed to fetch their wet gear.

"Lots more color turnin' up lately," Maude said, speaking of the slightly larger nuggets they'd been finding in the last couple of weeks. "Sure can tell the difference in a claim that ain't been worked out."

Charity grinned. "Maybe we'll find a big one this week."

"Ya never can tell. That's what keeps it interesting."

Well, looking for gold was definitely not boring. She thought of the Stampeders, then thought of the search she wanted to make for her ancestors. That made her think of Call and she found herself biting her hangnail again.

She wondered what he would say if he knew she was falling in love with him.

* * *

Call stalked into the living room and sat down in an overstuffed chair. His mood was grim. Earlier, he had spoken to the FBI about the problems at Datatron. Apparently the Feds were satisfied that the firewall breach was accidental. That was the good news. The bad news was, the companies involved still intended to sue.

"You going over to see her?"

Call turned at the sound of Toby's voice. The kid stood at the window, staring off toward ol' Mose's cabin, sunlight shining on his dark red hair. "The guy who was there is gone, you know. I saw him drive down the hill this afternoon."

"It's none of my business whether the bastard is there or not." Trying to concentrate on the copy of *Newsweek* Toby had picked up for him in town, trying not to think of Charity and what might have happened between her and Hauser, Call turned a hard look in the kid's direction. "It's not your business, either."

"He came all this way to see her. I wonder why he left so soon."

Call was wondering that, too. Especially since he had obviously spent the night with her. The thought of another man in Charity's bed made his stomach squeeze into a knot.

Especially *that* guy. Jeremy Hauser was too good-looking, too polished, too obviously New York. Call had disliked him on sight.

"You don't suppose she left with him."

That brought him out of his chair. Tossing the magazine aside, he stalked over to the window, reached up to the shelf, and dragged down his binoculars. He hadn't used them in weeks. Now he focused them on the cabin but saw no movement. He swung the lenses down toward the creek and there she was, working the dredge with Buck and Maude.

A trickle of relief filtered through him but the anger remained. He had no right to feel it. He had no claim on Charity Sinclair—had, in fact, warned her he had no interest in any sort of relationship beyond a few hours in bed. If she wanted more than that from a man, he had no right to stand in her way.

He stuffed the binoculars back in their case and tossed them back up on the shelf. "I'll be in my office. I've got some work to do."

"But what about Char—"

Call slammed the door in his face.

CHAPTER SIXTEEN

She had to talk to him. She owed him an explanation. As Maude and Buck finished work and left for the night, Charity climbed into the shower, shampooed the day's grime from her hair, then put on a pair of black slacks and a lightweight blue cotton sweater. As soon as she was dressed, she grabbed her jacket and purse and headed out the door.

The path was well-lit. With twenty-some hours of daylight, it wouldn't be dark for hours. She was still having trouble getting used to it, but with the makeshift blinds she'd had Buck build for the bedroom, she managed to get the room dark enough to sleep. She hated to think what it must be like up here in the winter, when the day was only four hours long.

Traveling the path, it didn't take long to reach Call's house. Smoke ran up to greet her as she climbed the stairs to the porch and she ruffled his thick, silver fur. She knocked on the door and a few minutes later, Toby pulled it open.

"Hey, Charity! Come on in."

"Hi, Toby." She glanced around for Call but didn't see him.

"How's your head?" Toby asked.

"I'm fine. Thanks for taking such good care of me."

"Call's in his office. He's been holed up in there all day. I'll tell him you're here."

She nodded, her nerves inching up. "I'm not interrupting dinner or anything, am I?"

"Nah, we eat pretty late this time of year." Toby disappeared and a few minutes later, Call walked into the living room.

He needed a shave. His jaw looked tight, his features dark and intense. "Your boyfriend leave already?"

She glanced toward the kitchen, saw Toby disappear out the back door, leaving them alone. "He isn't my boyfriend. At least he's not anymore."

Hard blue eyes bored into her. "So what then? You just invited him in and gave him a farewell fuck?"

Oh, dear. He was madder than she thought. She wasn't sure if that was a good sign or bad. "I let him spend the night, but I didn't sleep with him."

"Yeah, right. And the New York Yankees are gonna lose the pennant this year."

"I didn't sleep with Jeremy. I didn't want to. I don't have those kinds of feelings for him anymore."

"So I'm supposed to believe the two of you stayed together in a two-room cabin and he didn't wind up in your bed."

Her own temper heated. "I'm not a liar, Call. I especially wouldn't lie about something like that."

He stared at her for several long moments, then a weary sigh escaped. "I'm sorry." He walked toward her, dragged her into his arms, and very thoroughly kissed her. "I just . . . I didn't like the idea of him being over there with you."

Her legs felt weak. How could he do that with just a single kiss? He let her go but she wished he hadn't. "I had no idea Jeremy was going to show up on my doorstep. If I'd had the slightest idea of his intentions, I would have tried to head him off."

"What exactly *were* his intentions?"

She kept her eyes on his face. "Jeremy came here to ask me to marry him."

His jaw went hard. Call walked over to the window, stared off toward the cabin. "Yeah, well, he looks like a pretty good catch. Expensive shoes. Wall Street haircut. Oozing with slick New York polish. What'd you say?"

"What do you think I said? I said no, dammit. I'm not interested in finding a 'good catch.' I wouldn't marry a man unless I loved him. I don't love Jeremy Hauser."

Call said nothing. He gazed out the window, then slowly turned to face her. "Look, Charity. Even if you aren't interested in Hauser, maybe it's just as well this happened. After you left, I started doing some thinking. We were getting pretty involved. You know how I feel about that."

"Pretty involved? We spent the weekend together, Call. We slept together. We enjoyed ourselves. It wasn't any big deal." If he could dish it out, so could she. And she could tell by the scowl on his face that she had hit a nerve.

"No big deal?" His expression was dark as he strode toward her, hauled her back into his arms. "We screwed like minks for hours and you call it *no big deal?*" She gasped as his mouth crushed down over hers.

Charity clung to his shoulders. God, the man could kiss. Her body responded as it always did, turning warm and liquid. Her arms went around his neck and she kissed him back, opening to the slick feel of his tongue. In seconds she was hot and wet, aching for him to be inside her.

The roughness of his day's growth of beard abraded her cheeks, but Charity didn't care. His tongue was in her mouth and his hands were all over her, dragging up her cotton sweater, pulling it over her head, unhooking her bra and tossing it away.

He filled his hands with her breasts, took her nipple into his mouth, sucked hard on the end. He unzipped her slacks and shoved them down over her hips, leaving her in her white lace thong bikini.

"No big deal?" he repeated between scorching kisses, urging her backward till her shoulders came up against the living room wall. She heard his zipper buzzing down, felt the hard, thick weight of his erection. "I'll show you *no big deal*." He didn't bother to remove her panties, just reached between her legs and jerked the material aside, found her soft heat and thrust himself in.

A rush of pleasure tore through her so strong her knees nearly buckled beneath her. She was slick and hot, instantly on the verge of a climax.

"Oh, no, you don't. Not yet." Lifting her legs, he wrapped them around his waist, eased himself out, then plunged back in. Setting up a rhythm, he surged hard inside her.

"Oh, God . . ." Charity gripped his shoulders and hung on for dear life. Call kissed her deeply, filled her again and again, pounded into her until the pleasure was simply too much and she went off like a rocket, shooting over the edge. Bliss poured through her, sweet and warm and heady. Charity cried out his name and a few seconds later, Call's muscles tightened as he followed her to release.

For several long moments neither of them moved.

"Damn." He let go of her legs and she slid the length of his long, hard body. "I didn't mean for that to happen."

She managed a wobbly smile. "I think I've heard those words before."

Call raked a hand through his hair. "What is it about you?"

She sighed. "I don't know, but I hope no one was looking in the window."

He glanced across the living room. "Toby's out back." But he reached down and picked up her clothes, handed them over.

"Mind if I use your . . . ?" She tipped her head toward the powder room in the entry.

"Go ahead."

Charity started in that direction, stopped, and whirled back. "Oh, my God, Call! We didn't use protection!"

Call's eyes met hers across the space between them. "Christ."

"It . . . it isn't really that big a problem . . . at least not as much of one as it could be. I'm on the pill. The doctor prescribed it years ago to keep my periods regular. In regard to the other, Jeremy insisted we both be tested and we were fine. And you haven't had sex in years.''

Instead of responding, Call glanced away, faint color rising beneath his lean cheeks.

Charity knew that look. Every woman did. She gripped her clothes a little more tightly in front of her. ''That's what you said. You told me you hadn't had sex in four years. You didn't lie about it, did you?''

His eyes returned to hers, unnervingly blue and intense. ''It was the truth . . . at the time.''

At the time? Obviously something had happened in the weeks after that. Charity said nothing more, just went into the bathroom and closed the door. Dampening a washcloth, she sponged away the remnants of their encounter, then put on her slacks and sweater, trying not to think about Call making love to another woman.

Oh, God. She felt used and cheap and slightly sick to her stomach.

''Charity?'' Call rapped softly on the door. ''Are you all right?''

She swallowed, took a deep, steadying breath, pasted on a smile, and opened the door. ''I'm fine,'' she said far too brightly, trying very hard not to cry. ''Hopefully, you've been practicing safe sex with everyone else you've been sleeping with so today won't be a problem.''

She brushed past him and started for the door, desperate to get away from him. Call caught her before she could make her escape.

''It's not the way you think. It was you I wanted. I knew you weren't the kind of woman who played around. I was trying to stay away from you. I thought if I slept with someone else, I'd be able to leave you alone.''

Tears welled. It was ridiculous. He had warned her he was only interested in sex. Why hadn't she been smart enough to listen?

"I left something on the stove," she said. "I think I smell it burning. I have to go home."

"Dammit, Charity, I hadn't had sex in years. I thought it wouldn't matter. I thought any woman would do."

Her chest ached. She took the last few steps, opened the door and stepped out on the porch, dragged in a cleansing breath of air.

She heard Call's footsteps behind her. "It wasn't the same, Charity," he said softly. "She wasn't you."

Tears burned her eyes as she started walking. She wanted to turn around and go back, wanted to walk into his arms and put her head on his shoulder. She wanted to tell him it didn't matter. But the truth was, it did.

Call didn't want a relationship. He had said so half a dozen times. How much clearer could he make it?

She didn't look back, just kept on heading up the path to the cabin. Call made no effort to follow.

Work started early the following day. It was getting warmer all the time and the sun seemed to burn forever. Maude rolled in a little after six and her granddaughter, Jenny, arrived with her.

"It's nice to meet you, Jenny." Charity hid her surprise at the tiny gold ring in one of Jenny's nostrils. Both ears were pierced in multiple places and held gleaming studs, and a little rose tattoo rode on the back of one hand.

She looked down at the ground, then lifted her eyes back to Charity's face. "Grama said you might have some work I could do." She seemed shy or reticent or a combination of both, her curly, light-brown hair forming a halo around her head and hanging just past her shoulders. She wore tight faded jeans and a yellow tank top beneath an open denim shirt.

She was a pretty girl with an incredible figure. Charity couldn't help wondering what she was doing way up here.

"Actually, I could use someone to do odd jobs and help me clean the cabin. I always keep it picked up, but it hasn't

had a good, thorough cleaning in quite some time. I'll pay
you the going rate. Interested?''

Jenny just nodded. ''Thanks.'' Charity took the girl inside
and showed her where the rags and supplies were kept, then
returned to where Maude waited at the bottom of the front-
porch stairs.

''Pretty girl,'' Charity said.

''Her dad's been worried about her. Said she was hangin'
around with some no-account tough guy three or four years
older. Said he was afraid she was gonna do somethin' stupid
if he didn't get her away from him.''

''So he sent her up here.''

Maude glanced toward the cabin. ''I'm glad for the company.''

Charity could imagine how lonely it could be way out
here. It hadn't really happened to her, not yet, but this was
all still new and she knew she wouldn't be staying up here
that long. ''You rarely mention your son. Does he ever come
up for a visit?''

''Robbie's pretty busy. He and Fred were always close.
Couldn't blame the boy for wantin' to live with his dad. I
sure do miss him, though.''

''Did you meet Fred in Dawson?''

Maude nodded. ''He worked for one of them big minin'
companies what were up here some years back. I'd lost my
husband, Will. Fred was younger'n me and it was plain
almost from the start it wasn't gonna work. Robbie was an
accident, if you want the truth. Then Fred and I divorced.
Robbie went to live with him a few years later. Jenny wasn't
born till Robert was older.''

''What about her mother?''

''She and Robert divorced. She's livin' up in Modesto,
California. Jenny doesn't see her much anymore.''

''I hope Jenny likes it here.''

Maude turned toward the cabin. ''She used to like it when
she was a kid. Can't say how she'll take to it now.''

Charity had hoped that she and Jenny might be friends,
but the girl rarely talked and stayed mostly to herself. Charity

thought there was something troubled in her expression. She wondered what it was.

All week, the days seemed to drag and Charity's mood grew darker and darker, until Maude began casting speculative looks her way.

"You want to talk about it?"

It was late Friday afternoon. They had just finished cleaning out the sluice box, their take in nuggets the best so far. She should have been ecstatic. Instead, she couldn't quite muster a smile. "I don't know what you mean."

"I think you know dang well what I mean. You and Call. He still mad about that Jeremy fella?"

"No, and even if he were, it wouldn't matter." She had paid Buck's weekly wages and sent him home early. For some unknown reason, he'd been more surly than usual all week and she was glad he was gone. She was beginning to wish Maude and Jenny were gone for the weekend, too.

"Why not?" Maude asked.

Unexpected tears suddenly welled. "Damn him." Charity wiped the embarrassing wetness away. "I thought he cared about me . . . at least a little, but . . ."

"Well, sure he does. Any fool can see that."

Charity shook her head. "Call slept with another woman."

Maude stared off down the creek toward where he lived. "Now ain't that just like a man. How'd you find out?"

"He told me."

"He told you? Why on earth would he do that?"

"It's a long story, Maude. Something to do with trying to stay away from me—or at least that's what he said. I guess he figured if I wouldn't go for a one-night stand, he'd find someone who would."

"You're sayin' this happened before you two . . . you know . . . before you—"

"I guess so, yes."

"Well, honey, I always figured what happened in the past ought to stay in the past. What matters is what happens from here on out."

She looked up, hope springing into her chest. "You really think so?"

"I sure do. If he was plannin' on doin' something like that again, I don't think he'd have said a word. Those kind never do."

The hope unfurled. *It wasn't the same, Charity. She wasn't you.* Maybe he really did care about her. God, she hoped so.

"The way I see it, Call's still tryin' to find his way back from that awful place he's been. It ain't been easy for him— no siree. But I think you been a real big help. And I think he cares a whole lot more for you than he's wantin' to admit."

Her heart eased. For the first time in days, Charity felt like smiling. Maude was right. The past didn't matter. What mattered was where they went from here.

"You're a good friend, Maude Foote." Charity untied the leather work-apron she had been wearing over her jeans and tossed it over the porch rail. She pulled the clip from her hair and shook it out, ran her fingers through it.

"You goin' where I think?"

"He said I could use his computer. I plan to hold him to it."

Maude chuckled.

Jenny stepped out on the porch and walked up next to her grandmother.

Charity waved at both of them. "See you guys on Monday."

Maude grinned. Jenny's pretty mouth edged up in a rare, shy smile, and Charity smiled back, for the first time actually looking forward to the weekend.

Call paced his office. He needed to speak to the law firm in Seattle that was handling the Datatron case before the office closed for the weekend and catch up on his e-mail, but he wasn't in the mood.

He'd felt better yesterday and the day before when he'd

been working outside, off with the salvage crew that went after his plane. With the use of a logging helicopter, they had lifted the Beaver out of the lake in pieces and left it with Bob Wychek at Superior Air West, the local airplane fix-it shop. It would take a while, but sooner or later, Wychek would find the problem that had caused the engine failure.

Call's mind did an instant replay of the crash and a shudder rippled through him. In the last four years, he had wished himself dead a hundred times, but not this time. This time, Charity had been with him and she had a right to live.

He was thinking about her, wishing they could have parted in a less painful manner, wishing he hadn't hurt her.

He was wishing he didn't miss her so damned much when he heard Toby's voice in the living room, then footsteps approaching his office.

The door was ajar. Charity appeared in the opening, shoved the door open, and stepped inside.

"You said I could use your computer. I'm holding you to it."

Myriad emotions rolled through him: the powerful sexual attraction he always felt when he saw her, but mostly a staggering relief that she was there.

He cleared his throat. "You want to do some on-line genealogy, right?"

"If I'm going to find out if my theory is correct, that's what I need to do."

He took a step toward her; he couldn't help himself.

"Hold it right there. I'm still not happy about you sleeping with another woman."

"It was before we ever made love, and I didn't exactly sleep with her. She gave me, um . . . she gave me a blow job."

Charity drilled him with a glare. "Oh, that's right, I forgot—blow jobs don't count. Where do you think you are, the oval office?"

He looked away, embarrassed. He couldn't remember the last time a woman had embarrassed him until Charity had come along.

"I came here to work," she said. "For a while, at least, I think it's better if we keep our distance."

"Okay. Yeah, all right, then." It was what he wanted, wasn't it?

Sort of.

"Which one can I use?"

He strode over and flipped a switch on the computer at the far end of the walnut counter. It didn't take long for the screen to light up. He whirled a small, wheeled office chair over in front of the machine and Charity sat down.

"I have no idea where to start so I guess I'll just plunge in." She went on Internet Explorer and Refdesk.com came up, one of her favorite sites. In the Search box, she typed in *genealogy.* "I figure getting an overview is as good a place as any."

"That's what I'd do," he said.

The list the search engine brought up on the screen was substantial: www.genealogy.com; familysearch.org; ancestry.com; genetree.com. Then there were breakdowns by nationality, sites like Irish Genealogy On-line; sites for marriage and birth records, or cemeteries and cemetery records at www.internment.net.

"This isn't going to be easy," she said.

"You actually thought it would be?"

"I guess not." She clicked on a site that read *Genealogy for Beginners* and typed in her grandmother's name, Pearl Ann Sinclair. A list of names appeared on the screen and Charity sucked in a breath.

"Call! Look at this! There are four different Pearl Ann Sinclairs but this one here's my grandmother. Her maiden name was Ross before she married."

He pulled up a wheeled stool and sat down next to her, wishing he wasn't so glad she was there. "You sure it's her?"

"Married February 2, 1945, to Richard Charles Sinclair. He was my grandfather. God, this is great."

Great for her, Call thought, breathing in the floral scent of her shampoo. Not so great for him, since he was beginning to get hard just sitting next to her. He ought to get up, go into the other room, but her excitement was contagious. He was beginning to feel the thrill of the hunt himself.

"I'm calling my dad when I get home. I want to know everything he can remember about our family."

"Good idea. Why don't you call him from here? You can use my satellite phone."

She looked up at him. "It's pretty expensive, isn't it?"

He cast her a look. "Trust me, I can afford it. You can use it anytime you want. Consider it a payback for the little side trip you took on my plane."

She grinned. "Be nice to get something out of it besides a headache. Thanks."

"By the way, we brought it back to Dawson—the plane, I mean. It took a couple of days but we finally got all the pieces here."

"That's great, Call. I hope you can get it fixed—not that I'm in any hurry to go up in the thing again."

He didn't really blame her. "The mechanic who's working on it's a guy named Bob Wychek. He's the best there is, and in a place where there's so much mining, you can always get metal work done. It'll take a while, but eventually, she'll be good as new."

"Think you'll be able to figure out what happened with the engine?"

"We'll figure it out. We won't stop looking until we do."

CHAPTER SEVENTEEN

Using Call's satellite phone, Charity called her father at his office on the Boston University campus.

"Charity?" The minute he heard her voice, he went on instant alert. "Is something wrong, honey? You never call me here."

"Nothing's wrong, Dad." She didn't mention the plane crash. She knew he would worry and she didn't want that. She would save the details of that particular adventure for when she got back home. "I'm working on a project and I was hoping you might be able to help."

She told him she was researching her family tree and wanted to know the names of her relatives as far back as he could remember.

"I know a little about them, not all that much." A little turned out to be his side of the family all the way back to his great great grandfather, Walter Sinclair, who had been born in the 1880s, but on his mother's side, the Rosses, he knew his ancestors' names only back as far as his great grandmother, Olga Conrads, born, he recalled, in April of 1902.

"The Sinclairs were Scots, but the Conradses were Norwegian. That's where you got your fair skin and blond hair."

"I remember you saying that when I was a kid. What about Mom's side of the family? There's Grandma and Grampa Whitcomb, of course." Her mother's parents, but they were no longer living. "I don't remember anyone Mom might have mentioned further back."

"I'm afraid I don't know much about your mother's side of the family. Your grandmother Whitcomb was a Doakes before she married. Your mom used to kid about being Irish. She thought that was pretty terrific. Tell you what—I'll get out some of the old photo albums and see what's written on the back of the pictures. There's a bunch of old newspaper clippings, too. I'll send you any information I come up with."

"Why don't you e-mail what you can? I'm borrowing a friend's computer to help with the research. He can relay the message."

"He?" her dad repeated, picking up on the word.

"My next-door neighbor." She didn't say, *my sexy next-door neighbor who is also my off-and-on lover.* "His name's McCall Hawkins."

"Why does that name sound familiar?"

Oh, God, she'd forgotten what a news junkie he was. "Long story, Dad."

"What's his e-mail address?"

"Hawkins@dawson.com," Call supplied.

She talked to her dad a little longer, briefly catching up on family news: her stepmother Tracy enrolling in night school to finish her master's degree, and Charity's sisters, Patience and Hope, both enjoying their summers, Patience working hard on the rodeo project she would start late next spring.

Ending the call, Charity went back to work, digging around the Internet for information on the Sinclairs and Rosses on her dad's side, the Whitcombs and Doakeses on her mother's.

For the next two hours, she studied dates and places

of marriages, dates and places of births, hoping something interesting might turn up that would link her to the Yukon.

"Any luck?" Call asked, walking up behind her. She could smell his aftershave, something with a hint of pine, and the urge rose up to press her mouth against the side of his neck.

"Nothing so far," she said, forcing herself to concentrate on the screen. "To inherit memories from someone, I'd have to be a direct descendant. The Gold Rush happened from 1897 to 1900, so my relative would have had to have been born somewhere around 1880 or before to be old enough to have gone. That would make him one of my great-great-grandparents.

Call sat down at his own computer. It didn't take him long to design a form she could use for her work. He punched the print button and a long sheet of paper rolled out, a family tree with boxes for each set of parents, grandparents, great grandparents, etc. He handed her the paper. "The diagram goes back four generations."

"I'm the fifth, right?"

"That's right."

She looked over the paper, thinking how few of the blanks she could fill in. It was typical of Americans to focus on the present and have little interest in the past. In England, families could trace their heritage back five hundred years.

"I'll input this into the computer you're using," Call said. "You can add information or make changes as you go along."

"Thanks, that'd be terrific." A few minutes later, she was typing names into the blocks, putting in her mother and father, grandparents, sisters, aunts, uncles, anyone whose name might appear during her research.

She looked again at the printed sheet of paper. "To be roughly the right age to have made the trip—people, say . . . fifteen to thirty years old, there are eight sets of great-great-grandparents who qualify as possible memory donors. The bad news is, any family members I know about were born and raised in the East."

"I guess the trick is to find out if you have any relatives who went west."

Charity thought of the force that had compelled her to come thousands of miles to live in the wilds of the Yukon. Until that moment, she hadn't realized how much she wanted the answer to be that she did.

"So what do you suggest?" Sitting in a cozy red leather booth at Dante's, a sophisticated locals' bar in L.A. and one of his favorite hangouts, Tony King talked to his inside man, Stan Grossman, on his cell phone.

"The guy lives out in the middle of nowhere," Grossman said. "Anything could happen in a place like that."

"Like a hunting accident, maybe?"

"Maybe, but it's the wrong time of year. Guy might drown, though. 'Specially a guy who goes off by himself all the time. Lots of lakes around there. Fella could just disappear."

"I'm sure you'll think of something."

"I need more time. I need to know his habits, what he does every hour of the day. A thing like this takes planning."

"Fine, but don't take too long. Something might break and once it does, everything's going to get extremely messy." Tony broke the connection, thinking of Peter Held and wondering what kind of progress the young chemist was making with his research. The fire in the lab had slowed him down but not nearly as much as they'd hoped. If Held discovered the combination that would lead to cheaper disk storage—and Tony knew he was close—he and Gordon were going to be in some very deep shit.

Held was the risk at present. Without him, Hawkins would be back where he was when Frank McGuire had died and it would take him some time to find another replacement.

Tony punched in a different set of numbers. Maybe it was time to make the threat to Held a little more personal. Tony knew just the guy to handle the job.

* * *

Saturday and Sunday, Charity spent most of the day pounding away on Call's computer. For a while, he worked beside her, but he never stayed more than an hour before he shut down his machine and left the house.

She might have felt guilty for intruding on his oh-so-precious privacy if it weren't for the way he kept looking at her. Whenever he glanced her way, she could see the hunger in his eyes, but there was something more, something deeper. She thought that in some secret part of himself he was glad that she was there.

The weekend days passed swiftly. In the afternoon, they took a break and went hiking up the trails behind Call's house. In the evenings, she returned to her cabin, still not comfortable with the idea of sleeping with him again.

Not that she didn't want to. The guy was a flat-out hunk and she was more than half in love with him. Just watching his long, rangy strides as he prowled the house made her want to drag him off to bed. But she had come to realize she wanted more from Call than just sex. She wanted a relationship, at least for as long as she stayed in the Yukon, wanted him to acknowledge he felt something for her beyond mere physical attraction.

On Monday she went to work on the Lily Rose thinking about him. Maude and Jenny arrived right on time, but Buck, usually even more punctual, didn't show up at all.

"His boy, Tyler, come home from college for the weekend," Maude said. "Maybe he stayed over or something."

"Buck was in a foul mood all last week—not that his attitude is ever very good. Still, he seemed worse than usual. I wonder if it had something to do with his son."

"Tyler's a handful, I can tell ya. Spoilt rotten. Buck was making good money back when the kid was born and he bought Ty anything he wanted. He's an even bigger bully than his dad and just as hard on women. He's been goin' to college for years, but I don't think he's ever gonna graduate. Just goes for the women and the fun."

Charity looked up the hill, wondering if Buck's son was the reason he hadn't appeared. Eventually, they gave up waiting and simply went to work.

It was a long, hot day, the perfect sort to run the dredge, but Buck usually did the heavy lifting and moving so they decided to use the metal detector and do some panning instead. Charity was tired by the time Maude and Jenny left at the end of the workday. She thought of going over to Call's but he would probably just leave and she couldn't face his reticence again today.

Instead she sat down to read the new Max Mason novel, *Vengeance at Cascade Park,* that had just arrived, but eventually she grew restless and went outside to feed the squirrels. A little brown-and-white one with a long furry tail was her favorite. She named him Salty and spread unsalted sunflower seeds in front of the tree he lived in.

When he saw them, Salty set up a grateful chatter and scampered round and round the tree trunk. Charity laughed at his antics.

It was getting late, nearly 8:30, when she started back to the house. As she passed the storage shed, she saw that the door stood open. Certain she had closed it after they finished working, she walked over to inspect the latch.

It wasn't broken, merely unfastened. Stepping inside to check things out, she gasped as a big, dark figure loomed out of the shadows.

"Buck!" Her heart thundered even as she felt a wave of relief. "Good heavens, you scared me half to death." He moved toward her, stumbled over a wooden bucket, and nearly fell, and she realized he had been drinking. "God, you're drunk as seven lords."

"So what if I am," he slurred. "What's it to you?"

Charity straightened, not liking his tone. "It isn't a damned thing to me—as long as you're not on my property—which, in case you haven't noticed, you are. You didn't bother to show up for work. What are you doing here now?"

"I come for my drill. Left it here last Friday." He held

up the drill and stumbled closer and Charity took a step away.

"I think you had better go home."

His big shaggy head came up. His nose and cheeks were red, his eyes heavy-lidded and bloodshot, his shirt buttoned crooked down the front. "Oh, yeah? Well, I'm sick and tired of you tellin' me what to do. Just like my wife, always naggin', tryin' to boss me around. I didn't put up with it from her and I ain't puttin' up with it from you." He took a threatening step toward her and for the first time, Charity felt a tendril of fear.

She was almost to the door of the shed. She thought about turning around and running flat-out back to the house, but she wasn't about to give him the satisfaction.

Instead, she stood her ground. "If you want to keep your job, Buck, I'd suggest you leave."

He set the drill down on the workbench. "That right? Well, you can take that job of yours and shove it up your tight little ass." She hadn't noticed him getting closer but suddenly he was towering above her.

She swallowed. "Fine, if that's the way you want it."

Buck gripped her arms, his big, blunt fingers digging into her skin. "I'll tell you what I want. The same thing you give Hawkins. That's all you women are good for." He shoved her up against the wall, knocking down an old horse collar that clattered on the floor, and real fear streaked through her.

"Let me go, Buck—I'm warning you."

Buck ignored her. "Just like Betty," he muttered. "I'll give you what I gave her." Charity screamed as he dragged her away from the wall, tripped her with his foot, knocked her down on the floor of the shed, and came down hard on top of her. Pain shot up her spine and the air whooshed out of her lungs.

"Let . . . go . . . of me!" She tried to push him off her, but it was like trying to shove a ton of heavy ore. One of his big hands groped her breast, ripping her light blue tee shirt, while the other fumbled with the zipper on her jeans.

Her heart pounded with fear. This wasn't about sex, she knew. Buck was drunk and angry, furious at the circumstances that forced him into a position he considered beneath him. If Tyler Johnson disliked women as much as his father, perhaps his arrival this weekend had pushed Buck over the edge.

His heavy weight pressed her into the rough plank floor. Charity worked to drag a breath of air into her lungs. "Let . . . me . . . go." She didn't wait any longer for him to comply, just brought her knee up hard between his legs.

Buck blocked the blow. She struggled, jerked one hand free, and raked her nails down his face, sending him into a fit of violent cursing. She could feel his erection pressing against her thigh and the bile rose in her throat. She felt him tugging on her zipper and started fighting harder, started to scream, though she knew no one could hear.

"Shut up!" Buck warned, slapping her hard across the face. "Goddamn women. You know you want it. All of you do."

Really frightened now, Charity twisted left, then right, brought her knee up hard a second time, and this time the blow connected. Buck grunted in pain and hissed air through his teeth. "Damn . . . you . . ."

A shadow appeared in the doorway. "What the hell . . . ?" Call's deep voice rang into the shed and an instant later, Buck's heavy weight jerked upward as Call hoisted the big man back on his feet. "You son of a bitch!"

Call hit him hard, a staggering punch in the stomach that doubled Buck over. Then a sharp blow to the jaw sent him reeling backward. Buck's eyes went wide as his head cracked hard on an exposed two-by-four and he slid down the rough board wall like a big sack of grain.

Call stood over him, long legs braced apart, fists still clenched, his eyes boring into Buck's slack face. For an instant, he just stood there. Then he released a shuddering breath, turned, and walked over to help her climb to her feet.

"God damn him." Gathering her into his arms, he held

her close and Charity clung to him. She was trembling, the last remnants of adrenaline still pumping through her blood, but eventually his body heat seeped through her clothes, chasing the chill inside her away, and she began to feel better.

"Are you all right?" He eased back a little to look at her.

She was shaking and her knees felt weak. Her cheek stung where Buck had slapped her. "More or less. I've never been so glad to see anyone in my life. Well, except for the day you saved me from the bear."

Call smiled, but his eyes still looked hard.

"What are you doing here?" she asked. "And don't tell me you were watching me through the binoculars because you couldn't see inside the shed."

He eased his hold a little more but still kept an arm around her waist. "I got an e-mail from your dad. When you didn't show up after work to use the computer, I thought I'd better bring it over." He glanced toward Buck and his hold unconsciously tightened. "That bastard. I knew the guy was bad news. I just didn't know he was this bad."

He sucked in a calming breath and she realized he was still angry and fighting to rein in his temper. "You had him on the ropes," he teased, though his shoulders still looked tense. "Another round or two, he would have been down for the count."

"Maybe. He's really drunk. But he's also strong as a bull and he was really pissed off."

Call raked a hand through his hair. "Toby said Buck's son Tyler was here this weekend. He and Toby went to school together. Toby says Ty hates women even more than his dad does."

Unconsciously, she shivered. "Buck said something about his ex-wife. He mentioned a woman named Betty."

"Betty Johnson ran off with a carpet salesman when Tyler was five years old. I guess neither Ty nor Buck ever got over it." He tipped his head toward the unconscious man crumpled against the wall. "I'll lock him up in here till the

Mounties arrive. I'll watch him while you go get your cell phone.''

Charity bit her lip, disliking the idea, trying to decide what to do. Then another shadow appeared in the doorway.

"Hi, sorry to bother you. I'm Tyler Johnson. I'm looking for my dad. I thought he might be over here." Tyler Johnson was as big as his father but a lot better looking, with his father's dark hair and brown eyes. The way Buck might have looked twenty years ago.

"Your father's over there in the corner," Call said. "He's about to go to jail for assaulting Ms. Sinclair."

Tyler took in her torn blue tee shirt, her disheveled hair, and dirt-covered clothes. "Shit. Excuse me, ma'am. I was afraid something like this would happen. He gets drunk like this every year on the day my mother left him. That's the reason I came home from college this weekend. I was hoping I could head him off." He shuffled his feet like a schoolboy, but Charity thought it looked a little contrived.

"I know it's a lot to ask, Ms. Sinclair, but do you think you might overlook his behavior just this once?" Ty gave her a pleading look and Charity had the feeling the younger Johnson was smoother than his father but not much different underneath.

Still, she didn't really think Buck was a danger, not once he sobered up.

"All right. You get him out of here and for now I won't press charges. But you can tell him he's through at the Lily Rose, and if he steps one foot on my property, I'll have the police breathing down his neck."

"I'll make sure he understands. Thank you, ma'am."

Call walked her outside, into the late evening sunlight, and his face looked hard again. "You shouldn't have done that."

"Probably not. But somehow I take more pleasure in knowing Buck owes me than I would in putting him in jail."

Call's mouth edged up but only a little. Then he frowned as she stepped out into the light and he saw the red mark on her cheek. "The sonofabitch clobbered you pretty good. I wish I'd hit him a couple more times."

Charity laughed. "You knocked him from here to Wednesday. I don't think he's going to forget the lesson."

"Just to make sure, I plan to have a little talk with him myself."

Charity said nothing, but a warm feeling spread out inside her. As they walked back to the cabin, Call reached over and caught her hand. It wasn't the first time and it occurred to her that before the accident, he must have been a very affectionate man.

He waited on the cabin porch while she brushed the dirt off her clothes, then he followed her into the house. Closing the door behind him, he pulled a sheet of paper from the pocket of his denim shirt.

"Your dad sent a list of family names—sort of a who-begat-whom of the Sinclairs and Doakes. I figured you'd want to see it." He handed her the e-mail message.

"Thanks." She didn't say more, didn't ask him to stay or suggest going back with him to his house. She thought he would leave, since he had completed his task, but he just stood there inside the door.

"Have you . . . um . . . eaten?"

She shook her head. "I thought I'd heat up some leftovers whenever I got hungry."

"Toby's frying chicken. The kid's getting to be a pretty good cook. Maybe you'd like to join us."

She wanted to and she didn't. Though Call hadn't pressed her, sexual awareness crackled between them whenever they were together. The attraction was getting harder and harder to resist and she knew sleeping with him would make her feelings for him grow deeper.

On the other hand, after what happened with Buck she wasn't in the mood to be alone. Still, she wanted to be sure he wasn't just being polite.

"I'm all right—if that's what you're worried about. You don't have to take me home like some stray kitten."

His mouth curved up as if he liked the image. "That's

not it. I just . . . I thought you might want to come over and work for a while and if you did you might like to join us for supper.''

He meant it, though she wasn't sure he liked that he did. Charity smiled and nodded. ''All right. I love fried chicken.''

Call's shoulders relaxed. ''Okay, then.''

''Let me get my purse.'' She still never felt quite complete without it. Grabbing a light, zip-up-the-front sweatshirt out of her room, she led him out on the porch and they started up the path to his house.

Seated at his computer, Call kept glancing over at Charity. He could still see the fading red mark on her cheek and every time he did, he got mad all over again. Damn Buck Johnson. He should have beaten the bastard to a bloody pulp.

He'd wanted to. The minute he had seen Charity on the floor of the shed and realized Buck's intention, he had wanted to commit bloody murder. And the fact that he had, scared Call to death.

Little by little, Charity was worming her way into his affections and his old protective instincts were coming back. It was the last thing he wanted.

He flicked her a glance, trying not to think about how glad he was he had gone to her house. The truth was, he had been looking forward to seeing her all day. He figured she would show up after work to use his computer and when she didn't, he was disappointed. The e-mail was just an excuse to see her.

The ruse had worked.

Charity was here, but now that she was, it was unholy torture. Every time he looked at her, he wanted to pick her up and carry her off to bed. He tried to tell himself it was better this way, better if they just stayed friends. But he couldn't make himself believe it.

Toby called out just then that supper was almost ready. Determined to think of something other than Charity and how much he wanted to make love to her, Call checked his e-mail one more time, pulling up a message from Bruce Wilcox.

Call frowned. He was so engrossed in Wilcox's message he didn't hear Charity walk up behind him.

"What is it? You look like someone killed your cat."

He rubbed his forehead. "More trouble at Datatron."

"Bad?"

"Apparently those two programmers, Shotman and Wiggs, also pierced the firewall of a big gaming consortium based in Antigua. Wild Card makes its money through gambling sites on the Internet."

"So is Wild Card suing you or what?"

"Or what is more like it. According to Bruce, the whiz kids discovered the consortium has been cheating. There are rules, you see, about gambling margins and profits and odds. When you gamble on-line—play poker, for example— there's a random engine . . . software, actually . . . that has over a billion combinations."

"I get it. The guys at Wild Card tampered with the software so it works more in the house's favor."

"Bingo. Illegal as hell in the States, but this is the Internet we're talking about, the laws—or lack of them—in cyberspace. Still, Wild Card could be in very deep trouble if the Feds find out and U.S. law prevails."

Charity leaned over to study the e-mail message and he could feel the soft weight of her breast against his shoulder.

"Interesting," she said. "International intrigue over the Net."

Call straightened away from her instead of turning around and pressing his mouth into the softness the way he wanted. He forced his mind back to the conversation.

"Worse than that, Shotman and Wiggs got greedy. They've been trying to trade their information back to the consortium for a cool million bucks."

"Blackmail?"

"That's what I'd call it."

"What will you do?"

"Fire Shotman and Wiggs, for starters. The FBI still thinks what happened was an accident. Maybe it was and it just turned into something else. They're still just kids. If they keep their mouths shut, they'll probably be all right."

"Then what? Turn the information over to the authorities?"

"We've got trouble enough already without adding to it. It's industrial espionage to break into confidential company files."

"I think I'm beginning to understand why you chucked the whole business thing and moved up here."

Painful memories stirred and something tightened in his chest. "Yeah." He didn't say he moved up there because he couldn't live with himself after what had happened to Susan and Amy.

They went in to supper and Charity said the chicken was delicious. Call could barely taste it. His appetite was gone.

CHAPTER EIGHTEEN

Tuesday morning arrived—a warm, sunny July day. This time of year the ground was drying out and the forests with it. There was always danger of fire, but so far they had been lucky. The heat felt good and the bright sun glittering on the hillsides helped wash away the bad taste left in Charity's mouth from her encounter with Buck the day before.

Maude and Jenny arrived right on time and Charity told them the story, relaying briefly what had happened in the shed.

"I don't really think he's dangerous," she said, "not unless he's drunk—but you might want to keep an eye out for him."

"You should have put the horny old bastard in jail," Maude grumbled, and next to her, Jenny almost smiled.

"Do you think we can find someone to replace him?" Charity asked.

"We can put an ad in the *Klondike Sun*, but it's gonna take time and we'll have to find the feller a place to live somewheres close by."

"Dammit."

"On the other hand, maybe we don't need him. Everything's up and runnin'. We got Jenny, here, to help us out. Maybe we ought to try it on our own.''

Charity's head came up. ''I don't know, Maude. Some of that equipment's pretty heavy.''

''I'm stronger than I look,'' Jenny said in a rare show of enthusiasm. ''And Grama knows lots about mining.''

Charity smiled. ''I know she does.'' She flicked a glance at Maude. ''You really think we could do it?''

''Won't know if we don't try.''

She grinned. ''All right, then. To hell with Buck Johnson. We'll run the Lily Rose by ourselves!''

And so they set to work, quickly discovering it wasn't as easy as they had first thought. Buck had done all of the really heavy work. The dredging machine weighed a ton. Even with the flotation collar, it was bulky and hard to move around, and none of them were very big women. Halfway through the day, they were wet and tired, their clothes and hair full of sand and grit. At least it was warm and they didn't have to wear their waders anymore.

They were standing along the creek getting sunburned, ready to slosh back into the water and restart the dredge, when Toby appeared on the path.

He waved and jogged toward them, a slender young man with freckles on his cheeks and a ready smile, making his way down the bank to where they stood.

''I saw you out here working,'' he said. ''Now that Buck's gone, I thought you might need an extra hand.''

Charity didn't ask *how* he had seen them. She had a pretty good hunch he'd been using Call's binoculars ever since Jenny arrived.

''Have you two met?'' She watched Toby's gaze slide in the younger girl's direction and a hint of color rose in his cheeks. ''Toby Jenkins, meet Jenny Foote, Maude's granddaughter. Toby works for Mr. Hawkins—or at least he did, the last I heard.''

''Nice to meet you, Jenny.'' Toby extended his hand and Jenny shyly shook it; then he returned his attention to Charity. ''I've got things pretty well under control next door.

Call said it would be okay if I came over a couple of hours a day to help.''

Charity rolled her eyes toward the heavens and flashed a grateful smile. ''There really is a God.'' She thought of the last grueling hours they had put in. ''What do you think, ladies? Can we use another hand?''

Maude grinned. ''I'd be darned glad to have ya.''

''Jenny?''

She glanced down at her feet. ''This is harder than I thought.''

''I'll pay you whatever Call pays, and be grateful for the help.''

Toby nodded, pleased to be so readily welcomed. ''I don't know much about dredging, but I'm more than willing to learn.''

''Well, let's git to it, then.'' Maude turned toward the dredge and they all set to work.

The afternoon progressed far better than the morning. With Toby's help, they moved several yards of gravel through the dredge and into the sluice.

''I can't wait to see what we got,'' Toby said, displaying the obvious symptoms of gold fever.

''We clean the sluice box every Friday. You'll have to wait until then.''

Toby looked disappointed and Charity fought a smile.

The day was coming to an end when another visitor appeared on the path. Charity recognized Call's familiar rangy strides and the big silver dog trotting along beside him. Another, smaller version of the dog raced along next to Smoke on the end of the leash in Call's hand.

''You guys wind it up,'' she told her crew. ''You've all done a great job—more than enough for today.''

Toby looked disappointed that they were quitting a few minutes early and Charity couldn't help a smile. ''See you tomorrow, Toby.''

The thought seemed to cheer him and he waved as he started toward home, passing Call along the way.

Charity started in that direction, her eyes on Call, telling her heart to stop that infernal clatter. Sometimes she wished the man didn't look so damned good.

"Hi," she said. A fairly lame attempt at conversation but she always felt a little tongue-tied when she first saw him.

"Hi." He didn't say more, just stared at her and she wondered if maybe he felt a little the same. "I brought you a present," he finally said. "After what happened with Buck, I figured you could use a good watchdog. Not that he's much of one yet."

He tugged on the puppy's leash and the little dog turned away from the beetle he was sniffing and raced toward her. He jumped up and down like a fuzzy pogo stick, rested his paws on her knees. He looked a lot like Smoke, but his tail curled up over his back and his long thick fur was tan streaked with black instead of silver.

Charity ran her hand through his warm, heavy coat. "Oh, Call, he's beautiful."

"He's a husky." Call smiled. "I couldn't find you a wolf."

Her own smile began to slip away. "He's a darling dog. I'd love to have him, but I can't possibly keep him."

"Why not?"

"They don't allow dogs in the apartment building I live in. What would I do with him after I got back to Manhattan?"

Something shifted in Call's expression and his features closed up. "I didn't know you were planning to leave."

"Not now, not until the end of October. I never planned to live here permanently. I subleased my apartment to my sister for six months. I'll be going back to New York when the lease is u.p."

"I see."

The words rang with a note of finality. For the first time she realized that part of her wanted to stay. Part of her didn't want to leave this beautiful country or the man she was trying so very hard not to love.

She forced herself to smile. "I thought I told you. All this time you were worried about getting too involved. Now you can see it isn't a problem." She kept her eyes on his face, but a lump was forming in her throat.

"Yeah. No problem at all."

No problem for him. But a very big problem for her.

He handed her the puppy's leash. "I'll take him when you leave. In the meantime, like I said, he can keep an eye on things over here."

Charity looked down at the beautiful husky puppy and the lump in her throat began to swell. "What's his name?"

"Whatever you want it to be."

She knelt at the puppy's side and buried her face in his fur. "He looks like a fuzzy little bear. I'll call him Kodiak . . . if that's all right with you."

Bright blue eyes gazed down at her. "Kodiak," Call repeated, his voice a little gruff. "That's a good name for a husky." He turned toward the path to his house. "You coming over to work?"

"I thought maybe I would."

"I'll see you when you get there." He didn't wait for her, just turned and started walking.

"Call?"

He stopped and turned. "Yeah?"

"Thanks for the puppy. I love him already." And she did.

One more thing to leave behind when she went home.

One more thing that was going to break her heart.

"You need anything from town?" Call stuck his head inside the door of his office. It had been a place of solitude, a place where he could relax and think.

Not anymore.

Charity turned away from the computer. "When are you going?"

"I'm leaving in about ten minutes." It was Saturday.

Charity would be working most of the day. Which meant he would be staying away from the house.

She leaned back in the swivel chair in front of the computer. "Actually, there are some things I need. Why don't I go with you?"

A muscle clenched in his jaw. *Because, dammit, you're the reason I'm going!* "I figured you'd probably want to work."

"Aside from the fact I've been at it for hours and have gotten exactly nowhere, I'm going stir-crazy staring at this screen." She got up from her chair and tilted her head back, stretching to work the kinks out of her neck and shoulders. Her breasts thrust forward and his jeans went tight.

Sonofabitch. "Yeah . . . all right. We won't be gone long, just a couple of hours."

Since the day she had told him she wouldn't be staying in the Yukon, Call had kept his distance. He told himself it was exactly what he wanted, told himself it was the answer to his prayers. In a couple of months, Charity would be leaving, returning to her old life in the city. He'd be safe again, his emotions out of danger.

It was the perfect solution.

Funny thing was, instead of avoiding her, he ought to be hauling her off to bed, spending as much time there as he possibly could. He knew she would let him. When he looked at her, he saw the same heat in her eyes she saw in his. Still, a purely physical relationship no longer seemed quite right, either.

The result was that he stayed away from her as much as he could and went around with a hard-on half the day. Sooner or later, something was going to snap. He just hoped it wasn't today.

He looked over Charity's shoulder at the computer screen, his hand itching to reach down and cup one of her beautiful breasts. "You haven't turned up anything?"

She swiveled her chair around and looked up at him. "Actually, I've turned up tons of information." She went back to the computer and pulled up the screen that showed the chart he had designed for her. More than half the boxes were filled in.

"I found most of my dad's side of the family all the way back to the 1880s. They were English, pretty straightlaced, follow-the-rules kind of folks so they were fairly easy to track. Walter Sinclair—my great-great-grandfather—was the first generation born in this country. The Rosses, on my dad's mother's side, lived in the East since the early colonial days and there's no indication they ever left."

"What about your mom's side of the family?"

"I'm working on that now, but the information is a lot more sketchy. So far none of it looks particularly promising."

"Maybe something will turn up."

"Maybe." She smiled, but he could see she was getting discouraged. It occurred to him how important this search was to her. She wanted to understand why she had felt so compelled to come here, and if she really did have memories of this place from another time.

"You ready to go?" he asked.

She nodded, reached down, and turned off the machine. He could see she was still thinking about her research, see the little frown lines on her forehead.

"If you feel like it later, maybe we could catch a movie or something." Dammit, why had he said that? The idea was to get away from her. *Wasn't it?*

Wishing he had kept his mouth shut, he followed her out the door, scooping up the cell phone he had begun to carry lately on the way to the garage and his Jeep. It rang as he slid it into his pocket. Call fished out the phone and flipped it open.

"Hawkins."

"Call, it's Peter. Something's come up."

"You sound funny. You got a cold or something?"

"Broken nose . . . among other things. That's the something that's come up."

Call's hand tightened around the phone. "What the hell happened?"

"Guy wanted my wallet. I didn't want to give it to him. Should have, I guess."

"How bad is it?"

"Nothing to worry about. A couple of broken ribs, lots of cuts and bruises. I'm gonna need a little time off."

"No problem. Take all the time you need."

"Thanks."

"Where'd this happen?"

"The park. It was late and I was jogging. Pretty stupid, huh?"

"Oh, I don't know. You kept your wallet. That's the important thing."

On the other end of the phone, Peter laughed through his bandaged nose.

"Take care of yourself, Pete, and stay in touch. Let me know if there's anything you need."

Peter signed off and Call hung up the phone.

"More problems?" Charity asked.

"Peter Held got mugged."

"Your chemist friend in Seattle?"

"That's right, the guy doing the research at MegaTech."

"Is he okay?"

"He's pretty screwed up. He's taking time off until he's feeling better."

"I guess everybody has their share of problems."

"Yeah," Call said, but he was thinking he was having more than his share lately.

Toby couldn't believe his luck. He had been dying to ask Jenny out all week but she was really shy and he didn't think if he did that she would say yes. Then early this morning Jenny and Maude had shown up in his mother's jewelry shop, The Gold Mine. Jenny wanted to sell the little cache of nuggets that were her wages, her share of the weekly take now that Buck was gone.

Toby treasured his own. He would never forget the thrill he'd felt when they emptied the sluice box yesterday afternoon and he had seen the little kernels of glittering gold caught between the riffles. But Jenny had come to sell her share and once the transaction was finished, Toby had casually asked her to lunch.

"I don't know ... I think Grama might need me to help her buy supplies."

"Don't be silly," Maude said. "I been doin' for myself for nigh on seventy years. You kids go on and have fun."

Jenny still looked uncertain, but Toby thought that she actually wanted to go so he simply took her hand and led her off down the street.

She's so pretty, he thought. Sexy, too. And even that silly nose ring couldn't take away from the sweetness he sensed inside her. Maybe she wore it and that tattoo to make her look tougher. If she did, it wasn't working.

"So ... how 'bout The Grubstake? You like pizza, don't you?"

She nodded. "Pizza sounds good."

He was still holding her hand. He liked the way it felt in his, so smooth and soft. He wondered if her lips would feel the same. It was way too early to be thinking about kisses, especially with a girl like Jenny, but the thought crossed his mind just the same, along with some other, more forbidden thoughts he tried not to let creep in.

The truth was, his attraction to Jenny wasn't just about sex. Her shyness intrigued him. He sensed that she was intelligent and he wanted to get to know her, find out why she had come to Dawson, ask if she was going to go to college and if she was, which school she was planning to attend.

He wanted to know everything about her.

Mostly, he wanted to know why she always looked so sad.

The drive to town was pleasant. The sun burning down on the canvas top of Call's fancy black Jeep warmed the interior and Charity relaxed against the leather seat. As they bounced over potholes, stirring up dust, she pulled out a sheet of paper she had stuffed into her purse.

"What's that?" Call asked.

"Something else I've been working on while I've been pounding away in search of my long-dead relatives."

"What is it?"

"An article on inherited memory I printed off the Net. I read something about it before, in a couple of different magazines. That's what got me thinking about it. I wondered what I'd find if I nosed around on the Internet." She unfolded the sheet of paper and started to read.

"What's it say?"

She looked over to where he sat in the driver's seat. "Have you ever read any of those stories about people who get organ transplants?"

Call cast her a sideways glance, his big hands wrapped around the leather-covered steering wheel. "What the hell do organ transplants have to do with memories?"

"Well, say you got a heart transplant, for instance. Sometimes the person who receives the heart starts having all sorts of personality changes. Like he starts to crave peanut butter when he hated peanut butter before. The reason is the heart *donor* liked peanut butter. The recipient now has additional DNA that triggers certain changes in his behavior."

"So you're saying . . . what?"

"I'm saying if getting someone's DNA through a heart transplant could trigger an urge to eat peanut butter, maybe the DNA you inherit could trigger an interest in certain things—like the Gold Rush—because the DNA donor—one of my ancestors—came to the Yukon to search for gold."

"That doesn't mean you could have real memories."

She looked down at the paper. "Did you know calves are born refusing to cross a set of lines painted to look like a cattle guard even though they've never seen one? Or that a cat will groom itself even if it's raised as an orphan?"

"Those are instincts, not memories."

"The article proposes that genetic memory and instinct are one and the same. DNA serves as the conduit by which genetic memory is transmitted. It says we pass our descendants much more than eye and hair color, that about forty percent of our personality traits are also inherited."

"And?"

"There are scientists who believe genetic memory can be passed from generation to generation in the form of actual memories." She started reading from the article. " 'Those sorts of memories cause people to recall places and events from another time, many of which have been proven to have actually occurred.' "

Call looked unconvinced. "Yeah, well, even if it's true, you still have to find someone directly related to you who came up here a hundred years ago. You do that, and I might give your theory a little more credence."

He was right, of course, and Charity fell silent, wondering if she actually would find a connection. Outside the window, the forest kept its silent vigil. A huge hawk circled overhead, then swooped down and disappeared among the branches of a pine tree along the road. The sky was so blue it hurt her eyes to look at it.

Call's cell phone rang and at the low speed they crept along the road, he didn't bother to pull over, just flipped it open and pressed it against his ear.

"Hawkins."

"Bob Wychek here. Any chance you could drop by my shop sometime today?"

"As it happens, I'm on my way to town right now. What's up?"

"I'd rather show you, eh? See you at the shop in what? Forty-five minutes?"

"I'll be there," Call said, and hung up the phone.

"One of your girlfriends?" Charity asked, casting him a look.

Call's eyebrow arched at the faint note of jealousy she hoped he wouldn't hear. "Bob Wychek. He's the guy who's been working on my plane. I think he may have figured out what went wrong with the engine.''

"I know what went wrong. It coughed a couple of times and turned itself off and the propeller stopped going around.''

"Very funny,'' he said dryly but both of them grinned.

A little while later, they turned onto the Klondike Highway, the main route into Dawson, crossed the river, and started up downtown Front Street.

"I'm getting hungry. I don't suppose we have time for lunch before we see your guy about the plane?''

Call passed the street sign for Midnight Dome Road and kept on driving. "I guess we can make time. I'll phone Wychek and tell him we're going to be a little late.''

He made the call but Bob was out in back so he left a message.

"Let's go to Klondike Kate's,'' Charity suggested. "They've got the best food in Dawson.''

"You want to go to Kate's?'' Call looked uneasy. "I was thinking maybe The Grubstake.''

"Just imagine one of those mile-high sandwiches at Kate's.''

"I admit the food there is great, but—''

"Terrific. Let's go.''

Call frowned but continued down the road in that direction, turning down King to Third and pulling up across from the yellow-and-white, two-story, wood-frame building on the corner. They got out of the Jeep and went inside and Call gave the hostess his name. The place was crowded. It always was, even, she had heard, in the winter.

Still, it didn't take long to get seated at one of the small, square tables. A busboy brought over glasses of ice water, then a pretty red-haired waitress arrived to take their order. She looked at Call and there was something in the smile she gave him that put Charity on alert.

"Hi, Call. Haven't seen you for a while.'' She was younger than Charity, maybe early twenties, with a wide mouth, sparkling green eyes, and a figure to die for. She made it obvious exactly how well she knew Call.

He shifted uneasily in his chair. "I've been pretty busy."

The redhead tossed Charity a look. "I can see that." She didn't say more and neither did Call. The waitress took their order and headed for the kitchen, and Charity pasted on a smile.

"I take it that's the blow job."

Call started coughing, trying to hold down the drink of water he'd just taken. He glanced around to see if anyone had overheard, then relaxed a little when he realized no one had.

"Is that any way for a lady to talk?"

"You're the one who said it first."

"Yeah, well, I'm a man."

"That's what Buck Johnson always says."

A corner of his mouth curved up. "Point taken."

The redhead returned a few minutes later with sandwiches made of fresh-baked bread piled high with cheese and meat. Alfalfa sprouts bulged from the sides and French fries crackled on the plate. The waitress glanced at Charity, then cast a look of invitation at Call.

"You get finished with your ... business, give me a ring," she said.

Call wisely made no reply.

They were leaving the restaurant half an hour later, walking down the boardwalk toward the Jeep, when Charity spotted Toby and Jenny walking toward them.

"Hey, you two!" Toby waved at them and grinned, but Jenny looked a little embarrassed. "What are you doing in town?"

"We had some errands to run," Charity answered. "And Call wanted to check up on his plane."

"How's it coming?" Toby asked him.

"On my way over to find out right now."

"You guys have a good time," Charity said. "See you on Monday."

They climbed up in the Jeep and Call fired up the powerful engine. A few minutes later, they drove through the high, chain-link gates of Superior Air West, where his plane was being repaired.

Call helped her down and they walked through the wide hangar doors leading into a big metal building. "I'm looking for Wychek," he said to a grease-covered mechanic in dark blue coveralls.

"Over here!" Wychek called out. He was short and bald, kind of round all over, with rosy cheeks and blue eyes, sort of a younger version of Santa Claus minus the beard. "I didn't get your message until a few minutes ago. I was beginning to worry you weren't going to make it."

"Sounds like this is important."

Wychek nodded. "It is." Walking toward the fuselage of the Beaver, he led them to where the engine lay scattered in pieces and parts.

"I didn't see it at first. I wasn't looking for something like this, eh?"

"What'd you find?"

The mechanic looked over at Charity as if maybe he shouldn't say anything in front of her.

"It's all right. The lady was up there when it quit. I guess she's got a right to know."

Wychek nodded. Reaching a greasy hand into a section of the engine, he pulled out the remnants of a tiny metal box.

"What is it?"

"Container for a small amount of explosive." He held the fragment of metal up to the light. "See how the box blew up from the inside out? Probably fixed to some kind of a timing device. When the charge went off, it severed the fuel line and the engine couldn't get any gas."

Call took the remnant of metal from Wychek's hand. "Are you sure about this, Bob?"

"Damn right, I'm sure. The fire melted the rubber tubing

that carried the fuel but see this here?'' He pointed to a length of line. ''The mesh was clearly blown apart, and this little piece of metal was still attached to the tube.'' Bob's round face looked grim. ''Someone wanted that plane to crash, Mr. Hawkins. And that's exactly what it did.''

No one said a word.

Charity's stomach suddenly felt queasy. She didn't need to hear any more. ''I think I'll wait for you in the Jeep, if that's all right.''

Call nodded. ''Go ahead. I'll be right with you.''

He appeared a few minutes later and she thought that his face looked nearly as pale as her own.

''I can't believe it,'' she said. ''Someone tried to kill us.''

Call cranked the engine. ''Odds are, they were after me, not you, and I've got a couple of ideas who it might be. Unfortunately, I don't know for sure. As soon as we get back to the house, I'm calling Steve McDonald. He's a private investigator and a good one. We'll see what he can find out.''

Charity turned away from him and stared out the window. Someone had tried to kill Call. It made her sick to think about it. They finished their errands in record time and started up the road toward home. The scenery was just as pretty as it was on the way down the hill, but this time Charity didn't notice.

CHAPTER NINETEEN

As soon as they got back to the house, Call went into his office and picked up his satellite phone. First, he dialed the private investigator, Steve McDonald, in Seattle and gave him the facts, which weren't many, and promised to send the remnants of the tiny explosive device that had been used to sabotage the plane.

Next he phoned Peter Held. Call didn't mention the plane crash or what Wychek had discovered. He had no idea how all this was going to shake out. He needed more information, needed to know whose loyalty he could count on. Instead, he asked if Peter was certain the mugging was random and Peter assured him it was.

"Like I said, I was running in the park. It was getting pretty late. That kind of stuff happens all the time in a city."

That was true enough. "Anything new turn up on the fire in the lab?"

"The fire department said the blaze was caused by a problem in the electrical system. The building was old. They think some of the wiring was probably faulty. With that many chemicals around it was easy for a blaze to get started."

A week ago he would have believed it. Now he had

to be sure. Ending the conversation with Peter, he dialed information and got the number for the Seattle Police Department. He asked for the head of the arson squad, a guy named Karl Miller, and asked him to take another look.

"Happy to, Mr. Hawkins." Four years might have passed, but in Seattle, where he had so much business, the name McCall Hawkins still carried plenty of weight. "You got reason to suspect foul play?"

"It's a possibility. I'd appreciate a second look around." Though Peter was close to a breakthrough, Call didn't really think MegaTech was enough of a threat to warrant a murder attempt. Which meant it was likely someone else.

Turning his thoughts in that direction, he phoned Bruce Wilcox for an update and any further details Wilcox might have on the Wild Card Internet gaming consortium.

"How long do you think they've known we were tapping into their records?" Call asked.

"I don't know. But they could have known almost from the start." *Not good news.* "Word is, these guys really play hardball. We've got to tread carefully with this one, Call."

No kidding. He thought of his plane, lying in pieces and parts on the hangar floor, and the tampering that had nearly caused their deaths. "See if you can arrange a meeting. We need to make sure these guys know Shotman and Wiggs were acting on their own. I'll try to come up with some kind of deal that will cover our asses and get them off our backs." *And keep them from killing one or all of us.*

"You got it, Call."

He wasn't sure Wild Card was behind the attempts on his life, but they were the strongest possibility. There was huge money involved in gambling and from what he knew, these guys were the kind willing to do anything to get it.

He was exhausted by the time he left his office and walked into the kitchen, and surprised to see Charity standing at the sink, wearing one of his oversized tee shirts.

She flashed him a smile that eased a little of his fatigue. "It's Saturday night and you've been working for hours. I figured you deserved a decent meal." She had tied an apron around her waist, hiking the tee shirt up and exposing her long, pretty legs and bare feet. Her breasts jiggled softly and her nipples formed shadowy circles beneath the fabric. He hadn't made love to her in nearly two weeks. Inside his jeans he went hard.

She must have seen him eyeing her clothes—or lack thereof. "The trip home was dusty," she explained, adding olive oil to the salad dressing. "I took a shower and put this on. I didn't think you'd mind."

He shook his head, not minding at all. He'd been so busy he had almost forgotten she was still there.

Almost.

"You look tired. Are you hungry?"

"A little, I guess."

She bent over to check the temperature of the oven, lifting the tee shirt even more, and his erection began to throb. He was hungry, all right, but not for food.

"Toby made spaghetti before he left for the weekend," she said. "I made a salad to go with it. I'm toasting some garlic bread, too."

There was an open bottle of red wine on the counter. Charity poured him a glass and handed it over.

"Thanks."

"Do any good in there?" She tipped her head toward his office and stuck the tray of French bread under the broiler.

"I got things rolling. It took a while."

"I've been thinking about what happened . . . to the plane, I mean. If someone wanted to kill you, they might try it again."

"They might. I'm trying to head them off before they get the chance."

"How will you do that?"

He told her Bruce Wilcox was trying to set up a meeting with the guys from the Wild Card consortium.

"There's a good chance they're the men behind the attempt. Datatron only has seven employees. I'm the head of the company. They probably figured I was the guy behind the million-dollar shakedown."

"How will you convince them you aren't?"

He arched a dark brown eyebrow. "Believe me—I can be very convincing."

But the worry didn't leave her face. "I was hoping you'd get some kind of bodyguard or something."

He probably should, but he hated the idea. He liked his privacy too much. And the wilderness was his domain. He was sure he could protect himself if it really came down to it.

"I don't think I'll need to go that far. Once Wild Card knows we're willing to come to the table, I don't think they'll give us any more trouble—at least not until they hear what we have to say."

"You're sure that's who it was?"

"Fairly sure. I don't have all that many enemies—at least not that I know of. And it's been years since I've been involved in the business world."

Charity pulled out his usual chair at the breakfast table. "Why don't you sit down and I'll bring you something to eat?"

He settled himself in the chair while she went over and filled a plate for him and one for herself. As soon as the French bread was nicely browned, she put it in a basket, brought the rest of the food to the table, and sat down next to him.

The food was good and he was hungrier than he'd thought. His mind was still spinning with events of the day and he didn't feel much like talking. Charity seemed to sense his mood. It was one of the things he liked about her. They could be quiet together and not be uncomfortable. When they finished the meal, she blew out the candles she had lit in the center of the table and cleared the dishes, insisting that she didn't need his help.

Instead he sat there watching her, wondering if maybe he could convince her to spend the night or if she would continue to keep her distance. She rinsed the dishes and put them in the dishwasher, then came up behind where he sat and began to massage his neck and shoulders.

"How's that feel?"

Her hands were soft, and warm from the rinse water she had used. He could feel her breasts rubbing gently against his back and his arousal returned, harder than ever.

"You've got good hands." Good hands and a wonderful, tight little body. Beneath the table, he was hard as granite, the blood running like lava through his veins. Damn, he wanted her, and if she kept touching him the way she was, he would take her.

He felt her lips against the nape of his neck and a shudder rippled through him.

"I've missed you, Call," she said softly.

It was all the encouragement he needed. Noisily he shoved back his chair and hauled her into his arms. "God, I've missed you, too."

He kissed her fiercely. A thorough, taking kiss, measuring the softness of her lips, parting the seam with his tongue, ravaging her mouth. She smelled of soap and flowers and tasted faintly of dark red wine. His hands ran over the tee shirt and he filled his palms with her breasts. They were firm as apples, soft as peaches. Charity made a little whimpering sound and hot need surged through him. Shoving the candlesticks out of the way, he lifted her up on the table and settled himself between her legs.

The tee shirt slid up. Sweet Jesus, she wasn't wearing anything underneath. Desire pulsed through him and he heard himself groan.

Kneeling in front of her, he ran his hands over her hips, testing the smoothness, the firmness, wanting to taste her. Charity leaned back, propping herself on her elbows as he eased her legs farther apart and began to kiss her knees, the inside of her thighs, making his way toward his goal.

"C-Call . . . ?"

There was something in her voice, a thread of uncertainty. *This is new to her,* he thought with a rush of male satisfaction, and his arousal strengthened. He urged her back on the table and slid the tee shirt up above her breasts, began to suck on her nipples. She was moaning as he moved lower, kissed her navel, her hipbones, moved through the downy triangle of gold at the apex of her legs, found the tiny bud of her sex and took it into his mouth.

"Oh . . . oh, dear God!" He felt her hands in his hair and for an instant she tried to pull him away, but he gripped her hips and simply held her immobile.

"Easy," he whispered. He could be a patient lover. In the past he had prided himself on it and he used that patience now, gentling her a little, kissing her breasts again, dipping his tongue into her navel, then returning to his objective.

This time she didn't fight him. She trusted him and he used that trust to give her pleasure. Her stomach quivered. Her hands returned to his hair and fisted there, but this time they urged him to stay. He felt the muscles in her thighs contract, felt her arching upward off the table, and knew she was nearing release.

He didn't stop until she climaxed. He watched her with awe and something more, something primitive and possessive. He took her with his mouth a second time, laving and tasting till another climax shook her.

She was limp and pliant by the time he slid her off the table onto her feet and eased her over onto her stomach. He gripped her hips and pressed himself against her, letting her feel how hard he was.

"Oh, God," she said as he slid into her, filling her, taking her so deeply she moaned. Her bottom was round and smooth, an incredible turn-on, and he could taste her in his mouth. His loins were on fire, the muscles across his chest so taut they quivered, and he knew he wouldn't last as long as he wanted. Each stroke took him higher, closer. Charity came again, her passage tightening sweetly around him. He drove into her until he couldn't hold back a moment more, then exploded over the edge into release.

It was the fiercest climax he could remember.

Afterward he simply stood there, holding her against his chest, his arms wrapped around her waist.

Charity turned to face him. And then she burst into tears.

* * *

The kitchen finally stopped spinning. The earth stopped shaking and Charity felt Call's mouth pressing softly into her hair.

"It's all right, baby," he whispered, "everything's fine."

Too fine, she thought. *Too unbelievably good.*

And since the moment earlier that afternoon when Bob Wychek told Call someone wanted him dead, Charity had known how totally, how utterly, how wildly she was in love with him.

"I'm sorry," she said, wiping away the wetness. "I just . . . That was just so incredible."

He looked down at her and actually grinned. "It was, wasn't it?" She could see he was pleased with himself. *Typical male,* she thought. He could be murdered at any moment and all he could think was what a great lover he was.

Still, she couldn't help smiling in return. He really was a terrific lover.

His jeans were unzipped. He buzzed them closed, then lifted her up and carried her into the living room. Call sat down on the sofa with Charity still in his arms. He was looking at her in that self-satisfied way, a corner of his mouth edging up.

"I take it Jeremy wasn't into oral sex."

She shook her head, a little embarrassed, wishing he hadn't brought it up. "Jeremy was far too fastidious for something like that."

He didn't say anything else and she eased herself off his lap and curled up next to him on the couch. The living room was beautifully furnished: leather sofas and hardwood floors, throw rugs for a hint of color. But like the rest of his house, it was a little austere.

"You don't have any pictures," she said, surveying walls hung with expensive landscapes but nothing personal, and the near-empty, polished-walnut tables. "I noticed that before. Not even any of yourself."

His gaze surveyed the room as hers had done. "I never put them up. It hurt too much to look at them."

It was the first time he had ever referred to the accident, and her heartbeat quickened. "But you brought them with you. You have them here."

He nodded. "In a chest of drawers in the bedroom."

He had them but he still couldn't look at them. It made her feel so sad. "Maybe someday you'll show me."

He glanced away. "Yeah ... maybe someday."

But she didn't really think he would. She took a chance then, knowing it was probably a mistake. "How old was your little girl?"

She was more than half certain he wouldn't answer, that he would close himself off again or maybe even get angry.

"Three. Her birthday was November first." He stared straight ahead, his eyes fixed on the big rock fireplace at the end of the room. "Susan had a party for her that day and we all wore those funny paper hats. She ... died not long after, just a little before Christmas."

Charity's throat felt tight. She forced herself to continue. The only way he would ever get past the pain was to bring it out into the open. "I know there was a car accident," she said gently. "What happened?"

Silence settled over the living room. Outside the window, the wind rustled through the branches of the trees. The sun beat through the panes, but the room no longer felt warm. Call thought about the question. For long moments, he didn't answer, though for some strange reason he wanted to.

The seconds stretched, lengthened. He tried to think of a way to explain, a way to speak of the unspeakable, but he couldn't find the words. He just sat there on the sofa, staring at the big, stone hearth, letting the memories slide in. The fire was long dead, the ashes grown cold, the hearth dark and empty.

Just like his heart.

The minutes ticked past and a stream of images began flooding in: Susan laughing at something he had said, Amy scampering around the house in her little pink party dress, her dark curls bouncing up and down on her shoulders.

"It was my fault," he heard himself say, though the voice didn't sound like his own; it was flat and bleak, as lifeless as the pain-filled words made him feel. "Every year we rented a condo up at Heavenly Valley. Susan loved to ski and it wasn't that long a drive from San Jose. I was busy . . . the way I always was. As soon as we got off the hill, I shut myself up in one of the bedrooms I had set up as a temporary office and worked on my laptop. I was always working. I had so much to do. That's what I always thought."

He swallowed past the lump aching in his throat. "At the end of the week, Susan decided she and Amy would go down to Sacramento to spend a few days with Susan's Aunt Mildred. I guess she got tired of sitting around every evening by herself, no one to talk to but a three-year-old child."

He hadn't talked about the accident in years. Now that he'd started, he couldn't seem to stop. "I was supposed to drive them down the mountain after we finished skiing that day, but American Dynamics was in the middle of a complicated, very profitable merger and a problem came up. At the last minute, one of the VPs set up a conference call. I thought it was really important I be there when it came in." He swallowed past the lump, felt the familiar burning behind his eyes. "I didn't realize back then . . . that nothing was as important . . . as taking care of my family."

He could see it all so clearly: Amy in her fuzzy blue jacket with the little plush-trimmed hood; Susan dressed elegantly, as always, in black wool slacks and an expensive black cashmere sweater. She kissed him on the cheek as he walked them to the door of the condo.

"I'm really sorry about this, Susan."

She smiled but he thought it looked a little sad. "Don't worry about it. I can drive myself down the hill. It really isn't a problem."

But the sky was overcast and getting darker by the minute

and he worried that it might be snowing somewhere farther down the road.

"Maybe I should cancel the call."

"I'll be fine. Amy, honey, give your daddy a kiss bye-bye before we leave."

The little girl grinned and raced toward him and he hoisted her up on his shoulder. "Who's little girl are you?" he asked, a private ritual they shared.

"Daddy's favorite little girl!" She giggled and hugged his neck and he kissed her cheek and set her back down on her feet. He put her in the child seat in the back of the station wagon and Susan started the engine. It was an all-wheel drive Mercedes, so when she drove away he wasn't really worried.

Call squeezed his eyes shut but the memory remained, seared into his brain like a negative image burned into film. Beside him, he felt Charity's hand slide into his and it was nearly as cold as his own.

"I watched them drive out onto that snowy street," he said, "but it was almost time for the conference call and I was eager to get back upstairs. I never thought of them again, not until the sheriff knocked on the door of the condo later that night. He said there'd been an accident. Susan's car hit a patch of ice and slid off the road. It was a dangerous stretch, he said. The terrain in that section was really steep. The car rolled over half a dozen times before it came to rest in a gully at the bottom of a ravine."

"Oh, Call . . ."

He tried to keep his voice even, knew he wouldn't succeed. "A trucker saw them veer off the road. He pulled them out before the car exploded but it was too late. Susan was killed instantly. Amy . . . Amy never regained consciousness. She died . . . on the way to the hospital."

His chest was aching. His throat hurt so much he had trouble getting out the words. "For days after the accident, I was numb. I couldn't think, couldn't feel. Then the pain set in. I tried to live with it for a while, but no matter what I did, it wouldn't go away. Finally, I just gave up. I quit my job and moved up here.''

His vision was blurry but he didn't realize tears were washing down his cheeks until Charity reached up and put her arms around his neck.

"It's all right," she said. "Sometimes it's good to get things out in the open."

"It was my fault. If I had gone with them, if I hadn't been so driven to make the next deal, Susan and Amy would still be alive." His voice cracked on the last and he shook his head, unable to continue.

"It wasn't your fault," Charity said, and he could feel her trembling. "Maybe you should have done things differently, maybe you made mistakes, but you didn't kill them. Life and death are in God's hands, Call, not yours. And that's exactly the way it should be."

He didn't answer. He wished he could believe her, wanted to more than anything in the world. Even if it were true, he knew the guilt would never truly leave him. The best he could do was learn to live with it day by day.

"I'm glad you told me," she said softly. "I'm glad you trusted me enough to share something so important."

He did trust her, he realized. More than he had trusted anyone in years.

The hard truth was—she probably shouldn't trust him.

CHAPTER TWENTY

Call's meeting with the Ransitch brothers, the owners of Wild Card, was set up for the coming Thursday. He felt a little safer, knowing the contact had been made and they were moving toward a resolution.

"We got lucky," Bruce Wilcox said. "The Ransitch boys were in the States, some business in Las Vegas, I gather. I pressed them to meet us in Seattle, the way you said, and they agreed. Their asses are out a mile on this and they know it. They wanted to meet somewhere neutral. I've got a conference room reserved at the Four Seasons Hotel for Thursday at 1:00 P.M."

"Good work, Bruce."

"I'll have a car waiting to pick you up at the private terminal when you get there."

Call had picked Seattle because it was a doable flight for him and not too far from Datatron in San Jose, where Bruce would be flying in from, and because he wanted to see Peter Held.

Call hung up the phone, thinking of myriad other calls he needed to make and beginning to miss his secretary, Marybeth Allen. Beth was beyond efficient and when he had left four years ago, had no trouble finding another high-paying job. He could sure as hell use her right now.

He smiled faintly. Somehow he doubted Marybeth would be willing to relocate to the Yukon.

Instead, he dialed a charter company called Mile High Air and asked to speak to Bill Bandy. Bill and his partner, Bing Wheeler, once flew private jets for American Dynamics. Now they owned their own small charter firm. They were crack pilots, but more importantly, he trusted them.

He scheduled a Hawker-Raytheon to pick him up in Whitehorse, the closest airstrip able to handle a jet, and asked them to arrange a chopper to get him there. He would arrive in Seattle Wednesday night, get a good night's sleep, and be ready for his meeting on Thursday.

In the meantime, he had a lot more phone calls to make. Call sighed and started hitting numbers.

The sun was still bright, though the afternoon was waning. Toby walked next to Jenny along the creek, listening to the sound of the tumbling water. They were finished dredging for the day, Maude and Charity sitting on the porch sharing a soft drink before Maude took Jenny back down the hill to their cabin.

Jenny paused on the bank and plucked a leaf off one of the bushes growing down into the water. She looked pensive as she twirled it in her hand.

"You're always so quiet," Toby said. "But sometimes I get the feeling you're not really that way. That you don't talk because you don't want to say what you're thinking."

Jenny looked out over the valley. It was a gorgeous summer afternoon, warm and clear, just a few puffy clouds floating by overhead. She didn't seem to notice.

"I used to be different," she said. "Happier, I guess. Things just got so screwed up."

"Everybody gets screwed up once in a while. I got into some trouble last year, fistfighting and drinking and stuff. I lost my scholarship. My mom didn't have the kind of money it took to put a kid through college, but I got lucky. I met Call when I was kayaking up on the river. Maybe we were both feeling so low we kind of bonded or something, I don't know. Whatever it was, a couple months later, he offered me this job. He helped me get into a college in Calgary starting this fall. Call's loaning me the tuition money, interest free. He says I can start paying it back when I get out of school."

"That's great. Mr. Hawkins seems like a really nice guy."

"He is. But Call's had his own share of trouble, just like everyone else." Toby took the stem from her hand, started twirling it in his own. "His wife and daughter were killed, you know. Really tore him up."

"Grama told me."

Toby smiled, handed her back the stem. "Okay, so now that you know my life story, what's yours?"

Jenny looked away. As she stared out over the valley, her pretty green eyes filled with tears. It was obvious something bad had happened and for a moment Toby wished he hadn't asked.

"If I tell you, you won't like me anymore."

Toby took her hand. It felt icy cold. "That's not true. There's nothing you could tell me that would make me not like you."

But Jenny just shook her head. "I gotta go. Grama's getting ready to leave."

He didn't let go of her hand. "Listen ... I'll be going into town after work on Friday night. If you went with me, you could stay overnight at our house and I'd bring you back home in the morning. My mom will be there. She'd like the company and I'd really like to take you out."

She looked like she was going to refuse.

"Don't say anything. Just think it over for a while and maybe you'll say yes."

Very slowly, she nodded. Toby watched her walk back down the hill toward her grandmother's beat-up old blue pickup. He wondered what she could have done that she was so ashamed of. Whatever it was, it was over and done. Bad things happened. Life went on.

Watching her climb up in the truck, he wished more than anything he could make her understand that. Maybe once she did, he could make her smile again.

Cell phone in hand, Charity walked up the hill behind the cabin. Trotting along at her side, Kodiak stopped once or twice to sniff the bushes along the path, then ran to catch up with her. Already, the darling little puppy was almost house-trained. He slept with her at night and every day wove his way deeper into her heart.

She reached down and ruffled his fur, then started punching numbers into her phone. As much as she loved her life in the Yukon, she couldn't help missing her family and friends. Nearly dying in a plane crash had shown her the fine line between life and death and she had phoned her loved ones more often since then.

She had also come to realize that as much as she embraced the majesty and thrill of living in the North, she could never give up the outside world the way Call had, not completely. She wanted a home and family, wanted children, wanted them to have that sense of community that she had enjoyed as a child. She tried not to think of Call and how much it was going to hurt when she left.

The phone began to ring in her old apartment but no one answered and eventually the machine picked up. Charity listened to Hope's voice, then left a message after the beep: *Wherever you are, I hope you're having fun. Love you— middle sis.* Next she called her dad at home in Boston.

"Did you get the stuff I sent?" he asked.

"I got the e-mail list of names. Thanks for sending them."

"I mailed a package of old newspaper clippings, too. They were in one of your mother's old family albums. I figured you might find something helpful in them."

"Thanks, Dad."

"So how's your friend—McCall Hawkins? I knew that

name sounded familiar. The guy's a member of the Forbes 400. I remembered reading about him several years back in *Time* magazine. Not a bad-looking man, if memory serves.''

She got the hint. Her dad was no fool. "I told you he's just a friend.''

"He kind of dropped out of sight for the last few years . . . some family tragedy, as I remember. I guess now we know where he's been.''

Charity made no reply and eased her father into a different subject. They talked a little longer, getting family updates, giving her dad a rundown on the amateur gold-mining business she was running. When she finally hung up, she dialed New York.

Her best friend, Deirdre Steinberg, didn't answer till just before the machine picked up.

"So you're there," Charity said. "If you're busy, I can call some other time.''

"No, no, now's fine. I, ah, had company, but he just walked out the door.''

"Anyone exciting?''

"Actually . . . God, Charity, I hope you don't get mad. It was Jeremy. We've been seeing each other lately. I wanted to call you, but you know how hard you are to reach. I should have sent you an e-mail or something, but it seemed so impersonal. I really feel bad about this but—''

"Look, it's okay, Deirdre. I'm not upset. In fact, I'm happy for you. I never really thought about you and Jeremy, but now that I do . . . maybe the two of you aren't a bad combination.''

The relief was clear in Deirdre's voice. "You think so?''

She considered the notion. "Yeah, maybe I do.'' Deirdre was definitely a nurturer, the sort of woman who was happiest doing things for someone else, certainly not the type to go off on an adventure by herself. She was intelligent, well dressed, and attractive. But Deirdre and Jeremy? Hard to say for sure, but maybe they would be good for each other.

"If Jeremy makes you happy, I think it's great. Tell him I said so, will you?''

They talked a little while longer, filling each other in. It was obvious Deirdre had worried about getting involved with her best friend's ex-lover, and that she was relieved their relationship was finally out in the open, and that it hadn't destroyed the friendship Charity and Deirdre had shared for so many years.

"So what about you and Paul Bunyan?" Deirdre asked. "Jeremy told me all about him. I can't believe you didn't mention you were seeing someone—and don't give me that 'just friends' crap, either."

Charity laughed. "Well, mostly we are."

"But you've slept with him. Jeremy was insane when he got back."

"I've slept with him, but the relationship—if there really is one—isn't going anywhere. Call's made that clear." She explained to Deirdre who Call was and about the death of his family.

"Paul Bunyan is McCall Hawkins—the billionaire?"

"One and the same, though he didn't look like much of one when I met him." She went on to say how badly Call had taken the loss of his wife and daughter and that there was a good chance he would never love anyone again.

"If that's the case, you'd better be careful, girlfriend, or you'll wind up getting hurt."

Now *there* was some good advice. Too bad it was too late to take it. "Thanks, Dee, I'll keep that in mind." They talked a little more, then she hung up and walked back down to the house.

Since last Saturday night when she and Call had made love on his kitchen table, they hadn't had sex again. She had been ending the workday early, stopping work on the dredge and going over for a couple of hours to use his computer, but she hadn't been spending the night. Perhaps talking about his family had brought up the barriers again, or maybe it was worry for her safety.

Though he hadn't said anything more about the attempt on his life, she thought maybe he believed staying there might be putting her in some kind of danger.

This afternoon, he had gone into town. He had checked her mail along with his and brought back the package from her father. As soon as she finished work, she started poring over the stack of newspaper clippings, hoping something of interest would turn up.

Charity stared down at the yellowed slip of newsprint, the Portland *Oregonian* dated August 18, 1869. For the first time since she had started this project, something actually had.

Up until now, she had spent most of her research efforts piecing together the Doakes side of the family, easier since they all carried the same surname, from Emma Doakes, her grandmother on her mother's side, all the way back to Campbell Doakes, whose father, David Doakes, had emigrated from Ireland to Tennessee in the 1860s.

It was darned hard to ferret out the information and though it was exciting to know who her long-lost relatives were, none had traveled to the Yukon or even crossed the Mississippi River. She was getting more and more discouraged, beginning to think maybe Call was right and whatever had compelled her to the North would forever remain elusive, that what had seemed like memories were nothing but a figment of her imagination. It bothered her more than it should have.

Until today.

Charity reached out to touch the stack of old newspaper clippings her father had sent. The one on top was more yellowed and tattered than the rest of the stack and when she had carefully unfolded it, it had simply fallen apart. With meticulous care, she taped the clipping back together, then sat down to read it.

The article centered around a man named Jedediah Baker. According to the clipping, after a trip on the recently completed Transcontinental Railroad, Baker had arrived in Portland late in the summer of 1869 to join his older brother, Nathan, who had earlier migrated west over the Oregon Trail. The brothers were reunited at a special celebration, the article said, held at the local Grange Hall.

Charity felt a bubble of excitement. Portland was one of the major starting-out spots for ships heading north to the Yukon. The clippings had been found in her mother's old family photo album. There was a good chance Jedediah and Nathan Baker were related to her somehow.

She was anxious to go over to Call's, see what she could dig up. For the first time in days, her spirits lifted. She couldn't wait to see what she might find.

When she got there, Call was packing. Toby told her as he let her into the house, getting ready for his trip to Seattle the following day. She didn't want to bother him so she motioned to Toby where she was headed, walked into the kitchen, and slipped quietly into his office.

Sitting down at her borrowed computer, she logged onto the Internet. A couple of clicks and www.ancestry.com popped up. Charity typed in *Jedediah Baker.*

For the next several hours, she searched one site after another: the Oregon marriage index, historicaltextarchive. com, familysearch.org, anything that might turn up information.

In some ways, trying to go forward in time was harder than trying to go backward. She found Jedediah's son, Thaddeus Baker, born in 1878, and saw where he had married a woman named Frances Fitzpatrick. Their six children were Jonathan, Sarah Thankful Baker, Melvina, Frederick, and Daniel.

One name sounded familiar. She scrambled for her notes, the printed chart she had been keeping that matched the one on the computer, and suddenly—there it was!

On May 3, 1920, Sean Doakes married a woman named Sarah Baker. Sarah *Thankful* Baker—it had to be. The connection of the Doakes to the Bakers was the reason the clipping had been in the album. Charity could feel her heart racing. The Bakers linked her family to the Pacific Northwest. Even more hopeful—Thaddeus Baker, Sarah's father, would have been in his early twenties during the Gold Rush era.

Had Thad Baker joined the Stampeders and set off for the Yukon, hoping to make his fortune? Had he seen the terrible suffering? Could some of his memories have been passed down to her?

It was still a far stretch, but it gave her a shot of hope. She wanted to race into the other room and share her discovery with Call, but he was still busy, and she needed to see what else she could find. Wiping her damp palms on the knees of her jeans, she started typing again, trying to find out if any of Sean Doakes and Sarah Baker's children were still alive.

She took each of the offspring one by one. Emma, her grandmother, Patrick, and Phillip were all deceased, but Annie Mae and Mavis, the eldest two children, had no date of death listed on their genealogy charts. She moved backward to where they'd been born and sucked in a breath.

Issaquah, Washington! Both Annie Mae and Mavis Doakes had been born in the West! Sean and Sarah must have lived in Washington for a while before heading east to Boston, where the rest of their children were born.

The women would be old, Annie Mae eighty-two and Mavis eighty-one, Charity calculated from their birthdates.

She glanced toward the door leading into the kitchen. Call would be flying to Seattle in the morning. Issaquah was only a few miles away. Charity chewed her lip. What would it take to convince him to take her with him? He wouldn't want to, she knew, but dammit, this was important.

Charity set her jaw. Call was taking her—he just didn't know it yet.

"Forget it, Charity. This is business, not a sightseeing trip."

"Come on, Call. What difference would it make if I came along? There's room on the plane, isn't there?"

"It's an eight-passenger jet. Room isn't a problem."

"Then what *is* the problem? I'll stay out of your hair—I promise. You said you know the pilots. It's not like we're going to crash again or anything."

He turned to her, planted his big hands on his hips. "Why is this so all-fired important?"

"You know why it's important. I've finally had a breakthrough. I've found a link in my past—at least to the Pacific Northwest." She explained about the two great-aunts she had discovered that she hadn't known existed. "There's a very good chance they're alive and living near Seattle."

He sighed, raked dark, suntanned fingers through his hair. "Even if they are, how are you going to find them?"

Good point. "I'll try the obvious first—long distance information. Maybe I can get an address before we leave. Or I can try to find them on-line. If that doesn't work, once I get there, maybe I can track them down through old courthouse records or something."

Call's face looked grim. It was obvious he didn't want to take her with him and it hurt to know he would rather go by himself.

"You'd be a whole lot safer right here," he said, and suddenly she wondered if protecting her was part of his motivation for wanting to leave her behind.

Charity altered her strategy. "Are you sure I'll be safer? I was on that plane, too. Until you know what's going on, I don't see how you can be certain of anything."

She knew she had him. She could see the worry creep into his face. His sigh held a hint of frustration. "All right, dammit, you can go. We're leaving early. The chopper will be here at six tomorrow morning."

Charity hid her jubilation. "Thanks, Call." She walked over to where he stood, went up on her toes and gave him a soft, nibbling kiss. "Maybe I can find a way to repay you."

Call's eyes turned a darker shade of blue. "Yeah," he said, hauling her into his arms. "Maybe you can at that."

She didn't return to the cabin until a whole lot later.

Six o'clock came early, but at least the sun was already shining and she was beginning to get used to the early hours up here. The chopper, a fancy red-and-silver model—a Bell turbo, Call said—set down exactly on time, and the two of them raced under the still-churning blades. They threw in their overnight luggage, climbed aboard, and strapped themselves into one of the four wide leather seats. Call said something to the pilot and the helicopter began lifting away.

An hour and a half later, they were walking across the tarmac in Whitehorse toward a sleek private jet.

"Good to see you again, Mr. Hawkins."

"Good to see you, too, Bill . . . Benjamin." Call shook hands with both of the men standing at the bottom of the ladder. Bill Bandy was lean and good-looking. Benjamin "Bing" Wheeler was taller, heavier through the chest and shoulders, with dark brown hair and a ruddy, weathered complexion. He wasn't handsome but he had a strong masculine appeal and Charity imagined neither man had ever had trouble attracting women.

"This is Ms. Sinclair. She's going with us."

"Welcome aboard, Ms. Sinclair," Bing Wheeler said.

"Thank you." They climbed the metal stairs and stepped into the cabin of the jet. It was luxurious, with five deep, taupe leather seats, a sofa that seated three, a bathroom, and a refreshment bar. Charity settled herself in a seat facing Call, her heart pumping with excitement, and listened for the roar of the engine. She had never been in a private jet and this was definitely a thrill. Call seemed unimpressed.

For the first time, she got a glimpse of what his life must have been like before the accident, of the man he had been back then. She cast a glance in his direction. He was wearing a clean pair of jeans and a yellow cotton polo shirt, the kind of clothes he might have worn at home. But his gaze was fastened on the *Wall Street Journal* the pilot had handed him when he first sat down and he was already completely absorbed.

There was something different about him today, had been since the moment he stepped out of the chopper in Whitehorse and crossed the tarmac toward the chartered multimillion-dollar jet. His strides seem to lengthen, grow more purposeful, and beneath the yellow shirt, his shoulders looked wider, straighter than they were before. There was power and authority in each of his movements, and a solid, unshakable confidence in the planes of his handsome face.

This was once Call's world and she saw how perfectly he fit into it. It occurred to her that no matter how much he loved the Yukon, some part of him must miss this and want to return.

The Seattle-Tacoma airport, one of the busiest in the country, was teeming with people when the jet rolled to a stop at the executive terminal.

"Nice ride," Call said to Bill Bandy, who stood at the door of the cockpit.

"We're scheduled to depart at ten A.M. tomorrow for the return trip to Whitehorse, but we're keeping things flexible, as you requested. Let me know if there's a change of plans."

Call nodded. Setting a hand at Charity's waist, he urged her down the aisle and out of the plane.

A long black stretch limo waited at the edge of the field. The chauffeur opened the door and Call watched her slide onto the soft gray leather seat. He followed her in and closed the door.

From behind a copy of *Newsweek*, Call saw Charity surveying the cavernous interior of the car, the tiny white lights illuminating the dark wood paneling and the crystal decanters in the built-in bar. "I can't believe this."

Call looked at her over the top of the magazine. "Can't believe what?"

"If someone had told me the first time I met you that I'd be flying in a private jet with you and riding in a big, black limo I would have thought they were insane."

A corner of his mouth edged up. "What? You mean the beard and the long hair fooled you?"

"That and that nasty disposition of yours." She cocked a golden eyebrow. "Sometimes you've got a really bad temper, you know."

He smiled at her teasing tone, then gave her a slow perusal that made color wash into her cheeks. "That's not all I've got, honey."

Charity laughed. Some of the tension he had been feeling began to ease and he set the *Newsweek* aside. "Ever been to Seattle?"

She shook her head. "I'm really looking forward to seeing it."

He relaxed even more, settling into the deep leather seat. "Good, because I'm really looking forward to showing it to you."

"You are?"

"Yeah, I guess I am." He'd meant to get his work done and leave, but if things went as planned, there was no reason they couldn't enjoy themselves a little before they went back home.

Charity looked at him and a brilliant smile broke over her lips. It was warm and sweet, and something expanded in his chest. It was a feeling that unnerved him and for a moment, he wished he hadn't volunteered. But the truth was, he wanted to show her the city.

He just hoped like hell his meeting with Wild Card would ensure it was a safe thing to do.

CHAPTER TWENTY-ONE

They checked into the Four Seasons Hotel in downtown Seattle, a magnificent, historic structure with a sumptuous lobby, marble columns, and an exquisite spiral staircase leading up to the second floor. After her weeks of living in the wilds of the Yukon, Charity felt like pinching herself to be sure she wasn't dreaming.

They crossed the lobby and walked up to the long black-marble registration counter.

"This place is really expensive," Charity whispered. "I never thought about that when I asked to come. Maybe I could stay in a cheaper—"

"Dammit, you don't have to pay for a room." His eyes moved down her body in a way that made the nerves beneath her skin come to life. "You'll be staying with me. Until this is over, I want you close enough so I can keep an eye on you."

Charity didn't protest. They might have had sex, but she had been spending her nights alone in the cabin. She wanted to sleep with him, curl up in his arms. She wanted to wake up next to him in the morning.

The reservation had already been made. It didn't take

long before they were walking behind a bellman into a magnificent corner suite on the tenth floor. It was spacious and beautiful, with deep beige, over-stuffed sofas and chairs, and a polished mahogany dining room table big enough to seat six. Charity grinned when the bellman showed her the two marble bathrooms and Call said she could take her pick.

"In that case, I want the one with the Jacuzzi."

"Fine," Call said, a wicked glint in his eyes, "as long as I get to share it."

They had a marvelous afternoon. Call insisted she buy something special to wear to dinner and she chose a simple black knit dress from one of the hotel shops. When she reached for the price tag, he caught her hand.

"It isn't important. I can't wait to see you in that dress."

She picked a pair of black high heels from the shoe store next door and they returned upstairs to the suite. A before-dinner soak in the Jacuzzi tub led to a slow round of lovemaking, which led to another.

In the end, the dress stayed on its hanger in the closet and Call had supper sent up to the suite.

"Don't worry about it," he said as if he knew she was thinking about the cost of the dress and shoes, which, of course, she was. "You can wear them tomorrow night."

Her head came up. "I thought we were leaving tomorrow afternoon."

He shrugged as if it weren't important. "One more night won't hurt. If everything goes right, once this is over we can relax and enjoy ourselves."

She went up on her toes and kissed his cheek. "That sounds wonderful."

They went to bed early, made love, and she drifted into an easy sleep. Once, in the night, she awakened to find Call standing in front of the window.

"Can't sleep?" she said. He was worried about the meeting, she knew, and considering how much was at stake, she didn't blame him.

He padded naked toward the bed, his strides long and rangy. "Maybe you can help me," he said. She purred as he joined her in bed, came up over her, and slid himself inside her. When they finished making love, this time both of them were able to fall asleep.

Charity awakened the following morning later than usual, her muscles a little sore, her body pleasantly sated. Call was already gone.

She found a note from him on the dining room table. *Had some errands to run. Meet me downstairs in the lobby at one o'clock.* It was signed simply, *Call.*

She had hoped to see her aunt in Issaquah. Tracking down the older of the two Doakes sisters had been surprisingly simple. Mavis Doakes was listed in the Issaquah phone directory. Apparently the woman had never married. If she had moved to Boston with her family as a child, at some point in time she must have returned to the place of her birth.

Charity hadn't phoned her yet. She had intended to do it this morning. She stared down at the message, which seemed an odd request. Call's business meeting was scheduled for one P.M. Surely he didn't mean for her to go with him.

Just in case, she dressed in the blue linen suit she had brought, one of the few New York outfits she had taken with her to the Yukon, and mentally postponed her meeting with her aunt until later in the afternoon.

Call was waiting in the lobby when she got there, an expensive belted leather briefcase in one hand. She almost didn't recognize him. His hair was shorter and perfectly groomed, and he was wearing what could only be Armani, a charcoal gray pinstriped suit, white shirt, and yellow power tie. He looked as comfortable in the expensive clothes as he did in his jeans and flannel shirt, and she couldn't help thinking of Max Mason, who wore a tux as easily as he did a camouflage commando uniform.

Call reached down and caught her hand and a little zing went through her.

"Come on," he said. "We need to get into that meeting."

He tugged her forward and she hurried to keep up, her low-heeled blue pumps tapping on the marble floors.

"Surely you're not taking me with you?"

"Actually, I am."

She set back, forcing him to stop. "Why?"

He sighed and turned to face her. "Because I want to make it extremely clear that you're under my protection." He started walking again and this time she didn't slow him down. He paused for an instant outside the door to the conference room, seemed to collect himself, then reached for the heavy brass doorknob.

Call settled a hand at Charity's waist, keeping her close to him as he ushered her into the conference room. As he had planned, the others were already there.

Bruce Wilcox stepped forward, a well-dressed man with sandy brown hair and perceptive green eyes. "Good to see you, Call. I hope this flight went better than the last one."

He smiled. "Much better, I'm happy to say. Good to see you, Bruce." Wilcox had been told about the plane. Being next in line at Datatron, the threat might reach him as well.

Besides Bruce, Charity, and Call, there were three other men in the room—two on one side, one on the other—big, brawny types who kept their backs to the wall and their eyes on the doors and windows. Two had arrived with Ransitch; the other, a man named Ross Henderson, with a thick neck and shaved head, had worked for Call before and was there as security for him and Bruce.

Wilcox introduced him to the small, black-haired man standing a few feet away, Fredrico Ransitch.

"I am happy to meet you," Ransitch said.

Call looked past him, searching for the missing man, taking in the elegant boardroom with its potted palms, gilt-framed pictures, and long mahogany table surrounded by twenty overstuffed chairs. "Where's your brother? He was supposed to come with you."

Bruce Wilcox answered. "Apparently at the last minute Marco Ransitch couldn't make it."

"Really? Well, then, I guess this meeting is over." Call picked up the leather briefcase he had set down on the table. "Perhaps another time."

"Wait!" Fredrico moved in front of him. "Surely you realize I have the authority to speak for my brother."

"Do you? The deal was for both of you to be here." Call eyed the small, dark-skinned man and a thought suddenly struck him. "Unless, of course, Marco isn't aware of the problem." He watched Fredrico's eyes dart nervously away and knew without a doubt that was exactly what was going on.

"My brother . . . he is not involved in this side of the business."

Translation: Marco Ransitch didn't know about the tampering being done on the Wild Card sites. Fredrico was pocketing the extra money and he was there to keep his brother from finding out. Call relaxed a little, knowing the odds had just shifted in his favor.

He gently urged Charity forward. "I'd like you to meet a friend of mine . . . a very good friend . . . Ms. Sinclair."

Fredrico made a polite bow of his head. "A pleasure, Ms. Sinclair." But he looked annoyed that she was there. The fewer people who knew about the cheating he had been doing, the better for him, as far as he was concerned.

Too bad, Freddy, old boy. You should have thought about that when you nearly got both of us killed.

"All right, now that the niceties are over," Call said, "why don't we get down to business?" Seating Charity in a comfortable beige chair, he took a seat beside her and pinned his gaze on Fredrico.

"We all know why we're here, so there's no need to go into detail. Suffice it to say that my employees' illegal intrusion into your business has ceased and will not be resumed under any conditions. Their actions occurred without my knowledge or anyone else's. Whatever information they gleaned is in this briefcase. It'll be returned to you . . . on one condition.''

Fredrico stiffened in his chair. "So now you want more money, is that it?''

"I don't want any of your money, Ransitch. I've got plenty of my own. And the business you're in is making you plenty rich, too.'' Call opened his briefcase, lifted out a thick manila file, and set it down on the table. "What I want is for you to cease your illegal manipulation of gaming software. I want you to run your gambling sites by the book, all nice and legal.''

Small black eyes fixed on Call. Ransitch gritted his jaw.

Call tapped the manila folder. "Oh, and there's one more thing. If anything should happen to me, anyone at Datatron, or anyone in any way under my protection''—he cast a meaningful glance at Charity—"a copy of the information collected will fall into the hands of the authorities . . . and also your brother.''

One of Fredrico's hands fisted on top of the table. For long seconds he said nothing. Then he made a faint, jerky nod of his head. "I will do as you request.''

Call pushed back his chair and stood up. "That's it, then.'' He didn't mention the plane crash or make any accusations. He had no proof and Ransitch would only deny it. "We shouldn't have any more trouble. Right, Fredrico?''

"No more trouble,'' he said.

Call shoved the manila folder toward him across the table. "There's a second copy of this in the hands of an attorney. He knows what to do with it if you don't comply with our agreement.''

Ransitch picked up the file. "I understand.''

Call watched the smaller man walk stiffly out of the room, followed by his pair of oversized bodyguards that dwarfed his small frame even more.

"Congratulations,'' Bruce said, once the door was closed.

Charity smiled at Call. "Yes, that was very impressive. You're a real mover and shaker, Mr. Hawkins, when you put on a suit.''

Call smiled at Charity, then glanced toward the door Fredrico had just gone out. "I didn't want to involve you in this, but the more I thought about it, the more I began to believe you'd be safer if they understood exactly where you fit into all this. To be honest, I felt a whole lot better when I realized what Fredrico was up to."

"You mean that he was cheating his brother."

"Exactly. Marco Ransitch has the reputation of being one tough customer."

"I think we should celebrate," Bruce said. "Have either of you had lunch?"

"I haven't." Call looked over at Charity. "You hungry?" In her pretty blue linen suit, her blond hair swept up and gleaming, she looked good enough to eat. Ah ... but that could wait until later.

"I was hoping to see my aunt this afternoon," she said. "But I suppose having lunch first would be all right."

Call snapped the latches closed on his briefcase, feeling as if they actually did have something to celebrate. "The Georgian Room is fantastic, but I was kind of saving it for tonight." Charity had wandered into the high-ceilinged room yesterday after they had finished their shopping and remarked on the magnificent crystal chandeliers. He had planned to take her there last night, would have ... if they hadn't gotten so pleasantly distracted.

He forced his mind in a different direction. "There's a great little bistro down the block that's usually good."

"The Oyster," Bruce said. "It is good. Charity?"

"Sounds wonderful to me. I'm getting hungrier by the minute."

"When we're done, I'll take you over to see your aunt ... that is, if you don't mind the company."

Charity gave him a dazzling smile and an odd pressure rose in his chest. "I'd love for you to come."

He glanced away, uneasy with the feeling. "All right, then." He turned his attention to the big man still standing, legs splayed, beside the door. "Thanks, Ross. That'll be all for now. I don't think the Ransitch boys will be much of a threat anymore.''

As he picked up his briefcase, he caught a glimpse of Charity's smiling face and his pulse took a leap.

The threat from Wild Card was over.

The biggest danger he faced right now stood only a few feet away.

Thinking how magnificent Call had been in the meeting, Charity turned her attention to the visit with her aunt she hoped to make. Picking up the phone in the conference room, she dialed the number she had found for Mavis Doakes, then crossed her fingers, praying her aunt would pick up, and suddenly she did.

''Hello?''

''Ms. Doakes? Mavis Doakes?''

''Yes?'' The voice sounded old and brittle but not unfriendly.

''You don't know me. My name is Charity Sinclair. I'm your great-niece, your sister Emma's granddaughter.''

A long pause on the other end of the line. ''Well, now, isn't it nice of you to call.''

''I was wondering . . . I'm in Seattle for a couple of days. I was hoping I might stop by and meet you.''

''Well, sure you can, dearest. Whenever you would like.''

Her pulse cranked up. ''How about this afternoon?''

Mavis Doakes agreed and Charity could barely suppress her excitement. Lunch at The Oyster with Call and Bruce Wilcox was interesting and fun, but while the men talked business, her mind kept wandering, straying toward the woman she would meet that afternoon. What would Mavis Doakes be like? What would she know about the past that might help Charity prove she was somehow connected to the Yukon?

''Come on,'' Call finally said. ''I can see the two of us are no competition to a recently discovered great-aunt. I'll have Joseph bring the car around and pick us up out front.''

*   *   *

The scenic drive to the base of the heavily forested Cascade Mountains didn't take long. The views along the way were majestic, with ropy clouds clinging to the hillsides and the air thick with mist. They arrived at the address her aunt had given her and Call guided her up on the old wooden porch.

If Charity could have imagined the perfect great-aunt, Mavis Doakes would have been it. Silver-haired and wrinkled, she was thin and slightly bent, but her smiling face carried a wealth of warmth and it surrounded Charity and Call the moment she opened the door.

"Charity, my dear, come in, come in." Mavis hugged her as she walked into narrow entry. "Emma's grandchild. I can hardly believe it. And look at this handsome man you brought with you. Who is he, dear, your husband?"

Charity's cheeks went warm. "He's a friend, Aunt Mavis, my next-door neighbor, actually. Call Hawkins."

"It's a pleasure to meet you, Ms. Doakes," Call said, gently clasping the old woman's hand in both of his. "I know how much Charity has been looking forward to seeing you."

The older woman actually blushed. "Well, both of you come into the parlor and make yourself comfortable. I've got the kettle on the stove. I'll make us all a nice cup of tea." She shuffled out the door in her lavender flowered housedress, freshly washed and neatly pressed, a little white Peter Pan collar at the neck.

The old, wood-framed house she lived in at the bottom of a hill was probably built in the '20s, the kind with the gabled roof overhanging the porch. The parlor had built-in bookshelves encased by lovely old leaded-glass doors. A colorful knit afghan spread across the back of an overstuffed sofa and hooked rugs covered the hardwood floors.

Mavis brought tea and poured it into pretty little china

cups while Charity told the woman something of herself and her family. She talked about her adventures in the Yukon, and the search she had been making into her past.

"My mom died when I was ten. I knew about Emma, my grandmother, but I only found out about you and Annie Mae a couple of days ago."

A shadow moved over the old woman's face. "I'm afraid my sister passed on last year. She's buried in a cemetery in Seattle."

"Oh, I'm terribly sorry."

The shadow lifted, slowly faded. "It's all right, dear. We all have to leave this earth sooner or later and Annie had a wonderful life while she was here." Mavis told her a little about the life her sister had led and Charity understood that the women had cared for each other deeply.

From there the conversation moved back into the past.

"From what I could piece together, your mother's maiden name was Sarah Thankful Baker. Is that right?"

"Yes, dear. She married my father—your great-grandfather, Sean Doakes—on May the third, in the year of our Lord nineteen hundred and twenty. I remember because they always celebrated that day as if it were very special to both of them."

"What about your grandparents? I'm particularly interested in Thaddeus Baker, your mother's father. I know he was born in 1878. He would have been in his twenties during the Gold Rush. I'm trying to find out if Thaddeus went north in search of gold."

"You mean to Alaska?"

"Skagway, yes. Then on to the Yukon."

Mavis chuckled. She took a sip of her tea, then set the cup back down in its saucer. "No, child, my grandpa never went much farther than that old farm of his just outside Portland. He dearly loved that place. They buried him under a pine tree up on a hill there when he died."

Charity's heart sank. She hadn't realized how much she was counting on this.

Call spoke up just then. "How about someone else in the family? Did anyone you know of take off for the goldfields?"

"Well, now, that's a different question altogether. Granny Frances—she was a Fitzpatrick, you know, Grandpa Baker's second wife—he married her after his first wife died of the pneumonia." She glanced up. "Where was I?"

Charity sat forward on the edge of her chair. "Granny Frances and something about the Gold Rush."

"Oh, that's right. Granny used to talk about her sister Rachael going up there."

Charity almost spilled her tea. "She did?"

"It was kind of a scandal at the time. Granny only talked about it after she got older. Guess it doesn't matter much anymore."

"Why was it a scandal?" Call asked.

"Well, Rachael wasn't married, you see. She fell in love with some no-account gambler named Ian Gallagher and the two of them ran off together."

"And you're sure they went to the goldfields?" Call pressed.

"Oh, sure enough, they did. I've got proof, you see." She levered herself to her feet and trudged out of the living room.

Charity looked hopefully at Call. "At least it's something—isn't it? You don't think it's just coincidence?"

"It's interesting. No doubt about it."

But she knew what he was thinking. Even if Rachael Fitzpatrick had gone to the Yukon, it was Frances who was her blood relation, not Rachael.

Mavis shuffled back into the room. "Rachael brought this back with her all the way from the Klondike." Taking Charity's hand, Mavis set a fat gold nugget in the middle of her palm. "She kept it all her life . . . gave it to Granny Frances just before she died. Granny never sold it . . . not even when times got tough. She said her sister paid a high price for it and she was gonna keep it no matter what. I always thought it was beautiful, so she willed it to me when she passed away."

Charity's fingers closed around the smooth chunk of gold, far bigger than anything they had found on the Lily Rose. She thought of the photo above The Miner's Bar, of the Stampeders trudging up the icy Golden Staircase, and imagined what Rachael must have suffered to get it.

"What happened to Ian? Did he and Rachael ever get married?"

"Not that I know of. Granny never mentioned him and I never thought to ask."

Charity held out the nugget. "Thank you for showing me." She tried to hand it back, but Mavis shook her head.

"I want you to keep it. I'm getting on in years. Never had any children of my own. It would make me and Granny Baker very happy if you would give it to your own children some day."

Charity's eyes filled with tears. "Are you sure?"

"Very sure, dearest."

"Then that's what I'll do—I promise."

Mavis rose from her chair to walk Charity and Call to the door.

"I don't have much family left anymore," Charity said to her aunt. "I wish I didn't live so far away."

"So do I, dear." Mavis turned to Call, reached her bony arms up and hugged him. "You take care of her, now, you hear?"

Call just nodded. Since the successful conclusion of his meeting, he'd been relaxed and at ease, enjoying their celebration lunch, smiling more often than Charity had ever seen him.

Now, with her aunt's harmless words, there was tension in his face once more. Charity sighed, knowing what that tension meant.

You take care of her. The words settled on Call's chest like a six-pound nugget as the limo drove along the hilly streets, returning them to the Four Seasons Hotel. Taking care of someone was a responsibility he no longer wanted.

He had failed at the task before and wound up getting his family killed. He never wanted to risk that kind of failure again.

He said little on the ride through the scenic mountain passes back to Seattle. When they reached the hotel, they left the car and went straight up to the suite. Charity cast him a glance as he walked over to the desk in the corner, sat down, and simply went to work.

Dialing Steve McDonald, the investigator he had hired, Call gave him a rundown on the meeting with Fredrico Ransitch, but didn't pull him off the job. Instead, he instructed the detective to continue his efforts, hoping to confirm Fredrico as the man responsible for the attempt on his life.

Though Call was confident he had put an end to the threat, he wasn't a man who took things for granted.

McDonald said that he would keep digging.

Next, Call dialed Peter Held. He had phoned Peter a couple of times before he left the Yukon, but Held wasn't there and the answering machine had picked up. He'd left a message asking Peter to contact him, but so far hadn't heard from him. With Held still recovering from his injuries, Call had assumed he'd be in town.

Dammit, if Marybeth Allen still worked for him, the meeting would have been set. She would have dogged Peter's tracks until she found him.

The hours slipped past. Determined not to fall into the old, hectic routine that had ruined his life four years ago, and feeling a little guilty for breaking his promise to show Charity the city, he left the desk and walked over to where she sat reading one of her adventure novels. She had changed into jeans and a lightweight sweater, perfect for what he had in mind.

"We've got a couple of hours before we need to get ready for supper. Why don't I have Joseph bring up the car and we'll take in a few of the sights, maybe stop at the Pike Street Market and look around a little?"

Charity gave him one of her heart-stopping smiles. "I'd

love to.'' She set her book down and took hold of his hand and he felt the jolt of awareness she always made him feel.

It was a shot of warning.

Call chose to ignore it.

At least until they got home.

CHAPTER TWENTY-TWO

Seated behind the sleek rosewood desk in the spacious office of his San Francisco headquarters, Gordon Speers turned away from the wall of glass and spectacular view of the Oakland Bay Bridge and turned his attention to his computer screen.

A couple of clicks of the mouse and the latest market data on platinum appeared on the screen in front of him. Today's value, given in U.S. dollars per troy ounce of weight, four hundred and twenty-five dollars.

Platinum, already one of the world's most expensive metals, was getting more costly every day. It was a soft, ductile material, resistant to oxidation and high temperature corrosion. And one of the valuable metal's most rapidly growing applications was in the production of hard-disk storage.

Somewhere around ninety percent of all computer harddisks contained platinum in their magnetic layers. With the constant need for more and more storage, the demand—and the cost—had no place to go but up. It was a dilemma all manufacturers faced, though ultimately the burden would be borne by the purchasers.

Unless someone discovered a way to use a cheaper metal with the same or even higher degree of efficiency.

In which case, Gordon's company, Global Microsystems, and every other manufacturer still forced to use the more expensive product, were going to find themselves in a world of hurt.

The thought stirred a thread of irritation. Reaching into the drawer, Gordon picked up his cell phone and dialed Tony King.

He answered on the first ring.

"I've been expecting to hear from you," Gordon said, letting his annoyance show. "What's going on?"

"Take it easy, everything's under control."

"Is it?"

"I said it was, didn't I? First of all, after a little friendly persuasion, Peter Held decided to take his girlfriend to Hawaii for a long vacation. That buys us some time."

Some good news, at any rate. "Even if it does, it won't stop Hawkins . . . not in the long run."

"I'm still working on that. I've got a man in place."

"The same guy you used before?"

"Stan's good. He just doesn't like being rushed. He likes things neat and clean and so do I."

"That makes three of us. Tell him to take his time. Tell him we want it done right this time."

"Anything else?"

"Everything on this end is running smoothly," Gordon said. "Give my best to Alice and the boys."

Gordon signed off, feeling a little better, grateful as always that Tony was on the job. They made a good team, the two of them. In the next few years, they were going to make millions of dollars. Far more than that, if everything went the way they planned. He could retire in the style he had dreamed of—hundred-foot yachts, magnificent villas, plush private jets.

And his wife's obscenely rich, old money family would finally have to give him the respect he deserved instead of looking down their noses as if he manufactured cheap suits instead of sophisticated software.

Smiling at the thought, Gordon relaxed and turned back to the computer. If he wanted this to go off smoothly, he had his own problems to solve.

At his office in the Bank of America building in downtown L.A., Tony King placed a call to Stan Grossman in Dawson City.

"I'm working on the problem," Stan said from his room at the Aurora Motel. "The guy's a little unpredictable. I've got a couple of possibilities in mind. I'm gonna have to play it by ear."

"I thought you liked to have everything in place."

"I do. Unfortunately, sometimes, you gotta be flexible."

"Held's left town for a couple of weeks. That gives us a little more time."

"Two weeks oughta be enough."

"Make certain it is." Tony hung up the phone. Stan didn't like his chain being jerked, but hey, shit rolled down hill.

He leaned back in his chair, looking at the small, silver-framed photo of Alice and his twin boys, Roger and Tony, Jr. Good-looking boys, he thought—a good-looking family, in fact. Opening one of the drawers, he pulled out a photo of himself and Bridget, his long-time girlfriend, taken last New Year's Eve. She was a tall, voluptuous blonde, a former starlet with tits the size of melons and a mouth like a silk glove.

He didn't keep both photos on the desk in case Alice walked in, but he had a fondness for that particular snapshot of Bridget. In the eye of his mind, he could see her seductive smile and shapely body. He thought of how much money it took to keep her happy and hoped to hell Stan finished the job this time.

*　　*　　*

Life returned to normal on the Lily Rose. The chopper had brought Call and Charity home late last evening, and Kodiak, who had been staying with Smoke and Toby, came bounding into her arms the minute he saw her. Charity hugged his small wriggling body and ruffled his thick brown fur.

Call walked the two of them home, but declined her invitation to stay for supper and the unspoken offer to join her for the night. Something to do with a project he needed to finish, he'd said, and she hadn't seen him since.

She knew it was the closeness. It was always too much for him. She could feel him withdrawing from the moment they left Seattle, knew he was ready to run, but she had hoped this time he wouldn't.

Though she worried about him, she left him alone and settled into her work.

Unfortunately, before they got started, the first problem arose.

"It's that durned dredge," Maude said, sucking on the stem of her empty pipe. "Somethin's wrong with the engine."

"How can there be something wrong with the engine? The darn thing's practically new."

"Well, sometimes you just get a lemon."

Charity walked up the hill with her cell phone to call a mechanic. D. K. Prospecting specialized in mining equipment, but the repair guy couldn't make it out till the end of the week.

"Fine," she said, "then we'll just have to bring it in."

With Toby and Jenny's help, they dragged the heavy dredge out of the water and up on the bank of the creek. It wouldn't fit in the back of the Explorer, so Toby went over to borrow Call's Chevy three-quarter-ton pickup. Call came back with him to help them load it—rather reluctantly, Charity thought—but with all of them lifting, they were able to get the engine into the bed of the truck.

Charity, Jenny, and Toby made the hour-long trip down the mountain to town to drop the engine at the repair shop.

As luck would have it, the mechanic found the problem while they were still there.

"Sand in the gas tank," he said. "Looks like somebody got careless."

Charity frowned. "That's all that's wrong with it?"

"Far as I can tell."

"I should have thought of that," Toby said. "We're always so careful I didn't think to look. I'm sorry, Charity."

"It's not your fault." She sighed. "Crummy buttons—that cost us a whole day's work."

Toby smothered a laugh and even Jenny grinned. "Crummy buttons?" Toby teased.

Charity tossed him a look. "What's wrong with that? It's what my mom always used to say."

Toby chuckled all the way to the truck.

With the dredge running again they decided to make a chow stop at Klondike Kate's—fortunately, the redhead was nowhere in sight—and pick up a few supplies before making their way back up the hill.

Call must have seen them driving past his house. He showed up a few minutes after their return to help with the unloading.

"That was fast," he said. "I thought you'd have to leave it a couple of days."

"Nothing but sand in the gas tank," Charity said.

"I'm surprised Toby didn't find it. He's pretty good with engines."

"I should have," Toby said regretfully. "We're always just so careful when we fill it."

Call helped them get the dredge back into the water, sloshing down from the bank in a pair of khaki hiking shorts that showed off the long, hard muscles in his terrific-looking legs. They were all soaking wet by the time they got the flotation collar back on the machine and had it positioned correctly in the creek.

Call's gaze ran over the wet tee shirt clinging to Charity's breasts, but he made no comment, just excused himself and walked back down the path to his house.

Two days passed. Work was going smoothly but she'd seen no more of Call. She wondered what he was doing, wished he would come over, but didn't really expect him to. She missed him more every day, missed sleeping with him, missed making love to him. It was dangerous thinking, she knew. Eventually she would be leaving the Yukon. Once she returned to New York, she would probably never see Call again.

The thought made her chest ache. It was the first time she had allowed the truth to completely surface and now that it had, it shook her to the core. She was in love with Call. Crazy in love, and she didn't want to leave him. But she couldn't stay in the Yukon forever and even if she could, Call wouldn't want her to.

Her mood grew darker. At night she had trouble sleeping and when she did, she dreamed. Earlier that evening, she had been thinking of her meeting with Aunt Mavis and perhaps that was the reason.

Rachael Fitzpatrick, Aunt Mavis had said, had gone to the Yukon more than a hundred years ago in search of gold. She had returned with a glittering gold nugget as proof of her journey. Rachael was not in Charity's direct line of descent, only a far distant aunt, but considering the search Charity had undertaken and her belief that she had some connection, perhaps even memories of the North, it was interesting nonetheless.

Perhaps thoughts of Rachael were the reason for the dream. Certainly the calm, rational side of her nature said that it was. That night, as she lay deep in slumber, she had dreamed of an avalanche, a crushing mountain of snow that cracked away from the rest and slammed down the hill. She had dreamed of a man dressed head to foot in heavy woolen clothes being buried beneath the tumbling weight of the snow. People rushed toward him, digging furiously in the place he had been.

In the dream, she seemed to be one of them. She could feel their pain and frustration, feel their terrible grief at his loss.

One woman in particular stood out, though she couldn't see her face. Even after Charity awakened, her heart pounding wildly and her nightgown damp with perspiration, she could see the woman frantically digging in the snow. Her skirt was wet and clinging to the soggy woolen petticoats she wore to keep warm, her fingers frozen, and her heart . . . her heart felt as if it were breaking in two.

Charity sighed as she thought about it later. Dreams were funny things. Anything could set them off.

Still, as she lifted the shiny gold nugget out of her dresser drawer and watched it gleam in the morning sunlight, she couldn't help wondering if she had missed something in her search, and if in some deep, hidden corner of her mind, the dream wasn't part of a long-ago memory.

Another day passed. Call never appeared and her black mood continued to spiral downward. Not one to mope around, she decided to do something about it and finally suggested they quit work early Wednesday afternoon, make the trip into town, and take in a matinee.

"Besides, we're getting low on vegetables and milk," she said to the small group standing at the bottom of the porch. "I should have picked some up when we went in to Dawson to fix the engine, but I was thinking about the dredge and I forgot. What do you say?"

"I need to check with Call," Toby said, "see if he needs me this afternoon. If I can get away, that'd be great."

Even Maude agreed to go. As soon as they spotted Toby returning down the path, grinning and giving them two thumbs up, they all jumped into the Explorer. Charity put the Ford in gear, circled around, and they were off.

They were crossing the rickety wooden bridge over the creek when she heard a loud, wrenching, groaning sound and the back of the Ford seemed to simply drop out from beneath them.

Charity and Jenny both screamed as the bridge collapsed at one end, a drop of about four feet, hit with a bone-jarring jolt, and the car started sliding backward into the stream. Water began rushing past the wheels, lifting the rear end up and moving it off the bridge, angling it sideways till the tires wedged into a cluster of rocks. Fortunately, it was summer and the water wasn't all that deep. Charity realized they weren't in any real danger and heaved a sigh of relief.

She glanced across at Maude, sitting next to her in the passenger seat. "Guess I should have got the bridge fixed like I planned," she said.

Maude looked out the front windshield, which angled upward, giving them a view of the sky. "Good thing it ain't the rainy season."

In the backseat, Jenny giggled.

Charity looked over at Maude and all of them burst out laughing.

They finally brought themselves under control and Charity sighed. "Come on, guys. I guess we aren't going to town after all."

They got out of the car, sloshed through the water, and climbed up onto the road on the opposite side of the property to study the problem.

"Got any ideas?" she said to the group.

"Call's got a winch on his Jeep. I'll go get him."

Charity's heart kicked up as Toby jogged off down the dirt road toward his house. She hadn't seen Call in days. She knew he would come to their aid and anticipation poured through her. Damn. She was in worse shape than she thought.

It wasn't long before Call's black Jeep appeared. When he reached the bridge, he pulled over and turned off the engine. Charity watched as he got out of the car to study the problem and raked a hand through his hair.

God, he looked so good.

"Can you help us get it out?" Charity asked, trying to act casual and praying that he could.

"Yeah, no problem."

Relief filtered through her and something more, something that made her heart flutter oddly. Dressed in a dark green tee shirt and khaki hiking shorts, he unrolled a length of cable from the big metal winch on the front of his Jeep, walked over to the Explorer, and attached the hook at the end of the line to the tow hook under the front bumper.

As soon as the controls were engaged, the wheel began to turn, recoiling the cable, dragging the Ford out of the water and back up on the bridge. Little by little, the winch hauled the Explorer up the ramp formed by the old wooden planking onto the dirt road on the far side of Dead Horse Creek.

"I should have had it fixed," Charity said, trying not to look at Call, afraid he would see how much she had missed him.

Call took off his hiking boots and socks, preparing to go into the water to examine the damage to the bridge. "I know it looked ready to fall down any minute, but ol' Mose had it all reinforced just a couple of years ago." Walking past her, he went down the bank and sloshed into the creek, pausing where the wood had broken apart, examining first one side and then the other.

"Come here and look at this, Charity."

She was wearing khaki shorts like his, the kind with all the pockets, her legs lightly tanned from working in the long hours of sun. She did as he had—removed her tennis shoes and socks and waded into the creek, which was still darned cold even with the hot July weather. "What is it?"

"This is where it broke. See how it splintered?"

"I see it."

"Look how smooth the wood is right here."

She reached down and studied the broken edge of the wood, felt a small, uneasy shiver. "It looks like someone cut it."

"Exactly. It's rough and uneven where it splintered, smooth where it was sawed. Someone cut it partway through. Eventually it was bound to collapse—and it did."

A little streak of fear slid through her. "You don't think this has anything to do with—"

"No. Even if the bridge had gone down all the way, this time of year, there wasn't much danger of anyone getting hurt." He took her hand and helped her climb back up the bank to the road where her Ford was parked.

"A couple of days ago, the engine on your dredge went out. Today the bridge went down." He looked up the hill toward the north side of the property. "I think someone wants to teach you a lesson."

Charity's gaze followed his and she knew in an instant who had cut the bridge. "Buck."

"That'd be my guess. He was furious the day you fired him. I guess he wants to pay you back . . . or maybe show you how much you need him to help you run the Lily Rose." Call started walking toward his Jeep. "I think I'll have another little talk with your former employee."

Charity fell in beside him. "I'm going with you."

He looked down at her and she thought he was going to argue. Instead, he nodded. "Let me unhook the winch and we'll go have our little chat."

Toby stood next to Maude and Jenny as the Jeep rolled up the hill in a cloud of dust. "Since we can't get Charity's car back to the cabin, why don't we drive it over to Call's, at least get it off the road. We can have something cold to drink while we're waiting for them to get back."

"You two go on," Maude said. "I'll just take myself on home. Can't get my truck 'cross the creek till the bridge is fixed, and the walk'll do me good."

"You sure, Grama?"

"Go on with Toby. Charity give us the afternoon off. Might as well make some use of it."

Toby could have kissed her. He had asked Jenny to go into town with him Friday night, but she had refused, and he had ended up waiting for Call to get home from Seattle and going in the following morning. It was obvious Jenny still felt shy around him, though he thought she was beginning to like him.

She sure looked pretty today, with her light brown curls all windblown and her cheeks glowing from the sun. He tried to keep his eyes on her face. Her tank top had gotten wet in the river and he could see the outline of her breasts and the hard little points of her nipples.

"You think Buck Johnson sawed down the bridge?" she asked as he helped her into the front seat of the Explorer, careful not to look at anything he shouldn't.

"He's the kind of guy who would." Toby slammed the door, rounded the car to the driver's side, got in and cranked the engine.

"He seems like a mean one," Jenny said. "I knew some-one like that once."

Toby flicked her a glance as he drove the Explorer down the dirt road and turned onto the sturdy metal bridge Call had constructed in front of his house.

"Who was he?" Toby parked on a pad beside the garage and turned off the engine.

"A boy I used to date."

When she didn't say more, he helped her out of the car and took hold of her hand. "What was his name . . . the guy you used to date?"

Jenny stared down at her hiking books. She had really small feet. "Gerald Rollins. Everyone called him Jazz." She looked up at him. "I thought he was really cool at first. He was four years older than me . . . so mature, I thought. He wore lots of leather and he smoked. I thought I was cool, too, just because he was interested in someone like me."

He tightened his hold on her hand. "Any guy with half a brain would be interested in you, Jenny. Don't you know that?"

They didn't go inside the house, but skirted the buildings and went out in the back. There was a cedar deck out there and a rocky little feeder stream that ran across the yard and drained into the creek. They sat down on the wooden swing and Toby began to gently rock it.

"Why'd you break up with him?" he asked, somehow knowing the guy she was talking about was involved in the sadness that seemed to haunt her.

Jenny looked down at her hands. They were dainty, just like her feet. "He beat me up."

Toby stiffened, stopped moving the swing.

"It happened more than once," Jenny said softly. "Every time it did, Jazz would say he was sorry, that he loved me so much he couldn't live without me. He begged me to forgive me and like a fool, I did. If it hadn't been for my dad . . ." She broke off, shook her head.

Toby's arm rested on the back of the swing and he settled it around her shoulders, easing her against him.

"Not all guys are like that, Jenny. I'd never hurt you. I'd never do anything to make you unhappy."

She leaned her head against his shoulder. "I don't think you would ever hurt anyone, Toby."

Her hair smelled like sunshine. He nuzzled his nose in the downy-soft curls, inhaled the clean fragrance. "Is that the reason you came up here?"

Tension crept into her shoulders. "One of the reasons."

She slowly eased away from him and he didn't try to stop her. He could see she had said all she would and he didn't want to scare her away.

"Still want that soft drink?" he asked.

Jenny smiled. "I'd love one."

Toby got up to get it though he didn't really want to leave. He glanced at Jenny one last time, saw her sitting there stiffly, the swing unmoving. Her smile was gone and the sadness was back in her face.

CHAPTER
TWENTY-THREE

Call drove up in Buck's front yard, stirring up dust as he slammed on the brake. He and Charity both climbed out of the Jeep and he led her to the door. The house was a simple, wood-frame structure painted gray with peeling white trim. What had once been flowerboxes sitting neatly beneath the windows were now overgrown with weeds. When Betty Johnson lived there, the place had probably looked a lot better.

Call pounded on the door but no one answered.

He hammered away again and heard the sound of Buck's heavy footfalls coming toward them across the living room floor. Dressed in a frayed white undershirt and a pair of dirty coveralls, Buck pulled open the door.

His busy dark eyebrows slammed together. "What do you want?"

Call's jaw hardened. "I think you know what I want. It seems Ms. Sinclair has been having some problems. I thought you understood what would happen to you if you gave her any kind of trouble."

Buck's barrel chest swelled. "I don't know what you're

talking about.'' Kinky brown hair on his back and shoulders curled around the straps of his undershirt.

"So you aren't the one who put sand in the engine of the dredge? You didn't go over there while she was out of town and cut the supports on her bridge?"

Buck's jaw went slack. He looked stunned. "No. No, I didn't. I didn't do none of those things.''

Call felt Charity's presence beside him. She stared past Buck into the darkness inside the house. "Where's Tyler?"

Buck's eyes darted over her head. "Ty's ... Ty's gone into town.''

Call's thoughts mirrored Charity's. "But he's staying here now. He's out here for the summer. He was here this week-end while Charity was away.''

Buck edged backward as if he wanted to run inside and slam the door. "My boy wouldn't do those things, neither.''

"Who're you trying to kid, Buck? Your boy's got a mean streak wider than the one you've got.''

"You're wrong. He's a good boy, Ty is.''

"Yeah, well, that good boy of yours is about to be carted off to jail.'' Gripping Charity's arm, Call turned and started walking.

"Wait a minute!'' Buck called after them. "You can't do that.''

Call stopped and turned. "Someone's stirring up trouble on the Lily Rose. Ty's been in this kind of trouble before, and since Ms. Sinclair fired you—his father—the week before, he's got a motive. You think the Mounties aren't going to know exactly who's behind this?''

Buck's glance flicked for an instant toward the living room and Call realized the kid must be inside.

"Listen ... Hear me out. Tyler's already on probation for some problems he had down in Whitehorse. You bring in the Mounties, they'll put him in prison.''

"He should have thought of that before he destroyed the bridge.'' Call tossed a glance at Charity and they started walking away.

"What if he makes it right? What if he fixes the bridge?''

"Not good enough," Call said. "Not this time."

"Okay, okay." Buck turned around and spoke into the darkened living room. "You better come out here, son."

There was some low, grumbling conversation, and a few minutes later, Tyler Johnson appeared in the doorway.

"All right, all right. Look, it was a joke, okay? A couple of my buddies came out for the weekend and we got a little drunk. We thought it would be funny."

Beside him, Charity's back went rigid. "I'm sure it was hilarious—to you and your friends. It wasn't a bit funny to Call, who had to spend his time winching my car out of the creek."

"Okay—so I'll pay you back."

"How?" Call asked.

"I told you, I got friends. I'll borrow the money from them."

"I'll tell you what . . ." Call gave him a smile that wasn't a smile at all. "You and your *buddies* go down to the Lily Rose and fix that bridge. You've got a week to get it done. If it isn't finished by then, we're calling the authorities and you and your friends can deal with them instead of me."

"Wait a minute!"

"And you'll also work enough to pay the cost of fixing that engine. Take it or leave it."

Tyler clamped down on his jaw.

Buck stuck a thumb beneath the strap of his undershirt and began to slide it between his thick fingers. "You'd better do it, boy."

Ty glared at Call, then dragged in a breath and slowly nodded. "All right, dammit. I'll fix the goddamn bridge."

"And you'll watch your language in front of Ms. Sinclair."

Tyler ground his teeth.

"You start in the morning. Be there at seven and don't be late." Call settled a hand at Charity's waist, wishing he could pop the little smart ass a good one. *That's what you get,* he thought, *when you let your children run wild.* If ever there was a kid who needed a good, old-fashioned licking, it was Tyler Johnson.

He glanced down at Charity, walking silently beside him. Her blond hair fell like a golden curtain around her slender shoulders and her waist felt small and curvy beneath his hand. He wished he wasn't so damned glad to see her.

"I'm sorry that happened," he said, hoping he had put an end to her troubles.

She looked up at him and smiled. "Thanks for helping."

"I don't trust that kid. For that matter, I don't trust either one of them."

"Neither do I."

"Ty's really pissed off. He might do something even more idiotic than cutting down your bridge. Maybe I'd better spend the night." The words were out of his mouth before he realized he was going to say them. The truth was, he wanted to stay. He wanted to sleep with her, wanted to wake up with her. He had missed making love to her and he didn't even mind Mose's too-short iron bed if Charity was in it. He hated feeling that way, but he did.

She was looking up at him, smiling so brightly his chest began to feel tight.

"I think that might be a good idea," she said, and he wondered if she had missed him, too. "I'll fix dinner if you bring over a bottle of wine."

He relaxed, found himself smiling back at her. Charity had made that easy to do when it used to be so hard. "Deal."

By a little after six, he was back at her cabin, sitting at the table in the kitchen while she worked at making them supper. She was wearing shorts and he admired her long, shapely legs, nicely tanned now, maybe a little more sleekly muscled from her hours of hard work. He wanted to run his hands over her delectable little body, along the inside of her thighs, right up under the hem of her shorts. He knew what he would find there, knew the softness, the dampness that would surface when he touched her, and his shaft went achingly hard.

He wanted her, dammit, wanted to forget about supper

and make love to her, but it didn't seem fair to Charity, not when he'd gone out of his way to avoid her all week.

He had never been so physically attracted to a woman, never felt the constant edge of desire she aroused in him, but he wasn't going to allow that attraction to become any more than that.

He reminded himself he had nothing to worry about, that Charity would be leaving in a few more months and that would be the end of the affair.

It should have consoled him.

It didn't.

They drank a bottle of wine and ate the pork chops she fried in an old iron skillet on the woodstove, along with a can of string beans. Not exactly the Georgian Room, Charity thought, but the food was filling and it actually tasted pretty good.

All through the meal, Call watched her and she wondered if he were wishing supper was over as much as she was. Whenever they were together, her sex drive kicked in big time. She had certainly never hungered for Jeremy the way she did Call. Maybe it was breathing all this clean, invigorating Klondike air.

Whatever it was, as soon as the dishes were cleared, washed, and dried, Call led her into the living room and kissed her and she melted into his arms. She didn't resist when he carried her into the bedroom, stripped away her clothes and his own, and settled her in the middle of Mose's old iron bed.

They made love greedily the first time, then again more slowly. The sex was great as always. Perhaps that was the lure that kept Call coming back.

Charity hoped it was more than that. And yet, even if his interest went beyond mere physical attraction, she wasn't sure what it would mean to either one of them. She tried not to worry about leaving, or whether Call would run from his feelings again in the morning. She tried not to think of anything but the feel of his arms around her as she drifted off to sleep.

The night hours slid past. Her slumber was deep and drugging, a dense sort of blackness that engulfed her, sucking her into some fathomless, dark netherworld unlike any she could remember. No dreams interfered. Call didn't use his marvelous skills to arouse her in the middle of the night. Even the creaking of the old log house didn't reach her.

In fact, nothing would have penetrated the heavy dark haze of her sleep if it hadn't been for Kodiak's sharp, unrelenting barking. She didn't hear it at first, lying there so deeply asleep, but eventually the piercing little yelps began to reach her.

Charity stirred, tried to open her eyes, found it nearly impossible. It felt as if lead weights were attached to her lids and ground glass scraped against her eyeballs.

Kodiak kept barking and Charity forced her eyes slowly open. They instantly filled with tears and her lungs began to burn. Her head swam and it took a moment to realize the room was full of smoke.

"Call! Call, wake up!" Her throat felt scratchy. She moistened her lips, dragged herself up on the bed, and started coughing. Through the open door to the living room, she could see the lick of bright, red-orange flames eating through the ceiling, and pure terror jolted her into action.

"Call!" She gripped his bare shoulder and shook him, coughing, fighting to breathe, her eyes watering, scratchy with grit and soot. "Call! The house is on fire!" He was as deeply asleep as she had been and it seemed to take forever for his eyes to crack open.

"The house is on fire!" She started coughing and wheezing. "We have to get out of here!"

He started moving then, saw the flames, started coughing, too. Reaching out, he gently squeezed her hand. "Grab something to put on and let's go." He picked up the jeans he had worn to supper and Charity grabbed the tee shirt, jeans, tennis shoes, and socks that she'd had on.

Call opened the window, lifted Kodiak out, boosted Charity out, then climbed out himself. They ran a safe distance from the cabin, their eyes still streaming tears, before they stopped and hastily pulled on their clothes.

They finished just as Toby came racing up the path carrying a portable pump and a length of fire hose.

Call turned his attention to her. "You have any fire equipment?"

"I don't know. I don't think so. Oh, God, I should have thought of it." Her hands were trembling. Kodiak had stopped barking, but his small body pressed nervously against her leg. She ran a trembling hand through his fur, thinking what would have happened if the puppy hadn't awakened them.

Call reached for the pump Toby carried and he quickly handed it over. "I'll start the pump," Call said. "Go see what you can find in the workshop." Toby raced off in that direction while Call carried the pump down the bank and plunged the apparatus into the creek.

A good-sized stream of water hit the house a few minutes later. Toby returned with a couple of fire extinguishers, and quickly set to work outside the cabin.

"Dammit, we need more water if we're going to put this out."

"How about the dredge?" Charity suggested, trying to suppress the sick feeling inside her. "Can't we use it somehow?"

"We could if we had an adapter of some kind."

She shook her head. "Not . . . not that I know of."

The flames were rising and Charity kept thinking of all the work she and Maude had done on the cabin, of Mose and how much the place had meant to him. Fresh tears burned and she clamped down on her jaw, determined not to cry.

Call kept spraying the house, but it was obvious they were losing the battle. The last person she expected to see running down the path from the north end of the property was Buck Johnson.

He and Tyler were carrying the same kind of pump and fire

hose Toby had brought and a couple more fire extinguishers. Buck plunged the pump into the stream and fired it up and water shot up on the burning porch. Ty moved toward the wall outside the kitchen next to Toby and started spraying foam around the windows.

In a corner of her mind, she had believed that maybe Ty had started the fire, but now she wondered. The cabin was old and things like that happened. As the blaze continued to burn and the men kept working, Charity sloshed into the water next to Call to help hold the pump, and little by little the flames began to weaken and come under control.

Over the hill to the east, the sun was coming up though technically it was still night, and she could see the smoldering remains more clearly. It seemed like a miracle that any of the cabin remained, but part of the living room still stood, the big rock fireplace, and part of the bedroom and bathroom.

Her throat closed up at the ghostly sight it made. Wet, smoke-blackened, and tired to the bone, Charity sloshed out of the creek, sank down on the ground, buried her head in her hands, and started to weep.

Exhausted and covered with soot, Call slogged out of the water. A little way farther down the stream, Buck Johnson hauled his fire gear out of the creek.

As Call dumped his equipment onto the bank, he could hear Charity weeping and it made his stomach churn. He needed to go to her but first there was something he had to do.

Jaw set, he started walking. "What the hell is going on, Buck?"

Buck looked up from where he knelt, repacking his gear. "What do you mean?"

"Come on, Johnson. Odds are, either you or Tyler started that fire. Why the hell did you come down to help put it out?"

Buck's thick eyebrows drew into a frown. "We didn't

have nothing to do with this. Both of us were sleeping. Ty got up to go to the john and he saw the flames.''

Call pinned him with a disbelieving glare.

"I'm not proud of what I did to the girl. I was stupid drunk. I know it isn't an excuse. I got a little crazy, thinking of Betty, I guess.'' He cleared his throat, glanced away. "I'm glad you both got out all right. I mean that, I really do.''

Call watched him closely, beginning to believe Buck was telling the truth. Maybe the fire was an accident. It wasn't impossible, and Buck had certainly done his best to help put out the blaze.

"Old Mose's cabin is practically a landmark up here,'' Buck said a little gruffly. "I couldn't just sit by and watch it burn. And the woman . . . she's paid her dues up here.''

Call nodded, surprised by the note of sincerity. "All right, for now, we'll assume that's the truth. If I find out something different, you can expect to be hearing from the authorities.'' He wasn't sure yet what had happened tonight, but he intended to find out. And Buck had better not be involved.

He spoke to Ty, got the same story told with what seemed actual regret, then returned to where Charity sat slumped over on the bank of the creek. He could see she was crying and a muscle tightened in his cheek. They had damned near been killed tonight. It made him feel shaky inside to think just how close they had come.

Too many accidents, he thought.

Though maybe this one actually was. The cabin was old, propane tanks leaked, chimneys filled up with soot, things happened. Or maybe it was another of Tyler's pranks that simply got out of hand.

Still, until he knew the truth, he wasn't taking any more chances. He would call Ross Henderson as soon as he got back to the house, have him get a security team up here as fast as he could.

With that decision made and Buck and Tyler headed back up the path to their house, Call sat down on the grass next to Charity and eased her into his arms.

"It's all right, baby, don't cry. The fire's out and we're safe. That's all that really matters."

She leaned into him, put her arms around his neck, and simply clung to him. He could feel her shaking with silent sobs and his heart squeezed hard.

She looked up at him, her face covered with soot and her eyes filled with tears. "It's over," she whispered in a husky, smoke-roughened voice. "We all worked so hard and now . . . in a matter of minutes . . . it's over."

He looked at the smoldering ruins of old Mose's cabin. "Did you have any insurance?"

She shook her head. "The cabin was worthless . . . to anyone but me." She dragged in a ragged breath and fresh tears ran down her cheeks. "I wasn't ready to leave. I wasn't finished with my adventure." She pressed her face into his shoulder and started crying again and it hit him that she intended to go back to Manhattan.

A dozen different emotions ran through him. Regret, loss, need—others he couldn't name. One thing was clear. He didn't want her to go. Not yet.

He stroked a hand over her hair, still mussed from their earlier lovemaking. "Don't decide anything now. You can stay with me until you get things worked out." He was thinking of her but also the cabin, thinking that maybe with his help she could rebuild. It's what old Mose would want.

Charity made a negative movement of her head. "I don't know, Call. Maybe I should just give up and go home."

He caught her chin between his fingers. "Is that what you want?"

She glanced down, twisted the hem of her water-soaked tee shirt. "I don't know anymore. I'll have to go back eventually. Maybe it would be better if I just left now."

He didn't like the way the words made him feel, as if the air was being squeezed out of his lungs. "You don't have to decide tonight. Take some time . . . a few days at least, then make your decision."

She swallowed, mustered a shaky nod. "All right."

He felt a sweep of relief that made him as dizzy as he'd

been in that smoke-filled room. Gathering her close against his chest, he thought again of the fire and their narrow escape. What if the fire had been set? If it wasn't Buck or Ty, it might be the same guy who sabotaged his plane.

Maybe Charity should go back to Manhattan. Maybe she would be safer.

Maybe she wouldn't.

He looked over at her and prayed that convincing her to stay was the right thing to do.

It was six o'clock that morning when Toby heard the knock and opened the door to a terrified Maude and Jenny.

"She's fine," he said, before they could get out the words. "They both are."

Relief swept over their faces and they hugged each other briefly. "Thank the good Lord for that," Maude said.

"Come on in. They're still asleep. I'm fixing them some breakfast, but I don't want to wake them yet."

"How'd it happen?" Maude asked.

"We don't know yet. They were sleeping. Kodiak woke them up."

Jenny's pretty green eyes went round. "Oh, my God, the puppy saved them?"

"Looks that way. Buck and Call used the fire pumps in the creek to put it out."

"Buck?" Jenny repeated.

"Yeah. Kinda weird. We were all sort of thinking maybe he set the fire, but it doesn't look that way."

"What about that no-account son of his?" Maude asked. "Charity said he was spittin' mad about havin' to fix the bridge."

"Call talked to both of them. He doesn't think they had anything to do with it."

"Maybe it was an accident," Jenny said.

"Maybe." But Toby didn't really believe it and he didn't think Call did, either.

"I guess we ain't got a job no more," Maude said with

a downcast shake of her head. "And we was just gettin' close to somethin' big. I could smell it."

Call and Charity wandered into the room just then, Call in a clean pair of jeans and a white cotton tee shirt, Charity wearing one of Call's robes.

"I don't see why you have to stop," Call said to her. "The dredging equipment still works. You didn't lose anything you need to run your operation."

Charity didn't look convinced. In fact, she looked downright heartsick. "I'll think about it."

"Buck called Mose's cabin a landmark," Call said casually, though Toby had the feeling it wasn't a casual remark. "Mose once told me part of the original structure dates back to the Gold Rush days. I think it'd make him feel real bad if it didn't get rebuilt."

Charity looked up at him, alert for the first time since she had walked into the living room. "I can't rebuild. I don't have that kind of money."

"I do," Call said.

"I can't take your money, Call. I won't. Not even for that."

"All right, if that's the way you feel. Maybe we could work something out ... an option or something. You're planning to leave eventually. I've always wanted to buy the place. Maybe you could agree to sell it to me when you're ready to head back to the city."

He said it as if the idea had just cropped up, but Toby knew him better than that. Call had the money to rebuild the cabin and he knew how much Charity had come to love the old place. And whether Call was willing to admit it or not, he wanted Charity to stay.

"I-I don't know."

"Grama and I would help," Jenny said excitedly. "And if Mr. Hawkins doesn't mind, I'm sure Toby would pitch in, too." She looked at him as if he were the kind of man she could count on and Toby felt an odd little quiver around his heart.

"Jenny's right," Toby agreed. "All of us would help. It

might be fun to build a real log cabin—and part of it is already there.''

"You've got time to decide," Call said gently. "You don't have to start building today."

"That's right," Maude said. "Next week would be just fine."

Toby looked at Jenny and both of them laughed. Charity actually smiled. Then her smile slowly faded. "I appreciate the offer, but I'll still need some time to think about it."

Call frowned and Toby inwardly grinned. McCall Hawkins hadn't become one of the most successful men in the country by taking no for an answer. Toby wondered how long it would be before the first truckload of logs came rolling up the hill.

CHAPTER TWENTY-FOUR

Though still hot in places, the blackened, water-soaked wood had cooled enough by late afternoon to allow them inside the cabin. While Call made a second pass around the burned-out shell, Toby poked around in the living room and Charity worked in the bedroom, trying to salvage some of her clothes and possessions.

"Hey, Call, come over here a minute."

At the sound of Toby's voice, Call tossed away the burnt piece of wood he was examining and joined the younger man in what had once been the living room. The kitchen was completely gone, the wood plank floor burned almost all the way to the fireplace. An area in front of the hearth remained intact and that's where Toby stood, holding a burnt scrap of carpet.

"What is it?"

"A piece of the throw rug Charity had in front of the sofa." He handed the blackened remnant to Call. "Smell it."

Call bent his head and took a whiff. His insides tightened at the distinctive odor of gasoline.

"The front-room windows don't have any locks," Toby

told him. "All you'd have to do is push them up and you could get in. I think the guy opened the window, threw gas on the sofa and curtains, and tossed in a match. This wasn't an accident, Call."

His fingers tightened around the burnt chunk of carpet. "No, apparently it wasn't."

Charity walked out of the bedroom just then, her arms filled with water-soaked clothes. She stuffed them into one of the plastic bags they had brought to hold anything they might be able to salvage. She pocketed the heavy gold nugget she had rescued from her scorched dresser drawer and looked up at their solemn faces.

"All right, what's going on?"

Call handed her the chunk of carpet and headed for the bedroom. Charity followed him in.

"This window is locked," he said, checking out the old brass mechanism, as solid as the day it was first put on. "The one we escaped through last night was locked, too. I remember having trouble with the latch."

He walked into the bathroom, found that window solidly bolted as well. "Did the kitchen window have a lock?"

"Yes, but it was broken. The living room windows never had them. I meant to put some on after what happened with Buck, but I never quite got around to it."

"Maybe you should have."

Her look turned uncertain. "Why?"

"Smell that piece of carpet you've got in your hand."

She took a whiff. "Oh, my God—gasoline!" Her hands started shaking. "You think Buck or Tyler—"

"No. To tell you the truth, I don't think they had anything to do with this. The things Ty did were pranks, fairly harmless, nothing as lethal as this. Of course, I could be wrong."

"But if they didn't do it, who did?"

"Maybe someone who wanted Buck or Tyler to take the fall. Or at least come under suspicion."

Charity frowned. "If that's the case, that person or persons would have to have been watching the house. They'd have to know about the sand in the engine and what Ty did to the bridge." He noticed that she was trembling and inwardly cursed, knowing he was probably responsible for what had occurred last night. The thought made his insides tighten.

"That's right, they'd have to know," he said. "And they would have known I was staying in the cabin last night."

She glanced around the blackened walls of what had been her home. "You're not ... you're not thinking this is the same person who sabotaged your plane?"

He followed her gaze around the bedroom and a memory returned of the little dog's frantic barking and the room filled with deadly smoke. "It's beginning to look that way. We figure out who tampered with my plane, we'll know the answer to this."

Charity came toward him, her face drawn and pale. "You're scaring me, Call. What are we going to do?"

He couldn't resist reaching out and pulling her into his arms. "Ross Henderson is already on it. He's putting together a three-man team. They ought to be here by tonight. Once they are, we'll have protection round the clock."

He led her outside, into the fresh air and sunshine. Though being outdoors made him feel better, he found himself surveying the surrounding hills. Knowing their assailant might be somewhere out there, he guided her behind the protective cover of a nearby tree.

"I've been thinking about what you said, Charity, about going back to Manhattan ..."

"You think I should leave?"

"It might be safer."

She looked up at him. There was something in her face he couldn't quite read. "It seems to me that *might* is the key word here. There's still no way to know for sure that the threat has nothing to do with me."

"No, there's no way to know that for sure. At least not yet."

"Then I'd rather stay here."

Call felt oddly relieved. As certain as he was that his pursuers were only interested in him, Charity *had* been involved in both attempts. He could set up protection for her in Manhattan, but if anything happened, he would be thousands of miles away. He felt better having her here, where he could watch out for her safety himself.

It bothered him to think that she was now his responsibility, that at least for the present her protection was up to him. Susan's image flickered in the back of his mind, but he forced it away. He wouldn't fail Charity the way he had Susan. No matter what it took, he intended to keep her safe.

With a hand at her waist, he led her back to the house, Toby walking beside them. Charity headed for the washing machine in the mudroom to launder whatever soggy, smoky clothes she had been able to retrieve from the cabin, and Toby went in to thaw something for supper.

As soon as the two were gone, Call checked the doors and windows to be sure they were secure, then took his rifle down from the gun rack. He checked to see that it was fully loaded and placed it back in the rack. He needed to get Toby down the hill and out of danger, but he wouldn't let the boy out of his sight until Ross and his men had arrived.

Knowing the security team was on its way and needing to do something useful, Call headed for his office. His first phone call went to the Dawson City police. The Mounties promised to get there as quickly as they could. Next he dialed a camera surveillance firm in San Jose that he had done business with before.

Thinking of another destructive blaze in the not-too-distant past and never a believer in coincidence, he phoned the Seattle Police Department and asked for Karl Miller, the head of the arson squad.

"I'm glad you called," Miller said. "We just wound up our investigation on that fire in your lab. You were right. We located a spot where the wiring was tampered with. It was an electrical fire, all right, but it had a little help getting started. The guy was a real pro or we wouldn't have missed it the first time."

With that information, several pieces of the puzzle slid into place. It wasn't problems with Datatron, Ransitch, and Wild Card that were behind the first attempt on his life.

Someone wanted to stop MegaTech from developing a cheaper, more efficient method of hard-disk storage.

He hadn't believed the discovery would be motivation enough for someone to want him dead. Obviously he had been wrong. First the lab had been destroyed, causing a temporary setback. Then Peter Held was mugged, putting the young chemist out of commission, at least for a while. But ultimately, it was Call they needed to eliminate.

The question now was, who?

"Any ideas who might have set the fire?" Call asked Miller, forcing his thoughts back to the man on the other end of the line.

"Not yet, but we're on it."

Call thanked the detective for his help, hung up, and dialed Steve McDonald. He told the P.I. about the arson fire at the lab and the nearly fatal blaze in the cabin.

"Sounds like we've been looking in the wrong direction," Steve said.

"That's what I'd say."

"You talked to Peter Held?"

"No, but I intend to. As soon as he gets back to Seattle. Unfortunately, I can't seem to find him. See if you can track him down, will you?" Call thought of the mugging Peter had suffered—or at least allegedly suffered. He was beginning to think Held knew more than he was willing to admit. Call had some hard questions for Peter. He wanted them answered—and soon.

As he disconnected the phone, he thought of Charity at work in the laundry and knew he wouldn't rest easy until Ross Henderson and his team arrived. He ran a hand through his hair and sighed, more tired than he should have been. He wouldn't get a good night's sleep until this whole thing was over and there was no way of telling when that might be.

Shoving back his chair, he made his way to the mudroom. Charity closed the dryer door, looked up at him, and he realized she was as worried as he.

"I guess going for a walk would be out of the question," she said.

God, he could use a good long walk himself. "It wouldn't be the best idea. At least not until security gets here." He reached for her, drew her gently into his arms. "Toby's working on supper. Maybe we can find something to do in the meantime."

She showed a spark of interest. "How about a game of King Cobra?"

Not exactly what he had in mind, but it would have to do. "I don't know if you could handle it. I'm pretty tough to beat."

Charity went up on her tiptoes and kissed his cheek, nibbled softly on his earlobe. "There's a different kind of game I'd like to play first." She caught his face between her hands and gave him a deep, open-mouthed kiss.

He didn't have time for this. He needed to go over the list of companies who would be hurt by MegaTech's hard-disk development project, but he had done it once already and he had let business ruin his life before.

Call kissed her back. Lifting Charity into his arms, he started toward the hall, mentally rearranging his schedule.

Stan Grossman stood hidden in the trees near the top of the sloping hill at the back of the house. Through the branches off to one side, he could see the burned-out remains of the old log cabin.

Stan swore softly. *Sonofabitch.* Tony was gonna shit a brick when he found out Stan had botched the job again. *For chrissake, who'da figured the damn dog would wake them up?* But Stan had heard the little dog barking. They must have gone out the window before the neighbors arrived to put out the fire. To make matters worse, the way Hawkins had been prowling around the place this afternoon, there was a good chance he had figured out it wasn't an accident.

Stan would have preferred to wait, take a little more time to prepare, but Tony was getting impatient and when the opportunity had arisen, it seemed like the perfect solution. Fire, in one form or another, was his favorite method of dealing with a problem. It was fast and neat, real reliable if a guy knew what he was doing.

He had taken the calculated risk that the old, dry logs would burn so cleanly there wouldn't be enough left to suspect foul play—or even if there was, the two bumbling fools on the property next door would get the blame.

Maybe they still would.

Stan fiddled with his cellular phone as he started along the crest of the hill toward his rental car, which was parked out of sight behind a copse of trees about a mile down the road. Stan knew he should check in with Tony, let him know what was going on, but he just couldn't make himself dial the number.

No telling what Tony would do when he found out he had failed again. Pull him off the job, maybe, or give him his walking papers—or worse. Tony paid him very big money, and most of the problems Stan was called in to solve were more easily dealt with than this one, more like what he'd done with Held.

Stan hated to lose such a lucrative position and in the back of his mind, he was toying with another idea, one that would solve everyone's problems.

Doyle Sanders and J. B. Brown were old ex-army buddies he worked with once in a while. He hadn't used them in a couple of years, but he knew where to find them. They didn't do the neat, sanitary work he usually liked, but they came fairly cheap and they were efficient.

Come to think of it, he had used them on the Hawkins job four years ago. It hadn't gone quite the way they'd planned, but in the end the result had been the same. Hawkins had holed up out here in the middle of nowhere; King seemed satisfied and let the matter drop.

Stan didn't like to think of that job. The way it turned out had always made him feel kind of bad. Maybe it was poetic justice that Doyle and J. B. come in on this job— make up for screwing things up before.

If Stan called them in, he wouldn't make as much money, but this time Hawkins would be out of the picture for good. Afterward, he'd arrange for a chopper to pick them up— Doyle always seemed to know someone with more greed than morals. They could disappear across some remote section of the Alaskan border and that would be the end of it.

Stan stopped in the shade at the top of the hill and began to punch in numbers.

The security team arrived around eight o'clock that evening. The sun was still up, would be for hours yet. Charity recognized Ross Henderson's bulky frame from the meeting she had attended with Call in Seattle. He and two other dark-suited men climbed out of a brown rental car and started toward the house.

"Good to see you, Ross," Call said, shaking the big man's hand as he walked through the front door. "You remember Ms. Sinclair?"

Ross tipped his head politely in her direction. "Ms. Sinclair." Ross's attention shifted to the two men with him. "This is Randy Smith and Jim Perkins. They've been with the company more than six years. You can count on them to know what they're doing."

Each of them shook Call's hand. "Nice to meet you, Mr. Hawkins," Jim Perkins said, a lean, sinewy man with black hair and a slightly pointed nose. Randy Smith was shorter, with a nice, vee-shaped build and curly blond hair. Both of the men had bulges beneath their coats, obviously weapons. Since handguns were illegal in Canada, Charity figured they must have had some kind of permit.

"We'll be pulling two-man, six-hour shifts round the clock," Ross told them. "That way everybody stays fresh and alert."

"The police were here earlier," Call said. "They're aware of the situation. They'll be keeping an eye out for anything that might look suspicious, either in town or on the roads leading up here."

"Good."

"There's something I'd like you to take care of before your men settle in." Call turned, motioned for Toby to come out of the kitchen doorway and join them. "This is Toby Jenkins. He'll be staying in Dawson with his mother until this is over."

"Wait a minute!" Toby looked at him as if he'd gone insane. "I'm not leaving. I'm staying here!"

"It's safer for you in town, Toby. If I could send Charity someplace safe I would, but we don't know exactly what's going on yet, and for the present I think she's better off here."

"But who's gonna cook for you? Who'll take care of the place while I'm gone?"

"I'll do it, Toby," Charity said gently. "It won't be for long. Call has a number of people working on this. They're bound to turn up something very soon."

"I want to stay. I'm good with a rifle. I might be able to help if something happens."

"Ross and his men are professionals," Call said. "They'll take care of things here. I'll keep in touch, let you know when it's safe for you to return."

Toby grumbled something but didn't continue to argue. Jim Perkins walked him out to his little house behind the main structure to collect his things, then they set off down the hill, Perkins in the rental car following Toby in his paint-faded, once-red, now rose-colored minivan.

As soon as they were gone, Ross pressed a yellow hand-held radio into Call's hand and gave one just like it to Charity. "Randy, Jim, and I all carry one of these. You'll be able to reach us at any time just by pushing this button." Ross demonstrated the use of the radio for Charity, depressing the key to speak, then releasing it so the other party could answer.

She clipped it onto the waistband of her jeans.

"We'll take a look around," Ross said, "get a handle on things up here. Just signal if you need us."

Call nodded, but his face looked grim.

''I hate this,'' Charity said.

''So do I.''

But for now there was nothing else they could do.

It was the following day that Toby sat in the Victory Gardens behind the museum in Dawson City. Work had been suspended on the Lily Rose as soon as the arson was discovered, but he hadn't expected his job at Call's to end as well.

''Crummy buttons,'' Toby grumbled. Thinking of Charity, he managed to come up with a half-hearted smile.

Maude, Jenny, and Toby had disagreed with her decision to shut down the dredge, but apparently Charity felt it was the right thing to do. Imagining the gold they might have found, Toby had been down in the mouth ever since.

Until this afternoon—when Jenny had driven up in front of his mother's jewelry shop, The Gold Mine, in Maude's battered old blue pickup.

Toby rushed out to greet her. ''Hey, Jenny!''

''Grama said I could come,'' she explained a little shyly though the window of the truck. ''I was feeling kind of blue, I guess. I liked working on the Lily Rose. Grama thought maybe you might be able to cheer me up.''

''I'm glad you came.'' One of the reasons he'd hated to leave the mountain was Jenny. He knew how much he was going to miss seeing her every day.

Toby opened the door of the pickup. ''Come on. Let's get something to eat.'' Helping her out of the truck, they headed down the street to The Grubstake. The place was crowded. They bought sandwiches and sodas to go, returned to the pickup, and drove over to the park. The summer weather was perfect—clear, blue skies and a warm, gentle breeze. Up here, everyone made the most of the few short months of heat and sunshine.

There were tourists in the park, milling around the grass.

Toby found a place off by themselves and sat down. Maude kept a blanket in the pickup for emergencies and Jenny had spread it open on the grass. As they ate hearty submarine sandwiches, they talked about the fire and who might have set it and about rebuilding the cabin, which both of them wanted to do. Then Toby asked Jenny about her plans for the fall.

"I-I'm not sure yet."

"What about college? I think the U in Calgary is going to be great. I'm really looking forward to it. Don't you want to go to school, too?"

"I did. I had the grades and everything. Now I . . . I don't know."

"Have you applied anywhere?"

"No, but my dad says I can go wherever I want. He's really been great. It's just that . . ."

"What?" Toby reached over and took her hand. "What is it, Jenny? You can tell me. You can trust me with anything. Surely you know that by now."

The muscles in her throat went up and down and her eyes filled with tears. "Something happened a few months back. Since then . . ." She shook her head, stared off across the grass.

Toby squeezed her hand. "Tell me, Jenny, please."

She swallowed, turned back at him. "I had an abortion," she said softly. "A month before I came up here."

His hand tightened over hers. "Jenny . . ."

"Jazz Rollins was the father. I thought . . . I thought we were being careful, but something went wrong and I got pregnant. My dad never found out. He's ultraconservative. I knew if I told him he would try to talk me out of it and I didn't want that."

"So you had the abortion on your own?"

"I knew a girl once who got pregnant. I knew where she had gone to have the pregnancy ended."

Toby looked at her, trying to read her face. "Are you sorry you didn't have the baby?"

Jenny bit her lip, shook her head. "I know—for me— what I did was the right thing to do. Jazz wouldn't marry me and even if he had wanted to, I didn't want to marry him. By then I knew the kind of person he was, the cruel father he would be. I love children, but I knew I couldn't take care of a baby—not yet—and the thought of carrying one inside me for all those months then giving it to strangers was even worse than not having it at all."

She looked up at him and the sadness was there in her face. "You probably think I'm a terrible person."

Toby reached over and gently captured her shoulders. "I don't think that at all. I told you before, nothing you could tell me could change the way I feel about you."

Jenny closed her eyes and leaned toward him and he gathered her into his arms.

"I mean it, Jenny." He could feel her tears soaking into the front of his tee shirt and it made his chest feel tight.

"It's just been so hard keeping it all a secret, being afraid of what people would say if they knew."

Toby eased back to look at her. "You never told anyone?"

She shook her head. "Not until today."

He drew her close again, felt that funny quiver in his heart. He smoothed tear-damp hair back from her cheek and knew he was falling in love with her. "Bad things happen to all of us, Jenny. That's just the way life is. We have to put those things behind us."

She gazed up at him, tears clinging to her thick brown lashes. "I think maybe I love you, Toby."

He tightened his hold around her and spoke past the lump in his throat. "I think maybe I love you, too, Jenny." She hung onto him hard, and God, it felt so good.

For an instant he thought of Call and the wife and daughter he had lost. He thought of Charity and wondered if the two of them loved each other and if Call would be able to put the past behind him and look instead to the future. He prayed that they would be safe and that they would catch the men who had tried to kill them.

Then Jenny gazed up at him, her heart in her beautiful green eyes, and his mind turned to his own future, one that might include her. Toby leaned over and very gently kissed her.

CHAPTER
TWENTY-FIVE

Charity rattled around the house, feeling restless and edgy. She was worried about Call. Whoever wanted him dead was persistent. She didn't think they'd give up until they finished the job—or someone finally stopped them.

Earlier that morning, she had cooked breakfast for Call and Jim Perkins, then put ham, scrambled eggs, and biscuits in the oven for the two men on duty outside. She hadn't really cooked in years, not since her mother had died and the three Sinclair girls had taken over the job of preparing the family meals.

Out of necessity, she had learned to do a decent job— nothing fancy, just good, hearty meals—and doing it now made her at least feel useful. But she would rather be working on the Lily Rose, seeing what treasure she might find in the stream. And thinking about the fire made her sad.

The cabin was lost. Call had mentioned rebuilding a couple more times, claiming the cost of reconstruction should be his since whoever had set the fire wouldn't have done it if he hadn't been sleeping there that night.

Even if she agreed, they couldn't begin until they found

the man or men who burned it down and she wondered if she shouldn't just go back to Manhattan.

Thinking about giving up her adventure and leaving in defeat left her even more depressed. She refused to consider that she would also be leaving Call and instead wandered out of the kitchen and into his office.

He was sitting at the keyboard in front of his computer, typing in a message. He hit the ''send'' button just as she stepped behind him.

''What's up?'' she asked.

''I'm e-mailing Bruce Wilcox at Datatron, sending him a list of companies that manufacture hard disks—the ones most heavily involved in production development and design. I want Datatron to go out over the Net and collect as much information on each of the companies as it can.''

''Legally, you mean.''

''Yeah. You saw what happened with Wild Card when things went further than that.''

''What are you hoping to find?''

''Someone who's in deep financial trouble, a company that is desperate enough to try to stop Peter Held, MegaTech, and ultimately me—at any cost.''

''Have you heard anything from Held?''

''Not a word. Which makes me wonder what he's up to.''

''You think maybe he's involved in this?''

''Maybe. As soon as we figure out where he is, I'm going to find out.'' Call drew her down on his lap. ''You doing okay?''

She nodded, managed to muster a smile. ''I guess so.''

''I get the impression you're not enthusiastic about being my new roommate.''

Charity wove her arms around his neck. ''Actually, that's the only part of this I *am* enthusiastic about. I love sleeping with you, Call—I freely admit it. I enjoy making love to you.'' *I like everything about you. I'm in love with you.* But of course she didn't say that. God only knew what Call would do if she did.

''I like making love to you, too. And it's a good thing

we both feel that way. Right now, there isn't a helluva lot else we can do.'' So saying, he kissed her. She heard the snap pop on her jeans and a few seconds later the jeans and her panties were lying in a pile at her feet. With one of the security guards asleep in the guest room and the door firmly closed, Call settled her astride him in the chair and they made love there in his office.

It didn't allay her fears, but it did postpone them for a while.

It was later in the afternoon that Charity returned to the office. With little to keep her occupied and worry constantly nagging her, she focused her mind on her aunt in Seattle and the woman, Rachael Fitzpatrick, who had come to the Klondike in search of gold so many years ago.

Turning on the computer, she pulled up the family tree Call had helped her create on ancestry.com and looked it over. She found Sarah Thankful Baker; Sarah's mother, Frances Fitzpatrick; and Frances's younger sister, Rachael.

Rachael. A woman with the courage to travel thousands of miles to a distant, forbidding land. Times were different now and Charity hadn't faced the sort of hardships that Rachael must have suffered, yet it had taken no small amount of courage for Charity to come all this way by herself.

She wondered what had happened to Rachael, then thought of Ian Gallagher, the man Rachael had followed to the goldfields, and suddenly wondered what had happened to him. Rachael had returned with a heavy gold nugget, but Aunt Mavis didn't know what had happened to the man Rachael had loved.

On impulse, Charity typed in his name and a list of people with the same name appeared on the screen. Knowing he had lived in the 1890s near Portland, she eliminated each person on the list by date of birth until she came up empty-handed. None of them were the right age to have lived during the Gold Rush. She searched ships' registries of the period, hoping she might find either Rachael or Ian's names, but she had no idea which ship they might have sailed on. Not all the registries were posted and again she came up with nothing.

On a whim, she typed in Chilkoot Trail, going with her hunch that the trail was somehow involved in whatever had occurred. Besides, the odds were fifty-fifty it was the Chilkoot and not the Whitehorse Pass the pair had traveled to Dawson City.

She went through maybe twenty different sites: History of the Chilkoot; the Chilkoot Trail National Historic Site; Reliving the Chilkoot Trail; more than a dozen others. Switching to another search engine, she tried again. Still no mention of Ian.

She thought of the day she had spent on the trail and the eerie sadness she had felt. She thought of her dream and backtracked, typed in *Chilkoot Trail deaths,* and waited.

The list of sites was interesting. She clicked on Explorenorth.com and her eye traveled down the list of subtitles to *Palm Sunday Avalanche.*

She remembered reading about it years ago and her pulse kicked up. Any student of the Gold Rush knew about the terrible accident on March 3, 1898, when a wall of snow fifty feet deep buried sixty to a hundred men and women. It had taken four days to dig out the bodies. She knew about the temporary tent morgue at Sheep Camp set up to hold the victims' frozen corpses.

But she hadn't thought of it in years and never connected it to her dream.

And she had never seen an actual list of names.

Now there they were, recorded in alphabetical order on a graph made from cemetery headboards in Dyea in 1979 and the April issues of the *Dyea Trail,* the *Alaska Mining Record,* and *The New York Times.*

The record was cloudy and the reason was apparent. Many of the victims the four sources named didn't match. The headboard, for example, read Peter Anderson, but the name was reported as Andrew Anderson in the *Mining Record,* and O. Anderson in the *Times,* and there was no way to tell if they were one and the same or three different people. To make matters worse, some names appeared in one of the records and not the others.

She moved down the alphabetical list and when she reached the names starting with G, her breath caught. No Ian Gallagher was listed, but a headboard in Dyea named an I. Galahad who was listed in the *Record* as Ian Galliher and in the *Times* as I. Gallaghar.

Her adrenaline was flowing. She knew it was he as surely as she knew her own name.

Charity jumped to her feet, eager to tell Call, then turned and slammed into his chest. He caught her against him and for a moment neither of them moved.

''I found him,'' she said in a breathy little whisper. ''He was killed in the Palm Sunday avalanche.''

He was staring at her mouth. ''Who?''

''Ian Gallagher, the gambler Rachael ran off with. Rachael would have been with him. She must have seen it happen.''

Call frowned. ''Tell me you aren't thinking that what happened to her is somehow connected to you.''

Her shoulders sagged, her excitement slowly fading. ''I don't know. The day we hiked the Chilkoot Trail, I felt like I remembered something. I even dreamed about it one night last week.''

''You dreamed about an avalanche?''

She nodded. ''It was frightening, and unbelievably sad.''

Call let her go and stepped away. He didn't say anything more and at the dark look on his face, neither did she. But Charity didn't believe in coincidences any more than he did, and the dream she'd had must have been amazingly close to what had actually occurred.

She and Rachael were connected in some way—she could feel it. She wondered if she would ever know the truth.

Call listened to Charity puttering around the kitchen. The house felt different since she had moved in, warmer somehow, not so empty.

In the mornings, when he walked into the bathroom and saw her hairbrush on the counter, saw her panties hanging over the shower door, it reminded him what it had felt like to have a woman in the house, how good it had felt to come home from work and know that she would be waiting.

At night, after they made love and Charity curled against him, he could feel her heart beating softly next to his, and a fierce yearning opened up inside him, the feeling so sharp and intense it was almost a physical pain. It reminded him of all that he had once had, all that he would never have again.

As she lay sleeping, he thought how good it felt just to hold her, thought how it might be if she were his wife instead of his lover. Charity wanted children and in the past so had he. Amy was the first, but he and Susan had planned to have more. If things were different, he and Charity could have the family they both wanted.

If *he* were different.

If he weren't afraid to love again.

But the hollow ache she opened kept yawning wider and he knew it wouldn't stop hurting until she was gone. Until the reminders she stirred of home and family were buried again, until the ache of longing was stifled once more.

Last night, as she had before, she had mentioned returning to Manhattan. This time he hadn't tried to dissuade her. As soon as he was sure she would be safe, he would encourage her to go.

Call ignored a sharp pinch in his heart. Turning away, he walked into the bedroom to retrieve the cup of coffee he had forgotten on the bedside table and for a moment his eye strayed to the dresser against the wall. He found himself walking toward it, kneeling to pull open the lowest drawer.

In a small, gold-framed photo in the bottom dresser drawer, Susan's face smiled up at him. Amy's baby picture was tucked into the left-hand corner of the frame. Call's throat closed up. How long would it take before he could look at their pictures and not feel the ache of loss? When would their ghosts finally stop haunting him?

In the other room, he heard Charity calling his name and for an instant he wanted to hold her so badly his hands started shaking. But the ghosts of the past still lingered. Instead he closed the drawer, shutting away the memories and the pain. By the time he reached the kitchen, his mask was back in place.

And his heart closed up once more.

Three days later, Call sat next to Charity at the round walnut table in the corner of his office. Ross Henderson sat across from him, a big, solid man who completely filled up his chair. So far, the security team had turned up almost nothing. Several sets of footprints had been discovered, belonging, in Ross's estimation, to a man of medium height and slightly heavy build wearing a pair of tennis shoes.

They had followed his tracks across the side of the hill toward the road but the footprints disappeared on a narrow rift of granite and they couldn't find them again. The same footprints appeared in an area around Charity's cabin but there wasn't anything special about them and neither Ross nor the police were hopeful.

The good news was the security cameras were in place outside. Against a wall of the office, a monitor showing pictures of four different areas around the house gave them surveillance twenty-four-seven.

It would be nearly impossible to penetrate the protective barrier they had set up. Still, Call was edgy. He wanted his life back to normal, wanted this over and done. He kept hoping something would break and when he went into his office and pulled up his e-mail, he thought that maybe it had.

As he sat there studying the screen, Charity walked up behind him, lightly rested her hands on his shoulders. She was an affectionate woman, he had discovered. Different from Susan in that way. He found that he liked that in a woman.

"What is it?" she asked.

"E-mail from Bruce Wilcox at Datatron. Remember that list I sent him?"

"Companies you thought most likely to be damaged by MegaTech's possible discoveries."

"That's right. Smaller companies who might be in financial straits or have sunk large amounts into their own development projects. He's attached the information Datatron retrieved off the Net."

"You think maybe they found something useful?"

"God, I hope so." Call clicked the mouse and opened the file. "There were ten companies on my list. Of course, there could be others, but none that fit the criteria." Call studied the screen. "From what it shows here, three of them lost money last year, but not all that much, two of them have been in the red for the past two years, but appear to be on the upswing." He sighed. "Looks like most of them are showing a profit or at least breaking even, and a couple are doing extremely well."

"So you don't think any one of them is in enough trouble to warrant a personal attack on you and MegaTech."

He surveyed the screen a moment more, wishing the numbers would somehow change. "No, from what I see here, it doesn't look that way."

"What about the development aspect? Maybe someone wants to cut out the competition."

"Could be. Trech Technologies and Sept Systems are both heavily invested in research programs to increase hard-disk storage, but from what it shows here, they aren't in over their heads."

"Is it the same kind of research Peter Held is doing?"

"No. No one's working on anything remotely similar."

"Maybe that has something to do with it."

"Maybe. But I know both CEOs. I can't imagine Vernon Switzer or Hal Hartman putting me on a hit list."

"No, but it's hard to imagine anyone you know and like putting you on a hit list."

"True."

He could feel her behind him, studying the information

on the screen, feel the heat of her slender hands on his shoulders, and his groin tightened. Dammit, how did she always manage to make him think about sex?

"Maybe this has nothing to do with losing money," she said. She pointed to a name on the list and he recognized the company, Global Microsystems. "What about this one? They're showing a very big profit. Maybe the company's on a roll and they want that roll to continue."

Call reread the name, old memories returning. "I know the CEO and chairman of the board, Gordon Speers. He's a real prick, but that doesn't make him a murderer."

She laughed. "That's for sure. If it did, I'd know about a dozen serial killers."

Call chuckled.

"When did you meet him?"

"Way back when, Gordon offered me a job as president of his company. I had just sold Inner Dimensions, my computer game firm. I was looking for something interesting to do."

"So why didn't you take the job?"

"I didn't like the idea of working for Gordon Speers."

"Why not?"

"He's way too controlling. His wife's a Stanhope. Gordon's always been obsessed with proving himself their equal."

"Looks to me like he's done a pretty good job."

"Yeah. Unfortunately, Gordon's net worth isn't a drop in the bucket compared to the billions his wife's family is worth."

She leaned forward, her breasts pressing into his back. He ignored a rush of heat and concentrated on the list.

"How about Transworld Design?" she asked. "Looks like they're making lots of money, too."

Call sighed, beginning to get discouraged. "Unfortunately, making a lot of money doesn't usually lead to murder." Charity stepped away and Call rolled his chair back from the keyboard. "Dammit, there's nothing here that points to any of them."

He felt her hand once more on his shoulder, the touch

comforting this time. "You've got a lot of people working on this, Call. Maybe your detective will come up with something or something else will break."

Call scrubbed a hand over his face, trying to ignore his disappointment. "Yeah, maybe."

And the very next morning it did.

He was back in his office when the telephone rang. He had just ended the conversation and hung up his satellite phone when Ross Henderson walked in.

"Steve McDonald has located Peter Held," Call said. "Apparently the guy's been off on a little vacation with his girlfriend in Hawaii. McDonald told him he could come back willingly—now—or the police would be out to see him with a warrant for his arrest."

"Held's returning to Seattle?" Ross asked.

Call shook his head. "McDonald's meeting him at the airport in Vancouver tomorrow morning. Since I want to talk to him personally, I'll be joining them."

"We'll need more security. Jim and Randy can stay here with Ms. Sinclair. I'll go with you and have a couple more men waiting when we get there."

Call pondered that. He didn't like the idea of leaving Charity behind any more than he liked taking her with him. He wished she wasn't involved in this at all but she was and for the present that wasn't going to change.

He felt her fingers gripping his arm. "I know you'd probably rather I stay but—"

"It's all right," Call interrupted, the look in her eyes helping make his decision. He turned his attention to Ross. "The lady's coming with me." He heard her soft sigh of relief. "The chopper will be here to pick us up at six A.M."

By the time Peter Held arrived with Steve McDonald at the Pan Pacific Hotel in downtown Vancouver, Call and Charity were waiting for them in a luxurious suite. Held had been given the choice of meeting them at the hotel or at the local police station. He had gratefully chosen the former.

Charity watched him walk into the room, a young, Eurasian male in his late twenties, handsome and well-dressed in a stylish gray suit, though at the moment his face was drawn, his eyes a little red-rimmed, making him look slightly haggard. Faint yellow traces of bruising still darkened the skin on his jaw and cheek. At least part of what he had said appeared to be the truth.

Wearing black slacks and a crisp white shirt, Call walked toward him, his necktie loose and his sleeves rolled up to the elbows. Charity noticed the tension in his shoulders, the rigid muscles in his forearms. "Sit down, Peter."

The younger man dropped into a chair as if his legs had been cut out from under him. Call braced his hands on the arms and leaned over him. "All right—now that you've recovered sufficiently from your supposed attack, you're going to tell me exactly what the hell is going on."

Peter's eyes widened. He sat up straighter in his chair. "I *was* attacked. Take a look at my face."

"Okay—let's assume that much of your story is true. You were mugged. Now I want to hear the rest of it."

Peter met Call's hard-eyed stare for several tense seconds. Charity wondered how long the younger man could hold out against his boss's determined will.

Apparently not long. Releasing a heavy sigh, Held cut his eyes away from the unforgiving lines of Call's face. "I'm sorry. I guess I should have told you the truth from the start. I was afraid for Melanie . . . afraid of what they would do to her if I did."

Steve McDonald stepped into the conversation just then, directing his words to Call. "His girlfriend's still in Hawaii. I've got a man watching the condo she's staying in. When I found out he had taken her along and had no fixed ticket to return, I had a hunch it might be something like this."

McDonald was an average-looking man, late thirties, brown hair, maybe five-foot-ten. Nothing special, except for the awareness in his dark eyes and the harsh set of his features that hinted at the difficult road he had traveled. They warned how tough he had become.

Call studied Held, then stepped back from the younger man's chair, giving him a little more space, but his gaze remained locked with Peter's. "Go on," he said far too softly.

"Mostly I told you the truth. I was out jogging in the park. It was late. Three men jumped me. Two of them held my arms while the other one worked me over. I was in bad shape when they finished."

"So what did you leave out?"

Peter released a heavy breath. Beads of perspiration appeared on his forehead. "That they warned me to leave town, to quit working on the MegaTech project. They said if I continued, they'd do to Melanie what they had done to me. One of them said he'd make sure he got a piece of her while he was at it." He looked up and Charity could see his fear. "They would have done it, Call. They warned me not to say anything. They said if I did, both of us would wind up dead. They weren't fooling around. I knew they meant what they said."

"So you decided to keep your mouth shut and just walk away."

Held looked even more uncomfortable, a spot of color rising beneath the smooth skin over his cheeks. "I was hoping you'd figure things out. I was sure once you did, you'd find a way to deal with whoever it was. That's why I didn't quit my job. I didn't want to walk away from the project."

His fingers gripped the arm of the chair. "I'm close, Call. So close I can taste it. Lately, we've been trying a slightly different technique, using organic molecules attached to copper atoms. We take the same metal molecules we used before and spin-coat them onto the surface of a silicon wafer, but this time we expose them to a light pattern formed by a different kind of optical stencil than we were using before. Wherever the light falls, the molecule combination breaks apart, releasing metallic copper that sticks to the wafer. Then we—''

"That's very encouraging, Peter," Call interrupted, ending the technical diatribe. "What I need to know right now is who was behind the attack."

Peter rested his elbows on his knees and hung his head, spilling heavy black hair over his forehead. "I don't know."

"None of the men said anything? Made any sort of remark that might give us a hint who they were working for?"

"No." He looked up. "They didn't say much of anything—just beat the crap out of me, told me to take a hike, and warned me what they would do if I didn't."

Call blew out a breath. "Then we're left right where we started."

Steve McDonald focused his attention on Held. "You realize—thanks to your silence—there have been two nearly successful attempts on Call's life."

Held looked stricken. "What?"

"That's right. He and Ms. Sinclair were both nearly killed when someone sabotaged Call's airplane and just a few days ago, there was an arson fire at Ms. Sinclair's cabin. They nearly died of smoke inhalation." McDonald filled in the details while Charity watched the growing horror on Peter Held's face.

"I swear to God, Call, it never occurred to me they might go after you. I figured as long as the project was dead in the water, they'd be satisfied. I feel terrible about this, I really do."

Call moved back a little farther, allowing Peter to get up from the chair. "I understand why you did what you did." He flicked an unreadable glance in Charity's direction. "You were trying to protect someone you love. Sometimes when we're frightened we don't always make the right decisions."

"Melanie means everything to me. I couldn't stand the thought of her getting hurt. I just wish there was something I could do."

"Maybe there is," Call said. "I want you to go back to Hawaii and tender your resignation from MegaTech. As soon as you do, I'll put word out over the Internet that we're looking for someone new to fill your position.''

''So you're firing me?'' Peter looked slightly sick.

''I'm taking you out of the loop for a while. In the meantime, I'm going to open an office in Seattle, begin to concentrate on MegaTech full-time.''

Charity felt a stab of fear.

''That might not be a good idea,'' Steve McDonald said, mirroring her thoughts exactly.

''I'm tired of putting my life on hold,'' Call said. ''There's every chance whoever is behind this will just sit back and wait. They might not do a damned thing as long as I'm holed up in my house like a rat in a maze. I'm going to make it easy for the bastards to find me. When they do, I'll have a little surprise waiting for them.''

Her worry heightened and a knot clenched in her stomach. ''You're going to set a trap and you're planning to use yourself as bait.''

He turned his attention to her. ''More or less. I'm going to stop hiding and see what crawls out of the woodwork when I do.''

''Why don't you just pin a target on your back and parade around downtown Seattle until someone shoots you?''

His mouth went hard. ''I'll do whatever it takes to make this end.''

''You know, you may be right,'' McDonald said, rubbing his chin. ''Give them some rope, maybe they'll hang themselves.''

''My thought exactly. We can work out the details when I get to Seattle.''

''I'll get things rolling as soon as I get back,'' McDonald said, and Call turned his attention to Charity.

''Now that we know for sure you're not involved in this, I think it would be safer for you to go back to Manhattan . . . at least until this is over. You can leave today, catch the first plane out of Vancouver heading for New York.''

She swallowed, the knot clenching tighter in her stomach.

"What are you talking about? What about Kodiak? What about the Lily Rose? I have things I need to take care of."

Call's hard look softened. "I'll take care of Kodiak and the rest can be handled long distance."

"What about my friends, the people I care about? You expect me to leave without even saying good-bye?"

"It's the smart thing to do, Charity, the safest."

Her throat ached. "What about you? Are you going back?"

"I have to. I've got plans to make, arrangements to take care of."

"Then I'm going back, too. I'm not leaving without saying good-bye to Maude, Jenny, and Toby." Charity crossed her arms over her chest and lifted her chin. She hoped her lips didn't tremble. Dear God, she wasn't ready to leave. She wasn't ready to give up her once-in-a-lifetime adventure and return to a lifetime of sameness in Manhattan.

She wasn't ready to say good-bye to Call.

Her chest felt leaden. Deep down, she had hoped he would want her to stay. She looked up at him, but couldn't read his face.

"I'm going back to Dawson, Call," she said even more strongly. "You might as well accept it."

He raked his fingers through his hair. "All right, but I want your word you'll leave no later than day after tomorrow."

She made a slight, jerky nod, wondering if it could possibly be that easy for him to send her away. "Fine, if that's what you want."

"It isn't what I want, dammit! I'm trying to protect you!"

Charity made no reply. The lump in her throat felt massive and it was simply too hard to speak. Call said nothing more, but his gaze lingered an instant on her face before he turned away.

"That's all for now," he said to Peter. "Stay safe and I'll let you know when it's time to come back to Seattle."

"Thanks, Call." Peter shook Call's hand.

Charity watched the younger man walk out of the suite alongside Steve McDonald and thought that if Call hadn't had a loyal employee before, he certainly had one now. Charity figured he could count on that breakthrough at Mega-Tech in the very near future.

She hoped it made him happy.

CHAPTER
TWENTY-SIX

CHAPTER
TWENTY-SIX

Traveling as they had before, by private jet and helicopter, they arrived back at Call's mountain home that evening. Jim Perkins, who had stayed behind to keep an eye on the property, stood waiting on the porch.

"Quiet as a church mouse while you were gone," he said, "though that puppy of Ms. Sinclair's managed to chew up one of my running shoes. Everything okay in Vancouver?"

"As far as it goes," Call said. "At least we know for sure this is somehow involved with MegaTech. That means we're finally hunting in the right direction."

Ross and Randy followed them into the house and the security men settled into their routine, six-hour shifts. Call disappeared into his office without saying a word. He'd been silent and brooding since they left Vancouver. The hard set of his features and little more than grumbling responses warned Charity to leave him alone.

The hour grew late, though the sun was still up and she wasn't the least bit sleepy. She went into the bedroom, curled up and tried to read, but couldn't seem to concentrate.

Finally, she gave up and wandered into the kitchen for a glass of milk.

Kodiak was out on the porch, where he and Smoke slept this time of year. She opened the door and the dog rushed up to greet her, bouncing up and down, wriggling with excitement, his fuzzy tail curling over his back.

"Such a sweetie," she crooned, picking him up and cuddling him against her, knowing it wouldn't be long before he'd be too big. She hadn't had a puppy since she was a kid and leaving him behind made her heartsick.

"You gonna miss me, huh, boy?" She ruffled his long thick fur. "'Cause I'm sure gonna miss you." She felt tears rising. Tomorrow she would say good-bye to her friends, and early the morning after that, she would leave this place forever.

She had never meant to make a permanent home in the Yukon. She didn't want to live such an isolated life, but she had always felt a connection to this place and now that she had lived here, she had come to love it. She would miss the mountains and the animals, the wildness and the beauty, once she was gone.

Mostly, she would miss Call.

The thought made her eyes burn with tears. She said good night to Kodiak, closed and locked the door, then glanced toward Call's office. He was still inside but Charity didn't join him. Instead, she returned to the bedroom and curled up in his king-sized bed.

Call came in sometime later. He didn't reach for her and she didn't reach for him.

It was the middle of the night and the phone was ringing. Through his deep haze of sleep, Tony King struggled for a moment to realize what it was. He slapped at the receiver, finally groped it into his hands.

"All right, all right, what is it?" Beside him, his wife Alice groaned and dragged the feather pillow over her head.

"I want to know what's going on." At the sound of the familiar voice, Tony rubbed the sleep from his eyes.

"Couldn't this wait until morning, Gordon?" But Speers suffered from frequent insomnia and when he did, he didn't seem to mind intruding on someone else's slumber.

"Something's happened," Gordon said. "One of my employees called tonight. He says MegaTech posted an ad on the Internet. They're looking to hire someone qualified in semi-conductor electronics to run their research and development project. The pay they're offering is extremely high. It looks to me like Hawkins is replacing Peter Held, cranking things up over there."

"So what? It'll take a while for him to find someone to fill the kid's shoes. By then it won't matter."

"Are you sure of that?"

Was he sure? Hell, no, he wasn't sure. Silently, he cursed Stan Grossman. Tony hadn't been able to reach the bastard in days. He had no idea what the guy was doing or even if he was still on the job. Tony was worried that Grossman was turning into some kind of loose cannon, trying to handle things completely on his own. If he was and he made a mistake, he could wind up shooting all of them down.

"Relax," Tony said, forcing a note of confidence into his voice he didn't feel, hoping to alleviate Gordon's fears. He wished he could ease his own. "Like I told you before, I've got everything under control. Don't I always?"

He could hear Gordon's breath of relief. "All right, then. I'll let you know if I hear anything else."

"Try to do it in the daytime, will you?"

Gordon chuckled as he disconnected the phone.

"Sometimes Gordon's a real pain in the ass," Alice grumbled from the bed beside him.

"That's the truth." But he was afraid Gordon might be right to worry. Tony wished he knew what the hell was really going on.

*   *   *

"You ready?" J. B. Brown slipped toward him through the darkness, silent as a whisper of wind.

"Yeah—how 'bout Doyle?" Stan asked.

"He's moving into position."

Stan searched the shadows around the house but saw no sign of him. He thought about the occupants inside. "I wonder where they went in that chopper this morning."

J. B. crouched beside him. "Don't make a rat's ass. They're back here now. Lights have been off in Hawkins's office for nearly half an hour. Give 'em another few minutes, make sure they're asleep, then we'll move in."

The plan was simple: take out the two outside guards using rifle-fired darts similar to the ones used to sedate big game animals. No blood on the ground, no noise, no mess. As soon as the perimeter was secure, they'd move into the house, use the same technique on the inside guard, Hawkins, and the woman in his bed. While Doyle and J. B. carried the outside guards inside, Stan would rig Hawkins's own thousand-gallon propane tank to fill the place with gas.

A few minutes later, with the help of a timed, burning trigger, the house and its sleeping occupants would be blown to smithereens. Along with the house, the cameras would be destroyed, as well as any photos that might have been taken. Even if foul play was suspected, there wouldn't be enough evidence left to prove it.

In the meantime, Stan, J. B., and Doyle would be headed back the way J. B. and Doyle had come—by helicopter across the border to nearby Alaska, less than an hour away. From there they'd head north for the airport in Fairbanks and return on a commercial flight to the States.

All of them would be safe and everything would be right once more in Stan's world.

All neat and tidy. Just the way he liked it.

"Time to go," J. B. said, checking the load in his 9mm Glock and sliding it beneath the flap of the holster at his waist. Both he and Doyle wore dark green camouflage fatigues, remnants of their days in the army. J. B. had streaked his face with greasepaint. Stan wore black, head to foot.

J. B. picked up the rifle and a supply of darts and started for the guard walking the perimeter on the north side of the house. Stan skirted the area, keeping well back into the trees, and spotted Doyle taking out the guard to the south. Not a peep, just a single soft grunt as the guy hit the ground. Doyle made it look easy.

Knowing J. B. would have done his job with equal efficiency, Stan began moving in. A few minutes later, both guards were down and dragged out of sight, and the spray paint Stan had used to black out the security cameras was tucked once more into his pack.

While J. B. headed for the back of the house, Stan and Doyle made their way to the front. The heavy door was locked and bolted. Doyle grinned as if it were some kind of game, then used a small, muffled, explosive device to blow the locks. The door swung open of its own accord.

Nothing to it, Stan thought as they stepped inside, beginning to get a little stoked himself. The house was dark and everyone was sleeping, just the way they planned. A few minutes more and it would all be over.

He was smiling, thinking how smart he was, when he heard a noise in the hallway. Looming out of the darkness, a hulking dark shadow appeared.

"Drop your weapons!" the shadow commanded. "Do it now!"

The strong beam of a powerful flashlight glared into Stan's face, freezing him on the spot. Next to him, Doyle's rifle hit the floor, but he was already pulling his pistol. Shots rang out, thundering in the confining space of the hallway. Beneath a constant stream of gunfire, Doyle dropped to the floor, rolled, and continued firing.

Stan slammed back against the wall, out of the line of fire, his heart hammering with the same rhythm as the spent bullet casings hitting the wooden floor. He pulled out his pistol, a Heckler-Koch, from the shoulder holster he almost never wore. Doyle kept shooting, changed clips, and started firing again. Stan heard the dull thud of a bullet entering flesh, followed by a harsh grunt of pain.

The shadow toppled over and the flashlight crashed to the floor.

"He's down!" Doyle shouted.

Pressed against the wall, Stan could hardly believe he was still on his feet.

"You all right?" Doyle asked.

Stan blew out a shaky breath. "Looks like." The gun felt heavy in his hand. He didn't particularly like packing a weapon, but there were times it was damned comforting to have one.

"You guys all right?" J. B.'s voice floated toward them from the other side of the kitchen.

"Fine," Doyle answered. "You stay here," he said to Stan. "I'm heading for the bedroom. Stay low and watch yourself. Hawkins might have a gun."

Doyle started down the hall, kicked open the first door he approached, two-handed his pistol and held it in front of him, then stepped inside the room.

Well, it won't be neat and clean, Stan thought with a twinge of regret. But the situation could still be salvaged. He just hoped nothing else went wrong.

Wearing only Call's knee-length terry cloth robe, Charity climbed out the bedroom window. Shirtless, barefoot, with only time to pull on his faded jeans, Call waited in the darkness to help her down. She was shaking, so frightened that she stumbled and nearly fell into the bushes beneath the sill. Call caught her and lifted her the rest of the way outside, then took her hand and gave it a reassuring squeeze. Tugging her forward, he led her silently into the cover of the pine trees.

It was dark outside the house, the brief hours of summer night having finally descended. Their assailants must have waited for the sun to set to cover their movements before descending like jackals on the house.

"Stay here," Call said softly. "I keep a rifle for emergencies behind the seat of my Jeep. I'll be back as soon as I get it."

Charity nodded, swallowed the knot of terror in her throat.

"Stay low and stay quiet," he warned as he slipped away.

In the darkness, the night sounds enveloped her. The hoot of an owl, the luffing of the wind through the trees, the rustling sound of some small animal in the bushes along the little feeder creek behind the house. Her gaze searched the darkness for Smoke or Kodiak but she saw no sign of them.

Her worry heightened. Why hadn't the dogs started barking when they spotted strangers coming toward the house? Where were the guards? She wondered if Jim and Randy were dead and prayed they hadn't been killed. She wondered if Ross was already dead or if he was lying there in the hallway bleeding to death with no one to help him.

A thumbnail moon appeared for an instant between two passing clouds and in the brief, weak flash of moonlight, she caught a glimpse of something brown lying in the dirt not far away. Moving quietly, Charity slipped into the darkness, heading for the object she thought she recognized as the pants Jim Perkins had been wearing.

When she reached the base of the tree, she saw him, his body sprawled in the shadows beneath some bushes. For an instant, Charity couldn't breathe. Forcing her trembling legs to move, she bent and hurried toward him, crouched in the shadows at his side. She spotted the needle stuck into the side of his neck, a dart of some kind. But his chest was still moving up and down, she realized with a shot of relief. The dart must have contained some kind of sedative. He was alive. At least for the present.

She hurriedly reached for the pistol he carried in the shoulder holster beneath his arm, but the gun was gone, the holster empty. If the other guard was still alive, his weapon had probably been taken, too.

Charity bit her lip. She started to slip back into the darkness when she thought of the knife she had seen Jim slide into a leather sheath he wore strapped to his calf. Jerking up his pant leg with trembling hands, Charity spotted the knife and pulled it out of the sheath. It wasn't that long. She hid it in the pocket of Call's blue terry cloth robe, which hung off her shoulder and drooped to the middle of her calf.

Anxious to return to the place Call had left her, Charity eased backward, away from the unconscious man. Moving quietly through the forest, she had almost reached her destination when a hand clamped over her mouth. Roughly jerked backward, she felt the hard steel barrel of a pistol pressing into her ribs.

"Well, now, I wondered where you'd slipped off to." His arm was a rigid steel band; the hand over her mouth nearly cut off her air supply. He was wearing a dark green camouflage suit, his face disguised beneath two black stripes of paint, and his breath stank of strong, unfiltered cigarettes. A jagged scar ran from beneath his left ear, down along his jaw, and disappeared beneath the collar of his shirt.

He jabbed her with the barrel of his gun. "Come on, sweetheart. You wouldn't want to leave the party so soon."

His hand came away from her mouth and she gasped in a breath of air, but the pistol remained in her side, a silent warning as he prodded her forward. Charity thought of the knife in her pocket, but she didn't reach for it—not yet. She glanced into the trees, searching for Call, but didn't see him. She prayed he was safe wherever he was out there in the darkness.

Call stood in the shadows behind the tree where Charity should have been waiting. Instead, in a thin slice of moonlight twenty yards away, he could see her being marched down the hill, his blue robe hanging off one slender shoulder, a pistol pressing into her ribs as one of the assailants led her away.

Dammit! He should have taken her with him. He never should have left her alone! His mouth felt dry. He forced down the fear that clawed at his guts and his fingers tightened around the rifle.

Take it easy, he told himself. The gun, a Winchester 30.06 he'd had since he was sixteen, was a very reliable weapon. And he was a very good shot.

He was thinking how best to approach the house when a sliver of bark flew off the trunk of the pine tree just inches from his face.

Call jerked backward, into deeper cover, swearing a silent curse. Shouldering the rifle, he scanned the forest in the area where the shot had come from. The powerful scope was useless in the dark, but it didn't really matter. The shot hadn't come from that far away.

Call glanced up at the sky, searching for an opening in the clouds. They were moving pretty fast, the wind picking up, beginning to rustle the branches on the trees. He counted the seconds and estimated the speed at which they traveled, made a guess how long it would take before they broke apart and a trickle of light illuminated the landscape below.

One, two, three. He shouldered the rifle and fired off a shot an instant before the roiling clouds parted. His opponent returned fire just as a thin coil of light swept down through the trees. Call squeezed the trigger and the man went down. It was a head shot. He didn't get up and he wasn't going to.

One down. Two to go.

His blood was racing, his palms damp, and yet he felt a strange sort of calmness settle in. The odds were evened up a little. At least they had a chance.

Or that's what he thought until he heard one of the men shouting his name from inside the house.

"All right, Hawkins! Fun's over! Throw down your weapon and come join the party—or your girlfriend is gonna dance her last dance."

Sonofabitch! Call closed his eyes and leaned back against the tree trunk, fighting for control. He'd been afraid they would use Charity as bait. She was the single lure he couldn't resist.

He hauled in a steadying breath. "All right, take it easy! You win! I'm coming out!"

"Call, no! They'll kill—" He heard Charity's terrified voice and the crisp echo of the slap that silenced her warning.

A trickle of sweat ran down his temple. Knowing he had no choice, Call tossed his rifle out into the open, watched it slide to a halt in the dry pine needles and earth. He raised his hands above his head, stepped out of the sheltering trees, and started walking across the clearing toward the house.

The wooden porch steps felt rough beneath his bare feet. The sweet scent of blooming summer flowers seemed incongruous in the moment. Call pulled open the door and the minute he stepped inside, the lights went on in the kitchen. Charity stood in front of a man in military fatigues, a pistol pressed against the side of her head. A second man, dressed in black with a stocky build and long, fine strands of hair combed over the top of his nearly bald head, stood just a few feet away.

Call drew closer, his attention fixed on Charity. Her face looked pale, except for the red mark on her cheek. His hands unconsciously fisted. "Are you all right?"

She swallowed then nodded.

"Your concern is touching, Hawkins," said the man in black. "Unfortunately, in a few more minutes, how well she's feeling ain't gonna make a damn."

There was something in the air, an unpleasant odor like rotten eggs that seemed to be growing stronger by the minute. *Propane.* Call's shoulders went tense. The men intended to blow up the house—with him and Charity in it!

"Get over here," the man in black commanded. He flicked a look at his friend. "Tie him to one of the kitchen chairs."

Stalling for time, Call didn't move. "If you're going to kill us, at least have the decency to tell me who hired you. Why was someone willing to go as far as murder to stop a little company like MegaTech?"

"I don't know why. King wants you dead. He's payin' me the big bucks to make sure it happens and that's what I'm gonna do. Now get over here . . . and don't do anything stupid or the girl gets it before you do."

Call started walking, trying to gauge when to make his

move. There wasn't enough gas in the house to go off with a gunshot but there very soon would be. And if he were going to die—if they were both going to die—he wasn't going down without a fight. He had just reached the man in black when he saw Charity start to turn. Her hand jerked upward from the pocket of her robe. She spun and slashed at the man behind her and blood erupted on his face.

Call leapt forward, slamming into the man in black, knocking him down on the kitchen floor, grabbing the hand that held the weapon. A few feet away, Charity stabbed her assailant again. He shrieked in pain as the knife sank into his shoulder and his gun went flying across the floor out of sight.

Call struggled with the man in black, both of them fighting for the pistol, first one on top and then the other. Call slammed the man's wrist down hard on the floor and the gun careered across the linoleum. From the corner of his eye, he saw Charity scrambling to pick it up. Call punched his opponent in the face, jerked him up, and hit him again. They were on their feet and slugging away. Call slammed a punch into the stocky man's stomach, hit him hard in the jaw. He went down like a fallen tree limb, his head banging the wall as he slid into a heap on the floor.

Call whirled toward Charity, saw that she had found the pistol and was aiming it in the middle of the unconscious man's chest. Her feet were splayed, both hands wrapped around the grip of the gun, but she was shaking so hard he thought if she fired she would probably hit him instead of her target.

Unfortunately, the man behind her, covered in his own blood, had also retrieved a weapon. It was pointing at the center of Charity's back.

Call stood frozen, every muscle tense. In the next few seconds, one of them was going to die and he vowed with everything inside him it wasn't going to be her.

"Get down!" he shouted, diving forward, knocking her onto the floor, covering her body with his. But the loud report slammed into the room before she could possibly have escaped the close-range, deadly bullet.

For an instant his heart just simply stopped beating.

Then his gaze swung to the man with the gun. For the first time Call realized the shot hadn't come from the assailant's weapon. His glance jerked to the front room window. In the shadows outside the living room, Toby stared down the barrel of the rifle he pressed against his shoulder, leveled at the men in the kitchen. Charity's attacker was dead, slumped against the wall, a bullet in the center of his forehead.

Call moved swiftly, lifting himself away from her, pulling her to her feet. Her face was completely drained of color, her fingers still wrapped around the pistol, but she was alive and safe. Relief hit him so hard he felt dizzy.

"It's all right," he said gently, pulling the gun from her stiff, shaking fingers. "Everything's going to be fine." He eased her into his arms and felt her trembling, tightened his arms around her, said a silent, grateful prayer.

Toby ran through the front door, hurrying toward the kitchen. "You two okay?"

"I don't know what you're doing here in the middle of the night," Call said, "but I'm damned glad to see you."

"I was over at Jenny's." The kid's face turned a little bit red. "She sneaked out to meet me. We heard the gunshots. I figured you might need some help."

Call felt the faint tug of a smile. "Open the rest of the doors and windows. The place is filling up with propane."

"Jesus!" Toby raced off to complete his assignment.

"Keep an eye on him," Call said to Charity, handing the pistol back to her, watching her hold it with a steadier hand. "Shoot him if he makes a move. I'm going out to shut off the gas valve."

By the time he returned, the windows were open, the house rapidly airing out. Toby held the pistol and Charity had gone into the hall to help Ross Henderson.

"I called the police," Toby said. "I told them what happened. They said they'd send an emergency chopper. It'll be here by the time it's light enough to land."

"Good work." Call and Toby tied up the man in black while Charity worked to stem the flow of blood from Ross's chest wound.

"His breathing's pretty even," she said when Call was finally able to join her, "but he's lost a lot of blood." He could see the red-stained towel she pressed over the wound.

"Help's on the way. Hang in there while I check on the others, find out if they're still alive."

"I think they are. I took the knife from Jim—I remembered seeing him strap it on his leg. I think they shot them with some kind of sleep dart."

Call went out to check on the guards and found, as Charity had said, they were unconscious but still breathing. Smoke and Kodiak had also been sedated, but seemed to be all right.

Call thought of how close they had all come to dying and along with the fury still seething inside him, a single word repeated itself in his head.

King.

Gordon Speers was in business with a man named Tony King. Call had never known exactly what role the man played at Global, but he was thinking he might know now.

It was going to be interesting to see what the guy in black had to say about Tony King.

"Call?" Charity's voice still sounded shaky as he walked back into the house.

"Both of them are still pretty deeply under," he said, "but they're breathing okay and their heartbeats seems steady."

"Thank God," she said. A memory surfaced of Charity standing in the kitchen with the barrel of a gun pressed against her temple, and his stomach rolled with nausea.

Call forced the memory away. He didn't want to think of the gut-clenching moment he had been certain that she was dead.

Or the way, in that moment, his heart had crumbled to dust inside his chest.

CHAPTER
TWENTY-SEVEN

The emergency helicopter arrived, its rotary blades whirling, stirring up dust and dirt. White-coated medics appeared and raced inside the house. Charity waited tensely as a second chopper arrived, setting down in a wide spot on the road across the creek. Uniformed officers streamed out of the chopper and over the bridge onto Call's property and immediately set to work.

Quickly assessing the situation, they began the mop-up procedure, dealing with the dead man outside and the one in the house, arresting the man in black, whose wallet identified him as Stanley Nathan Grossman, a resident of Los Angeles, California.

Standing next to Call, Charity watched as Ross Henderson, his condition stabilized, Jim Perkins, and Randy Smith were loaded efficiently aboard the hospital chopper. A few minutes later, its rotary blades began to turn, lifting it into the sky, carrying it off to the medical facilities in Whitehorse.

"It looks like they're going to be all right," Call said.

Charity's eyes stung with tears. "Thank God." All of them had come so close to being killed . . . so very close.

A detective named Murphy, a tall, heavyset man who

seemed to walk hunched over against an imaginary wind, began what seemed an endless round of questions. After the arson fire in the cabin, the police were aware of the possible threat to Call's life. He mentioned Grossman's reference to a man named King and told the detective he believed that stopping MegaTech from completing its research program was the motive for the attacks.

The sun was well up by the time the mop-up was near completion and Murphy asked Call to take another look at the three assailants.

"You sure you didn't recognize any of them?" the detective asked.

"Not much left to recognize of the one I shot," Call said.

"How about the other two?"

"I've never seen Grossman before."

Charity waited as Call walked with Murphy over to the stretcher where the second dead man lay. One of the officers had wiped off the stripes of black face paint the man had applied below each of his eyes.

Call frowned. "Now that you've cleaned him up, I think I've seen this one before." Charity watched as he examined the scar below the man's left ear. "Yes, I'm almost certain it's him."

"When did you see him?" Murphy asked.

Something shifted in Call's expression and his features seemed to close up. "Four years ago. Unless I'm mistaken, this guy did some handiwork in the condo my family and I were renting up at Lake Tahoe."

Call looked at Murphy and even from a distance, Charity could see the pain in his eyes. "My wife and daughter were killed in a car accident a few days later. After that, I stopped work on MegaTech and everything else." His voice sounded sandpaper-rough. "I was supposed to be in the car the night they were killed."

"I see." Murphy wrote something in a little spiral notepad as Charity walked over to join them. "So you hadn't worked on the project for years, but recently you started things up again."

Call nodded. "About eight months ago."

Murphy didn't say any more. The connection was obvious and Call undoubtedly saw it. His face was paper white and one of his hands had started to tremble. Charity reached over and caught his fingers. They felt icy cold.

"Are you all right?"

He swallowed, nodded. "Give me a minute." Turning, he walked away. She watched him disappear into the forest, out of sight among the trees, and an ache for him rose in her heart.

"Tough news to deal with," Murphy said.

"Yes, it is."

The detective fell silent and the minutes ticked past. When Call returned to where they waited, his features looked cast in stone.

"Anything else you need from me?" he asked.

"Not right now. We'll let you know what turns up."

He nodded. Murphy returned to his men. The detective left a couple of Mounties there just to be safe, though none of them expected any more trouble. Murphy and his men climbed aboard the chopper and a few minutes later, the helicopter lifted away. It rose above the trees and disappeared out of sight, and quiet settled over the house.

Toby approached from inside. "If you don't need me anymore, I'm going back to Jenny's. She'll be worried. I'll let her know everyone here's all right, then I'm heading back to town."

Call extended a hand. "Thanks, Toby . . . for everything." Toby returned the handshake. Call clasped the boy's shoulder, pulled him into a rough male hug, then stepped away.

"I'll talk to you later," Toby said gruffly. Turning, he walked back to his van where it was parked out of sight down the road, and except for the two Mounties some distance away, Call and Charity were left alone.

They didn't go back inside the house. Instead they went around to the back and sat down in the swing on the deck. Kodiak and Smoke had finally awakened, but the dogs were still groggy and slept off and on at their feet. Charity could hear the water in the little feeder creek trickling over the rocks and boulders, and a red-tailed hawk soared in the pale blue, early morning sky.

Murphy had suggested they should pack a bag and head into town. The policemen would accompany them. Call intended to stay in Dawson till the house could be cleansed of blood and death and put back in livable condition.

Charity wondered how long it would be until he actually returned.

For herself, she still had the plane ticket Call had bought her when they were in Vancouver. Tomorrow morning, she would catch the commuter to Whitehorse and from there fly back to New York.

The thought made her heart hurt. She looked up at him and knew he wasn't thinking about her leaving. He was thinking about what had happened to his family four years ago.

"It wasn't an accident," he finally said, sitting like a statue on the edge of the swing.

"No. They were trying to kill you even then. If you'd been in the car, they would have succeeded."

Call braced his elbows on his knees, bent his head and ran a hand over his face. "They must have forced her off the road. It was dark that night. Amy was in the back in her child seat. They probably couldn't see her. They must have thought I was the one behind the wheel."

"I wonder how they knew."

"The same way they knew I was staying with you in the cabin that night. Or maybe the phones were tapped."

"You said the car blew up afterward. That would fit their pattern."

"Yeah."

"The police are going to catch the men who did it," Charity said. Next to her, Call sat stiffly, his features drawn and tight, as if his skin were stretched over wire instead of bone. She wished she could touch him but she knew he would only pull away.

"Yes, I think they'll catch them." He looked tired, so

exhausted it was all she could do not to put her arms around him. If only he would turn to her, let her comfort him in some way.

"Once they're arrested," she said, "this will all be over."

Call straightened on the swing, making it rock back and forth. "Will it?"

"It will if you want it to be."

He turned away, stared off toward the mountains.

"I'll be leaving tomorrow," she said softly. Call made no reply and her chest squeezed hard. "I won't be coming back."

He turned to look at her, his beautiful blue eyes full of turbulence. Still he said nothing.

"I know this is probably not the time, but I don't think another time will be any better." She reached over and caught his hand, cradled it between both of hers. "I love you, Call. I know that isn't what you want to hear. I love you. I didn't plan it. I never wanted it to happen but it did and I couldn't leave without telling you."

Call's fingers tightened for an instant over hers, then he pulled away. "I care for you, Charity. You know I do. Tonight, when I thought you'd been shot . . ." He closed his eyes and shook his head, trying to block the image. "I care, Charity. But I don't love you. I won't let that happen. I won't love you or any other woman. I know what it's like to love someone and then lose them. I couldn't survive that kind of pain again."

Charity fell silent. A lump swelled in her throat and her chest ached. Her heart felt as if it were being torn to pieces. She was in love with Call Hawkins but he didn't love her in return and there was nothing she could say, nothing she could do to change things. He'd been honest from the start. He had told her that what they shared couldn't last.

She felt the sting of tears and stood up from the swing. "I'll go get my things. If you're ready, I think it's time we started down the mountain."

It was over.

She was going home, leaving without a word to Maude

or Jenny. It didn't matter. She didn't have the heart to face them. She knew what they would see in her eyes if she did.

Her farewell to the Yukon was more painful than Charity could have imagined. They spent the night after the shooting in separate rooms at a small motel in Dawson and part of her wished she could say good-bye to him there. The other part wanted to stretch out every moment, to memorize her last few seconds she would have with him, knowing they would be her last.

They arrived at the small local airport just minutes out of town and her throat closed up when she saw Maude and Jenny waiting on the sidewalk in front of the terminal.

"Toby told us what happened last night," Maude said. "He said you was leavin'." Maude was dressed in her usual flannel shirt and worn, faded Levi's, but her pipe was missing and her face looked lined and sad.

Charity tried to smile. "It's time I went home . . . back to the city where I belong."

Maude shook her head, moving the soft flesh beneath her chin. "Never was a gal fit in better up here than you. Maybe you'll come back some day."

But she knew she wouldn't. Her adventure was over. She thought of Rachael Fitzpatrick, who had come to the Yukon so long ago. Rachael's journey had ended in pain and heartache when she had lost the man she loved. Charity's adventure was over long before it should have been. The cabin was gone. Kodiak was staying behind with Call. Even the little puppy she had loved was lost. And her heart—her heart was irreparably broken.

"I have to go," Charity said softly.

Maude just nodded in that sage way of hers. "You'll do what's best, gal. Like you've always done. But we couldn't let you go off without sayin' good-bye."

Her throat clogged with tears. "I planned to come and see you before I left—then those men tried to kill us and . . ."

Her voice trailed off as she thought of the awful scene at the house.

"It's all right," Maude said. "We're here now. That's all that matters."

Tears welled in her eyes as she looked at her two dear friends. "I'm going to miss you both. I'm going to miss you so much." She hugged the older woman, hanging on longer than she should have, thinking how much she had come to love the tough old sourdough, thinking that Maude had become one of the closest friends she'd ever had.

Then she turned to Jenny. "I'm going to miss you, too. Be happy, Jenny. Life is short. Make the most out of every moment."

Jenny nodded, tears in her pretty green eyes.

"Take care of Toby."

"I will." Sunlight glittered on the small gold rings in Jenny's ears. The young girl smiled but Charity could see she was fighting not to cry. "Toby said to tell you he hates good-byes. He says he'll see you next time you come to the Yukon."

Charity just nodded. Her chest ached so badly she couldn't manage to speak. She knew it was time to go inside. Past time, really.

"Take care of yourselves," she said. Picking up the small canvas duffel bag Call had loaned her, loaded with her few remaining clothes and the nugget she had gotten from her aunt, she waited while he opened the door, then walked past him into the tiny terminal.

Call watched her in silence as she checked in at the counter, then returned to where he stood waiting. He looked even more exhausted than he had last night and she wondered what demons he fought inside his head.

It seemed minutes, it seemed hours, until the loudspeaker announced the departure of the Air North commuter flight to Whitehorse and she prepared to depart for the gate. She didn't try to be bright and sunny. She knew it wouldn't work. Instead she turned to Call and felt the warm, salty wetness of tears sliding down her cheeks. Though his eyes were a troubled dark blue, he was still the handsomest man she'd ever seen. She wished he would open his arms so she could walk into them. She wanted to hold him so badly she trembled.

She looked up at him, so tall and unbelievably handsome, and more tears trickled down her cheeks. "I meant what I said. I love you, Call. I probably always will."

Call didn't move. His eyes locked with hers and his throat moved up and down but he made no effort to speak. Then he reached for her, dragged her hard against him, and his arms tightened around her. She could feel his heartbeat, as ragged as her own.

"I'll miss you, Charity. I'll never forget you." He bent his head and very softly kissed her. "I wish things could be different. I wish I could be a different man."

She gazed at him through a well of tears. "Life is just hard sometimes."

"Yeah," he said, "life is just hard."

She forced herself to step away. "Good-bye, Call."

"Good-bye, Charity."

Charity bit down on her trembling lip. Turning, she walked away. She didn't stop until she got inside the plane.

If Call was still there, she couldn't see him.

CHAPTER TWENTY-EIGHT

Say! You've struck a heap of trouble—
Bust in business, lost your wife;
No one cares a cent about you,
You don't care a cent for life;
Hard luck has of hope bereft you,
Health is failing, wish you'd die—
Why, you've still the sunshine left you
And the big, big blue sky.
　　　　　　　　　　　　—Robert W. Service

Charity moved back into her Sixth Street Manhattan apartment. Her year-older, slightly shorter, red-haired sister didn't mind sharing the place. Though Hope had set up her computer in front of the window, she was rarely in the city. Lately she had been doing more and more freelance assignments and a number of them involved some sort of travel. Besides, with the two of them splitting the rent, the amount was cut in half.

Still, the apartment felt tight and confining after the wide-open spaces Charity had known in the Yukon. When she looked out the windows, she saw a sea of rooftops instead of majestic mountains, vast distant horizons, and glorious evergreen forests.

She had been back in the city three weeks but she hadn't started looking for a job. She knew she should, knew it wouldn't be hard to find one. Her sterling reputation in the publishing business and the industry's constant search for qualified editors assured her a job. The problem was, she just wasn't ready to return to the everyday world.

Since leaving the Yukon, she had no energy, no will to move forward with her life. It was a classic case of depression and she knew it. She also knew she would eventually work through it and things would return to normal. In time, she would stop thinking of Call. At some point in the future, she would stop remembering their time together, stop seeing him in every man on the street.

It was strange the way her mind seemed to conjure him. Two days ago, she thought she spotted him in the park, feeding the pigeons. Yesterday, for a single split second, he was wearing a dark gray suit and sitting at a table in a small Italian cafe.

But the men were always a little too short, their hair not quite the right chestnut shade of brown, their shoulders not nearly as wide as Call's. Still, she couldn't stop looking for him, couldn't stop hoping he would miraculously appear on the streets of Manhattan, there in search of her.

But Call had never phoned or even dropped her a note. As a celebrity of sorts and an extremely wealthy man, the newspapers had been full of stories about the attempts on his life, MegaTech, and the arrest of Anthony King and Gordon Speers. Stan Grossman had turned state's evidence, incriminating King, and King had rolled over on Speers, as the police had hoped he would.

Yesterday morning, she and Hope had been watching TV when CNN announced MegaTech's hard-drive storage breakthrough, the discovery Peter Held had been so close to making. Later that same day, more information was released. When the six o'clock newscast was over, Charity sat back on the sofa.

"My God," she said to Hope, "so *that* was Speers's true motive. For the past six years, he invested every extra dime he had and everything he could borrow in platinum futures. He was banking on demand from the software industry to drive up the price.''

''And he very nearly succeeded,'' Hope replied. ''According to that report, at the time he started investing, only fifty percent of all hard disks contained platinum. In the last five years, that number has nearly doubled.''

''And the computer market has barely been tapped. King and Speers were set to make billions.''

''The bad news was,'' Hope added, ''according to what they said on the news, MegaTech's new process uses copper, a far cheaper metal. No wonder they wanted Call dead.''

Charity looked over at Hope, who sat on the sofa with her legs curled up beneath her. ''Speers knew Call wouldn't stop,'' Charity said. ''Not when his company was so close to success. I guess they thought killing him was the only solution.''

Her sister cast her a glance, and Charity shivered. Call was safe now and that was a consolation, but it didn't make her miss him any less.

Thank God for my family, she thought. Her dad had called as soon as she got back to the city. Patience had phoned. Last weekend, worried about her, the two of them had taken the train from Boston to visit her for the weekend. They knew what had happened in the Yukon. Mostly they knew that she had fallen in love with Call and now her heart was broken. With one excuse or another, one of them phoned every other day.

And Hope was a rock in the tempest. With her constant prodding and determined cheerfulness, she forced Charity up off her duff and out of the house.

As she had earlier that morning.

''Deirdre called a few minutes ago,'' Hope said when she returned, having insisted Charity go down to the little French bakery in the middle of the block for a bag of croissants. Charity knew Hope was simply trying to get her up and doing something productive. ''She wants you to phone her back.''

"Did she say what she called about?" Charity reached over and picked up the phone.

"Something to do with a Literary Arts dinner. I think she wants you to go."

Charity groaned and started to hang up the receiver. Hope bolted over, snatched it out of the cradle, and shoved it into her hand.

"Oh, no, you don't. Call her back and at least hear what she has to say."

"The last thing I want to do is go to some boring dinner."

Hope just glared at her. Charity blew out a breath. "All right, I'll call." She punched in her best friend's number and listened to it ring. "Okay, Deirdre," she said the moment she heard her friend's voice on the end of the line, "what torture have you thought up for me now?"

"I need a favor. Jeremy's working late tonight." *Big surprise.* "I have to go to the annual Literary Arts Dinner Dance and he won't be able to join me there until later. Please say you'll be my date—at least until he arrives."

Deirdre and Jeremy were still an item. A very serious item. In fact, it looked as if wedding bells loomed on the horizon for her friends. Charity was happy for them. That didn't mean she wanted to spend a miserable night out.

"I don't know, Dee . . ."

"Please? I'm begging you. You know what those things are like. Say you'll come with me. It won't be so bad if I have someone fun to talk to."

Charity sighed, thinking even if she went, she wouldn't be all that much fun.

"Go on," her sister urged. "You'll know a lot of people there. It'll be good for you to see old friends. Besides, maybe someone will offer you a job."

Charity rolled her eyes, but she was weakening. She needed to get out, just as her sister and Deirdre said. "Black tie, isn't it?"

"Unfortunately, it is," Deirdre said.

"I'll have to dig out something, I guess."

"Yes!" Charity could almost see her friend's arm shooting into the air. "I've got a town car," Deirdre said. "The publisher is picking up the tab. I'll be there at 7:30."

"Fine, I'll see you then." Charity hung up the phone, already wishing she had refused.

"I'm proud of you, sis." Hope grinned, her smooth, dark-red hair swinging along her jaw. She looked into Charity's face and her smile slowly faded. "I know how you're feeling. I felt like that after I found out Richard was sleeping with another woman."

"It isn't quite the same."

"Call broke your heart. Richard broke mine. What's the difference?"

"Richard betrayed you. Call tried to warn me. He didn't hurt me on purpose."

"That doesn't make it any less painful." Hope gave her a reassuring hug. "In time, you'll forget him, just like I forgot Richard. Keep remembering that."

Only Hope had never really gotten over the fiancé who had cheated on her, and Charity didn't think she was going to forget Call anytime soon.

Wishing the heavy weight of misery sitting like a rock on her chest would ease, she headed into the bedroom to find something to wear to the party.

Seven-thirty arrived far too quickly. Waiting in the lobby of her apartment, Charity spotted the black Lincoln town car rolling up at the curb. Making her way across the sidewalk, she waited for the driver to open the rear door, then slid onto the gray leather seat.

"My God, you look gorgeous!" Deirdre Steinberg was all of five-foot-three with gleaming dark-brown hair cut stylishly to just above her shoulders. She was pretty and intelligent, and always well dressed. Tonight she wore a long black skirt with a gauzy, beaded top that showed her midriff when she moved.

Deirdre examined her, head to foot. "I can't believe you're finally wearing that dress." They had been together when Charity purchased the long, slinky, red-sequined gown. The dress was elegant and expensive, paid for partly with a gift certificate from her dad that she had gotten for her twenty-seventh birthday. It wasn't her usual conservative style, which was far less formfitting and usually black, and it was more revealing, the strapless gown leaving her arms and shoulders bare.

But it was hot in the city this late-August night and she was determined to get herself into a better mood.

"The dress is still new," she said, "and it's bright. I thought it might cheer me up."

"Good thinking."

Charity smiled. "Let's hope it works." But so far it hadn't and she wasn't convinced it would.

After a short ride up Fifth Avenue, they arrived at the party being held at the Plaza Hotel. Following colorful Aubusson carpets, they made their way to the elegant banquet room filled with cloth-draped tables and dozens of guests. Crystal chandeliers illuminated the hall and the rug felt plush beneath her strappy red satin high heels.

"Look—there's Bob DiForio." Deirde discreetly pointed toward the tall, silver-haired man. "He used to be the publisher at NAL. I hear he's an agent now."

"I know Bob." She waved and DiForio waved back. Irwin Applebaum from Random House was there and one of the great old gentlemen of publishing, Walter Zacharius from Kensington. Mostly the crowd was more literary, publishers of the Oprah sort of books, self-help and nonfiction.

She saw her former publisher, Judy Blaine, from Glenbrook, and recognized an immediate interest in the stately, black-haired, fortyish publisher who began trying to extricate herself from the conversation in which she was immersed.

"She wants you back," Deirdre whispered. "I knew they would."

"I'm not ready to go back yet. I want time to explore my options. Come on, let's get something to drink."

The night was as dull as Charity had worried it would be and even the several glasses of champagne she drank couldn't lift her dismal mood. She wanted to go home, to be miserable where no one would see her, but she didn't want to leave Deirdre alone.

Jeremy still hadn't arrived by the time the music started. Charity accepted a dance with DiForio and one with Jack Dolan, an editor she had worked with at Glenbrook. The orchestra was large and played a lot of '40s big band numbers. As she returned to her seat next to Deirdre, she caught a glimpse of a tall, tuxedoed man near the door.

For an instant, her heart took a leap. She looked again, knowing it was ridiculous, knowing it couldn't be Call, that it was just another of the many mirages that haunted her. She saw him disappear into the crowd and took another sip of her champagne.

"Would you like to dance, Charity?" It was William Kelsey, a prominent author of children's books. She didn't want to dance, but she didn't want to be rude.

"Of course, William." The band played a slow song and she smiled and let him guide her around the floor, her gaze searching for Jeremy, cursing him for being so late getting to the affair. The song came to an end and William walked her to the edge of the dance floor.

"Thank you," she said.

"My pleasure." He cast a glance at the orchestra, which had struck up a lovely waltz, and she was afraid he might ask her again. Not wanting to refuse, she started walking back to the table but a man in black stepped in front of her.

"Hello, Charity."

She looked up at the sound of his voice and for an instant, she thought her eyes were deceiving her again, that the tall, incredibly handsome man in the black tuxedo couldn't be Call. But his shoulders were so very wide, his hair exactly the same rich shade of brown, and his eyes were the bluest she had ever seen.

"Call . . ."

"May I have this dance?" He didn't wait for her to accept, just settled a hand at her waist, guided her out on the dance floor, and eased her into his arms. Her fingers trembled as he enclosed them in his and his hand rested on her back.

Call swept her into the rhythm of the waltz, his movements surprisingly graceful, guiding her as if they had danced together a thousand times. Charity didn't speak and neither did he, but his eyes remained on her face and she thought that he had never look at her exactly that way. She could smell the piney fragrance of his cologne, feel the texture of his coat beneath her fingers. Her heart was beating too fast, her hopes rising, and she was so afraid.

Why was he there? Was it simply coincidence? Some sort of business that had brought him to New York and this particular affair?

The dance came to an end far too quickly and he led her to the edge of the dance floor. "What . . . what are you doing here?"

He looked into her face, his gaze still unnervingly intense. "I came for a couple of different reasons." He started to continue on but Deirdre walked up just then.

If Charity ever wished her friend would vanish into thin air it was in that moment. Instead, Deirdre took a long, appreciative look at Call, gave Charity a conspiratorial glance, and smiled.

"I don't think we've met. My name is Deirdre Steinberg."

Charity cast her a look, hoping she would get the message. "Deirdre, this is McCall Hawkins. I believe I may have mentioned him."

Deirdre's eyes seemed to pop right out of her head. "Yes . . . yes, I believe you did." She turned a less certain smile on Call. "It's nice to meet you."

"It's nice to meet you, too," he said, but his glance strayed to the door leading out to the terrace and Charity thought maybe he wanted to go somewhere private as badly as she did.

"I think I see someone I need to talk to," Deirdre said diplomatically. "I'll see you later, Charity. It was nice meeting you, Call."

"You, too," Call said.

Charity remained silent, not trusting herself to speak. She was afraid she would throw herself into his arms and tell him how much she loved him, afraid she'd make a complete and utter fool of herself.

"Why don't we go out for some air?" Call asked gently, taking her arm and beginning to guide her in that direction. It was a good thing he did. Her legs felt like rubber bands and she wasn't sure how long they were going to hold her up.

Her heart was hammering. If he had come to New York on business and expected her to spend a convenient night in his bed, it wasn't going to happen. As much as she wanted exactly that, when he left she would feel even worse than she did already.

Call held open the door and she preceded him out into the warm night air. It was a little bit humid this evening, but not as bad as it had been the night before. She walked over to the rail, took hold of it to steady herself, and looked down into the crowded New York streets.

Call walked up beside her and she slowly turned to face him. "You were telling me why you were here."

Call picked up her hand, lifted it, and pressed a kiss into her palm. "Like I said, there are a couple of different reasons." Reaching into the inside pocket of his tuxedo, he pulled out a small canvas bag. The material was old and brown and water-stained, ancient-looking. She couldn't imagine why he was carrying something like that in his pocket.

"What is it?"

Call placed the bag in the palm of her hand. It was heavier than it looked. "Open it."

She gazed down, pulled the rotting string that held the bag closed, and poured the contents out into her hand. "Oh, my God—gold nuggets!"

"They belong to you."

"Me? You found these on the Lily Rose?

"In a manner of speaking. After you left, I got worried about someone getting hurt in what remained of your cabin.

It was pretty unstable, so Toby and I went over to pull some of the burnt walls down. When we did, we found a couple of small bags like this and four bigger ones filled with gold nuggets under the old wooden floors.''

"Oh, my God!'' She studied the glittering hunks of metal in her hand, then looked up. "Wait a minute. Why would Mose leave his gold behind?''

"The gold never belonged to Mose. If you recall, the older portion of the cabin was built during the Gold Rush days. For years after that, the place sat empty. Mose bought it through some kind of an auction. He fixed it up and added on to the original structure but he never found the gold. Since you own the cabin now, it belongs to you.''

Charity stared down at the glittering nuggets in her hand, far bigger than any she had found on the Lily Rose. "I can't believe this.''

"Some of them are even larger.''

She looked up at him. "If it's really mine, I want to share it equally with Maude, Jenny, and Toby.''

Call seemed pleased. "I thought maybe you would.'' He bent his head and very softly kissed her. "Congratulations.''

But finding the gold couldn't make up for losing Call. And seeing him again only made the loss more painful. "Thank you for bringing it. How did you know I was here?''

"Your sister Hope told me.'' He looked wonderful tonight. She'd never seen a man wear a tux with such aplomb or look so incredibly good in it . . . well, except maybe Max Mason.

"There's something else,'' Call said, taking the gold from her hand, dumping it back into the pouch, and setting the bag down on the railing. "The other reason I came. Something far more important than gold.''

There it was again, that little kernel of hope popping up just to taunt her. "What is it?''

"I came to apologize. I lied to you, Charity . . . that morning on the deck outside the house.''

"Lied? I don't understand. What did you lie about?''

"That morning I told you that I didn't love you. That

was a lie. I knew it even before I said the words.'' He took her hand. Call kissed her fingers and they trembled. ''I thought once you were gone, I'd be able to forget you, but I couldn't. I love you. I think I fell a little in love with you the first time I saw you on ol' Mose Flanagan's porch.''

''Call . . .'' Her voice broke on his name. She went into his arms and simply clung to him. She didn't ever want to let go.

''I knew I was in love with you,'' he said beside her ear, ''and I felt so damned guilty.''

She eased back to look at him. ''Because of Susan?''

''Because I never loved Susan the way I love you.''

Tears stung her eyes. Charity went back into his arms and held onto him as tightly as he was holding onto her.

''I love you,'' she whispered. ''Every day has been torture without you.''

''I don't want to be without you anymore,'' he said. ''Marry me. Come back with me.''

Charity bit back a sob. ''I'd love to marry you.'' Though she knew the life she was choosing would be hard. As much as she loved the Yukon, it was a solitary, rugged existence. She would do it for Call, do it because she loved him and she didn't want to live without him.

Call kissed her. She had forgotten how fiercely he could kiss, the way his mouth pressed into hers, hard and taking, soft and giving, all at once. She forgot the heat that swept through her body, the powerful surge of desire she had never known with anyone else. She came up breathless and wanting more, wishing she were in bed with him instead of out here on the terrace. She could feel how hard he was and knew he wanted that, too.

''When?'' she asked.

''As soon as we can make it legal.'' Reaching into the pocket of his tuxedo, he pulled out a small, velvet box with a silver Tiffany's label.

Charity opened the box with trembling fingers and her breath caught at the gorgeous, four-carat diamond engagement ring and diamond pavé wedding band.

"I thought about us a lot while you were gone. I figured if you said yes, maybe we'd go to Seattle. MegaTech is there and I've still got lots of business connections in the city." He looked down at her. "I'll never make the mistake I made before, Charity. I'll never let work come between us. Family is the most precious thing a man can have. But it's time I got on with my life. You helped teach me that." He slid the engagement ring onto the third finger of her trembling left hand.

"Oh, Call, it's beautiful. Magnificent."

"It shouldn't be hard for you to find an editing job if you decide that's what you want to do. We'll buy a house somewhere . . . Bainbridge Island, maybe. Not too far from the city but not too close, either. Someplace with a little room, maybe some acreage. The kind of place that would be good for raising kids."

He wanted to have children! Happy tears glittered in her eyes. "That sounds perfect."

"Come on," Call said, taking her hand. "Let's get out of here." As they made their way back inside the ballroom, heading for the door and Call's suite on the fourteenth floor, she saw Deirdre at the table sitting next to Jeremy.

Charity smiled at her best friend and held up her hand. She pointed to the ring and mouthed the words, "We're getting married!"

Deirdre said a not-so-silent, "Yes!" And in a highly undignified moment, shot her arm up into the air.

EPILOGUE

Charity leaned back in the chaise longue on the deck of her sprawling ranch-style home on Bainbridge Island. The white-washed gray-cypress house overlooking Puget Sound had a heavy shake roof, wide wooden decks, and lots of glass. They lived on fifteen secluded acres of pines and sycamores yet were only a few miles by ferry from the city. Close enough to keep in touch with Aunt Mavis, room enough for Kodiak and Smoke to play. And a great place for children, whenever they decided they were ready.

Charity loved the house. She loved Seattle. She loved being married. Mostly, she just loved Call.

"Hey, Charity!" He was working in his office, which opened out onto the deck a little way from where she sat in her yellow flowered bikini, enjoying the late spring sun. "There's something I want to show you."

Curious, she got up from the chaise and padded barefoot down the deck. Call opened the sliding glass door a little wider to let her in.

His gaze took in the skimpy bikini that barely covered her breasts. "Lady, you look good enough to eat." He hauled her into his arms. "Maybe this can wait till later." He gave her a soft, nibbling kiss.

Laughing, she pulled away. "You know I'm putty in your hands when you do that. First, I want to know what you called me in here to show me."

Dressed in jeans and a blue cotton tee shirt, he walked over to his computer and Charity followed. Call urged her down in the black swivel chair in front of the machine.

"I've been playing around with something. Take a look at this."

She studied the computer screen and realized he had pulled up one of the many genealogical sites available on the Net. "Rachael Louise Fitzpatrick," she read. "Born January 11, 1883. Died December 14, 1950." He clicked the mouse, bringing up another name. "Frances Fitzpatrick, born March 12, 1880." No news there. She wondered what Call had discovered.

He leaned over and clicked the mouse on a different site: www.marriageindex:Oregon.com. "Now look at this." It was Frances's marriage certificate.

"It says she married her husband, Thaddeus Baker, on August 10, 1902." Charity turned her head and looked at him over her shoulder. "So?"

"So I couldn't find a birth certificate for your great-great-grandmother, Frances's daughter, Sarah Thankful Baker, but maybe she was born at home and the records were lost or something."

"That wouldn't be unusual."

"No, but strangely enough, I turned up a record from a Boston hospital in 1903. It says a Sarah T. Baker made a visit there in May of that year. She came in with a broken arm. The record says she was three years old at the time."

Charity frowned. "That's impossible. Frances and Thaddeus had only been married a year. In those days, out-of-wedlock children were a very big scandal."

"That's right. But what if the records are right and Sarah really was three at the time? The only scandal your Aunt Mavis mentioned was the one Rachael and Ian Gallagher created by running away together. Combined with the fact that there is nothing that shows Rachael Fitzpatrick ever married, I'd say there's a chance the baby wasn't Frances's child. I think it's more likely little Sarah belonged to Rachael.''

Charity sat there staring, thinking of Rachael and Ian and their journey to the Yukon, thinking what might have happened to Rachael after Ian was killed. Had she been pregnant when her lover died? Was Rachael, not Frances, actually her long-dead great-great-grandmother? If she were . . .

''My God, Call, if Rachael was Sarah's mother, then I'd be her direct descendant. We would share the same blood and . . . and . . .''

''And maybe you could have remembered something that happened to Rachael in the Yukon?''

''Yes, maybe I could have. Maybe that's the reason I always felt so compelled to go there.''

''I guess you'll never really know,'' Call said. But in June they planned to return, to begin reconstruction of the cabin.

She would never know the truth about the past, but it no longer mattered. Rising from the chair, Charity turned and went into Call's arms. ''Thank you.''

''I love you,'' he said.

Charity thought of the Yukon, the dream of adventure that had carried her so far from her home, and the turn of fate that had led to the place she stood now, in the arms of the man she loved.

And she smiled.

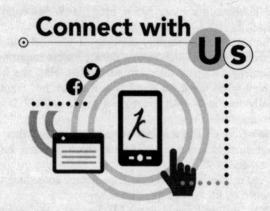

Books by Bestselling Author
Fern Michaels

___**The Jury**	0-8217-7878-1	$6.99US/$9.99CAN
___**Sweet Revenge**	0-8217-7879-X	$6.99US/$9.99CAN
___**Lethal Justice**	0-8217-7880-3	$6.99US/$9.99CAN
___**Free Fall**	0-8217-7881-1	$6.99US/$9.99CAN
___**Fool Me Once**	0-8217-8071-9	$7.99US/$10.99CAN
___**Vegas Rich**	0-8217-8112-X	$7.99US/$10.99CAN
___**Hide and Seek**	1-4201-0184-6	$6.99US/$9.99CAN
___**Hokus Pokus**	1-4201-0185-4	$6.99US/$9.99CAN
___**Fast Track**	1-4201-0186-2	$6.99US/$9.99CAN
___**Collateral Damage**	1-4201-0187-0	$6.99US/$9.99CAN
___**Final Justice**	1-4201-0188-9	$6.99US/$9.99CAN
___**Up Close and Personal**	0-8217-7956-7	$7.99US/$9.99CAN
___**Under the Radar**	1-4201-0683-X	$6.99US/$9.99CAN
___**Razor Sharp**	1-4201-0684-8	$7.99US/$10.99CAN
___**Yesterday**	1-4201-1494-8	$5.99US/$6.99CAN
___**Vanishing Act**	1-4201-0685-6	$7.99US/$10.99CAN
___**Sara's Song**	1-4201-1493-X	$5.99US/$6.99CAN
___**Deadly Deals**	1-4201-0686-4	$7.99US/$10.99CAN
___**Game Over**	1-4201-0687-2	$7.99US/$10.99CAN
___**Sins of Omission**	1-4201-1153-1	$7.99US/$10.99CAN
___**Sins of the Flesh**	1-4201-1154-X	$7.99US/$10.99CAN
___**Cross Roads**	1-4201-1192-2	$7.99US/$10.99CAN

Available Wherever Books Are Sold!
Check out our website at **www.kensingtonbooks.com**